WE SHOULD HAVE LEFT WELL ENOUGH ALONE

Selected Stories

By
Ronald Malfi

JOURNALSTONE
YOUR LINK TO ARTISTIC TALENT

JournalStone books may be ordered through booksellers or by contacting:

JournalStone

www.journalstone.com

ISBN: 978-1-945373-97-8   (sc)
ISBN: 978-1-945373-98-5   (ebook)
ISBN: 978-1-945373-99-2   (hc)

JournalStone rev. date: November 2, 2017

Library of Congress Control Number:2017951478

Printed in the United States of America

Cover Design: Neslihan Yardimli
Images: shutterstock.com/tr/image-photo/metal-blank-human-limb-on-black-538877989?src

Edited by: Sean Timothy Leonard

For Grandma, who showed me the truth inside a world of make-believe.

Table of Contents

WE SHOULD HAVE LEFT WELL ENOUGH ALONE

There was a café called le Sanglier near Paris and that was where many of the soldiers went to eat. It was a small café and rather dirty-looking, and the windows were grimy with soot from artillery fire. There were tiny wooden tables, circularly cut, placed about the cracked linoleum floor, and men crowded around these tables as if for air. Inside, nearing dark, it was always rowdy. If the weather cooperated, you could sit out back on the verandah and the waitresses would bring you French rum, which tasted old and distinctly of oak, and sometimes, if you were known to tip well, the waitresses would sit and talk with you for a while. Many of the soldiers did not know French and none of the girls knew English, but that did not matter, and it felt quite good just to have someone there and to look at someone pretty while sipping French rum.

THE DINNER PARTY

Two men in long black trench coats follow you into the supermarket. Aside from the coats, they wear wide-brimmed fedoras and mirrored sunglasses. They each have hockey stick sideburns that jet toward the corners of their mouths and black leather gloves on their hands. You don't know how long they've been following you or where they picked you up, but you are suddenly, fully, completely aware of them. Your heart sinks.

The baby is strapped to your chest in a wrap sling yet you hug him tighter, covering his small white head with one hand. It is a warm, soft ball, and you can feel his pulse thudding vaguely in his temples as he sleeps. Your hand is bigger than his whole head. That is good. You don't want the men in the trench coats to see him. Or you.

You lose them somewhere down the canned goods aisle. You know this because you can no longer hear their dry palm-slap footfalls, can no longer feel those mirrored sunglasses sizing you up behind your back. Absently, you continue to fill the grocery cart but you're not really paying attention now.

You think, *I have made a mistake.*

"Ma'am?" He is a teenager—brown-skinned, pimply, bespectacled—and he smiles with oversize teeth while he bags your groceries. His nametag says BYRON. "Help bring these to your car, ma'am?"

You shake your head. You can manage on your own.

Thinking, *When did I become a "ma'am"?*

Thinking, *Byron. Bad name.*

The woman ringing you up at the register smiles broadly and looks instantly like something out of a fairytale about distrustful cats. "What a little darling," she purrs. "Boy or girl?"

"Boy," you say.

"How old?"

Instinctively, you hug him tighter to your breast. Again, you're thinking of the men in the coats. "Three months."

The woman's smile widens. Inwardly, you cringe. "What's the sweetie's name?"

You tell her.

"That," says the woman, "is a beautiful name."

Before leaving, you glance around one last time for the men in the black coats. They are no longer there. Suddenly you are overcome by embarrassment, by the shame of paranoia. You nearly laugh, you are so relieved. Because you were wrong. Because no one was there to begin with.

I have made a mistake.

You strap the baby in his car seat in the back of the van. He wakes only briefly to work his mouth around soundless cries, his gray eyes blinking like castanets. You slide the door shut and dig through your purse for your car keys. But you can't find them. Panic slides a cold barb around your heart. Ridiculous conspiracy theories threaten to tear you apart. You rush to the door and tug on it, expecting it to be locked, horrible images of asphyxiation and blinking colorless eyes shuttling through your mind, but it slides open with a groan.

Gray eyes peep out at you. Pink fists jut through Oshkosh sleeves. There are giraffes on the sleeves, pandas on the plush insert of the car seat. You smile and think, *It's a jungle in there, kiddo.* You say, "Hey there." Say, "Hey there, big boy." Say, "Who's mommy's big boy?"

Thinking, *This is the funniest thing in the world. Michael would be laughing his head off right now. Michael would be calling me his paranoid pretty and would be laughing his head off. Nice one, girl.*

And there they are, in your hand: the car keys.

Back home, you breastfeed while the TV sits on mute. Michael said to expect them around seven, and it's still early, but you're not the greatest cook in the world and this is a big dinner. Promotion at work. Michael works hard. His boss, his boss's wife. Michael promised to bring a bottle of wine. A nice wine. You don't know the difference between nice wines and not nice wines except to watch the faces of those who drink the wine, but you're not worried about Michael and his wine. You are thinking of his boss and his boss's wife—their names. You wrote them down on the back of an envelope but now you can't remember where you put it.

The baby finishes suckling and begins to whine. You pick him up, dress him over one shoulder, thump his back with an open hand. You go into the kitchen, eyes darting about the countertop. The groceries are still splayed out, the grocery bags on the floor. No envelope. No names.

The baby burps. It's like a ghost vacating his tiny body. You kiss his head, holding him close to you. You are suddenly so close to tears you're frightened. The envelope, the fucking *envelope*—

Is on the refrigerator. Strawberry magnet.

"There we go," you whisper into your baby's ear. "See that? There we go. No sweat."

Tony and Eliza Sanderson. Great block letters, all capitals, in felt marker. You wrote it last night in the bathroom after Michael told you. Because you didn't want to forget. This is important to Michael, this dinner.

It's now three o'clock and you put the baby down for his nap. He goes willingly, already asleep before you set him in his crib. Cartoon lions with bushy brown manes caper on the spread and there is a mobile above the crib with colorful felt airplanes hanging from it. The room smells of baby powder, Desitin, ammoniac wet-wipes. In the crib, those pink fists uncurl, the baby snores his tiny snores, and you're already fretting about dinner.

You've done this before, though you're not the greatest cook. You prep the roast, adorn it with spices and cloves, set it in the pan, preheat the oven. You decide to do scalloped potatoes but, fuck it all, they come out looking like grimaces and you can't stand to look at them. So you smash them up in a ceramic dish and, *voilà*, they're mashed potatoes. You use your mother's recipe for green bean casserole, following the instructions like someone assembling a rocket, reading every line three or four times because you're terrified of getting it wrong. Twenty-nine minutes.

Behind you, the oven buzzes. Opens. Food goes in. You're sweating, but feeling good. Things are cooking now, ha ha.

Thinking, *Tony and Eliza, Tony and Eliza, Tony and Eliza, Tony and Eliza...*

Outside, a shape passes before one of the kitchen windows.

You freeze, your first thought, *Those men from the grocery store.* Your second thought: *The baby!*

You rush to the baby's room but he has not been disturbed. The shades are drawn over the nursery windows so you can't see out...but some instinct inside you tells you they are *out there,* walking around the house, trying to find a way in.

Suddenly, you wonder if you locked the front door.

Racing to the foyer, you make enough noise to wake the dead. You even utter a weak groan when you strike the front door and find that it's locked. It's been locked all along. Sweating, you listen, one ear against the door, but cannot hear anything. If there are men in trench coats circumnavigating the house, they are very good at remaining very good.

Or...

Or I made a mistake, you think.

You bring your hands up to rub the sweat out of your eyes, but when you look down, you are terrified to see fine silver hairs sprouting from your palms, so much it looks like you are grasping balls of very fine wire.

You scream.

But there is nothing there. Your hands are fine. A trick of the light, a trick of the eye. Michael's paranoid pretty, indeed.

Something smells. It's bad.

In the kitchen, something burns.

"Goddamn it." You rush in and it's the potatoes. Stupidly, you left a piece of paper towel stuck to the bottom of the ceramic dish. It burns as you fan pillars of smoke away from the mouth of the oven.

At the sink, you wash your hands, examining them for fine silver hairs, but you are okay. You are not a monster.

You cook. Check baby. Check windows for swarthy figures. You're able to do this calmly and simply now because you think of it as a routine. You think, *Lather, wash, repeat,* and try to keep from giggling. You think, *Tony and Eliza,* and you make a little song out of it in your head to the tune of "Frankie and Johnny."

The food is cooking now. Really cooking. With Michael's wine, it promises to be a fine evening. You set the table and actually feel good about how it looks. Outside, the stoop has darkened as the sun sinks below the distant trees. You go into the bathroom and begin to take a shower...but midway through the process—

(lather wash repeat)

—you panic about leaving the baby in his crib with those strange men outside. Naked, wet, soapy, you grab the baby from the crib, wrap him in his blue moose blanket and set him on the bathroom rug. You shower with the shower curtain open so you can keep an eye on him, keeping the water cold so the steam won't make it difficult for him to breathe. He has tiny lungs.

"There," you say in his ear when you are done. "Mommy's all done. She's going to dress now. Dress and look pretty."

And you feel his heartbeat echoing in his tiny skull.

In the bedroom, a man stands just beyond the window looking in. It is dark out now but you can see him clearly. He's dressed all in black, his white ghost-face seeming to hover in the air just beyond the windowpane.

"No," you say, holding the baby against your wet nakedness. "What do you want?"

The figure says nothing. Does not move.

"Leave us alone."

The figure does not leave you alone.

It takes all your strength but you manage to cross the bedroom to the window and pull the curtain closed. You can almost hear the stranger's heartbeat on the other side of the glass. Still clutching the baby to your body, you go to the nightstand and pick up the phone. You dial 911, listen to the rings. But when a woman's voice answers, you hang up. Because you're overreacting. Because, okay, maybe you're jealous of Michael a little too, and jealous of his taste in wine and his promotion and his Tony and Eliza, and 911 is your sabotage to the dinner party. But that's not true, either. Not really. Jealousy is just what you told the doctor. Because you had to tell him something.

You dress, put your makeup on, examine yourself in the mirror. Your breasts have gotten so big...but so have your hips. Your skin looks...grayer, somehow. You think of old photos of Jewish corpses stacked like cured meats. Could just be the lousy bathroom lighting. Briefly, you contemplate changing out all the light bulbs but don't think you'd have enough time before Michael comes home with your guests.

Still wrapped in his blue moose blanket, you set the baby back in the crib and smooth the fine hairs off his forehead. Soft, warm ball. Chest rises with respiration...and you are suddenly overwhelmed by your love for this little creature, this amalgam of you and Michael, of the successful attorney and the paranoid pretty.

Something stinks.

"Oh," you whisper over the baby, eyes wide.

The kitchen.

Stricken, you rush into the kitchen fearing the worst...but the food looks fine and it's almost done. It's just the smell—it seems to curdle in your nose and turn into solid waste in your lungs. You rush to the kitchen sink and gag into the basin. A foamy snake spirals out of your throat. After catching your breath, you run the water and wait as your hot, prickling skin goes back to normal.

When Michael comes home, you are sitting in the living room in the dark, sick to your stomach. The doorknob jiggles and you can hear people talking on the stoop, and the first thing you think of is the man with the ghost-face looking in your bedroom window.

"Hi, hon," Michael says. He's beaming, looking handsome in a camelhair suit and a shimmering red tie. He clutches a bottle of what you assume is nice wine. "Oh, you look beautiful."

You greet him with a kiss on his cheek as his boss and boss's wife file into the house. They are much younger and handsomer than you pictured them, Tony and Eliza, like a couple straight out of a glamour magazine. You think of horrible light bulbs and sallow, graying skin and are suddenly intimidated by these beautiful people.

"Tony and Eliza brought the wine," Michael says, carrying the bottle over to the wine bar at the far end of the room. "Dark in here." He flicks on a light switch as he goes. "Fix you folks a drink?"

The Sandersons agree that a glass of wine would be nice. Tony shakes your hand and Eliza smiles and looks suddenly hideous. How did you think this woman was beautiful only moments ago?

"Food smells wonderful," Eliza says. Her teeth are like the dented grille of a truck.

"It does," Tony says. He has silver hair at his temples and you quickly hide your hands behind your back in case that silver hair is contagious.

Michael returns with a glass of wine for Tony and Eliza. "You guys make yourselves at home," Michael tells them, motioning toward the loveseat. To you, Michael says, "Where's my little munchkin?"

"In the crib," you say.

"I'll wake him and introduce you," Michael says to the Sandersons.

"Oh," says Eliza Sanderson, "I've been dying to see him." And when Michael leaves, Eliza turns to you and says, "Is there anything I can help with, dear?"

You say no.

"You look wonderful," says Eliza. "That's a gorgeous dress." She winks, this aging medusa. "I can't believe you've just had a baby."

Tony just smiles and enjoys his wine.

Your stomach curdles. The smells from the kitchen are making you sick again. You think, *I made a mistake.* Think, *Byron. Bad name.*

Maybe there are men outside, maybe there aren't. Maybe you are jealous of Michael, just like you told the doctor, or maybe that's not true, either. You don't know. You wish Michael had never turned on the light switch and that you knew what wine was nice wine and that it didn't take you twenty-nine minutes to read the six lines on the casserole recipe because you had to make sure you got it right, got it right, got it right.

This is new to you. All of it. Three months new.

Michael comes up behind you but doesn't come down into the living room. You don't look at him; you feel him at your back like mirrored sunglasses. Eliza Sanderson cocks her head at a strange angle and stares past you, up at Michael. Tony Sanderson looks as well, and the expression on his face convinces you he smells how awful the food is, too.

You turn. Michael stands there with a quizzical look on his face—a mixture of confusion and bemusement, like someone who knows a joke has been told though he's missed the punch line. He stands there with the blue moose blanket in one hand and what can only be an uncooked pot roast in the other, and says, "Is this...hon? Some kind of...uh, hon?"

"I made a mistake," you say.

"Hon? Honey?"

You sit on the couch and smile politely at the Sandersons. In the kitchen, the oven's buzzer goes off.

LEARNED CHILDREN

Soon after, he began to question his sanity.

Holes, Paul Marcus thought. *Craters. A few more months of this and it'll look like a blitzkrieg.*

It was about the missing girl, of course. The scarecrow was a dream—he couldn't think of it otherwise without compromising his sanity—and he wondered how much of the actual digging had been done in some sort of fugue state, for he could only recall what he had done on the mornings that followed, waking in bed with mud dried to his feet. Once, he'd awoken in the field, his skin gritty with hours' old perspiration, his arms and shoulders sore from digging.

Digging holes, he thought. *Craters.* Trembling.

He was what the townspeople called "a distant"—a person from elsewhere who'd come to roost among them. A drafty old farmhouse with more bedrooms than he would ever need and a position of schoolteacher that needed filling were the things that brought him here. A *distant,* he supposed, was better than *intruder,* was better than *trespasser.* Nonetheless, he felt his own intrusion in his bones. His students did not make him feel any more welcome, either. Blank, moonfaced dullards, he often felt like he was preaching to a classroom of earthworms. Even creepier was when their slack disinterest turned to brazen effrontery.

"Can anyone tell me what Blake is trying to say in this passage?"

Ignoring the question, one of the piggish little gnomes toward the back of the classroom said, "They talk about you in church."

The comment caught Paul Marcus with his guard down. "I'm sorry?" He still did not know all their names, mainly because they refused to sit in their assigned seats. "Someone has been talking about me?"

"In church," repeated the boy.

"I don't understand," Paul said.

"Your car has a broken headlight," said one of the girls.

"Your shoes are funny," chided another.

And so on…

It was his students who first brought the missing girl to his attention. They kept her empty desk at the back of the classroom like a shrine; sometimes, after recess, some of the girls would bring flowers in with them from the schoolyard to decorate it. Hardened fingers of bubble gum hung like stalactites from the underside of the desk and someone had carved JANNA IS DED on the desktop.

Of course, since she was never found, no one knew for sure that she was dead.

"Who's Janna?" he asked upon first noticing the inscription. "What happened to her?"

"Someone got her."

"What does that mean?"

"She was here one day," said a boy as he dug around in one nostril, "and the next day, she was gone."

"When?"

"Month ago."

"Who took her?"

The boy shrugged. "Why is your hair gray on the sides but black up top?"

The students snickered.

There was no Janna on his roster. Were the little cretins messing with him? He didn't put it past them. There had been frogs in his desk and, disturbingly, a baby bird with its neck broken in his coffee mug one morning.

But they were not messing with him.

"It's true," said George Julliard one afternoon in the teacher's lounge. He was working around a mouthful of peanut butter and jelly. "Abduction is the sheriff's best guess."

"She isn't on my roster."

But he found out why later on: his roster had been carefully rewritten to exclude Janna's name. His roster was not the original. The original was found crumpled in a ball in Janna's desk, her name clearly legible. When Paul brought this to the principal's attention—a middle-aged woman with thinning silver hair—she only laughed and said kids will be kids.

"Did any of you change my roster?" he asked his students the following day.

"What's your favorite color?" asked one of the girls.

"Do you like cats?" asked a boy.

Holes, he thought. *And the scarecrow.*

It was a dream, surely. The scarecrow was just a slapdash thing strung to a post in the east field, its clothes tatters of flannel, its face a featureless burlap sack. Something so innocuous even the crows nested on its shoulders and pecked at it. Yet at night, in Paul's dreams—for surely they were only dreams—it would appear framed in Paul's bedroom window, its respiration—*respiration!*—impossibly fogging up the glass.

In a state of near-somnambulism, Paul would climb out of bed and, barefoot, follow the lumbering dark shape around the side of the house. That first night there was a shovel leaning against the porch. Paul took it as a weapon. The scarecrow—nothing more than a smudge of darkness—moved onward through the stalks of corn.

It wasn't until Paul reached a sparse clearing in the corn did he realize the scarecrow had disappeared. Something about the softness of the ground troubled him. The shovel, it seemed, was all too conveniently in his hands.

He dug, thinking of the missing girl, thinking, *Janna is ded.*

In the end, he found only an empty hole in the earth. And in the morning, despite the filth on his feet, he wondered if it had all been a dream.

But it was no dream. And it continued for the first month. When he tried to stay awake, the scarecrow did not appear. It was only on those nights where, bested by exhaustion, he would slump over in a chair only to awaken at the sound of the creaking porch as someone circumnavigated the farmhouse. A shape would lumber past the windows.

Scarecrow, he thought, shuddering.

He was supposed to find the girl—that much was clear to him. Each night, the scarecrow led him to a different part of the field. Often, Paul could discern patches of barren earth between the stalks, and he would commence digging. Other times, he found himself uprooting stalks to cultivate his craters. By the end of the month, and with the harvest moon now full in the sky, the field was pockmarked by his obsession.

"She lived in your house, you know," said one of his students...and how simple was he that he hadn't already come to this realization? It gave his obsession a heart and a soul.

"You're getting warmer," said another student, and this caused the hairs on the back of Paul's neck to rise. As if they were watching him at night while he dug like a grave robber in the cornfield.

He wanted to ask them, *Is the scarecrow real?* He wanted to say, *Is that what got Janna?* But he didn't. He would be driven out of a job for being a madman.

Again, night came. The scarecrow appeared shifting through the corn at the edge of the field. This night, Paul waited for it, sitting on the porch with the shovel across his lap. Again, he followed it into the field. When he lost sight of the creature, he began digging.

Janna is ded.

There was nothing beneath the ground.

Above, ravens cawed.

On a Tuesday, someone put a rotten apple on his desk. Someone else had stuck used flypaper in X formations across the windowpanes in the classroom. Again, the principal laughed and said kids will be kids.

"No one handed in their homework," he said to the class. This wasn't totally accurate—someone had handed in a ream of paper on which they'd pasted cutout photos from glamour magazines. Paul found this alarmingly sociopathic.

At the end of the day, as they filed out of the classroom, one of the girls smiled at him. Her front teeth were blackened and there was a bruise on her left cheekbone. "Tick tock goes the clock," she said to him.

"What?"

She smiled horridly then fled from the classroom.

He no longer waited for the scarecrow to make its appearance; he spent his evenings digging trenches in the cornfield. By the second month in the farmhouse, there was very little corn left.

Exhausted, sore, he dragged the shovel behind him back toward the house, stopping only when he saw the scarecrow hanging from its post in the east field. Its form was slumped under the weight of countless black crows. Despite his tiredness, he went to it. The crows were bold and did not fly off immediately. Paul scared them off eventually by swinging the shovel.

"Get," he said. "Go on."

It hung like wet laundry, its pant legs sprouting straw, its flannel shirt tattered. The featureless burlap sack of its face seemed to sag under the weight of its existence.

It does not exist. Not like that.

He reached up and pressed a hand to its straw-filled flannel shirt.

Not straw-filled.

Paul went cold. He dropped the shovel in the dirt.

Reaching up, he peeled the burlap face away to reveal a second face: a head turned funny on its neck, reminding Paul Marcus of the dead baby bird left in his coffee mug.

The next Monday, after a weekend spent at the sheriff's office filling out paperwork, he stood before his classroom. The earthworms were suspiciously quiet this morning. Nothing had been left on or in his desk. The flypaper had been removed from the cracked windowpanes.

"I want..." And his voice cracked. "I want you all to turn to chapter five in your texts," he continued, trying hard to sound in control. He was sweating through his tweed coat and his throat felt constricted. "I *want—*"

"Dogs can sense fear," said the boy toward the back, picking his nose.

"My mother had an abortion when she was a teenager," said one of the girls.

Paul Marcus offered them a wan smile and wondered, not for the first time, whatever happened to the schoolteacher he had replaced.

Knocking

Picture it: a squalid, self-deprecating little bungalow wedged like a rotting tooth in a mouthful of rotting teeth along the poorest side street of North London. Skies terminally gray, where the textured hues of an early morning are practically indistinguishable from those of a premature dusk, this little bungalow sat, undaunted, unfettered, deprived of everything yet feeling nothing in such depravity. On the outside the building looked like a construct stretched out of shape to resemble something from some child's fleeting nightmare. It looked gray and tired, the exterior stucco sheathing overcome by corded veins of ivy and ginseng where, in the springtime, sparrows nested. Despite the previous occupants' insistence to the contrary, the entire building canted slightly to the left. While ample space was provided for one to traverse the ivy-encrusted alleyway that separated our home from the building to our left, upon looking up while standing in this very alley, the proximity of our roof to the neighboring roof appeared to be less than six inches apart. Surely, following the passage of a few more years, the two roofs would eventually touch, the buildings bowing together like united lovers over an abyss. The listing was even more noticeable when glasses of water or bottles of wine were abandoned on tabletops, countertops, coffee tables throughout the place: it did not take much scrutiny to observe the not-so-subtle tilt to the surface of the given liquid. It was not something you felt, although both Tara and I found it difficult to fall asleep the first month of our occupancy, and after some casual discussion, we both decided our insomnia was due to our bodies acclimating themselves to the structural misalignment.

The interior of the bungalow was shabby and colorless, the atmosphere at times overtaken by a sort of chronic fatigue. The windows were too small, like the portholes in a ship, the panes dulled to cataract opaqueness. Standing in the center of the foyer and looking up revealed a gutted hollow that yawned to the second floor and, beyond that, the cathedral ceiling. It was like living in the gullet of some prehistoric reptile. The walls were an ancient alabaster, the woodwork and molding so old and arthritic, it seemed almost criminal to attempt any restoration, lest we upset some divine plan.

And for a while, it was perfect.

"This works, yeah?"

"It works," Tara said. "It all works."

"Tell me one thing you love about living here."

"One thing?"

"Just one."

She considered. "I love the way everyone says 'bloody.' It's very British."

I laughed. "All right," I said. "Now tell me one thing you hate."

She said, "I hate the bloody weather."

We moved to London from the States near the end of May, on our one-year wedding anniversary. It was different and new, all of it. I'd grown up in the suburbs of Washington, D.C., while Tara had spent her youth with a family of seven in the sun-baked scrublands of the Midwest. We had a good life in the States, but we were young and anxious and ready to take on as much of the world as we could. So we found the decrepit little flat in North London, and despite its ugliness (or maybe because of it), we loved it. We suffered the expected tribulations associated with any relocation—a missing box of dishes, a busted table leg, the discovery of items previously thought lost weeks after taking up residency—but in all, it went off without a hitch. Tara knew nothing about London but proved a quick study. She made it a point to venture into Camden, to patronize the neighboring shops and cafés and pubs in order to soak up the local custom. The discrepancy between U.S. dollars and

Ronald Malfi

British pounds was a cause for some mild frustration, but she soon got the hang of that as well. For the most part, we found the people to be mutually polite and reserved, displaying a sense of propriety and a respect for personal space that would have been mistaken back home for haughtiness or, in the least, some form of social maladjustment. I took a job teaching English at the university and Tara studied for her doctorate in child psychology while working part-time as a waitress at the Algerian.

Summer, the smell of the Thames was unrelenting. We would sleep with the bedroom windows open, falling asleep to the scent of the city. (This routine was abandoned, however, after a series of seemingly unrelated murders in the Heath transformed this humble pleasure into an act of recklessness.) We had a washer and dryer, but Tara took to hanging the clothes across a stretch of clothesline from the patio windows to the deck railing at the rear of the bungalow. One warm afternoon, we picnicked at Highgate Ponds and got drunk on cheap red wine. We laughed ourselves into stomach cramps when a group of middle-aged male locals appeared and stripped out of their clothing to sun themselves in the open quarter. Their nudity was severe and white, all ribs, stomachs, and wiry pepper-colored pubic hair.

The bungalow sustained two bedrooms off the ground floor, a foyer that communicated with a den that, in turn, fashioned off into a quaint kitchenette. The second floor contained the bathroom and another room that could have been forged into a cramped bedroom or an equally cramped study. At her pleading, I awarded the second-floor room to Tara, which she fashioned into a handsome little study of obsessive-compulsive neatness.

Once we'd settled into our respective roles, with North London starting to not feel so alien, I quickly immersed myself into the mix at the university. Tara attended her classes during the day, leaving the bungalow brooding and empty in our absence. On the nights she worked at the Algerian, I would sometimes visit for a pint; other times, I would stay home alone and listen to the encroaching silence of the bungalow while invisible clocks ticked in shadowed background.

One evening toward the close of summer, a soft rain falling in the streets, Tara appeared in the doorway to my home office door. I was perched over my desk, grading papers from my summer school class.

"Hon," she said.

"Yeah?"

"There's something upstairs."

"Hold on."

I scribbled a note in the margin of the paper I was reading then turned to face her. "There's what?"

"I don't know. Just come look."

I followed her up the winding staircase to the second floor. Through the slats in the balustrade, I looked directly down the gaping maw of the narrow little house, straight down to the foyer below. A soft rain pattered against the windows. I could hear a dog barking far off in the distance.

"Where?" I said.

"In the study."

We entered her study. The room was brightly lit and there was a Paul Desmond CD playing low on the stereo. Against one wall was Tara's desk, stacks of papers filed neatly on top. A spare bed, in case we ever found ourselves entertaining guests from far away who would require spending the night (though we could not see this happening any time soon), was pushed against another wall. Above the bed, twin windows glared at us like eyes.

"In the closet," she said.

"What is?"

"The noise."

"What noise?"

"The *noise*," she repeated with more emphasis, as if this would clarify anything. When I looked at her, she only shrugged. She'd dropped her voice to a whisper now, too.

I turned off the stereo and we stood together in the silence, unmoving. All I could hear was the fall of the rain against the roof. As if part of the conspiracy, the dog had ceased barking outside, too.

"I don't hear anything," I said.

"Harold, it was in the closet."

So I went to the closet and pulled the door open. Two file cabinets were tucked away here, as well as a plastic garbage bag full of winter clothes we had no room for in any other part of the house. But that was all.

"What did it sound like?"

"Like there was someone in the closet," Tara said. "Someone moving around in there."

"Who would be in the closet?"

"I'm just telling you what I heard."

"Well there's obviously no one here," I said, backing away.

Back downstairs, I poured what was left of the coffee into my mug and reheated it in the microwave. Standing in the darkened kitchenette, I watched the rain sluice against the window over the sink. The dog had resumed its tune, sounding closer now than it had before. When the microwave finally chimed, I carried my steaming mug back through the kitchenette and down the corridor toward my office.

Tara stood in the hallway, staring at me.

I paused. "What?" I said.

"Don't give me what," she said. "I know it's you."

"Me?"

"Cut it out."

"What?" I said.

"You're trying to scare me."

"I'm not doing anything."

"Liar."

"I swear it. I was making coffee." And I took a long, noisy sip to bolster my innocence.

"Well," she said, "I don't know what you're doing, or how you're doing it, but cut it out. I'm trying to study."

Back upstairs, I stood before her open closet door, peering inside. "I don't understand," I said. "What does it sound like?"

"Shuffling around. Sometimes like a knock, too. Like someone moving against the door from the inside."

"Well, then leave the door open."

"But that doesn't make whatever is doing it disappear, does it?"

"Maybe it's outside," I suggested. "Maybe it's the storm."

"It's not outside and it's not the storm." She was seated on the edge of the spare bed, looking past me and into the closet. "I heard it. It was right inside the closet, Harold."

I leaned forward and wrapped the old shave-and-a-haircut on the doorframe. "Wait for it," I said. "Wait…"

"Don't make fun," Tara said.

I sighed. "What would you like me to do, Tara? I don't hear anything."

"Do you promise you're not trying to scare me?"

"Of course I'm not."

"Because if it's you, just stop."

"It's not me."

"Swear it," she said.

"I already have."

"Swear it again."

"I swear it's not me," I promised.

"Harold?"

"Yeah?"

She said, "I feel funny."

* * *

As it will, time passed. Somehow, despite our hectic schedules, we managed to celebrate a reclusive yet cozy Thanksgiving together, fielding the customary telephone calls from our respective families overseas, and prepared for Christmas with the giddy excitement of two children set loose in a toy store. We were saving money—that was our promise to each other that year—and would keep gifts to a minimum. Pleased with myself, I managed to locate a well-made but inexpensive gold locket on a slender chain which I outfitted with a tiny photograph of Tara and me, taken back in the heyday of our courtship. I wrapped this gift in my pedestrian way (for the life of me, I could not wrap a gift) and decided to stow it in the attic of our little bungalow—a place, I was certain, Tara would never venture voluntarily.

I climbed the stairs and entered the dark maw of the attic. I had left Tara downstairs, busy decorating the Christmas tree; the house was draughty, the walls and floorboards thin, and the din of her soft, cheerful humming could be heard even against the whine of the wind in the eaves and the sigh of the cold winter's night against the framework of the house.

Scrambling for the dangling pull-cord that hung from the light fixture in the ceiling, my right hand swatted blindly in the dark. I managed a step forward. The pull-cord brushed by my face, sending tremors down my spine. I yanked the light on.

The whistling wind was a constant. I could hear the house groaning and creaking and rocking in its foundation. Fleetingly, I wondered if this would be the year our roof decided to crumble into our neighbor's.

I heard something move behind me. Spinning around, my eyes still adjusting to the gloom, I peered down the shadowy length of the attic, the ceiling low, the beams crisscrossing before me like the rank of raised swords in a military wedding. I could see nothing.

Yet unlike in the movies, where the protagonist must turn away from the noise before he hears it again, I *heard* it again: a labored, breathy sound, very much like respiration.

My own breath seized in my throat.

Then another sound: a dull thud. A *knock*. This was it—this was the sound Tara had heard coming from behind the closet door in her study. Quickly, I unfolded a mental blueprint of the bungalow and, sure enough, that section of the attic was positioned directly above Tara's second-floor study.

With mounting desperation, I was suddenly trying to recall whether or not the police had ever arrested anyone in connection with those unsolved murders in the Heath, and I was coming up blank.

Steeling myself, I walked along the floor beams toward the opposite end of the attic, toward the noise. The shadows deepened as I approached, but I no longer heard anything—

Something tittered and I caught a glimpse of a fleeting shadow swim across the far wall. This was not my imagination. I was certain of it.

Taking a deep breath, I reached the far wall and hunkered down to examine what appeared to be a narrow abyss in the attic floor, where the floor should have met the far wall. My fingers digging into the beam above my head for balance, I peered down into that narrow cut of darkness in the floor.

Poor construction. That's what I was looking at. Poor construction and, no doubt, the tilting of the house had caused the beams to split, to come apart, leaving a narrow little arroyo in the floor that just happened to drop down behind the wall of the closet in Tara's study.

The respiratory sound was undoubtedly the wind shuttling against the eaves. With such a separation in the framework, sound was bound to echo. That evening in bed, I explained what I had discovered to Tara, though she did not seem comforted by my revelation.

"I don't like that room," she said. "I don't like the noises that come from it, Harold."

* * *

Christmas came. I gave Tara the gold locket and she presented me with a handsome leather briefcase. We had a quiet dinner together in the drafty house then watched television until Tara went upstairs to shower before bed. My own eyelids growing heavy, I pulled an afghan up over my body and muted the television.

When Tara appeared staring down at me several moments later, I thought I was dreaming at first.

"What?" I muttered. "What is it?"

"It's back. Upstairs. Come listen."

Once again in the second-floor study, we both stood before the open closet doors, peering in at nothing by a couple of metal filing cabinets.

"That's the wind," I explained again. "If you'd seen the gap in the attic boards..."

"That isn't the sound I heard before." Tara looked frightened. "It was like something moving around on the other side of the drywall."

"Darling, there's nothing there."

"What if it's an animal come in from the cold? Living in the walls? A raccoon, maybe?"

"There's nothing up there, Tara."

She shivered beside me. "I feel funny. Strange. Like something is trying to get at me."

"Get at you?"

"Eat me."

"Tara, honey, there are no wild animals up in the attic."

"Harold, please..."

I sighed and promised her I would check again first thing in the morning.

But morning brings with it a breed of clarity that night disallows, and it took the passage of several more evenings before I agreed to once again climb up into the attic. Armed with a flashlight, a hammer and nails, and a few planks of wood, I promised Tara I'd chase out any animal intruder then board up the narrow gap in the floor, putting an end to this nonsense once and for all.

In the attic, I traversed the narrow beams until I reached the gap where the floor met the outer wall. Setting my implements down, I clicked on the flashlight and dumped the beam down into the open shaft.

Things twinkled at me from below.

The distance was too great to make out what they were, or to simply reach down and scoop them up. My curiosity mounting, I decided to climb down there and see what those items were. It was a tight squeeze, and I utilized the exposed beams as hand- and footholds on my way down. The dry smell of insulation caused me to sneeze. When I touched my feet down on solid flooring again, I was packed firmly behind the closet wall of Tara's second-floor study.

I trailed the flashlight's beam along the floor, illuminating those twinkling objects scattered about my feet...

Some items were easily identifiable as jewelry—necklaces, earrings, what appeared to be a collegiate ring with the jewel missing from the setting—while others were as enigmatic to me as matter floated down from space. There were also a few screws and things that resembled hammered ball bearings. I gathered up all these items and stowed them away in the pockets of my trousers. Then, climbing back up out of the gap, I covered the opening with the planks of wood. If any animal had sought refuge in this crevice, there would be no more re-entry.

* * *

For whatever unexplained reason, I felt compelled to hide the items I'd found in the gap from my wife. I put them all in a gym sock, which I stuffed toward the back of my underwear drawer.

* * *

It was very early morning, the sun not yet fully up, when I awoke in bed alone. Tara's side of the mattress was cool. I lay awake, staring at the ceiling, awaiting her return from the bathroom. But she never returned. And when I checked the bathroom, I found it empty and unused.

I searched the bungalow, calling her name. When the clock on the landing struck 5:15 AM, a dreadful panic had already set in. Hastily, I checked the windows and the doors—all of which were locked—and once again began thinking of last year's murders in the Heath. It was still an ungodly hour of the morning when I found myself pounding on neighbors' doors, asking if they had seen my wife. They all scowled and assured me they had not. Trembling, I returned home to call the police.

Two uniformed officers came, took notes, and conducted a cursory and disinterested scan of the bungalow. "Maybe," one of the officers suggested before leaving, "she just got bored, mate."

I called out of classes for the day and sat on the sofa for most of the afternoon, anticipating—hoping—that Tara would walk through the front door at any minute. By late afternoon, with a gray rain falling in the streets, I contemplated driving around town to see if I could spot her. I even pulled on my clothes without the benefit of showering and was in the process of lacing up my sneakers when I heard a banging sound echo down the stairwell from the second-floor landing.

"Tara!" It leapt from my throat in a strangled cry.

Racing up the stairs, I entered Tara's study to find the room empty. I listened again for the banging noise but heard nothing. My respiration was shuddery, my vision beginning to fragment. The closet doors stood open, the twin filing cabinets leering at me.

And then I heard it—a muted thump, like someone on the other side of the closet wall, pounding a fist. I pressed my ear against the drywall and listened, holding my breath. Nothing. Again, I called my wife's name. No response.

I grabbed the flashlight from the kitchen drawer then climbed up into the attic. When I turned the flashlight on, the beam shook in my unsteady hand. The attic appeared empty. Again, I called out Tara's name and received no answer. Crossing the catwalk of two-by-fours to the far wall, I wondered if somehow Tara had fallen down the gap between the walls. It was ridiculous, of course—what would she have been doing up here after all?—but what other explanation was there?

But no: the planks of wood were still nailed down over the opening.

I stood there, my heart slamming in my chest.

And thought I heard movement down below, in the gap.

"Tara!"

I dropped to my knees and began wrenching the planks of wood loose with my bare hands. Once I'd made a large enough opening, I directed the flashlight beam into the gap while holding my breath.

Of course, the space was empty. Had I really expected to find Tara down there?

My hands quaked. The flashlight's beam vibrated across the flooring at the bottom of the gap.

Again, something twinkled up at me.

After prying away more boards, I descended the gap as I had done once before, and crouched down to retrieve what I had seen from above.

Tara's locket. The one I'd given her for Christmas.

A terrible sickness overtook me. I thought I would pass out. Nothing made sense.

There were other things on the floor as well. Things similar to the hammered ball bearings I'd found previously...

* * *

I sit now on the spare bed in Tara's study, facing the open closet. In my lap is this notebook, in which I have detailed all that has happened, no matter how bizarre. Beside me is Tara's locket. The picture is no longer inside it; where it has gone, I have no idea. It's been three days since Tara's disappearance, and I am hearing the knocking behind the wall regularly now, much as Tara had.

What had she said? *I feel funny. Strange. Like something is trying to get at me.* But not just get at her. *Eat me,* she had said.

I'm done writing now. I'll sit and wait and see what happens. Tara was right—there is something here. Maybe not something *behind* the walls. Maybe it *is* the walls. The bungalow itself.

I don't know.

What I know is that I am scared I will never see my wife again.

What I know is that I am terrified of what is making that knocking sound.

What I know is that those hammered ball bearings I found are actually fillings from teeth.

We sat outside the café sipping hot espressos while watching the camouflaged trucks come down the dirt roadway. They looked heavy and were burdened with men, and the thick-treaded tires bit into the muddy earth and turned with much noise. There were five trucks in all, and they crept slowly past the café and down the rue boueuse, and behind them the sky was like gunpowder and acrid with the smell of smoke. From the café we could no longer see the smoke clearly, billowing up from beyond the veil of trees against the horizon as it had done for the past five days; after many days, the smoke had become part of the air itself, and it had mingled and dispersed. We were breathing it in with every breath. Omar said something about the water having turned gray and how the surface was covered in a gentle film of dust. You couldn't drink it, he said, because it would make you sick, and that it tasted very much like soot, and it coated your throat and made your throat and the back of your mouth taste very bitter and unclean. Many of the fish had died, too, and most were big fish and good for eating but no one would eat them now and anyway they floated at the surface of the dirty water like logs in filth. Not smiling, Omar said he'd seen children down by the bank of the river early in the morning and had watched them use long sticks to pull the dead fish close to the embankment. The kids, they made much noise, and it was very early in the morning for children to be outside. The water was too dirty for them to play in, also, Omar said. He said a lot of things about the water. He spoke more of the water than of the soldiers that had come into the town and shot the little girl in the street. Omar did not speak about the little girl, and of the way her mother had cried and screamed and how she had been shot, too. He said nothing about the little girl and her mother, and no one else did, either. It was easier to talk of nonsense and to talk about dirty, undrinkable water.

THE JUMPING SHARKS OF DYER ISLAND

They stayed in a small clapboard hut in Kleinbaai, which overlooked the black sea and the white flats and a jagged outcrop of glossy auburn stone. The air smelled of brine and fish, and there were many southern right whales beached down by the water during that week. Fishermen populated the flats in the early morning. Their tiny boats were like oversized shoes draped with chain-mesh fishing nets hanging over the sides. These men fished for hours beneath large, sweeping cumulous clouds, their bodies the color and texture of oiled saddle leather. Twisted bundles of muscle contracted in their backs and arms as they worked. Jay Conroy watched them from beneath the hut's portico every morning while seated in a rope-backed chair.

The last day of the week it rained, but the fishermen still came. Jay Conroy watched the dark men pilot their boats along the cusp of the beach through heavy sheets of rain. The whale carcasses had slowly been pilfered over the past five days; all that remained were the skin-stripped husks of their bodies, fin-less and fluke-less and ravaged by gulls. Janet did not approve of the smell and rarely sat beneath the portico with her husband. Jay Conroy, however, was invigorated by the fresh scent of death, and spent many hours in his chair, smelling the air and sipping from a mug of hot, spiced tea.

Janet stood in the doorway but did not come out. "You're going to catch cold, Jay."

Jay Conroy sipped his tea and watched gulls rip tendrils of meat off a whale carcass.

"Come inside and get dressed," Janet said. "There's fresh fruit on the table and it's warm inside."

The rain let up in late afternoon, leaving the air wet and the sky a mottled gray. From the clapboard hut, Jay Conroy could hear the waves breaking against the rocky shore. For lunch, Janet prepared a dried fruit chutney, which was very good and very sweet, and Jay Conroy ate two portions. Following that, he gathered some paperwork under his arms and slipped on a pair of rope-soled sandals. He examined his printouts and drew little red checks by several of the Fortune 500 companies listed throughout the printouts. Janet, breathing heavy through her nose and not saying a word to Jay Conroy, walked down to the beach. She steered away from the rotting whales.

By three o'clock they were hiking along the coast. It had gotten increasingly hot and the traveling was tedious. Several times Jay Conroy nearly slipped off a lichen-covered crag and spilled to the beach below. Janet laughed good-naturedly the first time, but grew progressively more impatient with him.

"It's too damn wet to walk these rocks," he said at one point. He wore, at his wife's insistence, a wide-brimmed safari hat and a long-sleeved chambray shirt. He burned easily in the sun.

"It's not too wet," Janet said, ahead of him on the rocks. She was considerably younger than him and in better shape.

"They're covered in algae."

"It's too nice to spend the rest of the day indoors, Jay."

There was a golf course on the southern tip of Danger Point, but Jay Conroy did not mention it now.

They joined a group of tourists near the mouth of a giant cave at one point. The guide was a handsome-looking young black man with narrow eyes and a length of hemp tied around his neck. He wore a bulky watch with a built-in compass on his left wrist. Jay Conroy recognized it as the same watch Janet had bought for him prior to the trip. He'd left it back at the hut.

"Over eighty-thousand years ago," explained the guide, "primitive man took up residence in these caves."

Many people snapped photographs and some applauded. The handsome-looking guide posed for a photograph with a few of the tourists. Jay Conroy, uninterested, lit a cognac-dipped cigarillo and looked out over the ocean. The brochure had promised this stretch of water between the coast and Dyer Island to be rife with whales, but the only whales he'd seen all week had been the dead ones along the beach.

"Jay," Janet said, "we should take a picture with the guide in front of the cave."

Jay Conroy watched the guide. Then he watched his wife watch the guide. "We have enough pictures," he said.

"What's the matter with you?"

"It's hot and I'm tired."

"It isn't hot," Janet said.

"Stand there," he said, slipping the compact Minolta out of his wife's hands and pointing at the yawning mouth of the black cave. "I'll take your picture."

"What about you? Jay, I want you in the picture, too. I want the both of us to be in the picture."

A pale-faced man in a baseball cap and reflective sunglasses smiled at Jay Conroy. "Let me help you," the stranger said, extending an open palm.

"Give him the camera, Jay," Janet said.

"That's not necessary," Jay Conroy said. He shook his head, looking at the man. "It isn't necessary."

"Oh sure," the man said. "Please." He said, "I insist."

Jay Conroy hesitated briefly before handing the little Minolta to the stranger. Some of the other sightseers were watching them now, along with the handsome-looking guide. They were smiling— all teeth, white and bright in the daylight. The guide's skin looked very black in the sun.

"Here," Janet said, plucking the cigarillo from Jay Conroy's mouth and posing with it hidden behind her back. "That's a filthy thing," she told him from the corner of her mouth.

The stranger examined the camera, held it to his eyes, grimaced, examined the camera again. Behind him, the guide held one tar-colored hand over his eyes. Jay Conroy thought he was looking at Janet. His eyes shielded, Jay Conroy could not tell where the guide was looking.

"Smile," Janet said at his side.

The stranger finally managed to take the picture, and again the throng of tourists applauded. Taking the cigarillo from his wife's hand, Jay Conroy missed his air-conditioned office with the magnetic dry erase board and the too-loud wall clock above his desk. He thought of Leib filling his monthly sales quota while he was here wasting time. Not for the first time he wondered how he'd allowed himself to be persuaded by Janet into taking this trip. And he silently cursed himself for bringing it up in the first place. It wasn't the first all-expense-paid trip he'd earned from the company following an outstanding year. There'd been a trip to Puerto Rico after he'd achieved ten CEO placements in only four months; there'd been the hiring freeze instituted by two of Leib's largest clients that made his record in 1992 all the more impressive, gaining him a weekend for two at a small bed-and-breakfast in New England; there'd been a trip to Ireland; to England; to the frozen valley of the Yukon. All those trips…

Jay Conroy looked up and saw his wife chatting with the stranger who'd taken their photograph. Laughing, Janet placed a pale hand on the stranger's shoulder. He couldn't see the stranger's eyes, so cleverly hidden behind the reflective lenses of his sunglasses.

The guide clapped his hands together and hastened the crowd to follow him — *carefully* — down the other side of the hill.

Janet did not wait for her husband; she began moving down the rocky slope with the rest of the crowd as Jay Conroy watched. She walked very close to the stranger who'd taken their picture, and very close to the handsome-looking guide.

Jay Conroy smoked his cigarillo down to the ember then flicked it out over the rocky precipice.

* * *

In the evening there was dinner and live music at an outdoor tavern on the crest of the hillside. Janet wore a tight-fitting floral summer dress and had her dark hair pinned back behind her head. Jay Conroy thought she looked very beautiful. In the carriage on their way to the tavern he could smell her body, warm and soap-smelling, and fresh like the band of air at the edge of the sea. They dined on exotic fish and great wedges of moist cake, and drank two cups of rooibos tea apiece. A calypso band performed beneath a grand arcade, the music predominantly percussion.

"Let's dance," Janet suggested.

"No," Jay Conroy said. "Let's just sit here awhile. I want to look at you sitting here."

"Why?"

"Because you're very pretty."

"You play so nice," she said.

"I'm not playing."

"Can I ask you something?"

"All right," he said.

"Did I make you jealous today?" she asked, smiling. She was so beautiful. Around her the night was dark and lit only by the moon and the nearby torches that were staked into the cold sand. "Did I make you jealous talking to that funny man? The one who took our picture?"

"I don't know," he said. "Maybe."

"And are you still unhappy we're here?"

"Not very."

"And you don't think about your office? You don't think about Milwaukee at all?"

"I can think of everything at once," he said. "I can think of you and me and also think of home, too. It's a talent."

She laughed. "You have such a lovely and interesting brain."

"And you have a magnificent body," he told her.

"Stop it. Don't tell me things like that. You'll make it go to my head."

"It's true," he said.

"Is that why you love me?"

"Yes," he said.

"Just because I have a magnificent body?"

"Yes," he said again.

"And for nothing else?"

"No."

She made as if to slap his hand from across the small table. "What a terrible thing to say!"

"Does that go straight to your head, too?"

"Not as fast as these drinks. Will you get us some more, Jay?"

"More tea?"

"No," Janet said. "Get something strong. Get us two drinks each and make sure they put a lot of coconut rum in mine. I love coconut rum. And a lot of ice, too."

Jay Conroy kissed his wife's hand, stood, and crossed the patio to the outdoor bar. He was in a good mood. The night was cool and fresh and made him feel clean. He ordered four mai tais, heavy on the rum, and gathered them awkwardly in his hands after the bartender placed them on the counter. There were a good number of people up dancing now, and he had to maneuver around them with some difficulty, careful not to spill the drinks.

Janet was not seated at their table when he returned.

He set the drinks down and scrutinized the crowd of dancers. His young wife was among them, laughing and dancing and twisting in her pretty floral dress. He watched her for what seemed like a long time before taking his seat and turning away. Beyond the hillside he could see the shimmering white lights of the fishing vessels pulling slowly across the sea. He could hear the whitecaps shredding themselves against the crags lining the shore. Without turning, he grabbed one of the drinks and brought it to his lips, sipped it. All he could taste, despite the extra rum, was grenadine and lime. He winced but took a second, larger swallow.

At one point a group of young women, Janet among them, began clapping and dancing around a handsome, middle-aged man with reddish skin and sharp, woodcut features. Jay Conroy watched Janet and she didn't see him. Then he watched the handsome man, who began dancing quite professionally. The crowd thought it was fantastic and cheered him on. The circle of women clapped louder and stomped their feet. Then the crowd applauded and cheered as the handsome dancer reached out and plucked a young woman from the circle. He spun her around twice, very elegantly, and bowed as she reclaimed her place in the lineup. Stomping his feet, the man twirled one hand above his head, eliciting shouts and laughter from the audience, and reached into the circle of women again. Janet was selected this time, and the handsome man pulled her up against him then pushed her away, rolling her down the length of his broad, sturdy arm. Laughing, Janet looked at Jay Conroy, winked, and gave him a small wave. He waved back, forced a grin, and clapped his hands off-tempo with the music.

When the dance ended everyone cheered and Jay Conroy stood and applauded. He'd finished two of the four drinks but he'd hardly noticed. The onlookers parted and Janet pranced across the macadam and took her seat at the table across from him. He sat as well, still smiling and clapping.

"Well," he said. "Look at you."

Blushing, Janet's smile widened. "I wasn't so bad?"

"Not at all. Your friend," he said. "He's very good."

"My friend?"

"Your partner. He's professional?"

"Oh," she said, bringing a mai tai to her lips with both hands, "I don't know. I don't even know his name."

"Well," Jay Conroy said, looking past his wife's shoulder, "here he comes, anyway."

Janet set her drink down just as the man approached their table. He was less alluring but still handsome up close. He wore a white cotton shirt, half unbuttoned, and the fabric was transparent enough for Jay Conroy to observe the tiny dark discs of the man's nipples.

"Thank you," the man said, smiling at Janet. "I thank all my dancers, but you were superb."

"I used to dance back in school," she said, staring up at him.

"You are not still in school?"

She laughed. "Oh, no! I've been out of school for a long time. I'm married."

"Yes," the man said with surprisingly little interest, and turned his eyes on Jay Conroy. "Mate," the man said, nodding.

Jay Conroy stood and shook the man's hand. "Please," he said, "have a seat."

"Yes," said Janet.

"I couldn't," the man said. "You're having a romantic dinner."

"Dinner is finished," Janet said. "Please sit. We can talk about dancing."

"Have a drink," Jay Conroy said, sliding the remaining mai tai in front of their new guest.

"Maybe just for a bit," said the man, and he moved to the nearest unoccupied table to retrieve a chair.

Jay Conroy watched his wife and smiled at her when their eyes met. Her skin looked pink in the nearby firelight and her eyes looked large and round and black. She was very beautiful and she *was* a good dancer.

"I'm Tommy McCurry," the man said, settling down in the empty chair.

"Janet Conroy," Janet said. "That's my husband, Jay."

"Husband Jay," said Tommy McCurry. "Your wife, she's a wonderful dancer."

"Thank you," Jay Conroy said.

"You are vacationing?"

"Yes. We're from the U.S.," Janet said. "Wisconsin," she added, "not New York." She laughed playfully. "It seems everyone thinks the U.S. is comprised of only two states—New York and Texas. It's just not true!"

"Yes," Tommy McCurry said, "I know your accents. I have been to the United States, but it was many years ago. I liked it very much."

"Do you live here?" Janet asked.

"Yes. I am from Kleinbaai. I have a flat there and work on the sea."

"You're a fisherman?" Jay Conroy said.

Tommy McCurry laughed. "No, no," he said, "I'm a tour guide. I didn't want to just say it that way. It sounds in poor taste, like I'm trying to get business from you. I'm sorry, that was rude."

"No," Janet said, "that's fine. We went on a tour of the caves earlier today. Didn't we, Jay?"

"We did," he said. "What do you tour?"

"Sharks," Tommy McCurry said.

Janet giggled and sipped her drink. "Don't lie! How can you tour sharks?"

"I've heard of it before," Jay Conroy said quickly, but neither his wife nor Tommy McCurry turned to look at him.

Tommy McCurry pointed out over the hillside toward the black sheet of water. "Look out past this koppie," he said.

Janet frowned but looked nonetheless. "Koppie?"

"This hillside. That water—do you see? That stretch that, in the dark, looks like outer space? That is Shark Alley." Smiling, he said, "Have you ever known sharks to fly?"

Janet's smile grew. Jay Conroy looked back over the koppie.

"They do," Tommy McCurry said. "Sharks fly here, Janet Conroy."

"Now you're talking lies," she said. "Now you're talking them for sure."

"Well, they jump, anyway," Tommy McCurry said. "These are the great white sharks. They are very large and very muscular fish. They are brutal predators, too, and at certain times of the day when the seals swim across Shark Alley from the island to the mainland, these sharks feed. It is unusual and magnificent to watch—and they soar straight up out of the water to catch their prey. It is really something. I am surprised you haven't heard more about these jumping sharks; it is what Dyer Island and Gansbaai are known for."

"I have heard of it," Jay Conroy said.

"Isn't it dangerous to be out there?" Janet asked Tommy McCurry.

"It is not very dangerous, but maybe a little."

"You sit on a boat," Jay Conroy said.

"Often," the man said, "we send shark cages into the water to watch them feed. I have taken tourists out into these cages many times. The sharks, sometimes they come up to the cage and bite at the bars."

"Oh," Janet said, wrinkling her brow, "that must be dreadful! How ridiculous."

"It's perfectly safe," Jay Conroy assured his wife.

"It's exhilarating," Tommy McCurry said, flashing white teeth as if doing an impression of one of the sharks.

"The cages are made of steel," Jay Conroy said from across the table. "It's not the nature of sharks to attack the cage. It was all in the brochure, Janet."

"I would like to see the jumping sharks," Janet said.

"Well," Tommy McCurry said, "I will do it at a special rate for you, my new mates."

"I don't know," Jay Conroy said skeptically.

"Jay!" Janet said, glaring at him. "Mr. McCurry said he'd give us special rates. It would be rude."

"There must be other, more peaceful things to do here…"

"There is golf," suggested Tommy McCurry.

"Jay loves golf," Janet added. Struck by an idea, her face lit up. "Tomorrow Jay can play golf and I will go and see the jumping sharks!"

Laughing, looking very handsome and rugged, Tommy McCurry said, "They are some sharks."

"It's supposed to be a beautiful day tomorrow," Janet said, running one finger along the rim of her glass. "It will be very warm and bright and beautiful. A great day for being out on the water."

"Or playing the golf," Tommy McCurry said, smiling at Jay Conroy. "It is a very fine golf course. It is a world course."

"I don't know what that means," Jay Conroy said.

"A world course," the man repeated. "People come from all over the world to play it. You will like it very much."

"I'm not really in the mood for golf."

"I don't think I could watch them eat a seal, though," Janet confessed, lightly placing her hand on the tour guide's arm. "I think it would make me feel bad."

"There are special ways around that," the tour guide said. "I have just the thing."

"What is it?" Janet asked.

"A surprise," Tommy McCurry went on. "Tomorrow you will see."

Janet laughed and finished her drink.

"This shark thing," Jay Conroy said abruptly, "it *does* sound interesting."

"Then it will be the three of us?" the tour guide suggested.

"Jay doesn't really like the water," Janet said.

"That's not true," he countered.

"There is always safari," Tommy McCurry said. "You could do that."

"He has bad knees, too," Janet continued.

"Stop it," he said to his wife. To the tour guide he said, "I don't have bad knees."

Janet frowned. "Of course you do, Jay!"

"The safari," Tommy McCurry said, "they take you around in a bakkie, so there is not much walking."

"What's a bakkie?" Janet asked.

"A truck," Tommy McCurry said and Janet laughed, reaching for the tour guide's untouched drink.

"This is such a beautiful country," she said, sipping from Tommy McCurry's glass.

"I don't have bad knees," Jay Conroy said to no one.

* * *

In the morning they had breakfast along the crest of the hillside. They drank tea and Janet ate several pastries. Jay Conroy ate nothing, as he did not feel well. They sat beneath a straw canopy and he could see the beach below. There was a circle of fishermen down by the docks, unfolding their nets and setting them in long, flayed strips along the bulkhead. Some young men stood watching the fishermen, snorkels and fins collected in their arms. These young men were abalone divers, Jay Conroy surmised, and he watched them watching the fishermen for a long while.

"You should eat something," Janet told him. "We're going to be out on the water all afternoon."

After breakfast they returned to the hut to bathe and dress. Janet dressed in a sheer cotton blouse and wrapped a floral-printed sarong about her waist. Jay Conroy dressed quickly in whatever clothes he came upon. He sat mulling over his paperwork beneath the hut's awning while waiting for his wife, breathing deep the salty air. Someone had come and dragged the rotting whale carcasses away from the beach. There were a number of other huts scattered around the point; perhaps one of the other guests had complained about the smell. But it hadn't bothered him.

By early afternoon they were trekking down the rocky slope toward the white sand flats. There were tall reeds in the grass and they whipped their legs in the strong wind coming in off the Atlantic. Below, several small charter boats crowded the few piers.

"Those are the boats?" Jay Conroy said. "They don't look too sturdy for shark hunting."

"No one's hunting sharks, Jay," Janet said.

Tommy McCurry's catamaran was small and peeling and looked rickety and uncertain. There was a cylindrical steel cage strapped to the front deck. His shirt off and his skin coffee-colored beneath the blazing sun, Tommy McCurry carried heavy white pails to the rear of the ship. He noticed them approaching and set the pails down and waved. He looked much younger with his shirt off, Jay thought.

"Watch your footing," Tommy McCurry said as they approached. He assisted Janet onto the boat. "She may not look like much," he assured her, "but she is a good boat." And looking back over his shoulder, he seemed surprised to see Jay Conroy. "Husband Jay," he said.

"Hello."

"So you've decided to come after all?"

He'd decided to come last night, but perhaps Tommy McCurry had had too many mai tais to remember. No, wait—Tommy McCurry hadn't had anything to drink all evening.

"Is it a long trip?" he asked, managing to climb onto the boat without any assistance. Tommy McCurry was already moving toward Janet at the rear of the boat, anyway.

"Maybe twenty minutes out," Tommy McCurry assured him.

"It's a wonderful day," Janet said. She'd seated herself on a bench outside the pilothouse and looked very young and very pretty with her hands folded in her lap.

"It is," the guide agreed. "Wait till we get out and away from the mainland here. The water is very clear."

"It's very pretty," Janet said.

Laughing, the guide said, "Yes."

Hugging the side of the boat with one hand, Jay Conroy made his way to the fiberglass bench and sat beside his wife. Without looking at him, Janet patted his hand. Jay Conroy thought she was watching their good-looking tour guide.

In the pilothouse, Tommy McCurry set aside a number of scuba tanks and started up the engine. It crackled and spat and roared and didn't sound too reliable. Jay Conroy wanted to ask if anyone's charter had ever gotten stuck in Shark Alley, but he said nothing. Tommy McCurry maneuvered the vessel out of its slip and directed it toward the wide mouth of the Atlantic. The boat cut quickly through the water, splashing spume and sea salt onto the deck and against the pilothouse windows. Janet laughed and dangled one hand over the side of the boat, reaching for the froth. Then she leaned forward and hollered something to Tommy McCurry. The tour guide laughed and rubbed at his ribs with one hand. Jay Conroy could not hear what they were saying over the roar of the boat's engine.

When the jagged peaks of Dyer Island appeared on the right, Tommy McCurry slowed the charter to a sputtering gallop. "The water," he explained, "it's shallow here in places. I have to be careful."

"Be careful," Janet agreed.

Jay Conroy looked around but could see no sharks. There were a few seals populating the island's coastline, sunbathing on the black rocks, and coal-colored cormorants perched in the high, reedy hills.

Tommy McCurry slipped from the pilothouse and went to the stack of white pails. He bent and popped the lid off one with a large knife then pulled on a pair of rubber gloves.

"What is that stuff?" Janet asked.

"Chum," Tommy McCurry said. "I spread it in the water to attract the sharks."

"Oh," Janet said, watching the tour guide work. She wrinkled her nose. "It looks like blood and guts."

Tommy McCurry said, "It is."

"And we want to do that? I mean, have them come up so close to the boat?"

"The closer the better," the guide said. He began scooping chum from the bucket with a plastic ladle and emptying it overboard.

"You should help," Janet told Jay Conroy.

"It's all right," Tommy McCurry said. "Just enjoy yourselves. This is your vacation. In fact, there are beers in the cooler."

"Where is the cooler?" Janet asked, looking around.

"You are sitting on it," Tommy McCurry said.

They stood and Jay Conroy fished out a cold bottle of beer for himself and his wife. Janet nudged him and he glanced over his shoulder and asked Tommy McCurry if he wanted one.

"Not for me, thank you."

"They're very cold," Janet said.

"Enjoy them," Tommy McCurry said. He finished with the chum and stepped back into the pilothouse to steer the boat in a half-circle. They proceeded to backtrack through their wake.

"This is prowling," Jay Conroy said into his wife's ear. "I read about this, too."

"You are magnificent," she said, and tasted her beer.

Something dark and plastic and the size of a small dog jumped from the pilothouse and slid across the boat deck. Janet jumped and cried out, startled, and Tommy McCurry appeared, laughing and raking his fingers down the xylophonic sides of his rib cage.

"Goodness," Janet said. "What in the world…?"

"This is Hester," Tommy McCurry explained, and picked up the object. It was a Styrofoam cutout covered in black latex that resembled a seal pup. There were ragged cuts and indentations along its body where the foam, white as bone beneath the latex skin, could be seen. Tommy McCurry held it up vertically, dangling it from the mossy rope that was attached to its snout.

"Look at that," Janet marveled.

"This is how we get the sharks to jump," Tommy McCurry explained. "We trail Hester here in the water behind the boat. Once the sharks get a whiff of the chum, they will come and follow the boat. When a shark sees Hester's silhouette swimming atop the water, it will spring up out of the water to catch her."

"How sad," Janet said, reaching out and stroking the seal's latex hide.

"It's fake," Jay Conroy said.

"Still," she said, "it's sad. Poor dumb fake dead seal."

"Those cuts along its body," Jay Conroy said to his wife, "those are from sharks' teeth."

Tommy McCurry smiled. "Not exactly," he said. "That's really just natural wear-and-tear. I'm afraid that if a great white got a hold of Hester, there would be very little left."

"Oh," Jay Conroy said.

"Poor Hester," Janet moaned, then sang: "Hester, Hester, beware the shark molester..."

"Lucky for Hester," Tommy McCurry said, "the big boys miss quite often."

With the latex seal dumped overboard, Tommy McCurry piloted the boat up and down Shark Alley. Jay Conroy was having serious doubts about spotting a shark, let alone a great white, when the tour guide shouted and pointed out over the dark, undulating waves.

"Look," the guide said. "See there? That's its dorsal."

A sleek, black mast rose from the water and streamed toward the boat. Janet began shouting and clapping and Tommy McCurry, grinning proudly, looped an arm around her narrow shoulders and gave her a familiar hug. Jay Conroy watched them then looked back at the shark. As it moved the dorsal fin dipped back down beneath the surface.

"Is that all?" Janet asked.

"Wait!" Tommy McCurry said, still squeezing Jay Conroy's wife. "Wait, Janet!"

There seemed to fall an eerie, foreboding silence. The cough of the charter's idling engine was all they could hear. Then the shark struck, spearing in a spray of glistening diamonds straight up out of the water, its body heavy and sleek and pure muscle, its jaws gaping and impossibly wide, reinforced with serrated, stone-colored teeth, each one huge and like the blade of a fan. It rotated its body until its jaws faced downward, its powerful crescent-shaped tail whipping from left to right, left to right, machinelike in its efficiency. Hester sprang up from the water and spiraled into the air, the rope taut then slack, spinning and twirling like an acrobat. The great fish came down and slammed through the surface of the water, shattering it. And with all its awesome, preternatural supremacy, it disappeared beneath the waves as if it had never existed.

"Good Lord," Jay Conroy uttered.

Janet broke out into cheers, wailing and clapping her hands. "Oh Tommy, that was *amazing!*"

"You see?" Tommy McCurry said. "What did I say?"

"You live such an amazing life, to do this every day! It is so beautiful here and the sharks are so impossibly wonderful! I never knew it!"

"I have much respect for the sharks," Tommy McCurry said.

"It is a very brave thing," Janet said.

Jay Conroy watched them and listened to them and forgot all about the jumping sharks of Dyer Island. He felt something hot and strong turn over in his stomach.

"I want to go down in the cage," Jay Conroy spoke up suddenly. "That shark cage at the front of the boat—I want to go down in it."

Their laughter subsiding, his wife and Tommy McCurry only stared at him.

"I want to go down," he repeated.

"In the *water*, Jay?" Janet said.

"Mate," Tommy McCurry said, "I'm afraid that's just not doable."

"I have money. I have cash right here with me, right now. What is it you people say? I want to do it *now-now.*"

"It's just not doable."

"Why not?"

"I don't have the proper equipment on board."

"The cage is right up front," Jay Conroy said, "and there are oxygen tanks in the pilothouse. I saw them."

Tommy McCurry started to laugh. "You are fooling with me, yes?"

"I'm serious. I want to go down."

"Jay," Janet said.

"It is a lot of work to send someone down in the cage."

"I'll help you," Jay Conroy said.

"Jay," Janet said, pulling herself to his side, "what are you doing? You can't go in the water."

"What needs to be done?" he asked Tommy McCurry.

The guide lowered his head slightly and smiled at Jay Conroy from beneath his dark brow. He placed his hands on his hips and flexed the muscles in his chest.

"First," Tommy McCurry said, "we need to lower the cage into the water."

"Jay!" Janet shouted.

"All right," Jay Conroy said.

"We let it sit in the water so the sharks will get used to it. I will then instruct you on how to use the scuba gear. Have you ever been scuba diving before?"

"No."

"You have bad *knees*, Jay," Janet reminded him.

"It is quite simple," Tommy McCurry said. "It will take no time for you to learn. Then," he said, "when the big fish have lost interest in the cage, I will send you down. There is even a camera I keep onboard for taking pictures underwater. You may use it, free of charge."

"All right," he said. "So let's put the cage in the water."

The tour guide's grin did not falter. "So let's," he said.

They unhooked the cage from the boat deck and secured it with nylon ropes to metal hinges along the catamaran's railing. Tommy McCurry strapped a diving cylinder to the inside of the cage and tugged at it. Jay Conroy stripped his shoes and socks off while watching Tommy McCurry through the meshwork of bars.

"It doesn't look like a strong cage," Janet said, hovering over her husband.

"It is a very strong cage," he told his wife, though he didn't think the shark cage looked very strong at all. "Isn't it?"

"Aye, sure," said Tommy McCurry.

"Jay, why are you doing this?"

"Go sit down on the cooler," he said to her, and watched Tommy McCurry watch his wife walk to the rear of the catamaran. Then Tommy McCurry turned and looked at him.

"You should not treat her that way," the guide said casually. "She is a lovely young woman and it is wrong."

"And you are a fine dancer," he responded.

"Oh?"

"You must make all the women very happy around here."

"I see," Tommy McCurry said. "This is a foolish thing, what you are trying to prove."

"I'm not trying to prove anything."

"Secure these ropes," Tommy McCurry said, tossing a coil of nylon ropes at Jay Conroy's feet.

The ropes tied to anchors running along the portside of the boat, the two men hoisted the cage up with little difficulty: it was not only small, but made of very lightweight steel. The two men lifted it and set it sideways on the boat's railing. Jay Conroy struggled with his end. There was a sliding, whistling sound. Tommy McCurry looked around and saw one of Jay Conroy's ropes had come untied and had slipped around the front of the cage. Jay Conroy saw it, too. It hung limply over the portside.

"Can you grab it?" the guide asked. "It is closer to you."

Jay Conroy reached out and overextended his fingers, but could not reach the rope. He chewed on his lower lip and was aware of his bare feet and he could not reach the rope.

"Balance the cage on your thigh," Tommy McCurry suggested.

Jay Conroy tried. "I can't," he said, his breath coming in short little wheezes now. "The cage is too heavy. It's too much weight on my knees."

"Then just hold it good and secure," Tommy McCurry said. The guide bent himself forward over the railing and snaked one bare arm around the outer portion of the steel cage, grappling for the fallen rope. Looking at Jay Conroy from the other side of the cage he said, "If I let my end go, can you support the weight?"

"No," he said. "Don't let go."

"But I cannot reach the rope," Tommy McCurry said.

"Wait," he said, "I'll call my wife over. She'll get the rope." But he didn't call for his wife and remained staring at Tommy McCurry through the bars of the cage. Tommy McCurry stared back and did not blink and Jay Conroy could see the glistening beads of sweat running like tears down his face and chest.

"No," Tommy McCurry said finally. "I can reach it."

He leaned further over the railing, stretching for the rope while balancing his side of the cage awkwardly with one hand and his left thigh. The rope hung loosely over the railing, thumping against the hull in the wind. So close to it, Tommy McCurry could almost reach it, almost swipe it with the tips of his fingers…

The cage shuddered then tipped further over the side of the boat. Tommy McCurry shouted at Jay Conroy to hold it secure, hold it, mate, but it was now unbalanced. The cage slid off the side of the boat and struck Tommy McCurry and caught his arm in the steel bars as it went down. The cage struck the water, pulling Tommy McCurry in with it, and Janet began shouting. Jay Conroy stood and saw Tommy McCurry's head rebound off the side of the cage, his arm still caught in the bars. The cage bobbed momentarily then began sinking slowly into the water. Tommy McCurry struggled and managed to get his arm free. Catching his breath, he began treading water with his one good arm while the cage sank next to him. He looked up at Jay Conroy and winced. The sun shone directly in his eyes.

"Well," Tommy McCurry said.

Janet rushed to the side of the boat and looked over. She said nothing.

Jay Conroy wound a length of rope around one hand. Slowly, with calculated lethargy, he began pulling the rope back onto the deck.

"Hurry, mate," Tommy McCurry said, water splashing in his face as he bobbed at the surface. Jay thought his voice sounded surprisingly calm. Blood oozed from a gash in his forehead.

"I'm sorry," Jay Conroy said, winding the rope back into a coil. "My knees…I'm sorry…"

Something flickered behind Tommy McCurry's eyes. Then he jerked his head to the left in time to see a blackish-gray dorsal fin cleave through the water. When he turned back to Jay Conroy, there was undeniable fear in his eyes.

"My knees gave out," Jay Conroy said. "You were right. The cage got too heavy and my knees gave out."

Wiping blood from his eye, Tommy McCurry said nothing.

Janet peered over the side of the catamaran at the submerged steel cage. She turned and looked sharply at Tommy McCurry. "It's an interesting and beautiful life," she said. "And I can't stop thinking of those sharks."

"Get me up," Tommy McCurry said.

"Look!" Janet said, pointing at the horizon. "There are two more!"

Jay Conroy looked. Indeed, two more dorsal fins wove through the surf toward the boat.

"Mate," Tommy McCurry said, his eyes pleading with Jay Conroy. He lifted one hand out of the water and held it out for him.

"Poor sad dead Mr. McCurry," Janet sang.

"Mate!" Tommy McCurry cried, though this time half the word was interrupted as the tour guide took on a mouthful of water as his head sank briefly beneath the surface. When he resurfaced, the guide looked around wildly. Blood streamed down his face. Another pair of fins appeared just a couple of yards away. "God have—" He went under again. This time, when he resurfaced, Tommy McCurry was screaming.

"Beware the shark molester," Jay Conroy said, then turned and headed across the deck toward the pilothouse. Peering over the portside railing, Janet laughed.

* * *

With the sun down, the beach was cool and breezy. They dragged a small folding-table through the sand and established it close to the rising surf. Jay Conroy started a fire on the beach and heated a handful of coals until they were red and glowing. He drove iron rods into the sand on either side of the fire and ran a rod barbed with tiny iron hooks between them. He cut strips of fish— what the Africans called "snoek"—and hung them from the little iron hooks over the fire. The smell was instantaneous.

Looking up, he saw Janet winding down the face of the cliff. She carried two candles, already lit to cast light on the stony path. She looked pale and ghostlike in the moonlight.

When the fish was ready they ate it at the little folding-table while admiring the rippling sea. The reflection of the moon in the water was large and blue and interrupted by many waves.

"The fish was very good," Janet said after a while. She'd cleaned her plate. "What is it called again?"

"Snoek," he said, pronouncing it *snook*. "Snoek braai."

"They sound like alien words."

"They do."

"What a marvelous day, and a marvelous trip. This will be a hard trip to beat."

"I think we can manage," he said. "Where would you like to go next?"

The Glad Street Angel

We stop for lunch at the Harbor Grill, although neither of us are really very hungry.

"You gotta get your act together now, Gideon, gotta keep your nose clean," my father tells me. I watch as he arranges a mound of crumbs into a straight line with his pinkie. "There are no more second chances."

"Yeah," I say.

"For real, man. You're eighteen now. Ride's over."

"Yeah," I say again, "I know."

I watch him take two bites of a hefty club sandwich from across the table. He chews slow and methodically, as if the act itself requires much thought, and his eyes alternate between me and the throng of cars along Pratt Street. My father and I don't really get along. Throughout my childhood, I maintained the constant notion of him as some brooding, elusive cloud on the horizon, rattling the ground below with thunder. I can remember watching him shave before the bathroom mirror, the sink half-full with water and clogged with shaving cream icebergs. He seemed so big. Once, I held a ladder for him while he scooped gunk out of the gutters of our duplex. I remember looking up and seeing straight up his shorts. His genitals looked like snarled, graying fruit.

"What are you thinking about?" he says suddenly.

"Mom," I lie.

"Well," he says, exhaling with enough zeal to send the queue of crumbs scattering like fleeing troops, "your mother, she's not feeling well. She'll be glad to see you, Gideon, but she's not feeling well."

"What is it now?"

"Her headaches."

"I thought she was taking something for that."

"She is," my father says. "The pills, they don't work like they used to."

"Is there anything else she can take?"

"Sometimes she can't even get up," he continues without hearing me. "You remember what she was like when she first started getting them? Goddamn migraines."

Suddenly, I'm thinking about pills. One day out of the blue, when I was a freshman in high school, I was struck by these dull, throbbing stomach pains, but not really in my stomach—more like on either side of my stomach, and just below it. The groin area. It felt like someone had stuffed two billiard balls just below the lining of my belly. My plan was to wait it out and not worry about it— tough it out like a man—but the pain wound up lasting for several days, and I grew increasingly frightened. All I could think about was my junior high sex education class and if there was a possibility I'd contracted some venereal disease from Jenna Dawson, even though we'd never gone all the way. So I panicked and wound up passing out one morning in the school bathroom, cracking the side of my head against a grimy urinal. I'd imagined my urine coming out in thick, coagulated, snotty ropes (it didn't) and that sent me swooning. I awoke sometime later in a bed at U of M with my father at my side. His first words to me had something to do with how real men don't whimper like little girls, and just what did I think I was doing in that bathroom anyway? Was I on something, for Christ's sake? When the doctor recommended I take pills, my father scoffed and told him I didn't need any pills. The pain went away after about a week, anyway. The problem was never diagnosed.

I sip my Coke and don't touch my roast beef sandwich.

"Anyway," my father says, "things are gonna change. They have to. You understand that, right? You understand that your mother can't handle your crap anymore?"

I tell him yes, I understand.

"And *I'm* through dealing with it, too."

I tell him I understand.

"I got you a job," he tells me, "doing some construction work for a friend of mine. This friend, he knows the deal—knows what you been through, I mean—and he's doin' me a favor by bringing you on. That means you don't embarrass me. I said it'd be okay if he gives you a monthly drug test or something. Told him I'd prefer it, really. I think that made him feel good about the situation. He's a good guy. Just don't screw shit up." He sighs and looks instantly miserable sitting out here on the verandah with me. Maybe he's thinking of my mom and her headaches. Or his construction worker buddy. Or whatever. "You start Monday," he says after too long a pause. "You better buckle down, Gideon."

I tell him thanks.

He is mulling something over in his mind. Caught in the throes of concentration, my father looks the way a washing machine might look if capable of thought, his brain all jumbled with faded chinos, polo shirts, worn house dresses stained with grease. "All right," he says finally, and there is some sort of resignation in his voice, "let's see 'em, Gideon. Up on the table." He says, "Let me see your hands."

I show him, holding them palms up, and there is no expression on his face. I feel I owe some sort of explanation. I say, "I haven't done it since I don't know when. A long time, anyway."

"Yeah, okay," he says, and only because he isn't quite sure *what* to say. He does not understand my hand thing. Neither do I, really.

A lumbering silence passes between us. I think of him shaving in the mirror again, his shirt off, his doughy paunch obtruding over the frayed band of his Fruit of the Looms, a wiry braid of black hair spilling out of his bellybutton.

"Can we stop at the gas station on the way home?" I ask. "I need to grab some smokes."

My father sets his hands in his lap, anxious to leave. I am familiar with almost all of his idiosyncrasies. And I am familiar with his hands, too. I start to think about the way he rolled his handgun around in his hands that night, sitting on the edge of his bed, his head down. I am still thinking about this when he finally opens his mouth and says, "Anything you want to get off your chest before we get home?"

"Like what?"

Casually, he rolls his shoulders. He looks goofy doing it. Simple, somehow. "Anything," he says. "Anything. Whatever."

I think about my time in rehab, almost laugh, then shake my head.

We leave.

* * *

There is something frightening about my mother. And I realize I haven't seen her in five months.

She is sitting in a green recliner in front of the television set, her white hands pressed firmly in her lap, her eyes glazed over. Her hair is pulled back into a bun, gray and dull in the slivers of daylight that slide in through the partially-shaded windows, and her mouth is drawn tight as string. Seeing her, I am suddenly reminded of my grandmother's funeral and the way my mother had pressed rosary beads into the palm of my hand, insisting that I pray as we stood before the casket. She pressed hard, leaving behind tiny pea-shaped indentations. I cannot recall her words, cannot recall what Nona had looked like packaged in her satin-lined mahogany tube; I can only recall the brush of my mother's hair against my cheek, frizzled and damp with tears, and the stale-sweet smell of her breath in my face. Funeral breath. Mourning breath. Breath that cannot be masked by a million slabs of spearmint gum.

She looks up and sees me and smiles in her medicated way. Struggles to get up. I picture scarecrows swaying in a corn field and feel something hard and sick and moist roll over in my stomach.

"Ma," I say, and advance toward her before she has time to rise. Too much movement and her headaches start up.

I bend down and she hugs me, kisses the ink-spot birthmark just over my left eyebrow.

"Gideon," she whispers, squeezing me tight. I can feel the dull knobs of her fingertips pressing into my back. She is crying now.

"Honey. You look too thin. Your father said you were being fed at that place..."

"I was fed," I tell her.

"Ralph," she continues, and her eyes—now wet and muddy in their sockets—shift beseechingly toward my father. She looks much older than I remember.

"They fed him," my father promises her from the tiny kitchen. He is searching through the refrigerator.

"How you feeling, Ma?" I ask.

She ignores me. "Are you angry with me for not coming to see you? I wanted to, I did, but your father, he said it would be too much, that I should stay home because it would be too much—"

"I'm not angry, Ma."

"I wanted to go and to bring you some food, some good food from home, and I can't image what..." She trails off. "My God, Ralph, they didn't feed the poor boy. Look at him, will you?"

"I've seen him," my father says back. "He's fine."

It's already too much. Five months at Crownsville and I've forgotten how easily people cry. Particularly mothers.

The apartment is smaller than I remember, too—much smaller than the old duplex. The carpet is an amber-colored shag, filthy and stiff with dried food and spilled cola, and the furniture looks cramped and uncomfortable against the paneled walls. There are only a few windows, the shades all half-drawn, and the room is musty and oppressive. I think of retirement homes and abandoned cars left on the side of the highway.

"I've been planning this all week," my mother says, finally pushing herself up from the recliner. She is all skin and bones, like a blouse and sweatpants threaded with pipe cleaners. "We'll sit down tonight, have dinner together like a family. I'll make something, cook it up. What would you like, Gideon?"

"You don't have to, Ma."

"It's your first day home. Tell me what you want."

I tell her hamburgers would be perfect, and that seems to make her happy.

While she busies herself in the kitchen, I move down the hallway and see my father staring without interest at some framed photographs on the wall.

"Look at these," he mutters.

"She doesn't look good," I tell my father.

"What are you talking about?"

"How long has she been this way?"

"What way?"

"So out of it," I say. "You can't tell?" I think maybe he's been around her too long to notice. "She needs to see a doctor."

My father finally looks up at me and his face is stern, his jaw set...yet his eyes seem hurt. I am not used to seeing him in this way. He says, "Your mother's fine." He says, "They're only headaches, for Christ's sake, Gideon. Just migraines." He says, "You worry about yourself, that's all you need to worry about."

Later, I go to the bathroom, urinate for what feels like an hour, then find myself standing before the bathroom mirror for a comparable amount of time. I have taken some of the clinic home with me, I notice: my face is pale like the walls, and peels like plaster. My cheeks are chapped and cracked and interrupted by a network of very faint blood vessels. My eyes look sucked into my skull, hollow like busted light fixtures. My skin is jaundiced, the color of the mashed potatoes served on Fridays. It is also the same color as my mother's skin.

Rinsing my hands at the sink, I scrutinize my palms. It used to amuse me the way my father would ask to see my hands, to hold them out for him. Yet today at the restaurant I found I only felt sorry for him. For whatever reason.

I stick my tongue out at my reflection, wag it back and forth, and go to the kitchen for dinner.

* * *

My bedroom seems alien to me, and I think it's only because we'd been living in the apartment just a few months before I was arrested. It's small and smells vaguely of turpentine. There are a few scattered comic books on the floor, some Star Wars figures still in their packages tacked to the drywall. A large poster of Jimi Hendrix covers the back of my door.

I lay on the bed in silence for a long while, thinking about my hands and that night on Glad Street. I remember thinking about my father the night I was arrested—sitting in the back of the police car, I had summoned the image of him on the edge of his bed, holding his handgun. It was odd to think of that then. Odd now, too.

Once my mom has gone to bed, I creep down the hallway and grab my jacket from the hall closet. It's been five months and I expect it not to fit, or to just feel strange, but it fits and doesn't feel any different than I remember. In the kitchen I load my pockets with matchbooks and stuff a pack of Marlboros into my jacket. Without having to look I can tell my father's watching me from the living room. He's seated in the recliner in front of the TV, but he's not watching television—he's watching *me*.

"What?" I say, not looking up. I pretend to busy myself with the zipper on my jacket. "What is it?"

"Where are you going?"

"Out for a while. That a problem?"

I can tell that it is, but he does not say so. Instead, he tells me not to stay out too late, that I need to keep my shit together and my head clear. He does not articulate his intentions very well, my father. What he really means is he doesn't trust me and that he's worried I'm going to fuck things up again. But what my father doesn't understand is that different people deal with things in different ways. My way had been to get caught up in shit, smoke dope, get laid, drink too much. Fine. Whatever. Everybody's got their own method of operation.

Not for the first time, I wonder what my father would say if he knew I saw him with his gun that night.

"Don't be home late," he calls after me, but I'm already out the door.

Outside, I am hit by a strong October wind. The air reeks of the harbor, even in the cold, and it is an unsettling chemical smell. The city streets are poorly lighted, surprisingly desolate, and uniquely Baltimore. There are a few Halloween decorations in some of the tenement windows. I walk and smoke, my destination premeditated.

When I get to Glad Street, I stop walking and just stand on the curb. I'm directly beneath a lamppost and my shadow is smeared across the empty street ahead of me. Someone has stolen a number of placards from the city's drug campaign—those ridiculous BELIEVE posters that do nothing but irritate property owners who remove them from their sidewalks whenever they appear—and a number of them now lay strewn in the street.

Shivering, I remain standing beneath the lamppost. Five months ago I was dragged across this street and slammed against the hood of a police car. My first offense, I had only to spend some time in rehab. So I was sent away and the city feels it's doing its job, getting punks like me off the street. Punks like me who pay no attention to BELIEVE posters. Whatever.

Something white flits through the darkness; I catch it from the corner of my eye. Turning, squinting down the blackened alleyway, I see nothing...but I suddenly feel much colder than I had just a moment ago.

No rest for the dead, I think, still trying to peer into the darkness. Looking for a shape, a visage...anything recognizable...

I see nothing. In the cold and the dark, I hang around Glad Street for forty-five minutes and still I see nothing.

* * *

Carter Johnson is my father's construction worker buddy, and he looks like someone stretched a pair of filthy coveralls over a city bus. His face resembles a burlap sack with eye-holes and his breath is an aromatic amalgamation of unfiltered cigarettes, peppered beef jerky, and steamed cabbage. He talks at an unnecessary volume and highlights every third sentence with profanity of a sexual nature. I immediately dislike him.

He's drinking beer with my father Saturday afternoon in our kitchen and my father introduces us.

"Good to meet you, Gideon," Carter Johnson says, rising and shaking my hand. It is like shaking a chainsaw. "Lookin' forward to havin' you come aboard Monday."

"I appreciate it," I say, and move down the hallway.

My mother is in her bedroom, propped up on the bed and staring blankly at the wall. It is the way my father sat that night while holding his gun. I enter the room quietly and pause at the foot of the bed, staring at my mother's profile. She doesn't turn to acknowledge me.

I say, "It's a nice day out, Ma. You should go out, get some sun."

She is slowly gnawing at her lower lip. I notice she isn't staring at the wall but peering out the window and down at the street below. She is watching a group of young black girls play hopscotch. My mother, she watches these girls like someone lost in a dream.

From the kitchen, I hear the dull boom of laughter.

"Ma..."

Without looking at me, she says, "You should eat something, Gideon. You look too thin. That's not a healthy thing for a boy your age."

"I been eating," I say. "I'm okay." I ask if her head hurts.

"No," she says.

But I can tell it does.

I spend the rest of the day hanging around Glad Street, but see nothing. People move by and it's like I'm invisible. Baltimore is good for that. I look homeless in my grimy sweatshirt and torn jeans, leaning against the PNC Bank with my head down and my hair in my face. I finish my final cigarette for the day and toss it in the street when I hear someone shout my name. I look up and see a girl rushing towards me from across the street, black hair streaming behind her, her right hand grappling with a shoulder bag that is slipping down her arm.

"It *is* you," she says, beaming, and hugs me awkwardly with one arm. "I thought I was seeing things."

The girl's name is Alicia Vance and we dated on and off prior to my arrest. She is thin, too thin, and her skin is so white you'd think if you held her up to a light you'd see her heart pumping through the wall of her chest.

She loops a bony arm around my neck. "When did you get back?"

"Yesterday."

"I've missed you." This is a lie. We were not really on speaking terms the night I was arrested. "What are you up to?"

"Nothing," I say.

"You should come by the loft sometime, see the guys. My God, Gideon, I feel like I haven't seen you in years."

"You still hang at the loft?"

"Sure. Come by whenever, we'll throw you a fucking party. It'll be like the old days. That's cool, isn't it? The old days, I mean. They didn't fuck with your mind too much in that place, did they? Crownsville, right? I hear it's real shitty, what they do to people there."

"It's cool," I say. "Wasn't too bad." I am looking past her and down Glad Street, only half-listening. She notices and mutters something. "What?" I say.

"I said, how 'bout a goddamn kiss?"

"Oh."

"What's the matter? They slip Soft Peter into your food or something?"

"I don't get it," I say.

"Never mind," she says. "Just kiss me."

* * *

Carter Johnson is excited about doing something important—in this case, contributing to the rehabilitation of a young urban drug abuser—so he personally shows up Monday morning to drive me to the construction site.

I sit in the passenger seat of his pickup in silence, watching the decrepit, ancient buildings of the city wash by the window in a blur. Carter Johnson, he is talking to me about nothing important, and I only pretend to fully listen.

"So you know," Carter Johnson says, "we give mandatory drug tests once a month."

This is bullshit but I don't say that. He's trying to play it simple, maybe save face, and I'll let him do it. I tell him that's fine, I have no problem with it.

"I mean, it's nothin' against you," he goes on anyway. "Just want you to understand that." Now he sounds like my father and it is suddenly very easy to comprehend their friendship. "All the guys—they all have to do it. It's a city regulation, Gideon."

"Sure," I say. Whatever.

Carter Johnson's men are erecting some office building on the outskirts of the city. The men, they all look like the construction worker cliché—burly, unshaven, flat faces with acne-pocked skin—but they are not. They work efficiently and mostly in silence. They take brief lunches and—surprisingly—are meticulous about washing their hands. A few attempt to engage me in friendly conversation, but something about my demeanor must blaze like an unwelcome torch, and they quickly relent.

I pay little attention to the work itself. Only when I taste grit and dirt do I remember I am sawing wood, am nailing nails, am carrying shit from trucks and whatever else.

Lunch, I slip away and find myself wandering closer to downtown. There are a number of people out at this hour—people in suits and people in cutoffs and other various people—and for the most part no one notices me. Hands in my pockets, my head down, I listen to my own respiration as I wander through the city.

And stop once I reach Glad Street.

There are people here, too. I recognize many of the buildings, have been inside many of them myself at one time (and not too long ago, either), but I hardly look at them now. I am more interested in the street itself. Glad Street. And the children. BELIEVE. The goddamn signs are everywhere now. It's like a plague. There are a number of residential tenements along Glad Street and there are a number of children playing in the street. It is a very different scene from the night before. I recall my mother sitting on her bed, half-gazing out the window at children playing hopscotch. I suddenly feel very angry. The BELIEVE signs—there's one so close to me, taped to the outside of a tenement door. I peel it off, getting my fingernails behind the placard, and hold it for a while at arm's length. Someone has punched two holes in the placard, each hole occupying the two enclosed bubbles of the B. I turn the placard on its side and hold it up to my face and wear it like a Halloween mask, peer through the holes at the children in the street. They are shouting and tossing a ball back and forth. They laugh and there is the *click-click* sound of a jump rope whipping the sidewalk.

BELIEVE. How can posters help if you don't know what they mean? And who wants to be preached at, anyway?

Looking through the B, I think I see an angel, a ghost.

I drop the placard and stare across the street, but there are only kids. No angel. No ghost.

And I am late returning to work.

* * *

The loft is really a basement. I don't know who named it or who actually owns it, but throughout high school it served as a private refuge where guys came to smoke dope and feel up their girlfriends. It is a large room, windowless and dark, lit only by the flickering illumination of a dozen or so candles. The floor is concrete, covered in places by mismatched rolls of carpet and fire-scarred furniture scavenged from various dumps. The walls are cinder-block and crowded with graffiti. Once, the loft had reeked strongly of mildew and animal feces. Now, only the acrid stink of marijuana exists.

Tonight Alicia is here, as are two other guys I don't recognize. I push through the loft's wooden double-doors and the two guys lethargically lift their heads from an arrangement of pillows on the floor, glance in my direction, then continue circulating a pipe. Alicia rises from a filthy-looking sofa and hugs me as I enter.

"You're soaking wet," she says, rubbing a hand through my hair. "Why did you walk in the rain?"

"I don't know," I say. I don't tell her that it wasn't raining when I left my building. I don't tell her that I hung around Glad Street for an hour before coming here, and that's when the rain had started. Anyway, Alicia wouldn't understand.

"Who is it?" one of the stoners shout.

Alicia takes me by the hand and introduces me to the two goons sprawled out like pharaohs on their pile of pillows. I immediately forget their names.

"You're the guy that got busted," mutters one of the pharaohs. "I heard about you. Some guy told me you got ass-raped in rehab."

"Someone told you that?"

"Yeah," he says. "That true?"

I shrug off my wet coat and fold it over the back of the filthy sofa. I say, "That's news to me."

"Yeah," the other guy says, "sure. I mean, that's what I figured." And he extends his little glass pipe. The inside of his arm is purple-black and covered in needle tracks. "Want a hit?"

"No," I say, shivering. I'm too cold and wet to think about smoking. Anyway, I'm still thinking of Glad Street.

"Come on," Alicia says, still holding my hand, and leads me down a narrow corridor that communicates with a basement-level apartment. Someone has spray-painted MIKE THE HEADLESS CHICKEN FOR PRESIDENT on the apartment door.

"Whose place is this?" I ask.

Alicia turns the knob and pushes the door open. "Mine," she says.

It is a small, one-bedroom job with worn carpeting and a toilet that runs continuous. It reeks of pot in here, too.

"Place is cool. You live by yourself?"

"Yeah," she says, but already I can see some guy's sneakers in the bathroom doorway, a couple pairs of unwashed boxer shorts lingering about the place. Beneath the pot smell is the undeniable smell of *male*. Yet I say nothing.

She takes me to her bedroom. It is as big as a closet, hardly large enough for the tiny bed that takes up most of the room, and the floorboards groan as if in pain when I walk across them. There is a window above the bed's headboard, facing Glad Street. I feel a chill rush through me—and then Alicia is there, peeling off my shirt.

"What?" I mutter.

"You're such an idiot," she whispers, and kisses my belly. I stare at the top of her head—at the pale white part down the middle of her hair—in the moonlight coming in from the window. "Come over to the bed."

I go to the bed. Alicia removes her shirt and stands in the semi-darkness half-naked. Her breasts are familiar to me. They are small and pale. Alicia's nipples won't appear until they're prodded and squeezed—and then they jut out like knots in bark.

She gathers me in her arms and pulls me toward the bed, down on top of her. We kiss and she tastes bad, like tonguing the bottom of an ashtray. I have difficulty getting aroused, mainly because I'm listening to the occasional car glide through the rain-swept street outside. Alicia works her way to the button on my jeans, tugs at the waistband, unzips the fly. She moans something but I'm not paying much attention. I feel her cold, thin-fingered hand slide into my pants and grip me forcefully. I am half-propped above her now, and I crane my neck to see out the window. But it's too dark and I'm positioned poorly, so I see nothing.

"What?" she says, irritated for the first time. "What? What is it, Gideon? You have to take a leak or something?"

"Yeah, I do," I say, which is not *completely* untrue.

"Get up, get up," she tells me, pushing against my bare chest with her hands. "Go use the goddamn bathroom, for God's sake."

I pull myself off her and stagger in the darkness beside the bed, my eyes still trained on the window. On the bed, Alicia scoots back against the headboard and props a pillow over her bare chest. As I move out of the room and into the darkened hallway I can hear her exhale with deliberate exaggeration. I do not turn and look in her direction, though that is what she wants. Instead, I continue to the bathroom, click on the bathroom light—wincing—and close the door behind me. Standing shirtless before the mirror, I look like some peeled fruit. Sickly, the way my mother looks.

There is a small window between the shower stall and the toilet. I go to it and lift the moldy shade, peer out. There is a BELIEVE poster covering the glass. I feel around the sill for the latch, find it, unlock it. Sliding the window open, I push the poster away from the glass; the driving rain quickly drags it to the sidewalk.

This is a basement apartment; the window is at ground level and striped with wrought-iron bars. I see the lamppost on the corner of Glad Street. The rest of the street is dark and motionless, yet I cannot pull myself away from the view. My eyes run the length of the street, pausing longest in the darkened, shadowy alleyways between tenements. I think I see something, even through the rain, even through the runnels of water running down the pane of glass, but it is too dark to be sure. I consider opening the window farther—it is one of those windows that push up and out—when I hear the door creak open behind me. I'd forgotten to lock it.

"Gideon…"

I turn after some hesitation. Alicia Vance stands shirtless in the doorway, her thin arms propped over her breasts, her thin-fingered hands tucked beneath her armpits.

"Gideon, what the hell are you doing? You've been in here for twenty minutes."

I go to say something, but suddenly realize there is something in my mouth. I cannot form words.

"Jesus Christ, Gideon, you're bleeding," Alicia says, refusing to move from the doorway. "You're still doing that?"

I catch my reflection in the bathroom mirror and see the heel of my left hand pressed firmly in my mouth. A single teardrop of blood trickles down my wrist toward the bend in my elbow. I am suddenly aware of my teeth biting through the skin. There is no pain.

"Maybe," half-naked Alicia Vance says with little emotion, "you should just leave."

A few minutes later and I'm back out in the rain. Hugging my sopping coat against my body, shivering, I stand outside Alicia Vance's apartment building for some time, unmoving, as a car passes slowly down Glad Street. I watch it turn at the intersection, its taillights glittering in the rain, before crossing the street.

And I catch movement off to my left.

I spin around, hair plastered to my forehead, rainwater coursing down my face, and catch the fleeting image of a small angel disappearing down one of the darkened alleyways. I see this and immediately cannot move. She is not a real angel—I know this—but, rather, she is a little girl dressed in a white satin gown with crepe paper wings and a pipe-cleaner halo above her head. It is fake; it is an illusion. I know this, too. She is just a little girl in costume.

Somehow, I am again able to move. I begin running in the direction of the angel, my Nikes crashing through puddles, my hair whipping my face, my heart slamming in my throat. Ahead, the angel has already vanished in the darkness and I can see nothing of her now. She is too fast. I have been waiting for her, expecting her since my return from rehab, but she continues to elude me.

I tear down the alley and crash into a wedge of metal trash cans. The sound is tremendous, rebounding off the brick alley walls. I spill to the ground, soaked, freezing…and think I almost hear laughter echoing from the other end of the alley. There is a street light at the other end—uninspired orange sodium—and its light falls across the mouth of the alley, but I cannot see the angel beneath the light. I hear her but cannot see her anywhere.

Catching my breath, my entire body suddenly sore and uncertain, I manage to pull myself to my feet and stagger back out onto Glad Street.

*   *   *

I am not sure where day stops and night begins. Things seem to be in a haze. In four days, the apartment has grown smaller and smaller. The air, it's like breathing motor oil. If I open a window my father comes around behind me and closes it. If I make too much noise in the kitchen my father stands with his arms folded in the small hallway and stares at me. I say nothing and try to do even less.

Carter Johnson calls the house on Friday and I answer the telephone. He asks me what's wrong and I tell him I'm sick and I'm sorry I didn't call this morning. He asks if I'll be in later and I tell him probably not.

"Is this about the drug tests, Gideon? You have to understand—"

I hang up.

My mother doesn't leave her bedroom. She sits there on the edge of the bed, mimicking the way my father sat that night with his handgun, and she stares silently out her bedroom window. Children play in the street. I, too, watch the children on occasion, but it just makes me angry. This whole city makes me angry. There is nothing to BELIEVE in this city, so who are they kidding? And these kids—there's no future here. So it just makes me angry, and although I'd lied to Carter Johnson about being sick, by Friday evening I am aware of a slight temperature working its way through my system. The result of moping around in the rain, no doubt.

Friday night, I move silently through the apartment toward the front door. I hear floorboards creak somewhere ahead of me and I freeze, imagining my father standing somewhere in the darkness. Down the hall I see shapes move.

"Dad," I whisper.

"Gideon." It is my mother. She steps into the living room, wrapped in a cloth robe, and her skin looks blue and translucent in the gloom. "Did you miss the bus?"

"What?"

"Will you be late for school?"

"I'm not going to school, Ma," I say. "I haven't been to school in a long time."

"I can pack you a lunch," she says. Her eyes are black and like two pits in the center of her head. Looking at her, I'm more conscious of my fever. "You don't eat properly."

"I'm going out," I say, and slip out the door. Hurrying down the stairs and out onto the street, I imagine my mother in the kitchen preparing me a bagged lunch to take to a school I no longer attend.

I make it to Glad Street in time to see the angel skipping down the sidewalk in the dark. I shout and feel something rupture deep in my throat. I pursue the little girl, my hands stuffed deep into the pockets of my jacket, my teeth rattling in my head. My body feels frozen and numb on the outside, aflame on the inside. I follow the angel toward the intersection of Glad and Charles. She pauses here and begins to spin with her arms straight out. The street is silent and dark and I can hear the scuff of her sneakers on the pavement. I shout again—I am shouting her name, although my brain hardly registers this at the moment—and I look around to see some tenement windows light up.

"Come here!" I shout, but the girl—the angel—does not come. Instead, she pauses and faces me, giggles…and vanishes into the night.

I am bad with time. I have no idea how long I have been out here shouting. But soon I hear police sirens tearing up the street. Like a thief, I hustle back down Glad Street and disappear down an alley. I run harder, faster, and break through to the cobblestone semicircle that is Water Street. My fever is rising and my lungs are fit to burst. I can't remember the last time I took a breath.

Two police cruisers sail past Water Street, their flashers on, their sirens blaring. I freeze in mid-stride. A sharp pain rips through my left hand and I taste blood. I am biting my hands again.

The little girl in the angel costume appears at the end of Water Street. She is staring right at me, waiting for me to see her, and when I do she turns and runs. I chase her, my legs pumping for all they're worth, my breath harsh and abrasive burning up through my throat.

I cross the street in pursuit of the little girl and I am suddenly aware of police sirens and flashing lights all around me. I am burning up with fever and am not all here. I feel I am floating somewhere just above myself. Turning down another alley I slam into a chain-link fence and quickly scale it, rat-style. I drop down on the other side into an alley swollen with garbage. This does not slow me down. I run faster, my heart about to burst from my chest.

The alley is a dead end. I come face to face with a brick wall, eye level with a BELIEVE poster. I tear the poster down, wrap it around my face, then hunker down in the swill. The poster pressed against my face, my breath strikes it and echoes in my ears. My eyes are pressed shut. I am thinking of our old duplex and my father scooping gunk out of the gutters. I am thinking of my mother's skin, brittle and yellow and like wax paper. I picture her now, at this very moment, searching for mayonnaise in the refrigerator.

I am suddenly aware of a presence beside me. I hear plastic trash bags shift and empty cans roll across the cement. I am not alone. Yet I do not remove the BELIEVE placard from my face. I hear the movement beside me and I feel my own hot breath against the cardboard. Mourning breath.

The girl, she giggles.

"What?" I whimper. And in my head I hear my father's booming voice: *Real men don't whimper like little girls, Gideon.*

More giggling. It's suddenly all around me.

"What?" I manage again. And think: *There's no rest for the dead.*

I tear the poster from my face and see the girl just a few feet from me, also hunkered down in the trash. She is forever young, her eyes wide and lost in innocence, and she is giggling behind a cupped hand.

"Stop," I tell her.

"Trick-or-treat," the angel whispers.

I reach out a hand to touch her but she quickly vanishes, and my hand goes right through the air, unobstructed. I touch the cold brick wall on the other side.

Police cars whiz by the mouth of the alley, and I pull the poster back over my face. My cheeks are burning. I can't tell if I'm breathing.

I wait for the sirens to die. When I remove the poster from my face and look around again, I see that I am alone. I remain crouched in garbage, unmoving, unthinking, until the first rust colors of dawn blossom between the cracks in the tenements across the street. Daylight, and I feel wiped out, exhausted. I toss the placard aside—had I really held onto it all night?—and stare down at my hands. My palms are covered in blood. There is a hunk of skin peeled away from one of my fingers, unrolled like a party favor.

I get up and start moving back toward home, feeling grimy and cold and sick. There is a dull pain on either side of my stomach, and just below the waist of my jeans. The groin area. By the time I reach our building, the pain is sufficient enough to cause me to pause halfway up the apartment stairs.

It is fully daylight now. I enter the apartment quietly. The place seems empty. I move down the hallway toward my parents' bedroom. I pause here and look at the framed pictures on the wall. There are two photographs in particular that attract my attention.

One, it's my mother and sister and me at the kitchen table in our old home, a melting ice cream cake bristling with candles in the center of the table.

The other photograph is from last Halloween. Having grown out of the tradition, I am standing against the railing of our home, looking slightly annoyed, slightly bored. My sister, dressed in her angel costume, smiles a gap-toothed smile at the camera. The sun must have been facing us that day because the shadow of my father, who is taking the picture, covers half my face. Only my sister is in full view.

I turn away and continue down the hall toward my parents' bedroom. My mother is there, sitting on the edge of the bed, staring out the window. My father is nowhere to be found.

"Ma," I say, "where's Dad?"

"Oh," she says, turning to see me in the doorway, "Gideon. Is it breakfast already? What would you like, dear?"

"Ma," I begin…but then say, "Eggs. Lots and lots of eggs. Do you think you can do that? I haven't been eating."

"Yes!" She says this with startling enthusiasm. "Yes, Gideon! I've been telling your father—that boy is not eating properly. That boy is getting too thin, just too thin, and he'll never make the football team. What did you say?"

"Eggs," I tell her.

She moves slowly off the bed and I stand in the doorway and watch. She pulls on her robe even though she is fully dressed and even though her skin is slick with sweat, then moves past me and out into the hall. When I hear pots and pans clanging from the kitchen, I cross the bedroom and open my father's top dresser drawer. His handgun is hidden beneath some socks. Beside the gun is a small box of bullets. I remove both the gun and the bullets and sit on the edge of the bed. It occurs to me that I must look just as my father had that night, sitting here with this gun in my hands. Last Halloween, a group of teenagers—most of them younger than me—were raising a commotion along Glad Street while I chaperoned my sister's trick-or-treating. City kids, they do things that even *they* can't fully comprehend, so how can I? And things just happened so fast. I heard gunshots before I even knew what they were. And when I went to grab my sister's hand, her hand was no longer there.

My sister. She was strewn across a pair of tenement steps, bleeding from the head.

Some many months later, after we'd moved from the duplex to this apartment, I walked in on my father sitting on the edge of this bed, turning this gun over and over in his hands. I watched in silence from the doorway, the heel of my right hand pressed firmly in my mouth, my teeth nervously biting down. I watched him without him knowing, and at one point I felt very certain he was going to do it—that he was going to put the gun to his head and end it.

But he didn't. He put the gun away and just cried for a long time.

I hear my mother humming from the kitchen. Her headaches started around the time of my sister's funeral. I think about that now as I load the gun. Before me, the single bedroom window looks out on a group of children playing in the street. Is there any hope for any of them?

Believe, I think. *Believe in what?*

I say nothing to my mother as I step out the front door. My belly cramping, my fever racing, it takes some effort to maneuver down the flights of stairs to the street. Outside, the sun is too bright and I wince. It hurts my eyes.

I carry the gun down the street, walking quickly for someone in such pain, and I think about my father shaving in his underwear. I think about his slow physical decline that started with my sister's death and continued throughout his visits with me at rehab. See, I was arrested one night on Glad Street with a bag full of weed in my back pocket. But the call didn't start out as a drug bust. The call started out as a disturbance. Apparently a number of people heard me shouting my sister's name from their apartments that night and called the cops. The dope—well, that was just an added bonus, I guess.

The sun is hot and I'm burning up. When my eyes adjust to the light, I manage to open them wide. It seems both sides of the city street are papered in BELIEVE posters.

I start to laugh. It hurts my belly but I laugh anyway.

City kids—they're all a bunch of hopeless animals when you get right down to it. The good ones are gunned down and the bad ones…well, the bad ones just grow weaker and weaker and smoke their lives away.

This is not a guilt thing.

Please don't think that.

I cross over to Glad Street and find it teeming with young children playing in the street. If their lives meant anything—anything at all—would they be so easy to end?

A ripping, agonizing pain tearing through my gut, I raise my father's handgun and begin shooting.

UNDER THE TUTELAGE OF MR. TRUEHEART

It's time, and I have secrets to tell, says Mr. Trueheart one sunny afternoon, still some months before Halloween night. *I'll tell them to you if you think you're ready, Warren.*

Warren does not have to think about it.

Warren is ready.

* * *

His mother said he looked pale but didn't pay him much mind after that. This was before he put on the makeup, which was supposed to make him look pale, look like a ghost. It was white greasepaint, the stuff clowns used, and he'd bought it a few days earlier at Strumsky's for ten bucks. It was expensive but he'd taken the money out of his mother's purse, just as Mr. Trueheart had instructed.

That evening, he dressed first so he wouldn't get greasepaint on his clothes, pulling the black sweatshirt over his head while staring at his reflection in the bathroom mirror.

In the den, his mother was sprawled out on the loveseat watching some old black-and-white movie on the TV, the shiny white helmet of one knee poking from the parted curtain of her bathrobe. In her lap was Laddie, a thing of silken black-and-brown hair with moist, runny eyes and, whenever someone came to the door (which was infrequent), a shrill bark.

She kept the liquor bottles in the kitchen, a whole legion of them. Earlier that day, Warren had emptied his school backpack, and now he stood peering into the cupboard at the assortment of bottles. At ten years old, Warren Enck knew nothing about alcohol, so he selected a bottle of amber liquid because it had a bright red turkey on the label. It was as good as any. In the den, the TV was loud enough to cover the sound of the cupboard door squealing closed, followed by the *zeeeet* sound of his backpack zipper after he'd shoved the bottle inside. Would the backpack raise his mother's suspicion? Who brings a backpack with them on Halloween? But no: she wouldn't be that perceptive. She was dancing at the back of her mind tonight.

Before leaving the kitchen, he paused and gazed at the block of wood on the counter with the handles of long carving knives jutting up from it. He thought about taking one. She would never notice. Even on a good day, she would never notice.

In the den, a creaky voice on the TV said, "Morgan is a savage. I must apologize..."

The sound of a glass bottle followed, clinkity clinking into another, then the dull thud of its heavy bottom striking the carpeted floor. His mother made a sound of frustration. Laddie yipped.

"Oh hush, now," said his mother.

He watched her for a time in the kitchen doorway, unobserved. He was small for his age, which accounted for the ease with which he could keep out of her periphery when he so desired, but tonight his stature had little to do with it. He watched her slouch forward, that ever-widening split in her robe exposing a flash of thick white thigh marbled with spidery veins and a patch of discoloration high up on the dimpled flesh. She groped for a bottle that spun in lazy revolutions on the carpet.

Laddie spotted him, let out a squeak.

His mother looked up sharply with a face comprised of right angles, her hair a spiky nest that fanned out like a peacock's tail at the nape of her neck. It took a second for her eyes to settle on him. "What's this?" she said, meaning his costume—the white greasepaint on his face, the black sweatshirt and cargo pants, no doubt the backpack strapped to his shoulders.

"It's Halloween," said Warren.

"Is that so? Is that what this is?"

He nodded.

"Where's my Warren?"

"Right here," he said.

She leveled an unsteady arm in his direction, finger pointing accusingly at him. "That," she said, "could be a lie."

"It's not," he said.

"It's your trickery," she said. "That's why you've got your face covered up in that paint."

"It's a costume."

"Yeah? What are you supposed to be?"

"The negative of myself," he said.

His mother didn't so much frown as her face seemed to tighten, all the parts pulling together as if by wires, forming creases along the rough contours. He had once heard a classmate's mother refer to his own mother as "unsightly," and then another mother responded with, "She has problems." Warren knew she had problems. He knew better than most. He certainly knew better than his classmates' mothers.

"Come here," she said. She wasn't an overly large woman, but she seemed twice as big when she was drunk, in the way her body seemed to move and reposition itself with great labored starts and stops: a car that kept stalling out in cold weather. Warren watched that single white knee roll like the pendulum of a clock, and he could see—or imagined he could see—from where he stood in the kitchen doorway the mad designs that made up her flesh, the permanent creases that reminded him of elephant hide, the shiny tautness of the knee that shimmered like a crystal ball in the TV's light.

"Come," she repeated.

He came to her, stood before her. Laddie spilled out of her lap and began scurrying in tight little circles on the floor. Yipping.

"You're going to leave me alone tonight," she said. It was not a question. She wore no makeup and her face looked like a mask made of latex, pulled taut over the angular bones of her skull. She smoothed a curl of hair behind his ear and said, "Do something nice for me before you go."

So he went into the kitchen and fixed her another drink—vodka from the cupboard mixed with a fruit punch drink box that was supposed to be for his school lunch. He returned it to her and she accepted it with a dreamy smile, her eyes droopy lidded, enveloped in some unseen fog.

"Kiss kiss," she said at him, her breath as eye-watering as turpentine.

He administered a swift peck to her right cheek. Her skin felt cold against his lips.

"Have fun with your friends," she called to him as he went down the hall to the front door. A silly thing to say: they both knew he had no friends.

Outside, it had just begun to get dark. The faces of jack-o'-lanterns gaped at him from his neighbors' porches, their eyes aglow with firelight. Young kids in dime store costumes were out with their parents, already going door to door. Warren knew his mother wouldn't answer the door tonight. Probably a good thing.

He hurried along Calabasas Street, his sneakers scudding across the loose granules of sand that lay scattered like birdshot along the sidewalk. An autumn breeze whispered through the trees, and when Warren paused to listen and watch the boughs wave and sway and dance above the quaint little houses that lined his street, he caught high-pitched devil's laughter trailing in the breeze's wake.

When he crossed the intersection of Calabasas and Greenmont, the devil's laughter grew louder. Warren glanced up and saw a group of older kids—sixth graders—crowded on the front steps of the house just ahead of him. They were dressed in raggedy clothes and were slapping each other with rubber monster masks. They all seemed to glance over and notice him the same moment he noticed them.

"Borin' Warren," chided one of the older boys, who either recognized him from school or the neighborhood.

"Fag," quipped another, less playfully.

Warren kept his eyes on his sneakers as he picked up the pace.

"Hey," one of the boys called to him. "Hey. Hey. We're talking to you. Where do you think you're going when we're talking to you?"

Warren moved quickly. He refused to look at them—ignore everyone, had been Mr. Trueheart's instruction—but he could see, from the periphery of his vision, that they were rising off the porch steps now. Some of them pulled their masks down over their faces. This troubled Warren deeply, as if some terrible act were about to take place, one the boys wished to execute anonymously.

"Hey!" the boy shouted, more urgently. "I'm talking to you, you piece of garbage!"

It was then that Warren felt something strike him, sharp as a kick, along his left shoulder blade. It was a rock, and it bounced down the sidewalk alongside him for a few steps, as if determined to trip him up. A second rock, much larger than the first, whizzed past his head.

Ignore them, Mr. Trueheart had instructed. Don't let them goad you. Don't let them suck you into their web. It's what they want. It's how they get you.

I know who you are, all of you, Warren thought. Briefly, he squeezed his eyes shut tight and willed the older kids away from him. *I know what this is all about. I'm not stupid. I'm smart, very smart.*

Warren's pace quickened to a sprint. He worried briefly that the older boys might give chase, but they didn't. *Maybe it's the white greasepaint.* However, he didn't slow down until he was several blocks away, standing in front of Mr. Trueheart's house.

Some of the kids at Robert F. Kennedy Elementary School said Mr. Trueheart's house was haunted. Indeed, it looked like something straight from a horror movie, with its siding overrun with leafy vines, its concave porch and slouching roof, its windows that were perpetually shuttered. There was a short wooden fence that surrounded the little postage-stamp lawn with its hip-high grass, PRIVATE PROPERTY, NO TRESPASSING, and BEWARE OF DOG signs posted every few feet along the pickets.

Mr. Trueheart did not have a dog.

Warren opened the gate, went up the walk, climbed the bowing porch steps, and knocked on Mr. Trueheart's front door. There were birds' nests bristling in the carriage lights on either side of the door and spiders' webs waterfalling like drapery from the eaves.

Mr. Trueheart's leaden footfalls on the other side of the door: *thunk, thunk, thunk.* This was followed by a single knock against the interior side of the door. Warren rapped two successive knocks against the door, waited five seconds—he counted them aloud under his breath—then knocked a final time.

The door wrenched open several inches. It was gloomy inside, and Mr. Trueheart's colorless, narrow face seemed to materialize out of the darkness and peer down at him. Something akin to a smile cracked the usually stoic veneer of Mr. Trueheart's face.

"Very good," Mr. Trueheart said, his voice a ruptured baritone that reminded Warren of the brass instruments in the music room of his elementary school. "You've done your face."

Warren nodded.

"Did you speak with anyone after leaving your house?"

Warren shook his head.

"What did you mother say?"

"She was drinking again," Warren said. This, he felt, was explanation enough.

Mr. Trueheart nodded, then stepped back so that Warren could pass through the narrow crack in the doorway. Once inside, Mr. Trueheart closed the door, bolted it, chained it, kept the palm of one hand against it for several seconds as though he were testing the temperature of the wood. Warren stood beside him and waited in silence. He was used to the routine.

Mr. Trueheart was seventy-one years old. Warren first met him over a year ago, when the members of his Cub Scout troop were tasked with assisting the elderly. Some boys went shopping for the elderly neighbors, others would read to them on the weekends. Warren had spent the first few visits helping Mr. Trueheart nail boards up over his windows and fill empty milk cartons with powdered dish detergent. Warren hadn't wanted to join the Cubs—it had been his mother's idea, a chance, she'd said, for him to make some friends—but he quickly took a liking to Mr. Trueheart.

Mr. Trueheart had a lot of wisdom to impart.

He saw things as they really were.

* * *

My name is not really Trueheart, says Mr. Trueheart during one of Warren's visits. *You can call me that, but it's not my real name.*

Warren asks him why he uses a fake name.

It's so I stay out of sight, responds Mr. Trueheart. *I keep hidden. They're always out there watching. Searching. It's necessary to be careful, Warren. And it'll serve you well to learn that quickly. I don't suppose anyone ever let you in on the big secret, have they?*

Warren shakes his head.

We must speak cautiously about these things, says Mr. Trueheart, dropping his voice to a conspiratorial whisper. *I will tell you, but this is the secret, the biggest one you'll ever keep. Is that something you can do?*

Warren nods.

Good, says Mr. Trueheart.

So Mr. Trueheart teaches and Warren learns.

In the end, Warren has made a friend after all.

* * *

Mr. Trueheart's house was unkempt and smelled funny, like the Campbell's tomato soup his mother sometimes made Warren eat. Tonight was no different, with the exception of something else borne on the air—a strangely pungent, medicinal smell. It made the air difficult to breathe.

Mr. Trueheart led him down the hall, past stacks of books on the floor, on chairs, piled on the stairs that went to the second floor. There were mounds of dirty laundry scattered about like strange alien pods that had grown up from the carpeting. Warren followed Mr. Trueheart down the hall and into the sunken den at the far end of the house—what Mr. Trueheart often called "the foxhole." There were windows that looked out onto a wooded backyard, a loveseat facing an ancient TV that still had rabbit ears, and a large wooden rocking chair outfitted in a beaded cushion. On this night, the furniture had been shoved against the walls to make room for the object that sat in the center of the floor.

"Is that it?" Warren asked.

"Yes. Would you like a closer look?"

"Is it safe?"

"For now," said Mr. Trueheart. "I haven't activated it yet."

Warren stepped down into the foxhole and walked cautiously over to the item in the center of the floor. It wasn't big—that was the point, really—and it hardly looked dangerous. It was mostly a tin coffee can, the words MAXWELL HOUSE clearly legible (although upside down) on the side, fixed to a thin square of wood. Colored wires spooled out on either side of it; some were soldered to the outside of the can while others disappeared beneath it, wedged between the can and the wooden board. A hole had been drilled through the top of the can—which was the bottom of the can—and what looked like a frosted Christmas tree light poked up.

Warren stared down at the thing for several seconds.

After a while, Mr. Trueheart said, "Would you like a Hawaiian Punch?"

* * *

They drank two glasses of Hawaiian Punch each, in the cramped kitchen where the sink overflowed with unwashed dishes and reams of unread newspapers blanketed the counter tops.

"Your face is very good," Mr. Trueheart said after sucking down the last of his juice. They were seated together at the kitchen table, which was actually a card table with wobbly legs. "That white paint has kept you safe."

Warren nodded.

"When you become your own negative, it makes you harder for them to see."

"Some boys from school saw me on the way over here tonight."

"What did they look like?"

"I don't know. I didn't look at them."

A smile stretched across the lower half of Mr. Trueheart's face. "Very good, Warren. You've really been paying attention."

"Of course. I don't want to get caught."

"Yes," said Mr. Trueheart. "I hope that's something we can avoid altogether."

Warren looked at his own empty glass. The sugary drink had upset his stomach. Or maybe he was just nervous.

"What is it?" asked Mr. Trueheart. "What's on your mind, Warren?"

Warren looked up at him. "I want to see them," he said. "See them the way you see them."

Mr. Trueheart's smile widened. "And tonight, dear boy, is that night. But first, we must be sure you understand what it is you need to do."

Warren nodded.

Mr. Trueheart rose from the table, went over to a cluttered breakfront, and rifled around through unruly stacks of paper. There were photographs among the papers, photographs that Warren had looked at several times before. They were of Mr. Trueheart and some other men, all of them in their twenties or so, in khaki military garb holding guns. From the background, it appeared they were in the desert. Whenever Warren would ask Mr. Trueheart where those pictures had been taken, he would always receive a different answer. "France," Mr. Trueheart sometimes said. "Africa," he'd offer. "Budapest," he said on a few occasions. And once, Mr. Trueheart (whose name was not actually Trueheart, not at all) said, "Mars, Warren. Those photos were taken on Mars."

Mr. Trueheart returned to the table with a large sheet of paper rolled up into a cone. He unrolled it and splayed it out across the table, then set their empty drinking glasses on two corners so that it wouldn't roll up.

Glued to the paper were a multitude of photographs, each one taken by Warren over a period of three months. Some of the photos showed Windell Street from various locations. Others showed Kennedy Park—the baseball diamond, the swings and seesaws, the wooded treeline that brooked the park and Windell Street. Other photos were of the streets and houses that surrounded the park.

"Tell me," Mr. Trueheart said. "What have you learned, Warren."

Warren leaned over the table, scrutinized the photos, then pointed to the one depicting the baseball diamond at the center of Kennedy Park. "Right here," Warren said. "That's where they'll meet up."

"What time?"

"Eight o'clock."

Mr. Trueheart glanced at the digital clock on the microwave. It was just five after seven. There was still plenty of time. Kennedy Park was only three blocks away.

"The baseball diamond is a good place, and it's certainly in the center of everything," said Mr. Trueheart, "but I'm concerned that it might be too conspicuous."

"What does that mean?"

"It's too out in the open, Warren. Too many people will be able to see it."

"Oh."

"Now," said Mr. Trueheart, leaning over the photographs, his shadow hovering like a bird of prey, "if you were to place it *here*," and he pointed to a low hedgerow that ran alongside the bleachers, "then we might be in business."

Warren nodded. "Yeah," he said. "I can do that."

"Wonderful." Mr. Trueheart straightened up. "Did you bring me what I asked for?"

"Yes." Warren leaned over and scooped his backpack off the floor. He unzipped it, procured the bottle of liquor from it, and handed it over to Mr. Trueheart.

"Thank you, Warren," said Mr. Trueheart as he studied the label then pulled the corked cap from the bottle. He poured a few inches into his drinking glass.

"Can I try some?" asked Warren.

"No, son. I'm afraid that would be inappropriate. Besides, you've got important work to do. And I'm not only entrusting you with one very invaluable item, but two."

"Really? What's the second one?"

"Only the thing you've been asking for since we started talking about this and making our plans."

Mr. Trueheart lifted his glass to his lips—the large sheet of paper speedily rolled up on the table—and took a sip. He grimaced and his teeth looked gray.

"Come," he said, and beckoned Warren to follow him back out

into the hallway.

* * *

Do you ever notice, dear Warren, how you are so frequently singled out in school or on the playground? That the children never seem to want anything to do with you? That sometimes they don't know you even exist? And the awful things they sometimes do when they do approach you...it's terrible, Warren. And do you know what else? It's unnatural. *Yes, that's right. Because these children aren't who you think they are. They're imposters, Warren. They've been replaced. Come—listen to what I have to tell you. Would you like some chocolate milk?*

* * *

From the hallway closet, Mr. Trueheart procured what at first looked like a hat or a rubber boot from the top shelf. It came loose in an avalanche of winter gloves and streamers of scarves, which Mr. Trueheart absently shoved aside with his slippered foot.

He handed the item to Warren.

It was a rubber monster mask, its fleshy face the color of pea soup, grotesque and alien in its countenance. The eye holes looked too narrow as did the slit within the mouth. It was like no monster Warren had ever seen on TV or in video games.

"That's Ru'ulgreg," said Mr. Trueheart. "I just call him Greg. But you can give him your own name. He's yours now."

Somewhat confused, Warren turned the mask over in his hands. He hadn't been expecting this.

"In truth, it doesn't matter what you call him. He's an *it*, Warren, just a thing. But a very *special* one. He who wears the mask sees the creatures in their true form. It's what you've been asking for all along."

Warren looked up at him. "Really? Just from wearing the mask?"

"Mind you, it's not instantaneous. It will take some time to...well, to grow on you. But soon you'll see them exactly as I do. They won't be able to hide from you anymore. And the mask will keep you safe, too. You can't run around painting your face white and pretending to be the negative of yourself forever, can you?"

Mr. Trueheart laughed—a brassy trumpeting sound that caused Warren to jump and then to join in with his own high-pitched laughter.

Once the laughter subsided, Mr. Trueheart placed a thin-fingered hand on Warren's shoulder and said, "We must hurry. You have to be there before the start of the parade. Otherwise people might ask questions. They might spot you and put a stop to the whole thing."

Warren nodded. "Okay."

"Come."

They returned to the foxhole and knelt down before the Maxwell House contraption.

"Look here," Mr. Trueheart said, and he pointed to a small toggle switch poking through an eyelet at the back of the coffee can. Warren hadn't noticed it until now. It was switched down, presumably in the "off" position.

"You flip it up to turn it on," explained Mr. Trueheart. "Then it will be alive."

"Will the light on the top come on?" Warren asked, pointing to the darkened Christmas bulb.

"No. The light was there only for the test runs. It wouldn't be prudent to have it lit up like a...well, like a Christmas tree, considering what we're trying to do. Am I right?"

"Sure."

"You'll need to switch it on once you've placed it in its spot. Do you understand?"

"Yes."

"And then you need to get far away from it."

"How far?"

"Back to the street, at the very closest. But you should probably just go home after switching it on. You don't need to be there when it happens. It's on a timer."

"How long is the timer?"

"It's set to go off exactly three minutes after it's turned on."

"Alive," Warren said.

"Yes. Alive."

"I can do it."

"Yes, Warren. I know you can."

Because they're monsters, Warren thought, *and they need to be stopped. They can fool everyone else but they can't fool us.*

He wanted to get outside and try out the mask.

* * *

Mr. Trueheart helped him slide it into his backpack. He helped Warren tug the straps up over his shoulders. The thing inside the backpack wasn't hardly as heavy as Warren had been expecting. He'd spent the better part of the year buying supplies for Mr. Trueheart—everything from powdered dish detergent to fertilizer, from soap to nine-volt batteries—but he didn't know exactly how Mr. Trueheart had built the contraption. What was inside the coffee can?

At the front door, Mr. Trueheart said, "I would do this myself, you understand, but I can't, Warren. I've grown too conspicuous after all this time to be out there among them."

"Out in the open for anyone to see," Warren added.

"That's right. No amount of face paint will protect me. No mask, either. Not anymore. So, you see, I must remain in the house. But that's okay, because this is where the second phase of the plan must take place. Phase one involves you at Kennedy Park. Phase two involves me right here in my home. Do you understand?"

He really didn't, not fully, but he trusted his friend so he said, "Yes."

"Excellent. Now run along, Warren. You've got a job to do. And you can't be late."

Out on the street, Warren pulled the mask over his face. It stank of mildew and it was hard to breathe through the tiny slits in the rubber, but he felt safe wearing it. The greasepaint hadn't been as effective as he had hoped—those sixth graders on the porch had noticed him—but the mask felt *right.* As if he could walk around all night, right through a crowd of people, and never be noticed by anyone.

This theory was reinforced when he arrived at Kennedy Park. It was still early, but there were already a few kids and their parents milling about, waiting for the Halloween parade to start. No one paid Warren any mind as he hurried across the field to the baseball diamond. Near the bleachers, he wedged himself between two of the bushes that made up the hedgerow. He was careful sliding his backpack off and unzipping it. He was even more cautious removing the Maxwell House contraption from it, and settling it down in the dusty sand behind the bushes. The thing was incredibly light. He wanted to shake it and see if things rolled around inside—he'd also purchased ball bearings, screws, and nails at the hardware store in town at Mr. Trueheart's behest just a few weeks ago—but he was afraid the thing might blow up in his hands. Instead, he covered it up with some dead leaves then climbed up into the bleachers to wait for the crowd to grow.

The mask still over his head, he watched the children execute cartwheels in the grass, watched a group of young girls play hide and seek behind a copse of trees, watched parents talking and smoking and looking at their cell phones. Despite whatever power the mask might have, they all still looked like regular people to him. Mr. Trueheart said it would take time—

It's not instantaneous. It will take some time to...well, to grow on you. But soon you'll see them exactly as I do...

Warren would wait.

He had always been a patient child.

* * *

Just about everyone has been replaced, Warren. Replacements fill your school, replacements walk up and down your streets. Let me ask you, Warren—have you noticed anything peculiar about your mother lately? No? Well, that's good. That's good. Maybe there's still time to save some of us, yeah?

* * *

At eight o'clock, the children gathered along the third-base line of the diamond at Kennedy Park, all manner of ghoul and goblin and witch and mummy in attendance. They kicked up plumes of dust with their sneakers, laughed raucously, swatted at each other with ninja swords, zapped random strangers with ray guns whose barrels lit up with sparks of flinty fire. Their parents climbed up into the bleachers, some taking photos of the festive lineup, others still busy on their cell phones. An infant's plangent cries echoed out across the darkening park.

No one noticed Warren Enck.

The mask was protecting him, just as Mr. Trueheart had promised, though whether it was actually hiding him from the horde, much in the way an invisibility cloak might work, or if it merely made him blend in with the rest of them, Warren didn't know. Maybe it didn't matter.

Someone blew a whistle. The costumed children grew quiet and listened to instruction from a large woman wearing bunny ears. They would march down Windell and through the town, trick-or-treating. The costumed children—the replacements— cheered. A few parents snapped photos and the baby continued to cry.

Warren clambered down the bleachers and crept behind the hedgerow unnoticed. Crouching down, he brushed the dead leaves from the Maxwell House contraption—

(the bomb)

—and slid his hand around the base of it until his small fingers found the toggle switch. He did not hesitate to switch it into the "up" position. Despite Mr. Trueheart's assurance, Warren held his breath, anticipating the Christmas light to wink on and give away his location. But it didn't. Relief washed over him.

Three minutes, he thought, crawling out from beneath the hedgerow. He could make it to the street with no problem, but he wouldn't go home. He wanted to watch the bomb go off, wanted to see the replacements, the monsters, die in the blast. With the mask on, he felt certain he would see their true selves as they writhed and died in the fire.

Warren ran across the park toward Windell Street. Street lamps blinked on in the dark, as if to illuminate his approach. Cars swooshed by, their headlights overly bright. There was a bench at the corner of the block, directly beneath a BUS STOP sign. Warren sat, readjusted his mask so that he could see better through the eye holes, and waited for the explosion.

He wore no wristwatch, but counted out the seconds, the minutes, in a low whisper. *Three minutes.* Many of the costumed children in the park had flashlights, and they switched them on now—dozens of bright little diodes fireflying in the darkness. They began to march toward Windell.

Warren counted out all three minutes.

Waited.

Nothing happened.

Recognizing that he could have been off by a few seconds, he waited, his palms sweating on the knees of his cargo pants, his sour breath filling the rubber mask. He could feel droplets of perspiration trickling down his temples, his forehead, his cheeks. His respiration sounded like an asthmatic's wheeze.

And still—nothing happened.

The queue of children—

(replacements)

—spilled out onto Windell, led by the large woman in rabbit ears. Parents followed. No explosion detonated by the baseball diamond. The world was unnaturally silent.

Warren watched the parade stomp by him. He took note of each costumed doppelganger, how they moved so convincingly like children, how their shrill voices sounded no different than they had a year ago. They were good at masking themselves and blending in. Mr. Trueheart had warned Warren that they would be.

After the parade had moved on down Windell and vacated the park altogether, Warren got up from the bench. Hesitantly, he crossed the field and approached the baseball diamond. Beneath the moonlight, the bleachers looked shiny and polished. The pitcher's mound was like a ghostly white humpback rising out of the earth.

Warren crawled through the hedgerow and stared down at Mr. Trueheart's bomb. He stared at it for a long, long time. He counted out 180 seconds, mumbling the numbers inside the mask, and still the bomb did not go off.

Summoning some courage, he flicked a finger against the side of the coffee can. It made a hollow *dong* sound. He lifted the whole contraption and shook it gingerly. Nothing rattled around inside. When he finally decided to pry the can off the wooden board, a part of him felt like a traitor to Mr. Trueheart. He also worried that the thing might blow up in his face.

But it didn't blow up; it came away from the board with little resistance, having only been tacked down with small, thin nails. Warren peeled the can off the board completely, the spools of wires pulling taut—Warren held his breath—and then he tipped the can upside down and peered inside.

It was empty.

The wires had been soldered to the interior of the can, but they weren't attached to anything. Similarly, the Christmas bulb poking from the base of the can was connected to nothing: it was simply held in place by two pieces of masking tape. The toggle switch was constructed in a similar fashion, having been pushed through a hole in the can but held in place by several bands of tape. There were no wires connected to *anything*. It was just a tin can nailed to a board.

Warren shoved the contraption further under the bushes then stood up. He remained standing there for some time, uncertain as to what this all meant and wondering what his next move should be.

"Phase Two," he muttered to himself eventually, recalling that Mr. Trueheart would be in the process of Phase Two at his house right now. Whatever Phase Two was...

* * *

I was overseas the first time I noticed something was off. We grabbed someone from the nearby village—someone whom I had been spying on, keeping tabs on, someone I recognized wasn't quite right—and we tied them up in a shed. Even when he cried and begged and screamed, I knew it was all a facade. Do you know what a facade is, Warren? It's a mask, just like the kind children wear on Halloween. This monster was wearing a mask, Warren, a human mask, but he hadn't fooled me. He hadn't fooled any of us.

Do you know what we did?

Warren does not.

We removed the mask, Warren. We cut it right off him and exposed him for exactly what he was. And that's when I was convinced. They are among us but they can't hide, not if we're vigilant and pay attention and have no fear. Do you have any fear, Warren?

Warren shakes his head.

Good, says Mr. Trueheart. *I didn't think you did. That's good. Because we've got a mission, you and me. Something we need to do.*

Warren asks what that is.

To save the world, Warren. To save the world.

* * *

He had to muster up some courage to mount the porch steps and knock on Mr. Trueheart's door. This wasn't one of their scheduled meetings and he'd never stopped by Mr. Trueheart's house unannounced before.

There were no footsteps on the other side of the door.

Warren knocked again.

He was perspiring like mad beneath the mask, but he felt calm inside it, protected, and he didn't want to take it off.

Warren waited, but there were no footsteps. No Mr. Trueheart. He began to worry, and wondered if something terrible had befallen his friend. Had the replacements caught on to their plan? Did that explain why their homemade bomb was nothing but a hollow shell? Had they gotten into Mr. Trueheart's house without him knowing?

This last thought sent a chill down Warren's spine. All species of terrible thoughts filled his mind. What, exactly, were the replacements capable of? Mr. Trueheart said they were terrible creatures that paraded as people, but what exactly *made* them so terrible?

For the first time, Warren's confusion bordered on self-doubt.

He reached out and turned the doorknob. Pushed. Mr.

Trueheart's door eased open with a squeal.

The smell of tomato soup struck him as he stepped inside, just as it always did...but now, there was something else. Something more rank.

It smells like a toilet, Warren realized as he walked slowly into the house.

"Mr. Trueheart," he called.

Paused.

No answer.

He peered into the darkened rooms as he passed by them on his way down the hall. They were all empty. He glanced into the kitchen and saw the cone of paper still rolled up on the kitchen table. Warren's empty drinking glass still stood at the edge of the table. Nothing looked unusual or out of place.

"Mr. Trueheart? Are you here?"

Mr. Trueheart *was* here: Warren found him in the foxhole, right in the center of the floor, in the spot where the Maxwell House bomb—

(not a bomb)

—had been earlier. He was sprawled out on the carpet, his body strangely crumpled. The smell of feces was stronger here. There was something on the floor near Mr. Trueheart's right hand. There was something on the carpet by his head, too. Warren crept closer for better inspection. The item beside Mr. Trueheart's right hand was a gun. The *something* by Mr. Trueheart's head was actually a puddle of blood, so dark in the poor lighting of the foxhole that it looked as black as velvet.

Warren stood over Mr. Trueheart and looked down at him. He was startled to find Mr. Trueheart's eyes still open, though there was an absence in them, something missing. There was also a small dime-sized hole at his temple from which two delicate streamers of blood issued. There were hunks of matter in the blood and on the carpet and, Warren noticed when he looked up, along the cushions of the nearby loveseat, too. Some of the chunks had Mr. Trueheart's hair stuck to them. Warren was suddenly grateful that Mr. Trueheart was facing the ceiling, for he feared the opening at the back of his friend's head was much larger and messier than the one at his temple.

Warren stared down at his friend's body for some time. He didn't count the seconds, the minutes, so he would never be sure how long he stood there, sweating inside that mask. Then, after a while, he adjourned to the kitchen, where he located the bottle of liquor on the counter—the bottle with the bright red turkey on it. He saw that there was only a little bit left in it.

Warren peeled the rubber mask up over his face, luxuriating in the way the sweat on his face grew instantly chilly in the air. He gathered up the bottle in two hands and brought the spout to his mouth. When the liquor hit his throat, he gagged and dropped the bottle on the floor. He thought he might throw up, and dropped to his knees, coughing.

After the feeling passed and he didn't throw up, he swiped tears from his eyes and, using one of the kitchen chairs for support, climbed unsteadily to his feet.

Before leaving the house, Warren peered back into the foxhole, though he didn't dare go down there again.

"I'm sorry," he called out to Mr. Trueheart's body. "I'm sorry they got you. We should have done something sooner."

In the foyer, Warren pulled the mask back down over his face and slipped out into the night.

* * *

He screamed when we cut his face off, Warren. But underneath! Oh, Warren, there was no hiding what that monster truly was! And we made him suffer. Yes we did, son. Yes we did.

* * *

It was late by the time Warren arrived home. The TV was still on in the living room, but his mother was passed out on the couch and snoring like a locomotive. Laddie was in her lap; his tiny black head popped up as Warren approached and, possibly because the dog did not recognize Warren in the mask, or possibly because he simply did not like or trust Warren, he began yipping shrilly.

"Quiet," Warren said. He went to the couch and snatched the dog up off his mother's lap. His mother didn't even stir.

Warren went through the kitchen and to the basement door. He opened the door and released Laddie onto the first step. The dog barked once then went silent. Warren closed the door on him. He locked it, too, even though Laddie could not use a doorknob. That was just silly.

Back in the living room, his silhouette silvered from the glow of the television, Warren stood for a long time above his mother as she snored on the couch. The longer he stared down at her, the more he could see the innate *ugliness* of her, the sheer *wrongness* of her. That angular face...the glistening trail of drool that purled from her open mouth...her meaty leg tented up from the part in her robe, the hue of unbaked dough...

"You can't fool me," Warren said, his voice muffled from within the mask. "You can't fool me."

But underneath! Oh, Warren, there was no hiding what that monster truly was!

He went into the kitchen for a knife.

THE HOUSE ON COTTAGE LANE

The Toomeys, who lived in the house next door, were always taking in weirdoes. My father repeatedly scolded me about using such a word, but that was the truth of it: the kids were weird. There had been the boy who sat in the yard all day trying on different women's hats, which he carried around with him in an old brown shopping bag from the A&P. There had been a girl of seven or eight who never came out of the house, though she would keep her pale white ghost-face pressed against one of the upstairs dormer windows, staring out at Luther Avenue with melancholia in her eyes, reminding me of fairytales about princesses held captive in stone towers. Last summer, the Toomeys brought home a girl of about eleven or twelve—my age—who seemed normal enough at first. She even came over to play a few times, and we would either go out into the yard and dig up larval ant-lions or play badminton (we have a net) or we would just stay inside and watch TV. But then one afternoon, while we were out digging in the yard for nightcrawlers, she bit me high up on my bicep for no reason. It was hard enough to draw blood. After that, my father said I didn't have to play with her anymore. When I asked him why she had done such a thing, my father's face grew dark, as if clouds were passing overhead, and he said, "Not all kids in this world are as lucky as you, Brian." He seemed saddened by my delight at not having to bother with the girl anymore. When she was finally sent off to some other foster home—or to wherever kids like her go—I was pleased.

The kids were weirdoes, all right, but that meant that the Toomeys were even weirder. What sort of couple brought kids like that into their home? I couldn't understand it. Jeremy Beachy's mom was constantly threatening to send Jeremy, her own flesh and blood, off to boarding school, yet Eric and June Toomey continued to take these strange kids into their home and pretend, at least for a little while, to be their parents. The Toomeys had no kids of their own, so I assumed this was their way of faking it. It was like an assembly-line: when one weirdo left, another one would show up. Over the years, I had lost count as to how many had come to stay at the Toomey house. My mother seemed to regard the Toomeys with an air of suspicion, but my father said they were good people and that they were doing a very good thing helping all those troubled kids. To me, they were weirdoes; to my dad, they were always "troubled kids." I failed to see the difference.

Their newest kid arrived two months ago. He was short and thin for a boy, and I originally guessed him to be a year or two younger than me. Turned out, he was exactly my age, and it wasn't long before my father started in with his not-so-subtle hints that I make an effort to befriend the kid. One afternoon, I went over to the Toomeys' house with a stack of comic books tucked under one arm. June Toomey's face lit up when she opened the front door to find me standing there. She quickly ushered me inside, and introduced me to the new kid. His name was Oliver, and he possessed the big face and widely spaced teeth of a jack-o'-lantern. Despite his slight frame, his clothes seemed too small. A large booger waved in and out of one nostril in rhythm with his respiration, like the hinged valve on a pipe. I asked him if he liked comic books and he just rolled those bony little shoulders of his. His shyness that afternoon would have driven me mad had I not decided to spread out on the Toomeys' living-room floor and read my books while Oliver, sitting Indian-style on the couch across the room, did nothing but stare out the windows.

At my father's behest, I ventured over to the Toomeys' on a few more occasions. Sometimes I brought my comic books, other times I took over my video game console, which Eric Toomey gladly hooked up to their TV, a smile on his face so stretched out of proportion that it looked like he was trying to hide something. Oliver sometimes played the video games with me, but he was so awful that it took much of the pleasure from it. Like pack animals, kids know when they're in the presence of a weaker member, and that was certainly the case with Oliver. I could sense his passivity like a stink coming off his flesh. In turn, I think my awareness of our hierarchy drove him into greater submission. I wasn't mean to him, wasn't a bully, but I couldn't help bark at him aggressively on the occasions when his timidity pushed me over the edge.

A week before Halloween, as I was about to sprint out the door to meet up with Jeremy Beachy and Cyn Cristo to play baseball in the park, my father suggested I see if Oliver wanted to join me. So I went next door, was greeted by June Toomey's strangely shocked smile, and ultimately asked Oliver if he wanted to come along. To my surprise and dismay, Oliver agreed to come. He didn't have a glove, so I ran back home and grabbed my old one for him.

At Shoulder Park, I introduced Oliver to Jeremy and Cyn, my best friends, while Oliver stared at his sneakers. Cyn said, "Hello," and spent the rest of the afternoon watching the strange new kid from the corner of her eye. Less understated than Cyn, Jeremy fired a barrage of questions at the boy—where did he come from? What happened to his parents (and were they dead)? Did he go to school? Had he seen June Toomey naked coming out of the shower?

Oliver's baseball skills made him look like a videogame wizard. He couldn't catch, couldn't hit, and he ran with the hobbled gait of someone learning to walk again after a markedly bad automobile accident. Jeremy was relentless in his torment, and never missed an opportunity to criticize. Cyn said nothing, but continued to stare at Oliver as if expecting, at any moment, his head to pop right off the skinny stalk of his neck. Later that night, over dinner, I commented on Oliver's maladjustments to my father. "There's nothing wrong with that boy, Brian," he said to me after I'd finished relaying how the kid had actually shrieked and ran away from a pop-fly. "Do you think everyone was born to be an athlete? I can't shoot a basketball to save my life. And as I recall," he said, winking at me while lowering his voice to a conspiratorial tone, as if he didn't want my mother, who was seated right beside him at the table, to overhear, "you were no Babe Ruth when you first started playing, either."

Given all this, it came as no surprise that my dad had me invite Oliver trick-or-treating on Halloween. I spent the afternoon assembling my werewolf costume, epoxying fake fur to my face and also to the flesh-toned T-shirt I planned to wear beneath a tattered flannel shirt. I had just finished coloring the tip of my nose black with a grease pencil when my mom called from the front hall to tell me Cyn had just arrived.

"Oh," my mother fawned over us both. "You two look fantastic! Let me get my camera."

Cyn was done up as Dracula, her face powdered white, rivulets of dried blood leaking from the corners of her mouth. Her dark hair was pulled back into a long braid, which she tucked down into the collar of her black satin cape, forming an impressive widow's peak at the center of her forehead. When my mom returned with the camera, Cyn popped in her plastic vampire teeth and growled as the flash went off.

We handed out candy to some of the younger kids while we waited for Jeremy to show up. When it started to get dark, I went into the kitchen and called his house. The phone rang and rang and no one answered. Irritated, I hung up. When I turned around, there was a terrible face framed in the center of the kitchen window—a peeling green zombie face. I cried out then relaxed as, on the other side of the glass, Jeremy broke out in bawdy laughter. He ran around to the front of the house and came swooping in through the front door, nearly trampling some little kids coming up the walkway in the process.

"That was priceless!" he howled. His face was done up in a base of green paint upon which he had affixed bits of rubbery latex that, when glimpsed through a window, looked remarkably like real loose-hanging flesh. "You should have seen your face! Oh my God!"

"Hilarious," I said.

Cyn poked her head over the half-wall that overlooked the foyer. "We gonna go or what?" she said around the plastic vampire fangs.

"Yeah," I said, grabbing the freshly washed pillowcase my mother had slung over the back of one of the kitchen chairs. "But we gotta stop next door first."

"Oh, no," Jeremy groaned, his ghoulish face suddenly going slack. "Don't tell me that little faggot is coming with us."

"My dad's making me."

"What horseshit."

"We don't have to hang out with him all night," I said. "He'll probably get tired early on and head back home. Then we can do whatever we want."

"You get more candy if you go to the door with less people," he hypothesized.

"You can go by yourself," Cyn said cheerily from over the half-wall, and Jeremy gave her the finger.

"Hey," growled my dad, passing through the hallway and catching the gesture. "Be nice, Jer."

"Sorry, Mr. Ganelin."

"And be nice to that kid next door."

"We will, Dad," I promised him, and hurried out of the house with my friends.

Next door, the three of us stood on the porch while I knocked. Jeremy took out his trick-or-treat bag and held it open. When I glanced at him, he shrugged and said, "What? Might as well make the most of it, right?"

The door opened and Eric Toomey's plastic smile greeted us. He held a Tupperware bowl in one arm. "Oh. Is that you, Brian? With all the fuzz on your face?"

"Yeah."

"I guess you're here for Oliver, huh?"

I nodded.

Eric Toomey turned and shouted into the house for Oliver. Then he faced back around, noticed Jeremy standing there with his trick-or-treat sack held open, and pulled a handful of pennies and toothbrushes out of the Tupperware bowl. He dropped the items into Jeremy's sack just as a shape moved in the gloominess of the hallway behind him.

"Oh," said Eric Toomey, stepping aside. "Your friends are here, Oliver."

Oliver was dressed as a ghost. A single white sheet covered his body, with two holes punched out for eyes. Along the sides of the costume I noticed strips of reflective material, like the kind you see on construction workers' vests. June Toomey had probably pasted them onto the sheet to ensure Oliver wouldn't get hit by a car. Oliver shuffled forward, thumped one shoulder against the frame of the door, and ultimately needed to be guided out onto the porch by Eric Toomey. "Okay," Eric Toomey said, that plastic smile never leaving his face. "You kids have fun, and be careful." He closed the door on us.

"Can you see in that thing?" I asked.

From beneath the sheet, Oliver shrugged his narrow shoulders.

We walked down the lawn and filed in among the other trick-or-treaters on Luther Avenue. Jeremy turned his sack upside down and emptied the pennies and toothbrushes into the gutter. "Those fuckin' whackos," he mused. "Seriously? Fuckin' toothbrushes?"

I gave him a quick kick to the shin and a look that told him to keep his voice down.

"Hey," Jeremy said, turning to Oliver, who bumbled along the sidewalk like a drunk. "Your foster parents are real cuckoos, you know that?"

Oliver turned his head and stared at Jeremy through the two holes in the sheet. He didn't say a word.

"Come on," Cyn said before we reached the intersection. "Let's start here. Mrs. Gisondi always gives out those supersize candy bars."

We hurried up the walk toward the Gisondi house, Oliver bringing up the rear. By the time Mrs. Gisondi answered the door and dropped a jumbo Mr. Goodbar into each of our bags, Oliver had just joined us on the stoop. He fumbled around beneath his sheet while Mrs. Gisondi smiled patiently at us. Finally, Oliver's small white hands appeared from beneath the hem of the sheet, holding open a plastic Ziploc bag.

"Oh," said Mrs. Gisdoni, dropping a jumbo Mr. Goodbar into Oliver's bag. "That'll fill up quickly."

The four of us hit the remaining houses along Luther Avenue, then hooked a right at the intersection onto Watchtower Street. Dusk had darkened the sky and the cool, crisp air was redolent with the smell of chimney smoke. Witches and trolls cackled as they passed us on the opposite side of the street. One house had a cauldron spewing clouds of dry ice on the porch, and a few of the neighbors had propped up fake tombstones in their front yards. At the Miners' house, prerecorded ghost-sounds issued out of hidden speakers. A troupe of ballerinas stared at us as we marshaled up Watchtower.

"Hey," Jeremy said, elbowing me in the ribs. "Check this out." He handed me a Tootsie Roll that looked just slightly thicker than normal.

"What is it?" I asked.

Jeremy laughed. "I wrapped up cat turds in old Tootsie Roll wrappers!"

"Gross!" I chucked the wrapped turd over a hedgerow decorated in orange pumpkin lights.

"Hey, Oliver," Jeremy called over to the walking white sheet. "You want a Tootsie Roll?"

Cyn and I laughed. Oliver stopped walking, his tattered sneakers sliding to a stop along a patch of wet black leaves. Those two eyeholes again fell on Jeremy.

"Ooh," Cyn crooned. "Cripple fight..."

"Shut up," Jeremy said, chucking another turd-wrapped-Tootsie at her. "Come on, Ollie. I'm just busting your balls."

Oliver said nothing. He didn't move.

"Dude, let's *go*," Jeremy groaned.

I nudged Oliver's shoulder. "Come on, man. There's more houses to hit."

Those two little eyeholes fell on me. Then Oliver faced forward again and continued down the street with us.

By the time we reached Chestnut Street, it was coming on full dark, and Oliver was showing no signs of tiring. Even when his Ziploc bag filled up, which didn't take long, he continued going house-to-house with us. At one point, when he stopped to lace up his sneakers, Jeremy and Cyn gathered around me. In a hushed voice, Jeremy said, "Let's ditch the freak."

"We can't ditch him," I said. "My dad'll kill me."

"Well, he won't kill *me.*"

"Yeah," I said. "But if you leave me alone with him, *I'll* kill you."

"Let's pretend we're tired and we're all going home for the night," Cyn suggested. She had a lollipop in her mouth. "When he goes home, we can all go back out."

"But he'll follow me home," I said. "And by the time I walk all the way there and then back out here, I'll miss all the good houses."

"Well, we gotta do *something,*" Jeremy said, picking some of the dried latex off his face.

I looked back over at Oliver, who had apparently stepped in someone's discarded chewing gum. He kept lifting his foot higher and higher off the ground, the gum stuck to its sole stretching like a tendon.

"I've got an idea," I said. "If we scare him enough, he might go home on his own."

"How do we do that?" Jeremy said, bringing the piece of latex to his nose and sniffing it.

"We take him to the house on Cottage Lane," I said.

It was a crumbling old A-frame, partially sunken into the earth and surrounded by woods. Beyond the trees and in the dark distance, the lights of the Naval Academy's communication towers pulsed red. The house had been vacant for the entirety of my lifetime, and it stood at the end of Cottage Lane in solitary confinement, cut off from the rest of the town. There were other houses on Cottage Lane, but they were huddled together closer to the newer developments at the bottom of the hill, separated from the crumbling old A-frame by several acres of black woods.

The four of us hit some of these houses at the bottom of Cottage Lane before I suggested, in a tone that sounded admirably spontaneous, that we check out the old abandoned house farther up the hill. Jeremy and Cyn pretended like it was a great idea. The two black holes in Oliver's sheet surveyed my friends before coming to rest on me.

"You'll love it," I told Oliver as the four of us proceeded to walk up Cottage Lane, leaving the well-lighted houses and the cacophony of trick-or-treaters in our wake. "It's creepy as hell."

"Like something from a horror movie," Cyn added.

"Tell him about the serial killer, Brian," Jeremy said.

"Oh, yeah. That's right. See, a guy used to live there. Like, a hermit, you know? Kept to himself, didn't have a wife. That sort of thing. Really weird."

"Weird like the Toomeys," said Jeremy.

"Quiet!" Cyn scolded him. "I want to hear this."

"Anyway," I continued, "it was a few years ago, in the weeks just before Halloween, when some of the neighborhood kids started disappearing. No one knew where they went, or if they'd just decided to run away."

"Paul Torvall tried to run away when he shit his pants in school and got embarrassed," Jeremy said, laughing to himself. "You guys remember that?"

"I said be quiet," Cyn reprimanded him again.

Jeremy frowned. "Sorry. Go ahead, Brian."

"Well," I said, moving in step with Oliver now, "kids kept disappearing all the way up to Halloween night. No one knew what the heck was going on, not even the cops. So all the worried parents and some of the cops started driving around the neighborhood, looking around to see if they could find clues as to what happened to all the kids. When one of the dads drove past the old house at the top of the hill, he noticed all these kids' costumes and bags of candy lying around on the front porch and in the yard. So he got out of his car and went up to the house. It was mostly dark inside, but he looked in one of the windows. And that's when he saw it."

Oliver sucked in an intake of breath and paused momentarily in his stride.

"The guy was inside the house, and he had his whole dining-room table set like he was gonna have a big party," I said. "Only instead of food on all the plates, there were all these kids' heads. The killer had stuck Halloween candy in their eye sockets and in their mouths, too. The dad, he runs back to the car and gets the police. When the police show up, there's like a shootout or something…and when they break into the house to apprehend the killer, they find that he'd escaped."

"Holy shit," Jeremy said in a small voice.

"Yeah," I went on. "And they never did catch him."

"There it is," Cyn said, and we all stopped in the middle of the street. The old house stood before us, blacker than a cave on the moon, slouching toward the earth as if terminally exhausted. Its windows were boarded up and there were great frilly hawks' nests in the eaves. Beyond the trees, the red lights at the tops of the communication towers throbbed.

"Pretty scary, huh?" I said.

Oliver stared at the house…then turned toward me. I waited for him to speak but he didn't. When he looked back at the house, I could hear his wheezy respiration once more.

"I dare you," I said, "to go inside."

Oliver's sheeted head turned back around to face me. He shook his head furiously.

"We all did it," Jeremy said. "You gotta go right in the front door, straight through the house, and come out the back. That's how we'll know you're brave."

"It would be the coolest ever," Cyn added, flashing a rare smile that hinted at her burgeoning femininity.

Oliver continued shaking his head.

"If you're too chicken," I said, "that's cool. But if you want to hang out with us, you gotta do it. Okay?"

Oliver looked back up at the house. I could tell his hands were fidgeting beneath the sheet, and his breath was coming in exaggerated gasps now. The reflector strips on his costume glowed in the moonlight like lines on a highway. One pale white hand appeared beneath the hem of his sheet, but then slipped back beneath it.

"We'll wait here for you," I told him.

Oliver nodded…then slowly made his way up to the house. The porch was overgrown with weeds, the wooden planks themselves rotted and cracked. He managed the stairs with little difficulty, but then paused when he reached the front door. When he turned back around to face us, I waved him forward. He turned back to face the front door. He pressed his hands against it, pushing.

"Shit," Jeremy said beside me. "It might be locked."

But it wasn't; apparently, even a pipsqueak like Oliver could manage to shove it open, if just several inches. A vertical strip of blackness seemed to ooze out. At that moment, I knew Oliver was going to chicken out, and we'd have to tote him along with us for the rest of the night…

Oliver's white sheet passed through the opening in the doorway, and went into the house. I glimpsed a final reflection of moonlight off his reflector strips before he was swallowed up by the darkness.

"Wow," Cyn said. "He did it." She looked at me, her eyes comically wide in her white-powdered face. "I wouldn't have done it."

"I'm gonna go around back and scare the shit out of him when he comes out," Jeremy said, and before anyone could say another word to him, he was jogging around the side of the house.

We waited.

"That was a cool story," Cyn said after a time.

"Thanks."

"Did you, like, make that up as you went along?"

"Yeah, I guess."

"Wow."

Crickets chirruped in the overgrown grass while the boomerang shape of bats arced across the face of the moon. A few blocks over, I heard the shrill, joyful cries of trick-or-treaters. They suddenly sounded very far away.

Something like ten minutes later, Cyn said, "What's taking so long?"

I shook my head.

"Maybe Jeremy's with him?" she suggested, sounding hopeful.

But at that moment, Jeremy appeared around the side of the house, his arms splayed out in a *what gives?* posture. "Where is he?" he asked as he joined us in the street.

"Don't know," I said. "He didn't come out the back?"

"Would I be here asking you where he is if he came out the back?"

"It's an old house," Cyn said. "Maybe he fell through some floorboards or something."

"I didn't hear anything," I said.

"But still," she said. There was panic rising in her voice now.

"Shit," I said, chewing fake werewolf fur off my lower lip. I handed over my pillowcase full of candy to Cyn. "Hold this. I'll go see."

"You're going *in* there?" she said.

I didn't respond. Slowly, I approached the house. Up close, the floorboards of the porch looked even more dangerous than they had from the street. Some were missing, revealing dark slats of space at intervals across the porch. I avoided these spaces and went right up to the door, which still stood slightly ajar. A smell like the interior of an old barn wafted from the opening, and I instinctively wrinkled my nose. *There are dead things in there.* The thought hooked me out of nowhere and refused to let go. *Dead animals...and maybe other things, too.*

"Oliver!" I called in through the open doorway. I could see nothing inside—just pitch blackness. "Hey, Oliver! Are you in there? Are you okay?"

My voice echoed off the walls inside the house, but then faded to nothingness. I listened. Not a single sound came from within that house...

I turned around, gripped by terrifying certainty that Jeremy and Cyn had fled, leaving me all alone. But there they were, standing together in the middle of the street, looking up at me. I hurried down off the porch and over to them, my heart strumming feverishly in my chest. "I called but he didn't answer," I said, frightening myself even more by the reedy, whiny quality of my voice. "I don't know what happened."

"What do we do?" Cyn asked, her eyes volleying between Jeremy and me.

"Maybe he's messing around with us," Jeremy said, though he did not sound convinced. "Like, maybe he's in there hiding, waiting for us to come in so he can jump out and scare us."

It didn't seem likely.

"We need to go home and tell my dad," I said finally.

Jeremy's eyebrows knitted together. "That's a bad idea."

"You got a better one? You wanna go in there and look for him?"

"No..."

"Then we've got no other choice." I snatched my pillowcase back from Cyn, who jumped at the suddenness of my action.

The three of us headed straight for Luther Avenue, not stopping along the way, and cutting through people's backyards when we knew the shortcuts. It was closing in on nine-thirty when we finally reached my house. The streets had grown empty at this deepening hour, and there were bits of candy strewn about the sidewalks and on people's lawns. As I opened the front door, Jeremy said, "I'm not going in."

"What are you talking about?"

"I'm going home."

"We gotta tell my dad what happened!"

"You tell him. It was your idea about the house anyway, Brian."

"You wanted to ditch him," I protested.

"Doesn't matter. I'm going home." He cast his eyes down then slumped off the porch. He lived only two blocks over, not far, but when he hit Luther Avenue, he started to run.

I exchanged a look with Cyn. "You wanna go home, too?"

"I don't know." Her voice was small.

"Go, if you want to."

I turned and went inside, calling immediately for my father. He came down the hall and into the foyer, wearing a sweater with black cats on it. He was smiling until he saw the panic in my face. "What is it, Bri?"

"We lost Oliver," I blurted.

"What do you mean you lost him?"

"He went into that old house on Cottage Lane, but he never came out. We waited around and I called to him but he never came out."

My father's eyes flitted past me and toward the front door. I spun around, hoping to find Oliver standing there in his sheet, but it was only Cyn. She looked too frightened to move from the stoop. My father waved her inside then told us to sit down on the couch. My mother appeared over the half-wall, plastic spiders pinned into her hair. She asked what was going on.

"Call the Toomeys and tell them to come over," said my father. Then he came over to the couch and said, "Maybe he went home."

"Yeah," I said, hoping it was the truth, but not believing it. We would have seen him leave the house. Jeremy had been watching the back door. Nonetheless, I held out hope.

Yet this hope was dashed the moment Eric and June Toomey filed into the house without Oliver. June looked frantic and Eric had a stoic, medicated look about him. He came over and sat down between Cyn and me on the couch, but he didn't say a word.

"What happened?" June said, first to my father and then to my mother. "Where's Oliver?"

My father relayed what I had told him. When he'd finished, June looked at me. She was visibly shaking. "He doesn't know the neighborhood," she said. "He's probably lost, wandering the streets."

"I'll call the cops," said my mom, who departed for the kitchen.

"Why in the world would he go into that house?" Eric Toomey said.

My father looked at me. I held my gaze on him for perhaps two heartbeats before I had to turn away. My face felt suddenly very hot.

Less than ten minutes later, two police officers showed up. They asked questions of my father and then of the Toomeys. When they asked what Oliver had been wearing, June Toomey said flatly, "A bed sheet. A goddamn white bed sheet. He was a ghost."

In a softer voice, Eric Toomey said, "The boy has problems. He's got special needs." His dead eyes looked over at the police officers. "You should know that, I think."

"We're gonna head out to the house," said one of the officers to my dad. "I'd like to take one of the kids with me, talk to them, if that's okay with you."

"Sure," my father said, his eyebrows arching. "Should I come, too?"

"No problem," said the other cop.

My father waved me up off the couch. "Come on."

"What about me?" Cyn said.

"You stay here with me, sweetheart," said my mom. "We'll call your parents."

Sedately, Cyn nodded.

My father and I followed one of the cops out to the patrol car, while the other cop stayed inside and asked more questions. The cop opened the passenger door for me. "Why don't you hop up front so we can chat? Brian, right?"

I nodded and climbed inside. My dad got in the back.

Once we had pulled out onto Luther Avenue and were headed toward Watchtower Street, the cop asked me to tell him again what had happened. I started to tell the same story Cyn and I had told back at the house when the officer cut me off in midsentence. "So you're saying your friend Oliver just decided to go into the house by himself? You guys weren't daring him or anything like that?"

"Well..." I said.

"I need to know the truth if we're going to find your friend," said the cop.

I looked out the passenger window, and at the glowing jack-o'-lanterns on all the porches as we drove by. The older kids were out now, safety pins in their shirts, black makeup over their eyes, tattoos. Some sat on cars parked up on lawns, drinking soda and smoking. They pointed to the police car as we drove by.

"Okay," I said, and told the truth.

When we reached the house on Cottage Lane, the officer took a flashlight out of the glove compartment and got out of the car. He went up to the house, completed a full circuit around the property, then went in the front door. I saw the flashlight's beam come slanting through the boards that had been nailed up over the windows.

I glanced up and saw my father's reflection in the rearview mirror. His jaw was set and his mouth was nothing more than a lipless gash just below his nose. When his eyes met mine, he looked quickly away, ashamed of me. He said nothing for the entire time we sat in the car together.

The cop returned a full ten minutes later. Sighing, he tossed the flashlight back into the glove compartment then geared the car into Drive. "There's no one in that house," he said. His demeanor had changed.

By the time we arrived back home, Mrs. Cristo's convertible Sebring was parked outside. As I got out of the police car, Cyn came out of the house, followed by her mother, and marched over to the Sebring without casting even the quickest glance in my direction. My mom stood in the doorway, her arms folded, looking cold and very thin. Apparently, the Toomeys had gone to the police station to fill out some paperwork. It promised to be a long night for them.

I went into the house and straight up to my room, where I dropped down on the bed and buried my face in my pillow. My father's voice ghosted up through the heating vents as he spoke with the police officer in the foyer. Once the cop left, it was my mother's voice that dominated much of the conversation.

After a while, I heard my dad creaking down the hallway toward my room. He opened the door and poked his head inside, where he remained for some time. I still had my face buried in the pillow, but I could sense him there like a spirit at my back. Eventually, he came over and sat down on the edge of the bed.

"Roll over," he said. "Look at me."

I rolled over and looked at him. My vision threatened to double.

"That story you told in the police car," said my dad. "Never in a million years would I have guessed that my son…" Disgusted, he let his voice trail off. It wasn't necessary for him to complete the thought. I felt horrible enough as it was. "Have you told the police everything?"

I merely nodded, not trusting my words.

"If there's something else, you better tell me now."

I shook my head.

"Speak," said my father.

"There's nothing else."

"All right." The bedsprings squealed as he stood up. "We'll talk more about this in the morning. You better pray they find that boy," he said, and left.

But they didn't.

They didn't find that boy.

I was questioned several times by the police, each time more thoroughly than the previous times. Cyn and Jeremy were questioned, too. Intimidated by the cops' authority, they did not bother lying. In the end, we all told the same story. We all told the truth.

The house on Cottage Lane was searched more thoroughly, too. The cops used dogs, and my parents, along with the Toomeys, joined in the search. But it was futile. There was no evidence found that even suggested Oliver had ever gone into the house. He certainly wasn't still there, hiding.

One Sunday, as we drove home from church, my mother said out of nowhere, "You should have never forced him to play with all those kids."

My father, who was driving, glanced quickly at her, a look of surprise on his face. Then he turned back to face the road.

"They're all problem kids," said my mom. "What did you expect?"

"They were just kids," said my dad.

"He could have just run away. Did anyone ever consider that?"

"It's possible," my father said.

"It's the Toomeys' fault, too," my mom went on. "This is a nice residential neighborhood. Who do they think they are, bringing children like that onto our street?"

"Geri," said my dad, his tone placating.

"Don't give me that," she spat. "There's enough blame to go around. No one's hands are clean in this, Roger."

My dad's eyes met mine in the rearview mirror. A confusing mix of compassion and disappointment greeted me.

"Maybe he'll show up eventually," said my dad as we pulled into the driveway.

But like I said, he never did.

Unless…

There's that old chestnut—a verbal crutch of sorts—that goes, *I told you all that to tell you this,* and I suppose that's the point we've reached in this story. I've told you all that to tell you this:

A year has passed since Oliver disappeared in the house on Cottage Lane. In that year, I have changed quite a bit. For one thing, I no longer hang out with Jeremy Beachy. We haven't spoken since that night, when he left Cyn and me standing on my front porch to face the music on our own. I'm sure he was scared and acting out of impulse, and in truth I don't really blame him for it; but the sight of him sickens me, because I see myself reflected in him. I see the way I may have provoked that girl into biting me on the arm, and how I teased the kid with all the hats in the A&P bag until he would cry. I remember one afternoon, troubled by that blank ghost-face peering down at me from the dormer window of the Toomey house, when I gave that little girl the finger. Most of all, I see the way I teased Oliver and tricked him and tried to scare him. Funny, how he wound up scaring us instead.

I still see Cyn at school, but she doesn't come over to the house anymore. Perhaps she sees herself reflected in me the same way I see myself reflected in Jeremy.

The Toomeys still live next door. Since Oliver, they haven't brought in any new kids. I hope they do eventually, because I could use the opportunity to absolve myself by changing my behavior. Maybe some of it is what happened with Oliver; maybe some of it is just a part of growing up. I'm thirteen now. I'm responsible for the stones I throw and the windows I break.

And then there's my dad. I won't be dramatic and say that, since that incident, he has looked at me differently, because that's not the case. True, I had disappointed him. True, it took some time to earn his trust again. But I *did* earn it back, and we share a good, strong, close relationship. My father is a good man, and it's funny how it took all these years to understand what that means.

So here we are, one year later, Halloween night. I didn't go out this year. I'm too old for that. Instead, I stayed home to hand out candy while my parents, dressed as Popeye and Olive Oyl, went to a party a few blocks over. Around ten-thirty, well after all the ghosts and witches and goblins had made their final rounds and ventured back home, I heard a knock at the front door. There was some candy left in the bowl, so I answered it.

A ghost stood on the other side of the door. It was a person just slightly shorter and thinner than me draped in a single white sheet with two eyeholes cut into it. The sight arrested me, and I stood there without moving, the bowl of candy gradually growing heavier in my hand.

A hand emerged from beneath the sheet, holding open an empty plastic Ziploc bag. The fingers of the hand were small and white, but there were crescents of black grit under the nails. There were specks of dirt on the plastic bag, too.

Finding my momentum again, I reached into the candy bowl, snatched up a handful of goodies, and dumped them into the ghost's bag. Apparently satisfied, the bag retreated back beneath the sheet. Yet my visitor did not move away from the porch. I stared at those two dark eyeholes, dark as roofing tar. Listening, I could hear the visitor's respiration, thin and wheezy, behind the sheet. I opened my mouth to speak, but no words came out.

The ghost turned and padded down off the porch. I watched it cross the yard and head down the driveway. When the sheeted figure reached Luther Avenue, I expected it to blink out of existence, but it didn't. It continued up the block, the reflective tape shimmering with moonlight on the sides of the costume, in the approximate direction of Cottage Lane.

There was a train that ran from northern France to a small village tucked down in the gray safety of a whitewashed valley. We spent most of the winter there, thankful to be away from the front and away from the beaches and away from northern France altogether. The train was calm and peaceful but shook rather furiously over the land, and the village itself was small and proud and did not seem very French. You would think of the beaches and think of the shelling on the beaches, then wake up and realize you were on the train all along. Everyone was still on the train. The bumping of the train did nothing to settle your dreams and you were only thankful for living once you were awake and able to understand it all, and able to understand living, and when you were able to see the little village up ahead through the dirty windows of the train. All of us drank hot coffee in the cafés and slept in two-story bungalows outside the village that had once been brothels. With the commencement of the war, the brothels emptied and became places of refuge for tired soldiers. Someone laughed at this and said we were all tired soldiers. Many of the men laughed, too. It was a strain to hear the laughter and I don't think it truly made anyone feel very good. Sometimes, we would move out of the cafés and into the streets and kick around a small leather ball with some of the village children. We all seemed to like it, sometimes more than the children. Some of the men spoke a little French, and the children would always laugh and point and call us américains bêtes, and it was all very much fun and all very European. But then at night you could hear the planes and think you could hear the gunfire and you forgot all about the children and kicking the leather ball around in the street. You forgot all about the hot coffee and the cafés and the bumping of the train. You would lay there and know that some man and woman had loved each other, albeit briefly and perhaps passionlessly, in the bed you were pressed into, and that did nothing to satisfy you. There was nothing any of us could do. And as the winter pressed on, the snow came, dirty and brutal, and buried the entire village. It was as if it never existed.

PEMBROKE

Pembroke's Used and Rare Books was, on the outside, a rather nondescript little enterprise tucked between a drab drinking establishment and the satellite office of a mortgage company along a brick-topped boulevard in historic Ellicott City. Its proprietor, Arthur Pembroke, had been in business at this location for the better part of three decades, yet despite the bookstore's prominence as a local fixture, few people ventured into the shop. In fact, few people even knew of its existence. This suited Pembroke just fine: a lifelong bachelor in his mid-sixties, Pembroke drew great pleasure from the quiet afternoons spent at the shop, untroubled by tourists or the occasional curioso who browsed the shelves but ultimately never made a purchase. His rent was cheap, his overhead low, and, with the exception of Tom DeLilly, who came in on Tuesdays and Thursdays to straighten the place up, Pembroke bankrolled no staff.

What kept Pembroke afloat were the few loyal customers with whom he'd cultivated a civil yet perfunctory relationship over the years—avid collectors of rare books who visited the bookstore on occasion to make specific requests (much in the conspiratorial tones and suspicious manner of someone inquiring about an illegal enterprise) of Pembroke. So-and-so has learned of a specific book on witchcraft—could he secure a copy? So-and-so is interested in a specific Romanian book of black magic—was it possible to place such an order? So-and-so fears that his wife has been unfaithful and has heard rumor of a book that might inform him one way or the other (with no harm coming to the unfaithful wife, of course)—was this something Pembroke could locate?

He was often fulfilling such exotic requests, so when he first saw the package on the front steps of the shop that Monday morning, he assumed it was one of the orders he'd recently placed. It was indeed book-shaped—large and blocky, like a dictionary, Pembroke thought—and it was wrapped in brown butcher's paper and bound with frayed bits of twine. The packaging was a bit out of the norm, but it wasn't wholly unusual—not enough to give Pembroke pause, anyway. What *was* unusual, he noticed as he gathered the heavy package up off the stoop and carried it into the shop, was that it bore no markings, labels, addresses, or postage. Pembroke puzzled over this for several moments after he set the book on the front counter and contorted out of his tweed coat. It then occurred to him that he could stand there puzzling over that nondescript brown paper for eternity, and so, with his wiry gray eyebrows arched above the lenses of his circular glasses, Pembroke untied the twine and removed the paper.

The book was bound between two roughly textured covers, greenish-yellow in hue and networked with what appeared to be tiny threadlike fibers. There was something very plantlike about the covers, reminding Pembroke of hand-rolled cigars, of which he indulged on occasion. There was no title or author's name embossed either on the front cover or on the very wide spine. This wasn't unusual per se; what *was* unusual was the absence of author's name and book title on the title page. Moreover, there was no copyright or publishing information. The book was sizable—perhaps 800 pages or so—but as Pembroke carefully turned page after page (the intensity and fervor of his page-turning increasing with each passing second), he saw that there were no printed page numbers, no headers or footers...no printed text anywhere in the book at all.

He stood there staring down at the blank book and wondered if this was some kind of practical joke. On occasion, Tom DeLilly took great pleasure in secreting rubber spiders among the stacks or hiding the self-help books so that patrons would, ironically, have to ask for assistance in locating them. This, however, struck Pembroke as something beyond Tom's wit or capability.

Perhaps it is a journal, he surmised, *or a sketch book. That would explain the lack of title, author, and text.*

Satisfied that was the answer, he closed the book and tucked it beneath the desk. Yet at the back of his head, he wondered about its mysterious arrival. If it *was* a journal or sketchbook, he hadn't ordered it.

* * *

Pembroke went about his business for much of that morning, calling customers to let them know their books had arrived and answering the phone whenever it rang, inevitably, with a wrong number. At one point, during the late morning, he found himself reclining in a creaky wooden chair at the back of the shop, the strange new book splayed open in his lap. He turned from page to page, examining the paper as if willing the words to materialize before his eyes. At noon, he took the book down the block and pawed through it while he sat by himself at an outdoor cafe. However, when the young waitress arrived and looked skeptically at the blank pages at which Pembroke had been staring with studied attention, he quickly snapped the book closed and glared at the girl. Perhaps taking it out of the shop had been a mistake.

He made a mental note to ask Tom about the book tomorrow; maybe he had ordered it for some reason. But when Tuesday arrived and Tom, cherry and bright-eyed, came bustling through the bookstore's front door—*ting!* went the tiny overhead bell— Pembroke was overcome by a peculiar sense of unease.

"Good morning, Arthur!"

Pembroke nodded at Tom as the younger man scooted down the narrow aisle and tossed his jacket over a rolling cart piled high with paperbacks. Pembroke had been turning the pages of the mysterious book when Tom had entered; now, he quickly closed the book and secured it back beneath the desk. He even went as far as stacking another book on top of it, as if to hide it. Not that Tom ever went behind the counter.

"Any new orders come in today?" Tom asked as he slotted paperbacks onto a nearby shelf.

"No," said Pembroke.

"I ran into Mrs. Teatree at the Giant," Tom said. "She's still fawning over that copy of *Mystical Methods* from last month." Tom snickered affably. "Strange old bird."

Pembroke nodded but said nothing.

At around three o'clock that afternoon, as Tom was in the backroom attempting to assemble a bookshelf, a man entered the shop, his presence causing the small bell over the door to tinkle. Pembroke, who was seated behind the counter balancing the stores books in a large ledger, looked up and took inventory. The man, who stood impressively tall, wore a long ash-gray overcoat and a Humphrey Bogart fedora of the same color. Beneath the fedora, his face was long, gaunt, angular, with a chin that appeared chiseled into a perfect rectangle. He possessed the distorted nose of a prizefighter and a firm mouth that was nearly a lipless slash. His eyes were small but alert—rodent's eyes—and they surveyed the tiny bookstore as the man stood unmoving in the entranceway.

"Good afternoon," Pembroke said, closing his ledger.

The man turned to face him, apparently startled by Pembroke's voice. His large, expressionless face creased into the approximation of a smile. Those rodent eyes twinkled like dollops of oil.

The man removed his hat, stepped toward Pembroke's desk, and said, "Good afternoon, sir. This is a lovely shop." His voice was smooth as satin.

"Thank you," said Pembroke. "Was there something I can help you find?"

"I hope so." The man's smile persisted. "I've got quite the specific request."

It was at that moment Pembroke knew what the man was looking for. A cool sweat broke out across Pembroke's forehead.

"It's a Book of No Name," said the man. "One of two, in fact. The yin and the yang, you might say." Impossibly, the man's smile widened, exposing teeth like a shark's. "The one I am seeking is quite large, and bound in a very rare organic covering."

"You'll have to be more specific," Pembroke said.

The man's smile faltered. "Will I?" he said.

"What's the author's name?" Pembroke retrieved a ream of

paper from beneath the desk, on which Tom had printed (from his personal computer) their inventory in alphabetical order by author.

"There is no author," said the man. The smile had completely vanished now. "Or, to be more precise, there are *many* authors. But I think, my friend, this book isn't something you'll be able to locate on your inventory list."

Pembroke slid the stack of pages aside. From the breast pocket of his tight-fitting oxford shirt, he removed a plain white handkerchief which he used to blot his brow.

"It is my understanding," said the man, "that this particular book may have mistakenly been delivered to this address yesterday morning."

Pembroke slowly shook his head. "We received no deliveries yesterday."

Almost imperceptibly, one of the man's long, slender eyebrows arched. He cleared his throat and said, "Perhaps we've started off on the wrong foot, Mister...?"

"Pembroke," said Pembroke.

"Pembroke," the man repeated. "My name is Selwyn, Mr. Pembroke. I work for a conglomerate of well-to-do academic types who reside throughout the world and who trust me to see to their personal, ah...affairs. This book, Mr. Pembroke, was in transit from one of my clients to another. Typically, I would oversee the transfer personally, of course, but that was not how this matter was handled. Unfortunately." He added that last part with unmasked disdain, as if somehow Pembroke was responsible for the book getting lost in the mail. "It would be most unfortunate for all parties involved, Mr. Pembroke, if I am unable to locate and reclaim that book." Again, that slender eyebrow ticked toward Selwyn's hairline as he repeated, *"All* parties."

At that moment, Tom came out from the backroom carrying the bookshelf. He paused as he saw Pembroke engaged with the man, a sudden look of surprise on Tom's face. But then Tom smiled his college-boy smile and bellowed, "Hullo! Anything I can help you with, sir?"

Selwyn's eyes never left Pembroke's. After a beat, Selwyn said, "No thank you, son. I was just leaving." Then, to Pembroke, he said,

"If you happen to come across this book, here is my card. I would appreciate a speedy notification. It would be best...for everyone...if this matter was put to rest sooner than later."

Selwyn set a small white business card on the counter, then placed his fedora back on his head and moseyed out into the daylight. Pembroke looked down. The only text on the card was the name SELWYN and an 800 number printed below that.

* * *

That evening, Pembroke could not get to sleep, his panic was so great. It was a mistake leaving the book overnight in the shop; he kept imagining that tall, gaunt stranger breaking in and stealing it. Around two in the morning, when his stress was causing his hands to shake, Pembroke dressed and slipped out onto the darkened street. At a quick clip, he covered the five blocks to the bookstore without incident, though he kept glancing over his shoulder, fearful that someone might emerge from the shadows and pursue him.

When he arrived at the bookstore, he went immediately behind the desk and reached for the book...but it was no longer there. Terror seized him, and he hurriedly loosened his collar so that he could breathe. Dabbing his forehead with his handkerchief, he peered into all the little shelves and nooks beneath the desk, wondering if he had misplaced the book himself, his panic rising when he still couldn't locate it. Yet the shop's door had been firmly locked and none of the windows were broken. That strange man would have had to use...other means...to have come in here and escaped with the book.

"I'll call the police, report a break-in," he said, pacing back and forth behind the counter, swiping that folded bit of handkerchief fitfully and repeatedly across his brow. He was unaware that he was speaking aloud. "Yes, yes—a break-in. An intrusion. And I can describe that strange fellow from earlier to one of their sketch artists." But even in his desperation, he knew he couldn't make such a call. The door hadn't been jimmied, the windows hadn't been broken. And nothing else was missing from the store except the stuff Pembroke had kept underneath the counter.

And that was when it occurred to him that *everything* from beneath the counter was missing—the printed inventory list, the books on reserve for particular clients, the shop's ledger. He took a moment to consider this. Unnerved by the strange man's presence that afternoon, Pembroke had left the shop early, leaving Tom behind to close up.

Expelling a gust of sour breath, Pembroke hunkered down and peered into the shelves beneath the counter more closely. When he saw something small and dark—a spot of black within the shadow of a cubbyhole—he reached for it, plucked it out. It was one of Tom DeLilly's silly rubber spiders.

A second bout of panic took hold of him—what if *Tom* had taken the book?—but then his gaze fell upon the rolling cart, and on it was the ledger, the printout, the patrons' reserved books, and the Book of No Name.

Relief washed through him. He rushed to the cart and yanked the book free, knocking several others to the floor. Carrying it against his chest in an embrace, he went to the small reading table at the back of the shop, turned on the museum light over the desk, and opened the book.

He spent the next few hours occupied with the book—it couldn't rightly be called "reading," for there were no words, but for all intents and purposes, that was exactly what Pembroke was doing. Because there *were* words on those pages, weren't there? There were stories, at least. Even without seeing the words, he could tell they were there.

Then he noticed two very strange things, back to back, as if one had been the product of the other. The first thing he noticed was that the tops of his fingers, the palms of his hands, and the underside of his wrists had gone smudgy and gray. Having handled old books for three decades, Pembroke recognized what this was immediately, though he was perplexed to think it had come from the book splayed out in front of him: it was the smudging of ink from the text printed on a book's page. Had he been reading any other book, it would have made perfect sense. With this book, however...well, there was no text to leave smudges.

Yet here they were.

The second thing he noticed was a dark brownish stain along the edge of one of the pages, near the lower right-hand corner. It was small, and may have been unnoticed by anyone other than Pembroke, who could not help but scrutinize every page, every nuance of the book. He had gone through every page of this book several times since he'd received it Monday morning, and he knew with certainty that the stain hadn't been there before. To Pembroke, it looked like blood.

* * *

The following day—Wednesday—Pembroke struggled to stay awake at the shop, having spent the previous night puzzling over that strange bloodlike stain on the book's page while also trying to clean the smudgy newsprint from his fingers, hands, and wrists. The smudges did not want to come off; in fact, they only seemed to grow denser and more pronounced, almost to the point that they resembled bruises. He tried to convince himself that the smudges had come from something else, but there was no denying what he believed in his heart—that they had come from the mysterious book.

When the bell over the door tinkled, Pembroke looked up from the counter—he had been examining that bloodlike stain on the page—worried that it was the man in the fedora again. Selwyn. But it was only Mrs. Teatree, red-faced and robust in a garish floral dress and rhinestone-studded handbag. They exchanged some pleasantries, much as they always did. Pembroke noticed the vast darkened pores in the flesh of Mrs. Teatree's face for the first time, each one glistening with its own tiny pool of perspiration. She had never repulsed him before, but now he was practically overcome by a discomfort at her proximity. It was all he could do to hand over her reserved books without touching her fat, short-fingered hands. As she waddled out of the shop, Pembroke unleashed a shuddery breath.

When the bell tinkled over the door an hour later, Pembroke looked up again. Selwyn came into the store, peering studiously at the floor-to-ceiling bookshelves much as he had done the day before, as if this was the first time he'd entered the store. When he turned and faced Pembroke, he removed his ash-colored fedora and delivered that sinister shark's smile.

"Well," Selwyn said, approaching the counter.

Pembroke had been in the process of wiping his hands with a damp rag. At Selwyn's approach, Pembroke tucked the rag under the counter, covering the Book of No Name which, thankfully, had been down there when Selwyn entered the store.

"Good afternoon," Pembroke said. His voice sounded jittery. "Mr. Selwyn, wasn't it?"

"Just Selwyn," said the man. He held his fedora in leather-gloved hands, running his long fingers around the brim. "I was hoping we might be able to approach yesterday's subject from a different angle."

"Oh?" said Pembroke. When Selwyn turned his gaze toward the smudgy marks on Pembroke's hands and wrists, Pembroke instinctively stuffed his hands in the pockets of his corduroys.

"You are a man who can get any book, no matter how rare," said Selwyn. "Is this correct?"

"For the most part," Pembroke said.

Selwyn's sharp smile flashed then vanished just as quickly. "I am trying to locate a book that has gone missing from one of my clients. It went missing en route to another client, and both are very upset. They are also very wealthy. I assure you they would pay any price if one were to locate the book and, say, sell it to them."

"I'd need an author's name and book title. Publisher's information, too, presuming they're looking for a particular edition. But of course," Pembroke added quickly, "I can't promise anything. Some books, I'm afraid to say, choose to remain elusive."

"That would be unfortunate, in this case," said Selwyn. And then Selwyn's eyes narrowed. He turned his head slightly to the left and, like a bloodhound on a scent, proceeded to sniff the air.

He smells the blood, Pembroke thought. *The blood on the page!* It was impossible, of course...but for some reason, Pembroke couldn't shake the certainty of it.

"Mr. Pembroke," said Selwyn, his voice lowering as he leaned closer to Pembroke over the counter. Pembroke could smell the man's cool, crisp aftershave...and was suddenly certain that the perfume was there to mask some headier, earthier smell. "We are playing a game with each other, yes? Allow me to assure you that there are other methods by which I could...obtain...what it is I am looking for. Those ways are much more difficult than a man's willingness to comply. What I mean to say, *Arthur*, is that it *is* possible for me to take the book from you by force. However, that would require certain...shall we say, 'policies'?...be violated. And my clients tend to frown on such tactics. Therefore I will leave you with this."

From within his overcoat, Selwyn procured a folded stack of paper money. He tugged several bills from the stack and placed them down flat on the counter. Ten hundred-dollar bills.

"Consider this as incentive," said Selwyn. "You will be able to name your actual price once the book is procured and turned over." Selwyn's thin lips pulled back from his teeth, and Pembroke could see without question that each tooth had elongated into a sharpened fang. There was something patchy and reptilian about the fleshy pockets beneath Selwyn's eyes, too. As if the skin there had turned to snake scales. "Because," finished Selwyn, "we are playing a game, yes?"

"I'm afraid I don't understand..."

"You've already been tainted," Selwyn said, his gaze shifting down at Pembroke's hands, which were still stuffed into the pockets of his pants. "It still may not be too late for you."

Pembroke said nothing as Selwyn replaced the fedora atop his head and, pivoting sharply on his heels, began whistling as he headed out of the door and onto the sidewalk.

* * *

He planned to take the book home that evening, but instead Pembroke wound up sleeping in the store, snoring loudly in one of the uncomfortable wooden chairs at the table near the back of the bookstore, the side of his face pressed against one of the open pages of the book.

* * *

"Mr. Pembroke?"

It was Tom DeLilly, shaking him awake.

Pembroke snapped up in his seat, his stiff back jolting with pain, his eyes bleary and still muzzy with sleep. When he glanced down at the desktop, he was mortified to see that the mysterious book was right there, its blank pages splayed open for Tom to see. He quickly slammed the book shut.

"Did you sleep here last night?"

"I guess so, Tom." He attempted to climb out of the chair but his back screamed in protest so he remained seated.

"I brought you a coffee," Tom said, setting the cardboard cup down beside the book. Steam wafted from the tiny opening in the lid. "Looks like you could use it, if you don't mind me saying." Then Tom's eyes narrowed. He leaned closer to examine the side of Pembroke's face.

"What?" Pembroke barked, suddenly repulsed by Tom's proximity. It was an invasion of his personal space. "What is it?"

"You've got a...I guess a bruise on the side of your face, Mr. Pembroke." Tom straightened up. He looked concerned. "Did you get in a fight?"

Pembroke laughed forcibly. "A *fight*?"

"Or maybe fall down from one of the ladders again?" Tom suggested.

"Nonsense." He touched the side of his face but felt nothing.

"Oh," Tom said. It came on the intake of air, as if Tom were suddenly prodded by something cold and pointy at the base of his spine. "Your hands."

Pembroke looked at his hands.

They were no longer covered in the smudgy bruises—or, more accurately, the smudges had coalesced to form a dense inscription of strange glyphs that appeared tattooed across the palms of his hands and circling around his wrists. They weren't so much words as symbols, but Pembroke knew, even through his horror, that words were exactly what they were. Words from some alien world, perhaps, or some alien time.

He thought of Selwyn's fangs and the snakelike skin beneath his eyes.

"Excuse me," Pembroke said, wincing as he rose from the chair. Hefting the book under one arm, he hustled through the small restroom door, which he promptly closed and latched behind him. Setting the book on the edge of the sink, Pembroke examined his reflection in the mirror. The lighting in here was so poor that, at first, he didn't notice the smudgy darkening of his skin along the left side of his face. But when he *did* see it, it was like strong, cold fingers were slowly closing around his throat.

You've already been tainted, Selwyn had said. *It still may not be too late for you.*

He looked down at the book. Momentarily, its organic green-yellow cover seemed to swell then deflate, as if respiring. Pembroke convinced himself it was just an illusion of the poor lighting in the bathroom. And as much as he didn't want to touch it again, his hands went to it and he gathered it up—lovingly—from the sink.

When he came out of the bathroom, Tom was still standing there, a mixture of confusion and concern on his face. Pembroke rushed past him with a curt nod, clutching the book to his chest. Tom followed him to the front counter, where Pembroke hurriedly stashed the book underneath in one of the shelves. A bright red rubber spider bounded out of the cubbyhole and cartwheeled across the linoleum floor.

"What did you do to your hands, Mr. Pembroke?"

"It's no concern of yours, Tom."

Tom frowned. He was holding his own cup of coffee, which he set down on the counter now. "What's with that book, anyway?" he said.

Pembroke reeled on him, teeth clenched as he said, "Do not *speak* of it!"

Tom shook his head and took a step backward. But he didn't let it go. "What *is* it? There's nothing on the pages...but then, the longer I look at it, I begin to see..."

"Enough," said Pembroke. "We will not talk about the book."

"And then the other night, when I was straightening up, I went to put the book on the rolling cart when it cut me." Tom held up his right index finger, which was capped in an adhesive bandage.

"A paper cut," Pembroke marveled, recalling that odd splotch of blood on the book's page.

"Yes, of course," said Tom, "only that's not what I thought at the time. Because when it happened, Mr. Pembroke—and this is going to sound ridiculous, I know it—but when it happened, my first thought was that the book had *bit* me. I dropped it on the floor like it was some wild animal. I've gotten my share of paper cuts working here, Mr. Pembroke, as you know, but this one...this one *bled.*"

"Tom," said Pembroke, trying to keep himself calm but also speaking as firmly as he could at the moment, "I think you should go home early today."

"I want to know what—"

"Please go, Tom. I'll see you next Tuesday."

Tom wanted to protest further—Pembroke could tell just by looking at the young man—but in the end, Tom snagged his jacket from the rolling cart and, whipping it over one shoulder, he hurried out onto the sidewalk. The bell over the door chimed. Outside, Tom paused momentarily on the other side of the front window, peering in at Pembroke, before continuing down the block.

After he was sure Tom wouldn't return, Pembroke picked up the telephone. Selwyn's business card was taped to the counter beside the phone, and Pembroke was halfway through dialing the 800 number when he froze, suddenly able to decipher the glyphs spiraling around his wrist. They were images quite similar to Egyptian hieroglyphics, but for some reason, Pembroke could now read them.

—for whether it resides in the well or in the dome, in the blackness of the void or the sprockets of the earth, in the soul of mankind or the blackened heart of the devil—

Very calmly, Pembroke hung up the phone.

* * *

When the man who called himself Selwyn arrived at the end of the week, Pembroke was propped in his wooden chair behind the front counter, his face waxen, his pallor the color of curdled cream. In just the past week he had lost about thirteen pounds and had pretty much stopped eating. His hands shook as Selwyn approached the counter, Pembroke's eyes rolling up to meet Selwyn's ratlike gaze beneath the wide brim of his ash-colored fedora.

Pembroke had the book out on the counter in front of him. He made no attempt to hide it as Selwyn approached. As it was, his arms were bandaged and in terrible pain; he didn't think he'd even be able to lift the book now if he wanted to. The only part of his body he hadn't been able to bring himself to cut was the left side of his face, where the smudgy bruise had solidified into a series of tiny symbols, running from his temple, down his cheek, and curving around the left side of his chin.

"You are in some shape, friend," said Selwyn, peering down at Pembroke's shaking hands and bandaged wrists and forearms. Blood had seeped through the bandages and stained the gauze a ruddy copper color. There was also dried blood on the counter and fresher puddles of it along the floor. The ream of paper that was the store's inventory was soggy and bloated with blood. Atop the inventory was a straight razor. Beside the straight razor was a bright orange rubber spider.

"I tried...tried getting the words off," managed Pembroke. Even speaking took much out of him. "They cloud my head. I can't stop reading them. And when I close my eyes, they speak directly to me."

"That's because you're a fool," said Selwyn. "Are you ready to hand the book over yet?"

"Y-yes," Pembroke stuttered. He attempted to slide the book across the bloodied counter to Selwyn, but Selwyn held up one hand and shook his head. Pembroke dropped his bloodied and ruined hands in his lap.

Selwyn peeled off one of his leather gloves, liberating a hand that was as pale as a cadaver's. His fingers, hideously long, were like the pale, segmented legs of arctic crabs. Selwyn ran his palm along the top of the book. His eyes momentarily unfocused and he actually released a faint, almost orgasmic sigh. Then his face went firm again. He gathered the book off the counter and tucked it under one arm.

"My clients will be most appreciative, Mr. Pembroke."

But Pembroke hardly heard him; he was busy staring at the small adhesive bandage at the tip of Selwyn's index finger. Selwyn followed his gaze then grinned at him like a feral dog.

"Oh, this?" said Selwyn. "Occupational hazard, I'm afraid." Then he nodded at Pembroke and headed for the door. He paused, however, halfway across the floor and turned back around to face Pembroke. "I almost forgot. Your commission. Have you decided on a price?"

"Please," Pembroke said. "Just help me. Get the words out of my head."

"I'm afraid that is beyond my ability. With any luck, you might recover. After all, it's only been a week, correct? It's not as if the exposure was unduly prolonged. Though do please remember, Mr. Pembroke—you brought this upon yourself. This was a mistake; it had nothing to do with you. You should have left well enough alone." With that, Selwyn nodded sharply, then left the store.

"Please," Pembroke shouted after him, still able to smell the man's cologne in the air like a calling card. "Please! Please!"

But there would be no salvation from that monster.

* * *

Pembroke's physical injuries cleared up over time. The scars left behind were terrible, ugly things, but they also served as a reminder that he had been foolish and careless and had committed himself to something that was beyond his comprehension. And after a bit more time, the voices in his head, much like the glyphs on his skin, began to fade. Soon, the only mantra he heard in his head were Selwyn's parting words: *This was a mistake; it had nothing to do with you. You should have left well enough alone.*

When Tuesdays and Thursdays passed without Tom showing up to work, Pembroke felt awful. He felt guilty the way he had left things with Tom, but he wouldn't let that guilt prevent him from making amends. Late one Thursday evening, he telephoned Tom's house. The phone rang several times before Tom answered.

"Listen, Tom, it's Arthur. I feel just terrible. I understand if you've got no interest in coming back to work here, but at least stop by and allow me to apologize and explain what happened."

"Geez, Mr. Pembroke, I really appreciate it," Tom said. "You know, I got another job, but I'd certainly like to stop by and see you in person. I don't like how we left things, either."

It delighted Pembroke that Tom was amenable to his apology, and the following Tuesday, prior to Tom's arrival, Pembroke bought a couple of coffees at the corner bakery and carried them back to the bookstore, a smile on his face.

Yet he froze midway across the street when he saw a man in an ashy-gray overcoat and matching fedora leaning against the front window of the bookstore.

Selwyn, Pembroke thought...but when the man lifted his head, he could see it was Tom's face beneath the brim of the fedora.

"Hello, Mr. Pembroke," Tom said, tipping a single bandaged finger against the brim of his hat.

In a Pet Shop

She was not very pretty and not very young and she did not say much about anything. An umbrella tucked under her arm, rain or shine, and dressed in a heavy wool coat and with a string of white pearls about her neck, she came just like that. There were many animals but she always went directly to the birds. There were many birds in the shop. She would stand for a long time and look carefully in all the cages and at all the birds. They were noisy and they smelled bad, but she did not seem to mind. Often, she would speak quietly to the birds as if she were speaking only to herself. Her lips were thin and were always painted a startling red. Her lips hardly moved when she spoke.

Once a day the birds were fed, and she was always there when they were fed. She never said anything and only backed up against the far wall and watched as John or I fed the birds. Once I asked her if she would like to feed them and she said no. She said this very quietly, and the way she said it made me feel ashamed and somewhat guilty for having even asked the question, for whatever reason. But I supposed it was all right. Anyway, she was not very pretty.

She came every day for two weeks, always in the black wool coat and always with the pearls, and she never spoke to anyone except the birds. One day I asked if she wanted to purchase one. They weren't very expensive. But she said she did not. I showed her one of our new cages, assuming she might like to see it and that she might then decide to purchase one of the little inexpensive birds, but she did not seem impressed by the cage and said nothing about purchasing a bird. On this day she left earlier than usual—just after John came out from the stockroom to feed the birds—as if my conversation had disturbed her.

"She is a crazy little thing," John said one day after the woman had gone. "What do you think she does it for?"

I said I didn't know.

"Why doesn't she hardly ever speak?"

I said I didn't know.

"How long do you think she'll keep this up?"

Again, I said I didn't know.

John said, "I'll bet she is senile." He said, "I'll bet she has dementia." He said, "I'll bet it's the early stages of Alzheimer's," only he pronounced it "old-timer's." Then he shook his head and pushed his glasses way up on his thin nose and kept his eyes on the science-fiction paperback he was reading. He said, "I'll bet she's a grade-A whacko."

Twice it rained when she came, but she did not use her umbrella: it remained tucked under her arm as it did on the days when it was clear and sunny. Her black wool coat was wet and it dripped rainwater onto the linoleum. She stood for a long time looking at the birds and I stood behind the counter for a long time looking at her. I watched her watch the birds through the thin metal piping of the birdcages. I watched her take out a small compact from her coat one afternoon, just before feeding time, and she opened it and held the mirrored section up in front of one of the cages, attempting to incite the birds. John saw this and told her not to be a nuisance. She did not look at John and only slid the compact back inside her coat. Then she stood against the far wall and waited for the birds to be fed.

"I have a feeling she is recently widowed," John suggested during lunch one afternoon. "Perhaps her husband had kept birds, and now that he is dead she comes here to remind herself of her husband and of her husband's birds."

Even if that were true, and her husband had died, I said, wouldn't his birds still be alive?

"How the hell should I know?" John said. He seemed slightly

incensed by my comment. "Maybe it was a house fire. Maybe they all burned up together." He laughed and said, "Rotisserie squaw."

Squab, not squaw, I told him. A squaw, I informed, was a term for an American Indian woman.

"Oh, sure," said John, snickering. As if I was trying to pull one over on him.

She came and was not very pretty and stood in front of the wall of birdcages. I wondered what she would do if she came in one day and all the birds were gone. What if John and I moved all the birds to the stockroom? What if we took all the cages away and there was nothing left for her to look at? Would she stop coming or would she continue to stare at the empty wall? Was it the birdcages or the space in the shop the birdcages occupied? Now I was confused; or was I making it more difficult than it really was? I did not know. Maybe she would sniff them out and discover their new location in the stockroom. Like a hound. Who knew? I thought about this and I did not know, and then she came into the shop and I thought about this some more. I said nothing to her, and she only stuck a knobby old finger between the slats in the birdcage. I said nothing. John was in the stockroom on his lunch break and did not see her stick her finger between the slats of the birdcage. Had he seen, he would have told her not to be a nuisance. To John, everyone was a nuisance.

I wondered if this was some sort of therapy. That maybe, as a child, she had been attacked by a bird of some sort, or perhaps even a flock of birds, and had sustained an irrational fear of them well into adulthood. Perhaps, I surmised, this was some sort of coping exercise for ornithophobes, prescribed to her by her therapist. Perhaps she was attempting to overcome this childhood phobia by sticking knobby white fingers through the slats of birdcages. It made me think of that old Hitchcock movie starring Rod Taylor and Tippi Hedren, the one where the birds start attacking people with no discernable rationale. What was the name of that film, anyway? I imagined flocks and flocks of birds blanketing the parking lot outside the shop, congealed in molting white clusters on the slanted roof of the In-N-Out Burger across the street, populating the roadway outside, studded in fowl straight up to the highway—so dense with birds, choked with birds, you could not see the pavement at all. Maybe this was the woman's therapy. When I was five I woke up to find a spider in my left ear. To this day, I maintain a severe apprehension toward spiders. The littler they are, the worse—because they can get into your ears, burrow in there (or do whatever it is that spiders do)—and how the hell are you even supposed to get them out? Thinking of this, I doubt there is enough therapy in the world...

The Birds, the film was called. Duh.

I watched her watch the birds and then it was time to feed them. I was reminded to feed them, in fact, by the way the woman shifted noiselessly across the floor and stopped against the far wall. She knew the birdseed was coming before I even remembered it. So I gathered the sack of seed and opened all the cages and poured the seed into the little white cups that hung suspended from the wire bars of the cages. She watched, and I could feel her little black eyes constantly on my back, boring into my back like spiders into my ears. It was as if she was looking directly through me to watch the birds eat. I could not understand her fascination. And not understanding it made it all the more fascinating.

I noticed one of the little brown finches dead at the bottom of the cage. This happens from time to time—there was nothing unusual about it—but then I thought of the woman, staring through me at the tittering birds, and wondered if she was slowly emitting some poisonous pheromone that was killing all the birds. Maybe, it occurred to me almost immediately, she was slowly killing me, too—John and me—and that this dead finch at the bottom of the cage served as the coalminers' canary. Was she here to slowly poison the shop's air? Was she slowly and silently murdering both John and me with each exhalation of breath?

Or maybe it was just the opposite: maybe she was here to *resurrect* the dead bird. Rise, finch, and walk. Christ incarnate. Maybe there was some greater, omnipotent divinity at work here. Perhaps the finch, in the scheme of mankind and the universe itself, played some vague but invaluable role, and this strange old woman was here to revive the dead finch so the prophecy—or whatever—could be fulfilled. If this was the case, I did not want to impede divinity, so I finished feeding the birds and paused with the sack of seed in my hands. I clutched it. I stood and did not move until I finally *did* move, stepping away from the cage to allow the woman access to the dead finch. Surely she had seen it was dead; she had been staring at them all morning. But she did not move and I did not move, either. We both stood like that for a long time. At one point I considered prodding her, asking if she had noticed the all-important finch was lying on its back with its stiff little legs in the air, but I did not say this. She would not move, so maybe I had been wrong about it all. I considered asking her why she was here and why she always came to look at the birds and why she liked to watch them eat. I was very close to asking this. I was very close to solving the whole mystery.

But then I didn't.

I said nothing.

I replaced the sack of birdseed back behind the counter and reclaimed my position on the stool in front of the cash register. Behind me, John came out of the stockroom. He was whistling and in a good mood. He was always in a good mood on Fridays. The woman stood for some time and watched the birds eat. It occurred to me that she had become a permanent fixture, and that it was no longer peculiar to have her stand there and watch the birds eat. I saw John eye her up, then shoot a conspiratorial glance in my direction.

"Hello," John said to her, not pausing in his stride.

The woman did not mutter a word.

"All right," said John.

I told him about the dead finch.

John backtracked, unfettered, and peered at the floor of the cage and at the dead bird. "Oh yeah," he said. "Look at that." Then he looked up at the woman. He did not say anything but I wondered if he was thinking the same thing I had been just moments before—that the woman had either murdered the bird with noxious bodily fumes or that she was perhaps here to bring the little creature back to life. However, if the importance of either concept registered with him, he was quick to dismiss them without further consideration. He said, quite unceremoniously, "Go flush it down the toilet."

The next day the woman returned, and wordlessly watched the birds eat. I had spent the early part of the morning, before John arrived, relocating some of the birdcages to the stockroom, just to see what the woman would do when she arrived and found them missing. Halfway through, however, I began to fear I was perhaps disturbing some otherworldly balance, and I moved all the cages back to where they belonged. I did not want to be responsible for the destruction of mankind and the world as we know it. You can't be too careful. Anyway, some of the cages were heavy and had broken casters, so I would not have been able to transport them on my own.

I watched the woman watch the birds. Again, I imagined the parking lot infused with birds, suffocated by birds, blanketed in a mass of feathers, all gray and filthy from pollution, and tiny clawed feet clicking on the macadam. I saw feathers floating lazily in the air, twisting and spiraling and manipulated by the wind. I envisioned them taking flight all at once, blotting out the sun and dropping all of Sacramento into premature nightfall. I saw them filing blindly into the turbines of passing airliners until the engines coughed and seized, and the planes plummeted, missile-like, to the ground. There would be mass confusion, car wrecks, explosions, looting, rioting, people flinging themselves from their office buildings. Rivers would clog with down; water would be rendered undrinkable. Massive piles of molted feathers, brittle and dried from the sun, would spontaneously combust in the heat, and the roads would be too congested with birds for the fire trucks to get through. The air itself, clogged with feathers, would make breathing an impossibility. It would be Armageddon. Suddenly, I did not like birds very much. And I could only sit perched on my stool and watch the old woman watching the birds. I could feel sweat cascading down from my armpits and along my ribs; I could feel hard, angry knobs of gooseflesh break out along my bare arms. And still I just sat there and watched her. The end of the world, and all I could do was sit and watch.

She was not very pretty and not very young and she was always dressed the same way. What was with that umbrella, anyway? I should have asked. I should have asked about the umbrella, I knew. But more importantly, I should have asked about the birds, all about the birds. It was such a bizarre preoccupation and I should have asked about it.

But after that day, the old woman never came back, and both John and I eventually forgot all about her.

COUPLES SEEKING COUPLES

At the restaurant, Jack Pagewater suddenly felt the urge to vomit. Lois was too busy fawning over the Capshaws to notice the sudden change of expression on his face, and the Capshaws themselves—well, their eyes hadn't lifted from their drinks all evening.

"Excuse me." He stood and accidentally bumped Lois's chair. She waved a hand at him without interest. He hurried down the hallway to the restroom where he leaned his head against the tiled wall, staring into the mouth of the toilet, breathing in great, wheezing gasps.

Behind him, two young men entered and straddled a pair of urinals. He could hear them talking through the stall.

"You run the marathon?"

"Oh, yeah."

"Marines?"

"Twisted some tendons in my left calf. You know how the—"

"Isn't it like the—"

"Twisted. And I had to stop at mid-mark."

"What do they do for that?"

"Massage."

"You can wear a brace?"

"Couple of weeks."

Five minutes later, Jack was back at the table. He hadn't thrown up, but his stomach had settled somewhat.

"Jack," said Mark Capshaw, "we were afraid you'd left us." Mark was forty and completely gray. His hands were slender and well-manicured. He wore French cuff shirts and 1940s swing-era tailored suit jackets with butterfly lapels. White teeth, shiny and even.

Lois patted Jack's hand. "Too much to drink, dear?"

"No," Jack said.

"We've got another round yet," Mark explained.

"*Several* rounds," Mark's wife, Miranda, insisted. "Jack, don't go all rubbery on us now, darling." She patted his other hand.

"He's been running lately," explained Jack's wife, as if apologizing for her husband's abrupt departure from the table. "Mornings, evenings…trying to reach—"

"Miss the youthful body, do you, Jackie?" Mark said. He thumped his own broad chest with a massive fist. "Miss your *jeunesse?*"

"Where do you find the time, dear?" Miranda asked. She gripped Jack's hand firmly, as if to offer condolence. She was an attractive woman in her late forties who did her best to present herself at half that age. Her fingers were cluttered with a wedge of sparkling rings—all real—and the perfume she wore was nearly cloying.

"Really, I haven't even been running all that much lately," he admitted.

"*Ne pas etre si modeste,*" Mark said.

The waiter returned, carrying a bottle of *vin rouge* and four snifters of brandy. Anxious to get at the drinks, Mark plucked the snifters from the waiter's tray without haste and distributed them around the table.

"Wine?" the waiter asked them. "Ladies?"

"None for me," Lois said. "My head is already spinning."

"Lois!" Mark Capshaw said. He was drunk enough to be too loud now. "Lois, please. It's on me tonight. Miranda and me."

"Well," she stammered. Jack watched her—watched her eyes—but she never thought to face him. To the waiter, she said, "Maybe just one glass."

"Two," added Miranda.

"And cigars," Mark said. He looked at Jack. "What's your preference?"

"Jack doesn't smoke cigars," Lois answered, wrinkling her nose. "Filthy, filthy things. That's a dirty habit, Mark Capshaw. Miranda—what's the matter with you, letting that fit man smoke such horrid things?"

"I am my own man," Mark the fit man said. Jack thought his eyes were beginning to look red and sloppy. "Jack, son, what flavor? Come on, now—a man shouldn't smoke alone."

"I don't know flavors."

"Don't do it, Jack," Lois harped...although she sounded like she really wanted him to.

"Robustos!" cried Mark to the waiter. "Two thick Robustos, son!"

Lois frowned playfully. The waiter nodded and slipped away.

"Did you tell Jack about your hunting trip, sweetheart?" Miranda prodded her husband.

"Yes," Lois said, "do tell it, Mark."

Mark finished his brandy and rubbed his thumb along the lip of the glass. "I own a Winchester Model 70 Custom African Express with walnut stock, ebony pistol grip, and adjustable front and rear sights. What's your make, Jack-o?"

"I don't own a gun."

"You don't *hunt?*"

"I have twice before..."

"Well, you should *take* him, Mark," said Mark's wife. "Jack would love it. You would love it, Jack."

"Back-ended a two-hundred-pound buck last week. I was perched in a tree, maybe twenty yards from the ground, and I'd been sitting there for—oh, I'd say forty-five minutes. Quiet. I felt like an Indian."

The women laughed.

"Waiting is the hardest part," Mark explained. "It takes a lot of patience and skill to wait in silence, and to keep alert. And then this beautiful animal strides out onto the fairway—magnificent, with a rack the size of...well, the size of this table, no doubt."

"No doubt," Miranda agreed.

"A spectacular head," Mark said. "You wait for the precise moment. Too soon and you might scare it off; too late and you're out of the picture. They move like lightning and will be gone just as quick. Snapshot, Jack. Like a camera flashbulb. You watch it, you try to become part of it. You breathe when it breathes. You blink when it blinks. Swear to God, if you had a tail, you'd both be flitting them in synchronization. Do you know what it's like to bring down such a beast, Jack? To pull the trigger and feel two tons of power ricochet in your arms, and see such a beast go down?"

"I've only been duck hunting."

"Oh, now!" Mark bellowed. *"Ducks?* What's a duck? That's *insignificant.* I mean, when that great buck went down, I could *feel* it, as if it were a part of me. Do you know what I'm saying? So strong. You have to kill it to appreciate such a thing, Jackie. I mean that, son. Superb."

"All right," Jack said.

"The first thing you do," Mark continued, "is heft the antlers. You just *feel* them, delicately but with force, too, like the way you'd feel a breast, and you can surmise the entire weight of the creature just by the thickness of its headgear. Experienced hunters can, anyway. Then you wait for it to stop breathing—you can see its chest heave. Once, twice—then like a blowup raft that's gradually losing air. Again, experienced hunters know how to snap the neck if you don't want to wait it out. But sometimes waiting it out is part of the reward. You've *ended this thing,* Jack. You've conquered. You've *earned* it."

"Jack caught very nice ducks," Lois said.

"Shot ducks," Jack corrected quietly.

"Hmmmm?"

"You don't catch them," he said, "you shoot them."

"Break a duck's neck in a similar fashion," Mark said. "You shoot and wing it, wait for it to fall, then find it in the brush. Grab its head and give the bugger a twirl—"

"Mark Capshaw!" Miranda cried playfully, swiping at her husband's shoulder. "At the *table?* Is it really necessary?"

Smiling, Mark did not take his eyes off Jack. "Forget duck, Jackie. A nice buck is the way to go."

"I've never even eaten venison," Jack said.

"Eat it? No—you *mount* it. The head, anyway. I mean, you can have it stripped, gutted, and cleaned if you want, but I never eat it."

"No?"

"I don't enjoy it."

"Red meat doesn't agree with Mark," Miranda said.

"You see, it's a sense of pride, Jack. Every man should kill a buck once in his lifetime. You're almost not a man unless you mount that head, Jack. You need to heft those antlers and let that creature know why man is the superior being. Do you understand what I'm saying?"

"Yes," Jack said.

"It's important that you do."

"I understand," Jack said.

"Take him hunting sometime," Miranda insisted.

"*Heft* them," Mark said. He mimed grabbing a rack of antlers, but it looked more like he was gripping an invisible steering wheel. Then, grinning, he finished off his wife's brandy. "Just feeling it— it's like a surge of power."

"Power-power-power," Lois muttered playfully.

"What happens if the buck gets away?" Jack asked.

"What do you mean?"

"If you shoot and miss. Or if you just injure it and don't kill it."

Mark laughed. "You can't *miss*, Jack. I mean, maybe with *ducks* you can miss, but who bothers with ducks?"

"What's a duck?" Lois said, giggling.

When the cigars came, Mark's face lit up like a child at Christmas and proffered one to Jack. "No, no," Mark insisted as Jack stared at the smoke. "You've got to clip the end."

"Bite it off like they do in the movies, Jack," Miranda said, winking at him.

"Don't bite it," Mark said. He produced a silver cutter from the inside pocket of his jacket and clipped the tip of his cigar. "Snip. See that? Can't bite it. How can you be such a damn fool, Miranda?"

"Oh, Mark…"

"Really, she's such a damn fool sometimes."

Lois and Miranda giggled.

When Jack and Lois first met the Capshaws two months ago, the Pagewaters were in awe of the couple. They were clever and mysterious and utterly *refreshing*. They used words like "hence" and "moreover" and "therefore," and occasionally used the word "summer" as a verb. Now, two months later, Jack had fallen out of awe. Lois continued to be intrigued by the couple (with each passing day, Jack thought, Lois loved them more and more), but Jack now only acknowledged the Capshaws with the mild curiosity of a weary movie-goer. Sixty-two days since their introduction and the Capshaws were no more interesting that a pair of glossy insects scuttling across a piece of dirty linen.

Mark clipped Jack's cigar, lit it while he puffed, then handed it across the table to Jack.

"Puff," Mark said. "Don't inhale. You don't inhale cigars."

Jack puffed. The cigar tasted vaguely like cinnamon but mostly like wet leaves and tar.

"Give it here, then," Lois said, grabbing it from Jack's mouth and popping it in her own. She sucked the life from it, then coughed. "Really," she sputtered, "you men are so primitive!" She thrust the stogie back at her husband.

Just when the check came, Jack began to feel nauseous again. He rose, plodded off to the bathroom, and hung himself over the toilet again. The cigar hadn't agreed with him. Also, he was light-headed and dizzy from all the drinking they had been doing.

Mark entered the bathroom, his voice booming some operatic song. He adjusted his silk tie in the spotted bathroom mirror.

"Jack," he said, "do you have any idea how much Donn Mason Mutual cleared for me last year?"

Jack shook his head.

"Up thirty-five percent. That's more than ten percent better than the New York Life return, did you know that? *Thirty-five.* I cleared about fifty grand in eleven months. That's what thirty-five percent will do for you, Jackie. Why do you waste your time floundering with real estate, anyway?"

Mark Capshaw was drunk. With the exception of the house he and Lois lived in, Jack had never touched real estate in his life.

"I'll tell you one thing, though," Mark Capshaw said. "If I could do it all again—pharmaceuticals. That's the way to go, and you better believe it. *Pharmaceutique,* Jack. Generic medicines. Your Tylenol, Advil, Whatever-the-Hell. You botch one tiny micro-atom or whatever you call it, modify the prescription, drop below the high-profile drugs by eighty percent—Christ, Jack, you'd have the whole goddamn market. And that's what it's all about: marketing. Can't you see that? And here you are, puckering around in real estate. It really is quite pitiable."

Mark wet his hands beneath the sink, then ran his fingers through his silver hair. He examined the closeness of his shave in the mirror as Jack became suddenly ill and vomited into the toilet.

"No embarrassment," Mark said. "An old Army buddy of mine threw up the first time he smoked a cigar." He produced a joint from his coat. "Here's the real treasure. You want to smoke before sex, Jack?"

Jack shook his head.

"It'll make you feel better, son."

"No," Jack managed. The letters of the wall graffiti blurred and doubled before his eyes. In his spinning head he heard Mark Capshaw's phantom voice say something about antlers, hefting antlers. "I don't think I could stomach it right now."

"What's the matter, anyhow?"

"I haven't been feeling well lately."

"Have you said anything to Lois?"

"No, but she knows."

"You should speak with her, if it's serious."

"She knows. And I don't know if it's serious."

"You should tell Lois," Mark said. He lit the joint and took one long drag. "She's looking very nice tonight, by the way. She's lost weight?"

"Lois?" Jack said. His head was still spinning. He flushed the bowl so he wouldn't have to look at what he'd just brought up.

"Her thighs have gotten less and less..." Mark paused, searching for the perfect word, *"messy.* She's a lovely woman."

"Thank you."

"How long have you been married?"

"Fifteen years," Jack said. He righted himself against the wall, took three deep breaths, and pushed his way over to the sink beside Mark. The stink of the marijuana made his stomach growl.

He thought of Mark Capshaw, naked in the glow of the fireplace except for his dress socks and his expensive wristwatch, nestling his groin against Lois's buttocks while his knobby red knees pressed into the worn plush of the Pagewaters' living room carpet. Lois laughed and said something while craning her neck back. Her breasts, slightly drooping with middle-age but still suggestively round, dangling from her as she held herself up on all fours. Miranda Capshaw, half-nude against the far wall, watching and clapping and cheering them on. And Mark Capshaw, his face ruddy in the firelight and glistening with perspiration, a thin smile on his lips, saying, *The world is waiting for you, Jackie! The sexual revolution is at hand!*

"She's just so lovely," Mark said, snapping Jack back to the present. Mark's reflection winked at Jack in the bathroom mirror. "We brought the van," the reflection said, "because I know how you and Miranda groove to it. It's right out in the parking lot."

"That was thoughtful."

"Will Lois and I be going to your home?"

"Ask her," Jack said. A sharp pain, needling and white-hot, jabbed at his belly.

"Just the same to me," Mark muttered, and stepped out of the restroom.

Twenty minutes later, Jack stood pale and naked in the back of the Capshaws' van, with Mark's wife sitting cross-legged and shirtless on the floor in front of him. Unlike Jack's wife, Miranda was all nipple and no breast.

She stood, gathered his neck up in her arms, and pushed herself against him. Her body stank of weed and sweat and baby powder. Jack was certain he stank of vomit and cigar smoke.

Miranda kissed him hard on the mouth. Then pulled away.

"Is something wrong?"

"Why?"

"Well, you...your..."

"I'm fine," he said, and kissed her back, much gentler than she had kissed him. His eyes closed, the dense heat of the van pressing against his bare skin, and he imagined himself tucked up in the high branches of a great tree, the walnut stock of a Winchester rifle pressing against his right thigh. Below him in the brush, sticky with fresh blood that still pumped from him, an injured and naked Mark Capshaw tried dragging himself through the blood-sodden thicket. Part of Mark's head had been blown away, revealing a pulpy, spongy arrangement of brain and skull that glistened in the sun. At one point he imagined Mark Capshaw rising to his knees, righting himself with one hand—his expensive wristwatch hand—against the gray and peeling body of a tree, his tanned and muscled back streaked with blood. Then falling dead in the tall grass.

"There we go," Miranda cooed, now smiling and fondling him. "Now we've got it."

Jack opened his eyes, blinked, and smelled the pot-stink of the Capshaws' van.

"I want you to do the behind-me stuff tonight," Miranda said.

"All right."

"Are you cold?"

"No."

"You *feel* cold."

"I'm not."

"Okay, then."

"Okay."

"Start with my nipples. I like when you start with my nipples."

"All right," Jack said, and lowered Mark Capshaw's wife to the floor.

THE GOOD FATHER

"Was it because we were bad?" Tim asked, suddenly looking up from his plate. The boy had been quiet throughout all of dinner, and this sudden question came as sudden as a handclap.

Michael set his fork down on his own plate. They hadn't been talking about her, but Michael did not need his son to be more specific. "Of course not," he said. "Why would you think such a thing?"

"Sean Allington's mom ran away last year, and Sean and his brothers are always getting into trouble," Tim said, and now Gertrude was looking at him with rapt, wide-eyed attention.

"Mom didn't run away," Gertrude chided her older brother. "She's coming back." She was six years old and spoke with a sibilant lisp.

Tim, who had just turned ten last month, regarded his younger sister with a look that conveyed both pity and frustration—an eerily adult look, Michael thought as he watched the boy.

"Let's get something straight," Michael said, sliding his plate to one side and folding his hands on the tabletop. "Your mother didn't leave because of anything either of you did."

"Then why did she go?" Tim asked.

"I don't know, Tim. Because she wanted something different, I guess. Because she wanted to change her life."

"Sean Allington said she fell in love with some guy and wanted to live with him instead."

Michael smiled sourly.

"Was it something *you* did, Daddy?" Gertrude asked.

"Enough is enough," Michael said, getting up from the table. "Finish your dinners."

* * *

Marybeth had been gone over a month and the house still mourned her absence. The floors creaked and groaned even when no feet tread upon them, as if the house were sobbing in its grief. Similarly, the bedroom she had once shared with Michael had grown chamberlike and inhospitable. Memories of their early years of marriage in this house frequently accosted him since her disappearance—the children, then only babies, cradled between them in the big bed, or the way Marybeth would fall asleep on the sofa with a book tented across her chest on Sunday afternoons— but he knew he had to be strong for the children. He had cried only once, after the weight of it all had come down on him and he understood what her absence now meant for him and the children. The tears had come in the sanctuary of the cold and inhospitable bedroom, the bed suddenly too big, the room itself like some great damning proclamation in all its matrimonial furnishings. For his children's sake, Michael did his best to keep his emotions well-guarded. Of course, he would never let the children see him cry over it.

Gertrude had cried. It had been a constant—every night since Marybeth had gone—for the first week. Normally it was around the time she had to go to bed—ruminations were violent and unforgiving things at night, Michael knew—but just last week he had to pick her up from school when she had broken down into a flood of tears. In an effort to alleviate the girl's grief, he had swung by the McDonald's on Tamarack Street, and he was grateful that the box of chicken nuggets and the ice cream sundae worked their magic. Back home, he had wanted to talk to the girl about her feelings—ironically, something Marybeth had always been better at than he—but Gertrude had seemed contented enough by the time they had reached the house that he was disinclined to bring up the issue with her.

Tim did not cry over his mother's departure. Michael would have preferred crying to the strange blank-eyed fugues that seemed to overcome the boy from time to time, as if he were being channeled by some spiritual undercurrent Michael himself could not tap into. The boy asked very few questions of him, seeming satisfied with the half-truths and rumors dispatched to him from his friends at Robert F. Kennedy Elementary. Occasionally Tim would ask a question, though they always struck Michael as scheming and byzantine in nature. Did Mom have a lot of money in her pocketbook? What was her middle name? How many pairs of shoes did she own? Michael wondered about the basis for such questions, though he never asked the boy. He figured it was better the boy was asking *something*, that he was *talking*, regardless of how peculiar Michael may have found these questions.

Michael Clement loved his children. Marybeth had loved her children, too. Michael knew this. Even when he questioned why she had done what she'd done, he knew that she loved her children. Which made the whole thing all the more perplexing.

"It's been a month," Duane Sullivan said later that evening. They were both on the back porch, working through a six-pack of Natty Boh. Duane was the local sheriff's deputy and one of Michael's closest friends. They had gone to grade school together. "I'm worried about you and the kids."

"We'll be okay," Michael assured him.

"Ran into Keith Dowry at the Crab Crawl two nights ago," Duane said, staring out across the Clements' rear field toward the distant trees. Stars blazed in the black heavens, speckled about a moon that looked like someone's white face peeking through a partially-opened door. "He said you keep calling his place and hanging up."

Michael said nothing. His fingers worked with agitation at the beer can's pull-tab.

"You can't keep doing that," Duane finished.

"Are you telling me as a cop?"

"I'm telling you as your friend," Duane said. "But, yeah, as a cop too, if necessary."

"I could kill the son of a bitch."

"What's done is done," Duane said. "Would that really fix anything now? Does that even matter anymore?"

"It matters to me," Michael said.

"Does it?" Duane asked, turned half his face to him. Moonlight silvered his jowls. "Does it really?"

Michael didn't know.

* * *

Breakwater had always been a friendly town, but since Marybeth's departure, everyone seemed just a bit nicer to Michael. At first he was pleased and grateful. After a while, however, he began to feel as though he were being pandered to, or indulged like some petulant child. He believed he could see the falsity behind the smiles, the judgment behind their eyes. What were people saying about him? *He must have done something wrong for her to just pick up and leave like that.* What did they know? He had been a good husband. He had never strayed, had always worked hard and provided for his family. Soon, he began to despise going into town. Offers of support and kinship from the Breakwater locals had started to sound like derision to his ears. Lately, he had been sending Tim to the market whenever they needed things for the house.

Yet he couldn't always send Tim. On a Tuesday, while both kids were in school, Michael drove into town and ran a few errands. Like someone wanted by the police, he wore a baseball cap tugged down low over his eyes. He stopped over at the supermarket where he picked up a few three-ring binders, which Tim needed for school. As he hurried past bags of charcoal briquettes and tubs of lighter fluid on his way to the stationary aisle, he considered going home and setting a bonfire of all Marybeth's belongings. There were closets filled with her clothes; there were her old yearbooks, college textbooks, and paperback novels squirreled away in the basement; there were her childhood toys packed away in one large steamer trunk hidden beneath the basement steps. All of it—one grand salutary conflagration. It would be a rite of passage, in a way. In his mind's eye, he could clearly make out the newspaper headline—MAN FINDS COMFORT IN BLAZING INFERNO. This thought, at least, brought a smile to his lips.

He hit the liquor store on Kaymore Avenue where he purchased a gallon of whiskey, another six-pack of National Bohemian, and two Slim Jims. Keith Dowry was in the wine aisle, bent over while reading the label on a bottle of merlot. Michael paused halfway down the aisle as he recognized Keith, a fine sweat suddenly prickling the hairs on the back of his neck. Before he could turn around and head toward the register down a different aisle, Keith looked up and saw him. Keith's small mouth came tightly together. His eyes widened the slightest bit.

Michael turned to move down the next aisle.

"Please," Keith said. "Wait."

He ignored Keith and went straight to the register. The man behind the counter, Melvin Jones, said, "Hey, Michael," as Michael set the jug of whiskey and the six-pack on the counter.

Michael felt a shadow fall against his back.

"Michael." It was Keith Dowry's voice.

"Don't worry," Michael said. "I won't be calling your house anymore."

"I want to talk to you," Keith said. "Please."

"I've got nothing to say to you," Michael assured him, not turning around to look at the man. Behind the counter, Melvin Jones watched their interaction with something akin to distaste. Breakwater was a small town. Everybody sniffed around in everyone else's business.

"Need a bag?" Melvin asked.

"No, thanks." He tucked the six-pack under one arm then hefted the jug of whiskey off the counter, anxious to be out of the store and rid of Keith Dowry. Yet to his consternation, Keith followed him out onto the sidewalk.

"Michael, please…"

"Go to hell," Michael told him.

* * *

That night at dinner, Tim said, "Did Mom dye her hair?"

"No, Tim."

"She wasn't getting all gray like you?"

Michael closed his eyes, took a breath, then opened them again. "What is with all these questions?" he asked his son.

Tim shrugged. "Was just curious."

"About whether or not your mom dyed her hair? How is that important?"

"Don't yell at him," Gertrude said in a small voice.

Michael looked at her and could see she was very close to tears. The suddenness of her change in emotion troubled him. "I wasn't yelling, hon."

"You're so mean," Tim said.

"Hey," Michael said. "How am I being mean?"

"You just are."

"You just are," echoed Gertrude.

This is wrong, Michael thought. *This is all wrong. I'm a good father. I'm here. I didn't do anything to hurt these children. I'm a good one.*

"I think you two should go to bed early tonight," he told them.

"No fair," said Tim, though he looked down sourly at his plate, his tone void of genuine confrontation.

"No fair," Getrude repeated.

After dinner, the kids took their baths then climbed into bed. Michael kissed them goodnight, and while Gertrude had warmed up a bit, Tim was still cold. He apologized to the boy and said he would answer any questions he might have about his mother in the future. Tim nodded, averted his eyes, then quickly rolled over in bed.

It was around nine o'clock when Michael heard someone outside on the front porch. He flipped on the porch lights and watched a dark shape slide past one of the curtained front windows. When he opened the front door, he expected to find no one there—surely the passing silhouette had been only in his mind—but instead he found Keith Dowry standing there, his longish hair greased and neatly parted, curling just a bit behind his ears. He wore a chambray shirt tucked into a worn pair of dungarees and cowboy boots with crosshatched stitching.

"I can't believe you're standing here," Michael said.

"It's taken me some time to summon the courage," Keith said. "I owe you an apology."

"You owe me more than that."

"You're right," Keith said. "I do. Can I come in?"

"No."

"All right." Keith stuffed his hands into the too-tight pockets of his dungarees, cleared his throat, and said, "I had no right to do what I did. She was your wife and I should have respected that."

"I thought we were friends."

"We were." Something cracked toward the back of Keith's throat. "I'd like us to be again someday, though I know that's probably impossible."

Michael tried to laugh, but all that came out was a miserable croak.

"If I knew where she was, I'd tell you," Keith said. "I swear it. I didn't even know she was...she was seeing someone else..."

The phrase *seeing someone else* caused fireworks to go off in the center of Michael's skull. It was all he could do to keep himself from taking a swing at the son of a bitch on his front porch.

"I think you better leave," he said through his teeth.

Keith nodded, turned around, and sauntered down the porch steps. His pickup truck with the rusted quarter-panels had been left running in the driveway. Michael watched Keith climb behind the wheel, saw the reverse lights come on as he executed a three-point-turn. A moment later, all he could see were the taillights receding into the blackness of the trees.

* * *

Two nights later, over beers on the back porch of Duane Sullivan's house, Duane said, "You gotta give the guy some credit."

Michael said nothing. He'd hired a babysitter for the evening and planned to drink himself into a coma.

* * *

One week later, when he heard more footsteps out on the front porch, Michael jerked open the door, expecting to see Keith Dowry standing there again. But this time it was not Keith Dowry. This time, Marybeth stood there. She was wearing a white blouse, dark jeans, sensible shoes. They were the clothes he had last seen her in— the clothes she had been wearing the night of the argument, after he had found out about her infidelity with Keith.

"Can I come in?" she asked.

He could only stare at her.

"Michael," she said, and though her dark eyes were pleading, questioning, there was no question in her voice. She spoke his name as a statement, a declaration.

Footsteps thundered down the stairs. Michael turned and saw Tim and Gertrude spill down the staircase, rush through the foyer, and shove him aside as they both quickly embraced their mother. Marybeth smiled warmly down at them, running her hands through their hair as they buried their faces into her. Yet her eyes never left Michael's.

"I knew you'd come back!" Gertrude cried. "I knew you wouldn't leave us for good!"

Michael stepped aside as Marybeth entered the house, the children still clinging to her. They all went into the family room, where Marybeth sat on the sofa and collected her children about her, still stroking them.

I'm a good father, Michael thought angrily.

"Are you back?" Tim asked her. The boy's eyes were wet. "Are you staying?"

"I am," Marybeth said. Tenderly she touched the boy's cheek.

Michael wanted to scream at her to get out, that she couldn't be here…but he knew that he could not say such things in front of the children. Instead, he went into the kitchen, knocked back a glass of scotch, then stabilized himself with both hands planted on either side of the kitchen sink. Out in the dark yard, an owl hooted.

Fifteen minutes later, Michael reappeared in the family room. "Okay, guys," he said to the children. "Time for bed."

"But *Dad*," Tim moaned.

"No buts," he countered, unwaveringly. "There'll be plenty of time to sit with your mother tomorrow. Now off to bed."

Both Tim and Gertrude planted a kiss on their mother's cheek. Then they dropped down off the couch and, without uttering a word to their father, moved past him and out into the hall. He listened as their footfalls thumped up the stairs then moved swiftly across the ceiling.

He looked at Marybeth.

"You're not here," he said to her.

Marybeth smiled. For one horrible instant, he could suddenly see the splotches of blood that had fallen across her white blouse, and the vertical lightning-bolt gash at the right side of her forehead where, in the heat of betrayal, he had smashed in her skull with a hammer and killed her. But then those things vanished just as quickly as they had appeared, and he was staring at her unmarred face again. She was suddenly, fearfully beautiful.

"Oh," she said, "I'm here. I'm here for good. I'm staying, Michael." Something akin to a smile came across her pale white face. "It's best," she said. "For the children."

THE HOUSEWARMING

Mark and Lisa Schoenfield spent the afternoon preparing for the party.

They scurried about their spacious new home, making sure the floors were spotless and the large bay windows were free from smudges. Lisa prepared guacamole, miniature tacos (chicken, beef, and vegetarian), cocktail wieners wrapped in flaky croissants, fruit salad, a Caesar salad, and a variety of cookies fanned out like playing cards on a gorgeous Wedgwood serving tray. Mark made the liquor store run, and returned with a carton of assorted bottles and several cases of low-calorie beer. They squabbled playfully over what playlist to select on their shared iPod, with Lisa preferring classical selections to Mark's more modern pop sensibilities. In the end, they settled on a rotation of up-tempo jazz numbers, and finished preparing for the event amidst the brassy intonations of Coltrane and Davis.

Mark was forty-two years old, in good shape, and had all his hair and teeth. He was a musician by trade, having once toured the East Coast with a group who played original Americana in the styles of Springsteen, Mellencamp, and Seger, though for the past decade or so he had found a comfortable little niche composing and recording the scores for independent studio films. This afforded him the luxury of working from home, which made the soundproofed basement the biggest selling point of the new house, at least as far as he was concerned.

Lisa was thirty-eight and was in equally good shape as her

husband. She maintained her figure with a steadfast regimen of aerobic exercises, proper dieting, and an overall positive outlook. She was an attorney who specialized in contract law, and she had recently taken a position with a downtown firm who lured her away from her previous employers with promises of partnership in the not-too-distant future. The new job was the reason for the relocation, and for the new house.

And the house itself? It was a neoclassical Victorian with great flow and four bedrooms at the end of a quaint suburban cul-de-sac. The lawns were blindingly green, the driveway like a black satin ribbon winding in serpentine fashion up the gradual incline of the property toward the two-car garage with the carriage-house lights. At the topmost roof, a weathervane fashioned in the shape of an archer's arrow spiraled lazily in the cool summer breeze. It was the first house the Schoenfields visited, and they had made their offer—quite a generous offer—the very next day.

Now, two weeks after they had moved in, the place had begun taking on some semblance of home. In tandem, Mark and Lisa had spent much of the previous week visiting their nearest neighbors, introducing themselves in their cheerful and overzealous way. The neighbors all seemed friendly enough, and pleased to have a seemingly normal-looking couple move into the neighborhood.

"We're having a housewarming party this weekend," Mark and Lisa would take turns saying, "and we'd love it if you'd come by."

Nearly everyone on the block agreed, and seemed enchanted by the prospect.

The first guests arrived that night at precisely eight o'clock. They were a young couple named Baum, the man in spectacles and the woman in a swoopy floral sundress.

"Hey," Mark said, fervently shaking the man's hand while grinning to beat the band. "Great! You guys are the first to arrive. Can I get you a drink?"

Mark fixed a vodka tonic for Mr. Baum and a glass of merlot for Mrs. Baum, which he handed off to the respective guests with his smile still firmly in place. In the parlor, Lisa raised the volume of the iPod in an effort to make the atmosphere livelier.

Soon after, more guests arrived. Mark immediately made no promises to himself that he would remember all the names of his visitors, though he did intend to conclude the evening having memorized the names of at least three of the couples. The Tohts, the Nancers, the O'Learys, the Smiths, the Barrows—they were all young and handsome and well-groomed and cheerful. Each time the doorbell went off—a plangent *cling-clong!* that sounded to the Schoenfields like a church bell—a new wave of bright faces filed into the foyer. Lisa was pleased to see that many of the women brought food. Mark was pleased to find that a number of the men brought liquor.

As is the custom at such events, the men eventually gravitated toward one end of the house and remained huddled in a tight little group away from the women. They clutched cans of beer or rocks glasses and spoke of the neighborhood's comings and goings with a sense of pride and stewardship Mark Schoenfield admired. They were straight enough to be proper but loose enough to laugh at the occasional crass joke, which endeared them all the more to Mark. When one of the wives swooped by, the respective husband would slip an arm around her waist and plant a quick little peck on her check.

Lisa led an expedition of inquisitive women through the house—up and down the stairs, in and out of all the rooms. Closet doors were opened and bathroom shower stalls were subjected to intrusive scrutiny. One woman even possessed the audacity to peer under the bed in the master bedroom. A few women marveled over what the Schoenfields had managed to do with the place in such a short amount of time.

"We've hardly begun," informed Lisa.

"Nonsense!" said a woman named Tracy Birch. "The place is lovely!"

"Hadn't any of you been in the house before, when the previous owners had lived here?" Lisa asked the gaggle of women.

"Of course, dear," said Sandy O'Leary, "but they had gotten so *old,* and their tastes were so *old.* It's good to have fresh young blood back on the street."

Downstairs, the men had become garrulous in the absence of

women. Mark was pleased to fetch them drinks and returned to the parlor at one point balancing a bowl of guacamole in one hand, drinks in the other, and a bag of Tostitos wedged under one arm. The men applauded his foresight then tore into the bag of chips like a pride of lions descending on a carcass.

"Do you play golf?" asked Bob O'Leary.

"On occasion," Mark said.

Bob O'Leary beamed and clapped him on the forearm. "Brilliant! There's an exceptional course less that fifteen miles from here. It's right on the bay. Gorgeous!"

"Gorgeous," echoed Milton Underland, who stood close by, his mouth full of guacamole. He held a beer in each hand.

The doorbell stopped ringing, yet the guests continued to arrive. The Nevins, the Copelands, the Wintermeyers, the Joneses, the de Filippos. Mark took snapshot photos of each of their faces by blinking his eyes. *Gotcha.* Heavily perfumed women kissed him wetly on the cheek, their scents floral and fecund and delightful. Each man shook his hand while gripping his upper arm in a familiar but not unwelcomed embrace. Mark realized that it had been a long time—since college, maybe—that he'd had a group of male friends with which he could so casually bond.

At one point during the evening, Mark and Lisa bumped into each other in the hallway. The rooms were choked with people and there were more walking up the flagstone path, but they didn't care: they kissed, and it wasn't a brief and perfunctory act. It was meaningful. The stress of the move sloughed from Mark's flesh; the anxiety of switching jobs seemed to burn off Lisa's shoulders like steam off hot blacktop.

The Quindlands, the Hamms, the Dovers, the MacDonalds, the Kellers, a second pair of Smiths—they kept coming. In the kitchen, fresh plates of food replaced old ones. Beer coolers were replenished with new cans and bottles then covered in a shower of ice cubes.

"What is it that you do?" Ted Hamm asked him.

"I'm a musician," Mark explained. "I compose and record the soundtracks for indie films."

"Fantastic! Any films I would know?"

"The most recent was called *Oglethorpe and Company*," Mark said, though he confessed that it had had only minimal distribution. "The most popular is probably the *Sledge* series of films."

"You mean those over-the-top horror movies where all those nubile young waifs get clobbered by the masked maniac wielding a sledgehammer?" Ted Hamm's eyes blazed with what Mark interpreted as pure enchantment.

"Yes," Mark said. "Those films."

"I *love* them! I go hog-wild for those movies! They're so ridiculously bloody, I don't know whether to laugh or scream in terror."

"Thank you," Mark said, unsure if such a comment should be taken as a compliment or not, "but I didn't make the movies. Just the soundtracks."

Another man—someone Mark hadn't yet met—appeared beside Ted Hamm and began humming the discordant title theme from the *Sledge* series of films. Ted grinned, nodding like an imbecile at the man, then turned his blank and grinning face back to Mark.

"Yeah," Mark said. "That's it, all right."

One of the wives also appeared before him. She was a slim brunette in a stunning red dress. She addressed the small upright piano toward the rear of the parlor with beautifully manicured fingernails. "You must play it," she told him. "Oh, please?"

"Yes!" boomed Ted Hamm. "You must!"

It seemed that he was carried toward the piano on a wave of arms. Before being deposited onto the piano bench, some invisible pair of fingers administered a sharp pinch to his midsection. The keyboard cover was thrust open, revealing a mouthful of grinning alabaster teeth. Temporarily disoriented, Mark did not begin to play until some of the guests began humming the theme song. He came in midway through the second bar, his fingers first fumbling over the keys before finding their rhythm.

"There it is!" one of the men shouted. "You've got it now!"

Mark laughed and continued to play. It was all minor chord progressions and jangly high keys—a simple but recognizable melody that had helped secure the *Sledge* franchise some status among horror movie aficionados.

When he finished, the room applauded. Yet when he tried to get up, hands appeared on his back and shoulders, forcing him back down onto the piano bench.

"Please," a woman's voice pleaded. "Once more around the mulberry bush, Mark."

So he cracked his knuckles and played the piece again.

Meanwhile, in the kitchen, Lisa found herself listening to the neighborhood gossip with mild voyeuristic pleasure. Which husband was sleeping with which wife; whose children were just *awful brutes;* what local restaurants were known swingers' joints.

"Is it something you've ever done?" one of the women asked Lisa.

"You mean Mark and me?" Lisa said, hearing Mark at the piano in the next room the instant she spoke his name. "Have we ever…?"

"Not even once?" another woman asked. She was meatier than the others, with great silver streaks in her otherwise raven-colored hair.

"No," Lisa confessed. "Not even once."

"This is so distasteful," said a third woman. Lisa thought her name was Betsy. "Such talk. Who are we, anyway? This isn't *Desperate Housewives,* you know."

A few of the women chided Betsy, though good-naturedly.

Lisa heard the piano stop again…then start up a third time. The same tune. She recognized it as the theme from those horror movies Mark had composed.

The patio door off the kitchen slid open and two good-looking couples came in. They ignored Lisa, and went to embrace some of the other women gathered around the kitchen. All of a sudden, Lisa felt like a stranger in her own house, and in her own life.

"The house is beautiful!" said one of the new women. "We love what you've done with the place. Show us around?"

"Yes," said the other woman. "We'd love the grand tour."

Again, Lisa took the women in and out of rooms, down hallways, opened closet doors. One of the women seemed to take exceptional interest in the cleanliness of the toilets, stopping to peer down at her reflection simmering on the surface of the water in each bowl.

After a while, Lisa packed away the food, leaving only the desserts on the counter. She brewed some Sumatran coffee and decided to forgo her good china cups in favor of the Styrofoam ones Mark had picked up yesterday at the grocery store. There were too many people and she didn't have enough china to go around. As she handed out coffee to extended hands, her guests smiled warmly at her.

"We love what you and Mark have done with the house," Sheila Duggan said.

"Your taste is exquisite," Sallyanne Monroe said.

"Oh," Lisa said, "we've hardly had a chance to do a thing."

The Bostons, the Daleys, the Fritzes, the Loans filed into the house, cheery-faced and smelling of colognes, perfumes, deodorants.

In the parlor, Mark struggled up off the piano bench. More hands gripped him and tried to force him back onto the bench, but he slid sideways and marshaled decisively through the crowd. Several of the guests issued boos at his departure, until someone else claimed the piano bench and began playing a fairly commendable rendition of Joplin's "Maple Leaf Rag."

Mark found Lisa in the doorway between the parlor and the kitchen, her back toward him. He sighed into her hair and muttered, "My fingers are burning."

Lisa turned...and it wasn't Lisa at all. Another woman in the same dress, her hair done up in a similar fashion. The strangeness of her appearance caused Mark to utter a small cry.

"Hello," she said, smiling prettily at him.

"I'm sorry. I thought you were my wife."

"She's delightful," said the woman. "You both are. Was that you on the piano just a moment ago?"

"It was."

"You play so well. You are a professional?"

"Yes, I am."

"So wonderful to have such a talented new couple join the community."

In the kitchen, Lisa waved to him over a sea of bobbing heads and grinning faces. Mark excused himself and navigated through the crowd until he reached his wife. She looked tired.

"Coffee?" she asked him.

"I'm too tired for coffee," he said, "if that makes any sense."

"They keep coming," she said.

"They love us," he responded, though without the satisfaction expected with such a sentiment.

In the parlor, "Maple Leaf Rag" segued into "The Entertainer." Voices boomed in pleasure. A few of the women in the kitchen began dancing with each other, their coffee cups held up above their heads while they twirled each other around with their free hands.

A perky redhead approached the Schoenfields dragging behind her a man in a pressed oxford shirt and pleated khakis. "My husband Michael and I missed the tour of the house," she said in a nasally, almost pleading voice. "Is it too late for us? We'd love to see all the work you've been doing."

"We really would," Michael added.

"We haven't done any work," Mark advised the couple.

"Everyone is bragging about the upstairs," said the woman, as if she hadn't heard him.

"It's nothing," Lisa cut in.

The redheaded woman cheered with glee, clasping her hands together. "I bet it's outstanding!"

Mark and Lisa exchanged a look. "I'll take them," he offered, then led the couple up the stairs. The three of them wandered around the hallway, dipping in and out of unfinished bedrooms, bathrooms, closets. The redhead paused before one bathroom mirror to examine her reflection, then—astoundingly—she readjusted her cleavage while Mark stood gaping at her in the bathroom doorway. The woman's husband didn't seem to notice; he was too preoccupied examining the grout in the shower stall.

A few minutes later, as Mark led them back down the stairs, he noticed that the pianist had abandoned Joplin in favor of plucking out random sour notes on the keyboard. It was as if the piano player had suffered a stroke while on the bench. Nonetheless, the guests still cheered on the abysmal playing.

Exhausted, Mark looked around the kitchen for Lisa, but could not find her. It seemed more people had showed up while he had been upstairs, which was strange because it was awfully late for new arrivals. He glanced at the wall clock above the sink and saw that the clock had ceased working at 8:39 p.m. He then glanced at his wrist before realizing he hadn't worn his wristwatch.

Someone began playing "Chopsticks" on the piano. Badly.

Mark shouted, "Lisa?" but doubted she could hear him over the cacophony of their guests, the piano, and the muddled jazz coming from the detachable iPod speakers. His head throbbed. "Excuse me, excuse me," he mumbled, cutting through the crowd. When he reached the parlor, he saw men dancing with men, women dancing with women, and a huddle of striped polo shirts standing around the piano. "Chopsticks" ended abruptly and the guests began haranguing the pianist. Mark saw the pianist try to stand, catching a glimpse of the familiar hairdo and dress, and thought, *Lisa.*

It was. She sat before the piano, several hands on her shoulders as if to hold her in place, while her hands sat now in her lap. A terrified expression was etched across her face. She did not know how to play the piano—barring, apparently, a rudimentary rendition of "Chopsticks"—and when she met Mark's eyes, he could see all the fear bottled up inside her. He reached out and she grasped his hand...but then *other* hands shoved him down onto the piano bench beside her.

"Play 'Heart and Soul,'" someone shouted.

"I want to get up," Lisa uttered very close to Mark's ear.

"Lean on my shoulder and I'll play," he told her.

After he had played "Heart and Soul" twice, he grasped Lisa's hand and tugged her up off the bench. Hands tried to shove them back down but Mark swatted them away as he dragged Lisa toward the kitchen. There were so many people in the parlor now it was becoming difficult to breathe.

"I'm so tired," Lisa said. "I don't think a single person has gone home yet."

"They just—" He was about to say *keep coming* when the patio door swooshed open again and another bright-eyed, pleasant-smelling couple appeared in the doorway.

"Hello!" boomed the man.

"So *nice* to finally meet you both!" cried the woman.

Lisa smiled at them wearily. Mark paused to shake their hands. To his surprise, the woman leaned in and kissed him on the corner of his mouth. The kiss lasted longer than it should have, and although it was dry and unobtrusive, she exhaled into his nostrils before pulling away. It was like tasting her breath. Instantaneously, Mark felt an erection threaten the front of his pants.

"I'd love to see the upstairs," the woman said to him, her stare hanging between them like cabling.

"In just a minute," he said, excusing himself, and dragging Lisa into the kitchen.

"Do you mind if we put on another pot of coffee, Lisa, dear?" said Betsy, coming up and breathing in Lisa's face.

"Well," Lisa said, her eyes skirting the room. "Do you think people will—"

"You're a peach!" said Betsy, then twirled away to address the coffee pot on the kitchen counter.

"I'm exhausted," Lisa moaned to Mark again. "It's got to be close to midnight."

"The clock is dead," he told her, glancing up at it again. Only now, it read 8:42 p.m. As he stared, he could see the second hand moving at nearly imperceptible increments. "Or," he amended, "it's *nearly* dead."

"Excuse me," Lisa said to Betsy. She pointed to the woman's sparkly gold wristwatch. "What time do you have?"

"Oh!" Betsy cooed. "Don't tell me you two are bushed already!" The woman glanced at her wristwatch. "Why, it's not even nine yet!"

Lisa said, "I'm sorry—did you just say it's not even *nine* yet? Nine o'clock?"

"This coffee smells so *good*," Betsy said with a wink, then turned back to the coffee pot. She began shoveling spoonfuls of coffee into the percolator.

From the parlor, someone shouted Mark's name. When Mark

turned, he saw a man he did not know waving him into the room. "I hear you're a regular Liberace!"

Mark just shook his head, a drawn expression on his face.

A woman in a dark blue beret appeared in front of Mark and Lisa and said, "I think you were a bit premature putting the food away. Do you mind if I break it back out? The Wilsons haven't even shown up yet, and they'll be ravenous!"

Lisa just blinked at the woman dumbly.

"Have at it," Mark interjected, then dragged Lisa out into the hallway.

Yet the hallway was cluttered with people, too. Hands extended to shake theirs, to pat their backs, to congratulate them and welcome them to the neighborhood. Again, those invisible fingers gave Mark's abdomen a pinch. This time he whirled around to address the culprit...but found himself staring at a wall of tightly-packed people, any of whom could have been the violator.

Claustrophobia tightening around his neck, he pulled Lisa toward the staircase. Together, they bounded up the stairs to the second floor...yet froze at the top of the stairs as they saw the queue of people standing in the upstairs hallway. Wide eyes peered into the bedrooms. People murmured as they examined the bathrooms, the hall closets. A man in a tweed sports coat and a corduroy necktie stood before one open closet door, one of their bath towels in his hands. As Mark and Lisa watched, the man brought the towel to his nose and sniffed it.

"Enough," Mark called out. "It's getting late. We're going to have to ask that we at least keep the party downstairs. We'd appreciate it if—" But he cut himself off when he realized no one was listening to him.

"Mark," Lisa said, and touched his arm.

Angry, he stormed back downstairs—

"Mark!"

—and shoved through the guests in the hallway on his way to the front door. It took nearly a full minute for him to reach the door, grasp the knob, yank it open.

A man and a woman stood on the stoop, a platter of cookies in the woman's hands. They both smiled warmly at Mark, their teeth big and bright. Mark could see lipstick on some of the woman's teeth.

"Ah," said the man. "You must be Mark Schoenfield. Welcome to the neighborhood, old sailor."

Hands grabbed Mark around the forearms. Fingers snatched at his shirt and the legs of his pants. He craned his neck around to see the ghoulishly smiling faces of the men from the parlor breathing down his neck.

"You're quite the virtuoso," said Bob O'Leary. There was spinach dip stuck in his teeth. "Come play us that horror theme again, will you?"

Mark yanked one of his arms free.

"Aw, come on, now," Bob said, frowning playfully. "Don't be a spoiled sport." Bob checked his wristwatch. "It's early yet."

Lisa appeared on the stairwell. Mark met her eyes. She opened her mouth to say something to him, but was immediately approached by the young couple who had come through the patio door and requested a tour of the house. Mark saw Lisa shake her head. Nonetheless, the couple advanced on her, ascending the stairs. Lisa slowly backed away from them, moving up the stairs herself. She glanced one last time at Mark before her head disappeared beyond the ceiling. He watched her legs move backward up the stairs as the couple continued to advance on her.

Bob O'Leary and some of the other men dragged Mark through the kitchen toward the parlor.

"Seriously," Mark said, trying to shrug them all off. "I'm in no mood to play. It's late. Everyone needs to go home now."

"Coffee's on!" Betsy trilled from the counter. A wave of people flowed toward her.

"Late?" Bob O'Leary said. Then he pointed to the clock above the kitchen sink. "What's the matter with you, Mark?"

The clock read 8:50 p.m.

"That clock is wrong," Mark said. He gripped the countertop and kicked at some of the more aggressive hands. They let him go. "It's late," he said, his breath coming in labored gasps now. "That clock is wrong."

Bob O'Leary's face seemed to crease down the middle with

frustration and, Mark thought, something akin to anger, too. He thrust his wristwatch in Mark's face. Mark stared at the digital numbers. "Is *my* watch wrong?" Bob O'Leary wanted to know. "Is it, Mark?"

Bob O'Leary's watch read 8:50 p.m. As Mark stared at it, he saw the dual numbers indicating the seconds hang on 32. As he watched, the seconds did not change...did not change...did not change...until *finally* the 2 turned into a 3. It took what felt like a full minute for one second to tick by.

Mark shook his head.

"So," Bob O'Leary started up again, that cheerful smile back in place, "how about regaling us with some tickling of the ivories?"

"Oh, yes!" chirped a woman in a houndstooth scarf. "That would be lovely!"

The hands returned, gripping him high up on the forearms, at the wrists, around the waist. Someone clenched him hard high on the thigh. Bob O'Leary winked at him...then reached down and tweaked Mark's penis through the front of his pants.

Upstairs, something heavy tipped over and smashed to the floor. A moment later, someone cranked the volume on the iPod.

"No!" Mark shouted as his guests dragged him toward the parlor and the piano. "No! Leave me alone! Let me go!"

"It's so early, Mark," Bob O'Leary said.

"We've got all the time in the world," said another man.

"All the time in the world," the woman in the houndstooth scarf echoed.

Mark Schoenfield screamed.

"Party pooper," Bob O'Leary said, laughing.

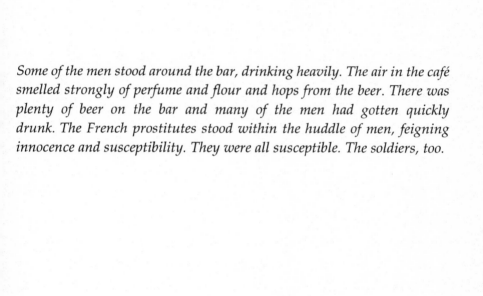

Some of the men stood around the bar, drinking heavily. The air in the café smelled strongly of perfume and flour and hops from the beer. There was plenty of beer on the bar and many of the men had gotten quickly drunk. The French prostitutes stood within the huddle of men, feigning innocence and susceptibility. They were all susceptible. The soldiers, too.

Chupacabra

I am a nervous wreck coming into Salinas Cove, my sweaty hands slipping on the steering wheel. I have come from Durango, down through Mesa Verde and across the Rio Grande toward Las Cruces, and the air is warmer. Even at twilight.

I peer through the windshield at the oncoming darkness.

It is a rundown motel outside the city. An illuminated sign promises its employees speak English. I pull into the parking lot and turn off the engine. It ticks down in the silence. There is less light out here, outside the city. Mine is the only car in the parking lot.

The girl who signs me in is dark-skinned, pretty. She definitely does not speak English. I scribble my signature on a clipboard and fork over my driver's license. Behind the counter, a wall-mounted television set flickers with the black-and-white, static-marred image of Cary Grant.

And for a moment, I zone out. I hear the man with the ironworks teeth saying, *You do not look like him.* He says, *Your brother—you do not look like him.* Yet he extends his hand anyway—

The room is bleak, tasteless, the color of sawdust. The shower stall is filthy and ancient, and there is the distinct impression of a foot stamped in grime on the shower-mat. Sketches of hunting dogs and wind-blown cattails cling to the walls in spotty frames. The bed looks miniscule, like something from a child's fairytale about a family of bears, and it is packaged in an uncomfortable-looking bedspread adorned with fleurs-de-lis. The ghosts of cigarettes haunt the room. Yet none of this troubles me at the moment. I stand in the center of the room and look at the miniscule bed and am nearly knocked over by the sudden strength of my exhaustion.

Immediately, I strip. I go straight for the bed and do not turn down the comforter and do not turn out the lights, for fear cockroaches will trampoline on my body in the dark. So I remain in bed, my hands behind my head, listing to my own heartbeat compete with the chug of someone's shower through the wall. And despite my utter exhaustion, I cannot find sleep.

I am thinking of the man with the ironworks teeth, and how he extended to me a set of pitted brass keys. *Keees,* he pronounced it. *Keees, chico.* And then I think of my brother, of Martin, and the way he looked after returning from the Cove, like some vital fluid had been siphoned from him. When he first saw me at the trailer park, he tried to smile, but his smile was all busted up, his lips split, his teeth jagged. His eyes were bulbous, swollen, amphibian in their protrusion. *They did me real good, bro.* Sure they did. Sure.

Somehow, I become hostage to a series of dreams. They all have the sepia-toned quality of old movies. Shapeless, hair-covered creatures shuffle along the periphery of a nightmare highway; each time I try to look at them, they break apart into glittering confetti.

At one point, I awake. I think I hear Martin talking somewhere in the distance. He speaks with the marble-mouth distort of a stroke victim. Because I cannot sleep, I rise and do calisthenics just beyond the foot of the bed in the half-gloom. I am too wired to sleep.

Before I know it, morning breaks through the half-shaded window across the room. I shower with the dedication of a death row inmate. Brushing my teeth with my finger, I try to think of old songs on the radio to hum, but I cannot think of anything.

With some detachment, I dress. And it is still early morning by the time I'm back in the car. I drive for some time without seeing anything, then finally pull over at a gas station to refill the tank. I purchase a cup of black coffee and a chocolate chip cookie nearly the size of a hubcap. The gas station is practically a ghost town; only a mange-ridden mutt eyes me from across the macadam. Back in the car, I drive for an hour and breeze by the twisted carcasses of chupacabra along the side of the highway.

I glance out the window to my left and watch the mesas watch me. I'm surprised I haven't seen any border patrol vehicles yet. This relaxes me a bit. I cross into Mexico with little difficulty, sticking to the route previously outlined for me by the man with the ironworks teeth.

I pull into a deserted parking lot outside a diner somewhere west of Ciudad Juárez. An ice cream truck sits slumped and tired-looking in the sun, mirage-like in a halo of dust. The sun seems to be at every horizon. I park alongside the ice cream truck and step quickly from the car to survey the vehicle. It could be an elephant. Or maybe a bank safe. Its color suggests it was once a pale blue, the color of a robin's egg. But both the desert sun and the passage of time have caused it to regress to a monochromatic gray, interrupted by large magnolia blossoms of rust and speckled with muddy chickenpox. Cryptic phraseology has been spray-painted along one flank. Reads, "Sho'nuf." Reads, "Denis Does Daily." Its windshield is grimy but in one piece and the tires, all four of them, look new.

Inside, I sip a glass of tasteless soda while picking apart a *sopapilla* stuffed fat with beans that look like beetles. I wait. Soon, a young, scarecrow-faced man with a too-wide mouth and baggy dungarees materializes beside my table. He introduces himself as Diego. He seems friendly enough. He sits across from me and orders a 7-Up. To quell my nerves, he tells me about a helicopter ride into the Grand Canyon and how there is this entire Indian tribe living down there, just tucked away like a secret behind some waterfall, and I listen with mild interest. Then around noon, just when I think nothing is going to happen, I catch a glint of chrome on the horizon morph into a prehistoric Impala as it draws closer to the diner.

"That's him," Diego says.

His name is Caranegra and his face is indeed almost black as tar. He does not smile—not like the man with the ironworks teeth, the man who gave me the *keees, chico*—and he tries hard to be stoic when we first meet. He wears a tattered Iron Maiden concert tee which I find somewhat comical and his knuckles are alternately covered with tattoos and intricate silver rings.

"I'm Gerald," I say and am not sure if I should shake this man's hand or not. I opt for a slight nod and leave it at that.

Caranegra acknowledges both Diego and me with a grunt. "You are Martin's brother?"

"Yes."

"You do not look like him."

"Yeah, that's what the other guy said."

"Pinto? Who gives you the keys?"

"Yes. Pinto." I hadn't known his name.

"You look nervous to me, boy," Caranegra says. And before I can answer, he says, "Your brother, he was not careful. That is why his face looks like it does. He has been doing this for a long time, *muchacho*, and he got careless. If you get careless, then the bad things can happen. If you do not get careless, *muchacho*, you will not have a face that looks like his."

"I won't be doing this for very long," I say quickly. For whatever reason, I feel I need to make this clear. "I'm just working off what Martin owes."

"Why?"

"Because he's my brother."

Caranegra leans back in his chair. I can smell marijuana about him like body odor. His face is heavy with lines and creases, like a map that has been folded too many times, and I cannot tell if I am looking at a genius or an imbecile. "Martin, your brother, was not a stupid man," he says. "He was a smart man. He just got careless. Did he ever tell you about his last crossing?"

"Some of it."

"Not all?"

"He told me enough. He just left some parts out."

"I would bet," says Caranegra, "those are the parts that make him look careless." And he smiles sourly.

"I have to piss," Diego says and rises automatically from the table. "Can we hurry this along? I've got things."

Caranegra watches Diego cross the diner and, when he is out of earshot, says, "He is my sister's boy. He is the good kid." Then he leans toward me over the table. Suddenly we are ancient friends and longtime conspirators. "How old are you?"

"Twenty."

"You look younger."

"I can show you my driver's license."

Caranegra waves uninterested fingers at me. "This is the delicate work, *muchacho*. Do you understand?"

"You don't have to worry about me."

"You have the map?"

I remove a roadmap from my rear pocket and splay it out across the table. With a fat red thumb, Caranegra presses down on a section just southwest of Guerrero. "Debajo Canyon. Up here, then up here, then—do you follow? Then up here." His eyes never leave mine. "But this is the delicate work, *muchacho.*"

"You don't have to worry."

Caranegra thumps his thick bronze fingers on the tabletop. Says, "Come with me."

Outside, he pats the side of the ice cream truck. "Pinto give you the route, no? The directions?"

"Yes."

"That is the best route. Pinto knows all the best routes. You stay on that route and you will have no worries."

"What's in the truck?"

"Your brother was careless," Caranegra says. "Also, he started to ask many questions."

Diego saunters out into the broad sunshine, hitching up his too-big dungarees. He smiles when he sees us as if happy to see old friends.

"Diego will take you to Debajo Canyon to get the I.D.," Caranegra says. "From there, you will travel alone."

Awkwardly, I move to shake his hand.

Carangera just laughs. Says, "You do not look like him." Says, "Get lost now."

No more than a minute later, Diego and I are kicking up dust in the ice cream truck, leaving the ruddy-faced Caranegra standing in the parking lot of the diner, his ridiculous Iron Maiden tee-shirt flapping in the breeze. The truck drives horribly, and I can feel every bump and groove in the roadway. It gives off the distinct aroma of burning steering fluid and someone has spilled M&M's

into the radiator ducts; they rattle like ball bearings from one side of the dash to the other with each sharp turn.

Debajo Canyon is due south, near Guerrero, and we are closer to it now than I thought we were. Diego stares at the map and talks to himself and hums hair metal songs under his breath while drumming his fingers on his knees. Having driven all this way by myself, his presence is practically suffocating, despite the fact that we hardly speak to one another. Then, finally, Diego mentions Martin.

"Did he ever tell you about this?" he asks. "About the job?"

"A little."

"He ever say what he carried in the trucks?"

"I don't know."

"Didn't you ask?"

"Sure."

"Frankenface didn't tell you?" And he seems pleased with himself for coming up with the name.

"I just assumed drugs," I said. "Or guns. Something like that."

"Do you know who did that to his face?"

"No. He never said."

"It was Pinto," Diego says. "Used his big fists."

For whatever reason, this upsets me.

"They sure banged him up pretty good," Diego continues. "Had a B.A.G."

"What's that?"

"Busted-Ass Grille."

"Let's drop it."

Something flickers just to the left of my line of sight. My breath catches. Immediately my mind returns to the dreams, and to the shapeless beasts that scale the highways. Chupacabra. Goat-suckers.

"What?" Diego asks, sensing my sudden unease.

"Chupacabra," I say. "Martin used to scare me with stories of the chupacabra when I was little."

"He raise you?"

"Our parents died when we were young, yeah."

"So now you feel you need to pay him back? To finish what he started?"

I roll my shoulders. "I don't know."

"This is not the business for that, bro."

"It's just this one time."

"Christ." Diego sinks down into the passenger seat. "Chupacabra's a myth. They're coyotes. Your brother saw coyotes."

"I saw something large and hairy dead on the side of the road coming down here. Looked too big to be a coyote."

"You're ridiculous," Diego says.

Am I? Because I am thinking of the horror stories Martin used to tell me when I was younger and he'd return from weeks and sometimes months on the road. He would tell me of the chupacabra and of the way they drained the fluids from livestock and how, sometimes, they drained the fluids from people, too. Of course, I know now that there are no such creatures, but seeing the dead coyote along the side of the road and thinking, too, of Martin instill within me a certain disquiet. Suddenly, I feel like turning around and driving the hell home.

It is late by the time we pull into Debajo Canyon. It is nothing more than a sandstone bluff overlooking a scrub grass valley, milky in the oncoming darkness, interrupted at intervals by ramshackle hovels and peeling, sad-looking campers. I have no idea what to expect from Diego's associates, but I can sense an urgency in Diego the moment we cross onto the rutted gravel roadway leading toward the semicircle of campers. In the distance, a small bonfire winks at us. The sky is dizzy with stars.

Diego has unraveled a worn slip of paper and looks at it now the way an explorer might scrutinize a treasure map. Says, "Pull off to the left here, Gerald."

I pull off to the left. Say, "Which one is it?"

Diego points past the windshield. "Straight ahead. One with the lights on." It is a beat-up trailer with automobile tires nailed to the roof. It is one of the few with lights in the windows.

Diego pops the passenger door and climbs down from the ice cream truck. For the first time, I catch a glimpse of a pistol butt jutting from the waistband of his dungarees, hidden beneath his shirt. "Let's shake a tail feather, bro. I got things."

I pop my own door and hop down, kicking up dust with my sneakers, and follow Diego to the trailer. Diego mounts the two abbreviated steps to the door then knocks and waits. Knocks again. My discomfort increases and I take a step back. Across the sandstone courtyard, very few lights are on in any other homes, and even the distant bonfire has disappeared. I scan the horizon for a sign of civilization beyond the trailer park, but I am kidding myself. We are alone.

The trailer door opens and we're suddenly scrutinized by a barrel-chested Mexican in a wife-beater, his thick, hairless arms as red as the sunset. His matted, corkscrew hair informs me we've just woken him from a nap.

Briefly, Diego and the man exchange pleasantries in Spanish. I understand very little of what is said. It isn't until I recognize my brother's name that I feel I am included in all this, and the big man in the wife-beater grins bad teeth at me.

Inside the trailer is like being in a coffin. The air is stale and palpable. It is a home for papers and paperwork, of overflowing manila folders and spools of adhesive tape, an ancient reel-to-reel recorder that blindly stares, and the like. Unwashed plates are stacked like ancient tablets in the sink. The whole place smells not of a structure of human residency and occupancy but, rather, of mildewed library cellars and wet paperback novels and discarded and forgotten towers of time-yellowed newspapers.

"*Aquí*," the barrel-chested man says, and quickly directs me to stand against one wall. Suddenly, I am looking across the cramped trailer at the lens of a digital camera. The man rattles off a succession of photos then, moments later, perches himself in front of a computer monitor.

Startled by movement in a darkened corner of the trailer, I squint to find a set of dark eyes staring back at me. An ancient Mexican woman, nearly skin and bones, watches me from a Barcalounger across the trailer. She has a knitted afghan pulled over her legs, and her hands, like the talons of a prehistoric bird, sink into the divot of her lap. Like a ghost, she watches. I suddenly taste my own heartbeat.

Then she starts cackling.

"Here," says the barrel-chested Mexican, stabbing a freshly-minted driver's license in my direction. He has something else in his other hand—something that quickly steals Diego's attention. It's marijuana, a few ounces of the stuff, in a Ziploc bag.

"Hey, Frodo," Diego says. "Go wait in the truck."

Cold, uncomfortable, I climb back into the truck and punch off the headlights. I sit in the simmering quiet of a desert night. I wait for decades. Soon, Martin is seated somewhere behind me in the truck, whispering my name. He makes me promise to be careful and to not ask too many questions. I call him an idiot and tell him I'll be home soon. He asks if I've seen the chupacabra and I snort…but deep down inside I am that lost, little boy again, fearful of the goat-suckers, of the desert vampires. *You know they don't exist, Gerald, right?* he soothes me now. Yet I frown and tell him it's too late, damn it, that he has already poisoned me with his stories, years of poisoning, years of waiting in my own sad little trailer for him to come home and raise me and act like a responsible adult. Is it fair that I should have to act like the responsible adult for both of us now? Is it?

It was an accident, he whispers. *I drove a truck into a river.* Then: *They did me real good, for driving the truck into the river. They did me real good, bro.*

Sure they did.

Sure.

Across the bluff, Diego spills through the trailer door. He staggers to the ice cream truck and motions for me to take down the window, which I do.

"Hey," he says, "you know where you're going, right?"

"I have the map."

"Yeah. Uh, I'm gonna crash here, all right?"

"I don't need to drive you somewhere?"

"Take it easy, Gerald."

I spin the wheel and pull back onto the main road, this time heading north. I drive for nearly forty-five minutes, the only living creature among miles and miles of desert. And when I think I see something shapeless and black moving alongside the highway, I can't help but slam on the brakes and straddle the highway's center line like a tightrope walker. And I think, *Chupacabra!* I am breathing heavy and sweat stings my eyes. Behind me, somewhere in the darkness, I hear Martin assure me that the chupacabra are not real. Vampire devils. Goat-suckers. His face, he says—what they did to his face is real, but the goat-suckers are not.

It is always brighter the moment you step out of a vehicle in the desert, no matter how dark it is. Now, it is cold, too. When people think of perishing in the desert they usually don't imagine themselves freezing to death, but that is the truth of it.

I step around the side of the ice cream truck, my ears keying in on every desert sound. The chatter of insects is deafening. I cannot seem to get my heartbeat under control. With one hand tracing along the body of the truck, I move to the rear of the vehicle and peer through the darkness. I am not shocked when I see the reflective glow of two beady eyes staring back at me from the cusp of the highway; rather, a dull sense of fatigue overwhelms me.

It is a coyote. I see it clear enough as it turns and scampers further down the shoulder of the roadway. And while I am relieved, I am quickly accosted by a delayed sense of fear that causes my armpits to dampen beneath my sweatshirt and my mouth to go dry. I turn and begin to head back to the cab when I hear a sound—some sound, some *thump*—echo from the rear of the truck. From *within.*

My footfalls are soundless on the blacktop of the midnight highway. There is no lock on the rear doors—just a simple bolt slid into a ring. Unhinging the bolt, I peel the doors open and stare into the black maw of the truck. The sick-sweet stink of decay breathes out. I climb into the rear of the truck. There are coolers affixed to the floor and metal boxes on shelves. There are a number of cardboard ice cream boxes lining the shelves here, too, but they are empty and so ancient that a slick, brown mildew coats every box. Looking down, I expect the coolers to be locked with padlocks, but they are not, and I am surprised.

Chupacabra? I wonder, and open one of the coolers. The hinges squeal and I fumble around my jacket pocket for a pen light. Shine the light into the cooler.

At first, it does not even register with me. And even after it does, I do not fully understand what I am looking at.

There are a number of them, bronze-skinned and wide-eyed, staring up at me, pressed so closely together that they are indistinguishable from one another. They reek of fear and sweat, their expressions just as uncomprehending as my own. Their clothes are filthy, their faces greasy with perspiration. So many of them, it is a wonder they can even fit. Finally, before I ease the cooler lid down, one of them says, *"Muchacho."*

"I'm sorry," I say…although I am unsure if I am actually speaking or am just hearing the words funnel through my head. And I hear Martin saying, *They did me real good, for driving the truck into the river.*

It is a long, quiet ride back across the border.

ALL tHE PREtty GIRLS

What do you know?

He knew where he was, for one thing. The day was hot and without wind, the jagged sandstone bluffs cresting like whitecaps above the darkened line of ponderosa pines. Sniffing the still air, Pablo Santiago could smell trout from the river, metallic and fishy, like ointment. Before him, Chama River Canyon lay undisturbed and contemplating, as if deep in thought. The hot sun beating down on his shoulders, Santiago fondly recalled the days of his youth fishing along the cusp of the winding river. On many occasions he'd trekked through the pinon-juniper woodlands, ensconced in the scenic hug of Apache plume and cliffrose and fendlerbush, only to arrive exhausted but content at the El Vado Lake Dam. In his youth, he'd spent many evenings watching the sun deteriorate beyond the horizon, bruising the sky with a multitude of pastel hues while sipping dandelion wine and smoking Pall Malls.

What do you know?

He knew about the car, too. And in many ways, despite all his years living off the land—despite the countless elk and coyotes he'd trapped and killed and eaten; despite his unwavering respect for the land itself—he knew the car was most important. How he'd come across it no longer mattered (anyway, he couldn't remember) and how it had gotten there, wedged between the blue-tinted firs along the cusp of the valley like a forgotten relic, was not important. What was important—what genuinely *mattered*—was what the car really *was*.

What do you know?

A lot, Pablo Santiago thought. Over time, he'd come to know a lot.

On the outside, it was a 1962 Mercury Comet S-22 Coupe with a two-tone black and red paint job, rusted and scored and pocked by the elements. Its windshield was grimy and covered in bull's-eye cracks. Its tires were flattened and flaking with rot and, over time, had become part of the earth. Its Mylar door panels were pitted and ruined, the bucket seats and loop carpeting torn and cancerous with mold. The front grille, with its busted-out quad-headlamps and deluxe chrome, was a mouth crowded with teeth, rusty and sharp for biting.

This day, in the hot sunshine, Santiago crossed down into the valley, the rising, rocky tumult of Albiquiu behind him, and paused beneath a tall stand of firs. They provided much shade in the summer, and he stood there for several moments while he mopped his brow with an oily hand towel. He thought of the trout in the river and the smell of them in the air. From where he stood he could not see the car, but some animal part of him could sense it. Santiago was not a stupid man, nor was he irreligious: he knew divinity when confronted with it. It was a power, he knew, which was even greater than the power of the land.

Leaving the stand of firs, Santiago advanced toward the lip of the canyon. From here, he could hear the din of the river and could smell brine in the air. Knowing the water was so close was enough to cool and refresh his body, and he found his legs suddenly pumping stronger and harder than they had just moments ago. Earlier in the summer, it had been a difficult hike with the equipment—the shovel, the spade, the rake, the pickaxe—but he'd soon gotten accustomed to his work and began stowing his tools in the Comet's back seat. The fresh earth smell left behind by the tools smelled better than the car's interior anyway, and it was easier for Santiago to breathe when seated behind the Comet's steering wheel. Smelled better than the stink from the trunk...

Ahead, a clearing opened up and Santiago could see the Comet's grinning grillwork behind a thin veil of kudzu. Shade from the surrounding firs made it look dull and dusty. Hitching up his dungarees, Santiago approached the vehicle, his eyes tracing the lines of the exterior, running over the chassis, hunting for a glimpse of reflected sunlight in the chrome. But there was none this day; there was too much shade beneath the trees.

If I could get you to run, Santiago thought, *we would not be so limited to Chama Canyon.* He thought, *We would not be limited to the grasslands up north and the Rio Grande and Albiquiu. If I could get you to run,* he thought, *we could travel and not be limited to any single place.*

But there was no way. Pablo Santiago was not a mechanic and knew nothing about getting old cars to run. The 6-cylinder engine beneath the Comet's hood could have been a birdcage or a ball of yarn or a series of intertwined coat-hangers. Often, Santiago found himself staring at the dead engine, one bronze and meaty hand propping up the hood, examining the intricacies of the object like a mathematician scrutinizing an equation. The engine, he knew, was the heart. If only he could get the heart beating again...

He shook his head and took a step away from the vehicle. He'd been staring at his mottled reflection in the grimy driver's side window. Beads of perspiration had broken out across his upper lip. He removed his hand towel from the rear pocket of his dungarees and blotted his face. The towel reeked of motor oil and dirt and something like copper and he quickly stuffed the towel back in his trousers.

Sometimes the car bled motor oil. In a black trail, it would slide down through the rocks toward the edge of the cliff. If he didn't blot it up in time, it would spill into the river below. And that wouldn't be good. Santiago did not know why he thought this, but he knew it just the same as he knew his own name. Something about that oil spilling into the river would be *muy mal.*

If I could get you to run, he thought now, *I wouldn't have to worry about this river.*

He stepped around to the rear of the car, one hand fisted around a tree branch for support, and examined the ground. There was no oil. He felt a wave of relief wash over him. Peering over the cliff, he could see the extended branches of shrubbery down the cliff-face, and could see the layers of colored rock, stacked like textbooks, dipping down toward the river and the canyon floor.

The river looked black and like gasoline in the sun.

What do you know?

He knew what to do. And he would waste no more time.

Santiago carried a slender metal prong on a key ring. He removed this device from the pocket of his pants now, examined it briefly in the hot sun, and moved toward the Comet's trunk. Here he paused, as if waiting for a signal. Listened. In his head, he counted: seven days. Always seven. He ran his eyes over the trunk. His reflection stared back at him from the black paint, dusty and pierced with tiny dents. Santiago ran two fingers over the trunk. Even in the shade of the firs, the steel was hot, warmed by the midday sun.

He slid the metal prong into the trunk's keyhole and maneuvered the prong around until he felt the lock give. There was a hollow metallic clang. Absentmindedly, he remained with one hand on top of the trunk, holding it down against the force of the springs. The trunk wanted to open, but the springs were weak with age and Santiago held the trunk down without difficulty.

There will be many black bears here before the summer is out, he thought without interest, his eyes focused on the wealth of trees and shrubbery through which he had come. *There will be plenty before the days get shorter and the nights get colder. I can remember all this land before it was government land, and how my father and grandfather had shot many black bears along this ridge. The bears,* he thought, *they are smart, smarter than we think, and if you shoot them and don't kill them, they will run for the cliff and run off and fall into the river and die. They will die either way but they do not want to die and bring satisfaction to the one bringing its death. They are noble that way.*

He thought he felt something thump against the bottom of the trunk and that made his heart skip in his thick chest. But no—it was all in his head, and he uttered a skittish, almost girlish laugh. Then opened the trunk.

At this point, something always overtook Pablo Santiago, and that was good. Not a spirit or any such thing but, rather, a certain *drive,* enabling him to function almost without senses: practically blind and deaf and without touch or smell. Like a long-distance runner. He operated like a machine, if only for the time it took to remove the carcass from the Comet's trunk and dump it to the earth, but that was time enough. That was the hardest part. The hardest part was always opening the trunk and seeing those dead eyes staring up from the black maw of the trunk...the gray cheesecloth look of the skin...the lips, always pulled back in a frozen snarl, the gums purple...fingernails shorn away...

Eyes slightly unfocused, Santiago exhaled heavily while wiping his forehead with the heel of one hand. He wasn't aggravated, not even disappointed anymore. Some part of him felt the tingling sensation of failure, but it was so minute that he hardly acknowledged it. Now was not a time to contemplate failure. Now was a time to be done with it and move on.

Santiago bent over the lip of the trunk and stuffed his large hands beneath the armpits of the body. The carcass was of a nude young woman, seven days dead, and soggy and heavy on the bottom where her remaining bodily fluids had come to settle. Such was the way with dehydration. Brittle skin, sunken eyes, soggy underside. The reek of urine and feces so strong from the trunk, it made Santiago's eyes water, and he worked quickly to hoist the body from the trunk and let it spill to the rocky earth. The body was not heavy, but even the solitary act of lifting seemed to wear him out. He removed a small bladder bag from his belt loop, popped the cap, and delicately sipped some water. It felt good and cold and clean. He poured some into his cupped left hand, then proceeded to dampen his brow and the sweaty nape of his neck. Some water ran down his shirt collar, chilling him.

Displeased with the smell of the trunk, Santiago quickly slammed it shut. The sound seemed to echo out over the canyon and across the valley like a gunshot. Looking down at the pallid, emaciated ruin at his feet, still vaguely female even in such a state, he was again prodded by that dull, throbbing sense of failure.

Is it me? he couldn't help but wonder. It was not the first time. *Do none of them take because of me?*

Her breasts had flattened to her chest, the nipples like two graying dimples of flesh. The abrupt mound of her pubis, sparsely peppered with fine black hairs, reminded him of the kudzu and the underbrush that made up the floor of Chama River Canyon. Her legs clamped together in a fetal stiffness, his eyes running over the twisted and bony knobs of her knees, Santiago was suddenly and frighteningly overcome by the urge to *separate* those legs, force them apart, and resume the act once again—one last time—if only to regain some sort of personal composure, some sense of self-gratification and accomplishment. Had he failed *again?* And how long until he proved useless and the car—

No. He wouldn't think about that. Anyway, there was work to do.

Retrieving his tools from the Comet's back seat, Pablo Santiago carried them to a remote tract of land further down the canyon ridge. Here, the ground was mostly rock and sand, difficult and tedious for digging, but devoid of any foliage that might appear suspicious if uprooted. He knew this land well, had grown up knowing it, and recognized each individual sandstone flat like a man recognizes old friends in a photograph. He knew the slope of the valley, the stonier parts of the earth. He also knew where the other bodies were buried, all those pretty girls, and was careful to weave around these sacred places when walking to a fresh spot.

He selected an undisturbed spot of land and dug a shallow grave. The sun was hot on his back while he worked and his mind was occupied with the sound of the rushing river in the canyon below. A portage straight to the heart of the Rio Grande, Pablo Santiago was quietly enraptured by the unmitigated freedom of the river, immune from obligation and unconstrained by a lack of duty. Unlike the sedentary Comet, the river could be anywhere in the world given enough time. *Anywhere.* The notion fascinated Santiago, and several times he paused during his dig to lean on the carved wooden handle of his shovel and contemplate the enormity of such a thing.

It was getting on dusk when he returned to the Comet for the woman's body. Propping it over one immense shoulder, Santiago carried the corpse easily to the fresh hole in the earth. He could feel the presence of the car boring into his back as he laid the woman's body into the hole. While he filled the hole with dirt he was aware of the wind whistling and sighing through the rust-holes along the vehicle's chassis.

We are getting close now, he promised the Comet. *I can feel how close we are getting. It is only a matter of time. We must be patient. It will work out.*

He filled in the grave and raked over the disturbed soil. Then, with the tools slung over his shoulder, he hiked back to the car.

The driver's side door stood open. He did not remember leaving it open, but that didn't matter. With the Comet, such things were not unusual. Carefully, he replaced his tools in the Comet's back seat, then—after a long pause—slid into the driver's seat and pulled the door shut.

He sat in silence, staring at the filth-covered windshield. He had been doing this for many months now, and still he was not quite used to it. Had he discovered the car one afternoon while driving his truck down the main highway? No; it was impossible to see the car from the highway, particularly in the summer when the forestry was in bloom. Had he spotted it one evening while fishing near El Vado Lake Dam? No; the car was hidden from sight at such a distance. One would require the eyes of a hawk. So he could not remember how he had found the car, but he could guess that he was probably drawn to it somehow, beckoned, summoned, called to it. Somehow. And he had come.

He sat behind the Comet's steering wheel for a long time. The interior smelled like urine and blood and dirt and mildew. At times, in the stillness of the car, his mind dredged up the sounds of all the pretty girls he'd struggled with in the back seat. He'd lost count of the bodies, each one a failure, each one unworthy. Or was *he* unworthy? Was his *seed* unworthy?

No, he told himself. *I was chosen. How could I be unworthy if I was chosen?*

But perhaps the car made a mistake...

"God does not make mistakes," he said aloud. His voice sounded thick and deep in the confines of the car and he did not like it.

Through the filthy windshield he watched the sun set behind the dark brown crags. His eyelids felt lazy and he wanted to sleep. But work was not done. There would be no sleep until work—

A low, electrical hum filled the car. Santiago could both feel and hear it. He gripped the four-spoked steering wheel with two hands and squeezed tight. He could feel the current—faint but undeniably there—tracing up his arms. The dash lights flickered, flickered, glowed, and the radio dial bled an eerie green light onto Santiago's lap. Static hissed from the radio. Santiago watched as the dial spun on its own, the vertical red pin sliding left and right and left again as if attempting to locate a signal. The static grew louder, rattling the ancient speakers. Santiago could feel the current in his teeth now, his back teeth and the bones of his skull.

"Are you angry, Lord?" Santiago half-whispered, his eyes locked on the illuminated radio dial. "Do not be angry." The car's shaking caused his voice to vibrate. "She was not the right one. I will find the right one. I need more time."

The *shhh-shhh* of static.

"How many?" Santiago asked.

Shhh-shhh.

"That many? Already?" Had he really gone through six women in all this time? He'd lost count, but he hadn't thought the number was so high. It bothered him to think he'd failed so frequently.

"There will be more," he promised the car. "It is summer. There are always more."

The static grew louder.

"Tonight?" Santiago said. "I think..."

The dashboard lights flickered and the radio dial spun wildly.

"All right," promised Pablo Santiago, "I will find one tonight." Then, as an afterthought: "But it is getting *muy* risky. Soon, there will be many people asking many questions. Too many girls, the police will surely start looking at me. It is only a matter of time."

The car shuddered, the dashboard lights flickered. The radio grew louder and louder until it crested, then died completely. The flickering lights went out. The car was once again silent and still.

Pablo Santiago's god was a 1962 Mercury Comet.

* * *

It was dark when Santiago returned to the Monastery of Christ abbey deep in the canyon. He pulled his pickup truck down a rocky path, got out, and headed directly to the *casa del rio* where he was employed as groundskeeper for the retreat's guesthouses. In his small one-room shack, Santiago washed his face and drank a tall glass of water. The water was good and cold. There was some frozen river trout in an ice chest. He considered broiling some fish but decided he was not hungry. Instead, he pulled on a weather-worn anorak, crept out of the shack, and used a set of keys to gain entrance to the main lobby of the guesthouse. Here, he moved quietly down the hall and slipped through an access door that communicated with a large, darkened room. It was here that the inner-workings of the guesthouse had been in operation before the monastery changed over to solar power.

There were some tools here, and some items in unlabeled mason jars on shelves. Pablo Santiago went directly to a crowbar hanging from a pegboard, pulled it down, and carried it back into the guesthouse lobby.

There were many rooms here. From behind a number of doors he could hear the shrill din of laughter, unintentionally disrespectful to the cenobitic life of the Benedictine monks. These were tourists, were visitors, were people who paid their money to stay at the monastery and go fishing and hiking and canoeing. *Los intrusos,* many of the locals called them. There were many small villages throughout Chama River Canyon comprised of several generations of Hispanic immigrants. These were people who had worked the land and had lived off it since their forefathers crossed the Mexican border. There were many girls there, ripe enough for Santiago and his god, but none of his victims ever came from these villages, and not out of any sense of heritage or pride or respect but—simply—out of concern that he would be caught too quickly. It was easier to forget about strangers when they disappeared.

Using another key, Santiago gained access to one of these rooms. They were small rooms, with a bed and a single window beside the bed, an adjoining bathroom, a closet for hanging clothing, a dresser opposite the bed, and a mirror on the wall above the dresser. Also, a hand-carved wooden cross on the wall. Modest yet expensive rooms.

There was a suitcase on the bed but no one in the room. Still carrying the crowbar, Santiago slid open the closet door and stepped inside. Behind him, he pulled the door closed but not all the way, allowing a vertical sliver of space through which he could keep an eye on the room.

They are out looking for mountain lion, Pablo Santiago thought as he sat Indian-style on the carpeted floor of the closet. *And why not? They come here from big cities and pay good money to see them. It is not as if they see mountain lion every day.*

Pulling up the hood of the anorak, Pablo Santiago waited. He had patience much like the mountain lion.

*   *   *

What do you know?

Sound. And opening his eyes he was aware he'd fallen asleep. Or almost. But it did not take him any time to recall his surroundings: on the closet floor in one of the guestrooms. The noise that had woken him: the sound of the guestroom door opening. Also, the gay sound of drunken laughter.

These tourists, Santiago thought, peeking through the space in the closet door, *all they know to do is drink. Litter and spend their money and drink-drink-drink.* Los borrachos!

Two figures moved past the closet. Lights were turned on. More laughter. A man and a woman. He tried to see the woman but he could not see her face. She moved too quickly. The man, though—he was young and handsome and, Santiago thought, very white. As he sat crouched in their closet, he could hear bits and pieces of their conversation...

"I've never seen so much food," the very white man said. "And all the wine! Have you ever seen such wine?"

"I didn't think it would be this way at all," said the woman. Santiago still could not see her. "I didn't want to come but now I'm glad we're here."

Si, Santiago thought, *as am I.*

"It is beautiful here," the woman continued. She moved across the room and went to the suitcase on the bed. Santiago could see her back. She was tall and slender with a petite waist and long, dark hair. Wringing the crowbar between his hands, he could feel the crotch of his dungarees tightening.

"Beautiful," the man agreed, "but very dusty. It's on all my clothes."

"You complain," said the woman.

"I'm sorry."

"It's nothing. It's perfect. Go and shower and then I'll shower."

"Yes, you're right," the man said. "It *is* perfect." And he disappeared into the bathroom, closing the door behind him.

From where he sat, perched and anxious as if on a ledge, Pablo Santiago watched the woman cross the room and advance toward the mirror above the dresser. In her maneuvering, he caught a glimpse of her reflection in the glass. She was very beautiful.

Weren't they all? he thought, watching her. *Weren't they all pretty girls?*

The woman began fixing her hair in the mirror. The sound of running water could be heard from the bathroom. Then the man's low, baritone singing. This made the woman smile at her reflection. She removed her blouse and unhooked her bra, tossing the articles onto the bed. Her breasts were small and neat and pink. Santiago watched as she moved again to the suitcase, rummaged around for something, then went over to the single window beside the bed and pushed it open a few inches. Santiago heard the click of a lighter and saw a spark. The woman lit what appeared to be a joint, gave it three quick sucks, then exhaled through the open window.

Breathing heavy, Santiago managed to stand in the cramped closet space. Holding the crowbar in one hand, the seat of his dungarees pulling tighter and tighter, he slid open the closet door. It made no sound; groundskeeper Santiago was meticulous about oiling all hinges and tracks. He moved across the carpet slowly, familiar enough to avoid every groaning floorboard, listening to the soundtrack of the very white man singing in the shower. A few paces behind the woman, his shadow not yet on the wall beside her own (he was very conscious of this), Santiago felt that same sense of *drive* overtake him, quite similar to the feeling that rushed through his body when he had to pull his failures from the Comet's trunk...and very nearly the same as how he felt when overtaking them in the Comet's back seat...

But no—he was thinking too much ahead of himself and that was bad. To think ahead was to pay little attention to the present. And after six failures, as the Comet had reminded him, he could afford no more—

The woman sensed him, turned around, and stared for what must have been less than a second. Yet it seemed like an eternity, as it always did, and Pablo Santiago was able to examine the split ends of her hair, the broken blood vessels in her sclera, the knobs of gooseflesh that had broken out along her body, and the erect state of her nipples. And he sensed a scream rising up her throat—but not of fear, merely of surprise, of utter ridiculous and absurd surprise—and he raised the crowbar and brought it down across the upper right side of her head. It stunned her, rocked her head back on her neck, but did not knock her out. It *did* kill the scream, killing it even before it came, like an abortion. One hand went back and slapped a palm against the wall while her other hand dropped the joint on the bedspread. Before striking the woman again, Santiago carefully picked the joint off the bedspread and pinched the cherry dead, as to not start a fire. Too many fires had devastated the land over the years, and they all began very small and very harmless.

"What do you know, *mi* paramour?" Santiago whispered, and struck the woman a second time. This time, she went down.

Santiago wasted no time gathering the woman's supine body from the bedspread and arranging her over one shoulder as if she were a small Christmas tree and he a lumberjack. Still listening to the singing man in the shower, Santiago crossed the room, opened the door, and looked up and down the hallway. It was empty, but he need not walk the length of it; rather, he darted into a second doorway that connected with a long corridor used only in case of fires. The woman was very light on his shoulder as he hurried along and he thought that she was perfect, that she would be the one, and there would be no failure this time. God would be pleased.

At the end of the hallway, Santiago pushed through the exit and out into the freezing night. It is a misconception that nighttime in the desert is mild and pleasant. If Pablo Santiago had a quarter for every story he heard about someone freezing to death in the desert, he would be a very rich man.

Crossing the rocky tarmac with the woman over his shoulder, her skin now cold to the touch in the frigid night air, Santiago hurried around a copse of pines and headed without pause to his pickup parked outside his tiny shack. There, he quickly wrapped the woman's body in a piece of tarpaulin, tied it, and eased her down in the bed of the truck. Crawling behind the steering wheel, he then turned over the engine, pulled the transmission into reverse, and rolled slowly backward down the gravel drive. Only once he was back on the main highway that overlooked the canyon did he begin to relax. It could have taken him an hour or fifteen minutes to wrap the woman in the tarp—he could not remember. And was she number six or seven? Or was he just getting confused with the seven days he had to wait before opening the trunk again? Damn it, his mind was going on him. Old age creeping, the dirty devil.

The drive to the canyon ridge where the car sat waiting was lonely. Above, the moon was full and pearl-colored. The road below was bumpy and could prove treacherous at night. Many times Santiago had not seen a jagged rock or mule deer carcass in the dark and had blown a tire. Now, he rationalized, would be a poor time for flats.

Once he reached the clearing, Santiago drove the pickup right up to the ridge of the canyon. Outside, the sky was dense with stars. Santiago went directly to the truck bed and quickly unraveled the tarpaulin from the woman's body. As the cold night air struck the woman's bare chest, she began to stir and moan and flutter her eyes. She was bleeding badly from the gash at the side of her head. Santiago hoisted her from the bed and carried her in his arms to the silent and brooding Mercury Comet. It looked smarter in the dark, the car, as if it had set aside all pretenses and fakery used to manipulate Santiago in the daylight. Now, in the dark, there was no need for such formalities. In the dark, things were what they were.

The woman began forming words just as Santiago slid her into the Comet's back seat. Hunching into the car himself, he planted one foot down on the business end of the shovel and the handle shot up and thudded against the roof of the car, startling him. Then he laughed nervously and pulled the tools from the car and set them against a tree. *Muy estupido.* It wasn't the first time that had happened.

Strewn out along the back seats, the woman brought a hand up to her face, her head. She was still moaning but was making no sense. Santiago knew he would have to be quick if it was to be easiest, and he leaned forward and proceeded to unbuckle her slacks. He tugged them off her hips, along with her underwear, and bent to remove her shoes—and saw that one of her shoes was missing. Surely she had been wearing both shoes when he carried her from the retreat, yes?

Not now, he thought. *Now is time for action, not thought. There will be plenty of time to think about things later.*

Yanking the remaining clothes from her body, Pablo Santiago remained poised and motionless above the woman, breathing deeply, his eyes creeping along her flesh. There was a sweetness to this act still, and that at least made it bearable, but there was also that goddamn *drive,* too, and that was now burning up inside him. Again, he could feel himself swelling inside his dungarees. The woman—her body was gorgeous and white and smooth and pink and perfect and firm and he could see the tiny faded scars along her blue-tinted flesh and the smattering of freckles and the fine white hairs covering her breasts and her belly, and the soft downy mat of dark hair between her thighs, and the gradual incline and *receive* of her legs and the way they bent and straightened and looked blue and white and perfect in the moonlight filtering through the dirty rear windshield.

Breathing heavy, struggling now with his own pants, Pablo Santiago said, "You may consider a retreat for your personal gratification. We are not beyond compassion. God is love." He had spoken these words many times before. "I recommend summoning the image of the great and mighty mule deer, dark and stunning and graceful and mysterious in nature." He'd had time to rehearse these words. "The mule deer is a powerful animal and is capable of many great things, *pero* the mule deer is also a gentle and serene animal who favors nature and peace."

His zipper undone, Pablo Santiago separated his victim's legs and forced himself between them. Beneath him, he felt the woman's body go stiff and knew she was about to start screaming, but that didn't matter out here. No one would hear her, not for miles. Just him. And God.

He continued, "The mule deer of this habitat run with a series of distinct leaps and bounds. This is called 'stotting,' and," he went on, his breathing labored now, his actions muddying his thoughts, "and...and this is significant because it is typical only of mule deer from...*from...*"

The car began to hum beneath him and just as he felt his seed lurch from him, completing the act, the car's radio came instantly to life, hissing and spitting with static. Eyes pressed closed, Santiago could hear nothing but that hissing *shhh-shhh* of static and the shrieks from the struggling woman pinned beneath his great weight. And he could feel nothing but the hum of the vehicle all around him and the wasted, shriveled sensation of release.

The woman screamed.

"What do you know?" Pablo Santiago shouted back. "Just tell me what you know!"

He dragged her from the car. She was kicking and struggling and moaning now, but her struggles were without power. The two blows she'd received from the crowbar had knocked something loose in her head, Santiago assumed. That, too, had happened before.

With little difficulty he carried her to the rear of the vehicle. The cold night air now felt good against Santiago's skin, freezing the sweat on his body. The Comet's trunk stood open. Santiago had not opened it. Sometimes this happened and sometimes it did not. It didn't matter now, anyway.

Santiago lifted the slumped and struggling woman up over the lip of the Comet's trunk and let her fall into the gaping black maw. Again he was accosted with the ripe, fetid smell of the trunk's interior. *Maybe not all of them have died from heat or cold or starvation,* Santiago thought now. *Maybe at least one died from that smell.*

But there would be no dying this time. This time, there would be no failure. He would see. After seven days, he would see.

Pablo Santiago slammed the trunk closed with the nude woman inside and remained with both his palms planted to the top of the trunk, motionless, for some time. Closing his eyes, he could still feel the vehicle humming beneath his palms, electrical currents juicing up his arms. He did not like to feel this, did not like to think of this. Instead, he thought of the river trout and the way they often swallowed lures and hooks and, most often, all the bait. There were nice size trout in the river, Santiago knew. He'd fished it for many years and the river had been kind to him and he, in turn, had remained true to the river.

He righted himself, gathering his tools, and piled them in the back seat of the Comet. Then, sitting behind the steering wheel, he said, "This time, my Lord, will be the time. I make these promises," he explained to the car, "because I know this to be true in *el corazón.*"

The car did not respond. All Santiago could hear was the muffled sobs and relentless pounding coming from the Comet's trunk. Such sounds hurt his ears. How at ease he would feel once his God was finally sated.

This time, he promised himself now, *this time. No more because it will be this time.*

* * *

He knew what to expect upon returning to the abbey. There were two police cruisers outside, their lights flashing, and many *policía* inside the monastery. This did little to disturb the composure of Pablo Santiago, and only when a policeman spoke his name did he look up at all.

"Pablo Santiago?" The policeman was young and hungry-looking, in the way most black bears get when they are late in hibernating and cannot find food. "Sir?"

"Yes," Santiago said, pausing just outside the circle of people in the lobby. He recognized the very white man among the *policía* and did not like the determined, frightened look on the pale man's pale face.

"I would like to have some words with you."

So this is how it ends? Santiago thought. He said, "What is this that has happened?"

"There has been another abduction," the officer said. "A young woman was attacked and taken from one of the rooms. I would like to discuss this matter with you."

"All right," Santiago said amiably enough. "Would you like I wait in my room?"

"You can wait here, please," the officer said, and that was when the very white man began shouting, shouting and pointing, and all of the officers and many of the monks and patrons who had gathered in the lobby all turned to look, and their eyes all came to rest on Pablo Santiago. Devout groundskeeper Santiago.

Although they all stared, no one—not even the police—seemed to understand what they were staring at until the very white man, in a hoarse and strained voice, shouted, "That shoe! That shoe! This is my Isabel's shoe!"

So Pablo Santiago followed their eyes and looked down and, sure enough, the woman's missing shoe had somehow managed to hook itself into one of the many loops of Santiago's work belt.

"Well," Santiago said, "I suppose you have found what you have found."

* * *

Chief of Police Tomás Barrera, looking quite dark and young and upset, entered the interrogation room and sat down at the table opposite Pablo Santiago. Santiago, in cuffs, looked up from the tabletop and smiled at Tomás Barrera.

"Your father and I," Santiago said, "we grew up on this land together. Your father was a good man, Tomás. I miss him now that he is dead."

"Mr. Santiago," Tomás Barrera began, "I have my men down at the car now. They have opened the trunk and they have started digging in the flats for the bodies. You have cooperated thus far, Mr. Santiago, and it may do you more good to cooperate further."

"I have told you," Santiago said, "I refuse to go back there. You have caught me and I have given up my God, but I cannot go back there and I will not show you the bodies. I have explained where they are buried and if your men are good diggers and hard workers, they will find them all."

"And how many will we find, Mr. Santiago?"

"*Seis.*"

"English, please," said Tomás Barrera. "This is not Mexico."

"Six," Santiago repeated. He did not tell the young officer that he was uncertain about the number.

"Why did you do this?"

"I have come to know things," Santiago said. "That is why."

"What do you know?" Tomás Barrera said.

"What I have found."

"And what have you found, Mr. Santiago?"

"*El Dios,*" said Santiago. "God."

"Is that so?"

"I have learned," Santiago said, "that God is always looking for a way to speak with us, Tomás Barrera. There are many ways but most times, people do not listen. Maybe it is true that I happened to be listening one day, and there is His voice for me to hear. God, He comes in any form, from the burning bush to the modern automobile. We have to be aware, Tomás Barrera. That is all."

"You raped those women and locked them in the trunk," the young officer said.

"It was God's will," Santiago explained. "We are now in preparation for the Second Coming of Christ. He will return as before in the womb of a young woman, a union of human seed and human egg. You do not understand, Tomás Barrera, that it was my job to select all the pretty girls and offer my seed. If it is as it should be, God will take the girl in her pregnancy and raise her in one of the many depths of purgatory. After seven days, God will decide whether He approves of my selection, my donation. He may then take the girl or leave her to die."

"In the trunk of the car," Tomás Barrera finished.

"What is a trunk?" Santiago said. "What is a car?" Clearing his throat, he continued, "Unfortunately, He has yet to approve of my selections. But this last time..." Santiago's voice rose a notch. "May I ask a question?"

"What is it?"

"When you opened the trunk tonight, what did you find?"

"I think you know what we found."

"I do not," said Santiago. "Do you not understand the words I've just spoken?"

"Isabel Fitzgerald was in the trunk, Mr. Santiago," Tomás Barrera said. "She was in the trunk dead and raped and half-frozen."

"Oh." There was no expression on Santiago's face. "She died quick. Was it the head injury?"

"Asphyxiation. She suffocated in the trunk."

"Well," Santiago said with mild interest, "that had never occurred to me."

Tomás Barrera stood and moved toward the door.

"Wait," Santiago said, and the young officer paused. "You must keep her in the trunk undisturbed for seven days. She is the one and the mission has been completed. You cannot remove her, or this will have to be done all over again."

"She has been removed," Tomás Barrera said coldly. "Anything else?"

"No," Pablo Santiago said, looking back down at the table. "Except, this has been most ignoble for me. Sitting here like this with chains on my wrists..." Santiago's eyes unfocused and for a moment it looked as though he had fallen into a deep sleep. Then, before Tomás Barrera could leave the room, Santiago said, "Yes, I think it would have been much better to go over the cliff like the black bear. Don't you agree?"

Tomás Barrera said nothing.

* * *

Cold, dark, late, and Chief of Police Tomás Barrera walked along the sandstone flat high above the canyon. Above him burned high-intensity fluorescent lights, stretching his shadow out along the scrub land and over the edge of the cliff. Around him, many men worked with high-powered drilling equipment to exhume Pablo Santiago's victims.

Finishing a cigarette, Barrera approached Officer Andy Lopez, who was crouched on his hams with a flashlight peering into one of the shallow graves.

"How many we got so far?" Barrera asked.

"Well, either Santiago was lying or just couldn't remember, but we got about seventeen corpses so far. All young girls."

Barrera thought he misheard the man. "For serious?"

"This summer only about three girls have gone missing, two of which were staying at the monastery. All these other girls—Christ, the guy must have been traveling and picking them up across the state."

"Seventeen?" Barrera heard himself repeat.

"What a mess," Officer Lopez muttered.

Slipping his hands inside his nylon coat, Barrera trudged through the underbrush back toward the highway, breathing in the cool, crisp night air. The dark, swarthy shape of the Mercury Comet, half-hidden in a copse of firs, caught his attention, and he headed over to it. Ran two fingers across its hood. Tomorrow morning, he would have a truck sent from the city to haul the thing away. *How in the world did you even get here?* he wondered, moving around to the driver's door. Cupping his hands about his face, he peered through the filthy glass into the car. With one hand he opened the door...and caught a whiff of ancient soil and blood and something stronger, more pungent, that reminded him of barnyards and cow shit.

Carefully, delicately, Tomás Barrera entered the vehicle and situated himself behind the steering wheel. He fingered the steering column, the horn ring, ran his palm along the dusty lip of the dashboard. Looking down, he noticed the radio dial beside his right knee. He jiggled the knobs, turning them, spinning the dial. Smiled. His father used to have a car like this. Not a Comet, but an old Mustang. And weren't all those old cars the same, anyway?

Officer Lopez turned his flashlight on Barrera's face. Wincing, Barrera waved him away.

"You been in there for over an hour," Lopez said. "Want me to call your wife and tell her you moved out?"

"Over an hour?" Barrera muttered. "What time is it?"

"After midnight."

"Jesus Christ."

"Something wrong, Chief?"

After a moment, Tomás Barrera shook his head and climbed out of the car. A weak sigh escaped him when Lopez slammed the door shut.

"One hell of a mess," Lopez said, hands on his hips. He was looking out over the darkened rim of the canyon. Below, the rush of the river was easily heard. "You want I should get a tow truck up here to take this piece of junk away?"

"No," Barrera said, and he thought the words came from his mouth too quickly. Unlike Andy Lopez, he could not take his eyes from the Comet. "Don't worry about it," he said finally. "I'll take care of it."

Officer Andy Lopez shrugged. "Suit yourself," he said, and headed through the ponderosa pines in the direction of the highway.

The shelling started. It shook the ground and many men rolled in the muddy ditch between the flats and the giant stone wall. Some were all right. The wall was very large and looked strong but would not provide much protection against the shelling. Further ahead, pressed low in the grass, I could see Omar with his head down and his hands laced together at the back of his helmet. He looked very dark and small pressed into the grass. He did not move. I thought of the men that had gone down during the march, ambushed by soldiers pressed against the flanks of the high road, and I found I could not take my eyes away from Omar. Even when a shell exploded just several yards to my left, I could not take my eyes from him.

Closing In

The hotel room was small, colorless, practically nondescript. Collie Burgess entered in a huff, tossing his duffel bag on the single bed, and immediately bolted the door. The room was dark, sunlight at the single window across the room obscured by a swipe of heavy curtains. Collie flicked the light switch beside the door, but the lights did not come on.

"Perfect."

Lifting up his sweatshirt, which reeked of sweat and was caked in hardening mud, he pulled the Glock from his waistband, ejected the magazine, and popped the extra round from the chamber. Then he unzipped the duffel bag and retrieved from it fresh clothing: a folded pair of jeans, clean underwear and socks, a Miller Lite t-shirt, and a button-down chambray work shirt. He buried the Glock and the magazine in the duffel bag, covering the items up with a section of last week's newspaper.

Briefly, he stood in the center of the room, his hands on his hips, his breath rattling his lungs. He could smell the grime on his filthy flesh—the smell of topsoil, of muddy trenches and human degradation. A shower. He could use a good, long, hot shower.

There was a television remote on the small table beneath the shaded window, resting beside an ancient rotary phone. Collie scooped up the remote and, aiming the device at the television set housed in a credenza facing the bed, prodded the power button repeatedly. Like the lights, the TV did not turn on.

"Piece of shit."

Setting the remote back on the table, Collie pulled back the curtain and peered out the window at the industrial ramparts and fire-blackened tenements below. Beyond, the sky was the color of sawdust, the sun a dwindling red ember sinking below the crenellated outline of the city.

Collie pulled the chair out from the table, banging it against the wall—the room was that small—and produced a slip of curled paper from the rear pocket of his dirt-caked jeans. Dropping down in the chair, Collie unfurled the paper and, picking up the telephone, dialed the number that had been scrawled in Maggio's childish handwriting.

On the other end of the line, the phone rang at least a dozen times before Dominic Maggio picked up. "H'lo," Maggio growled in his typical disinterested tone.

"It's Collie."

"Where you at?"

"A hotel." He knew better than to give Maggio anything more specific. Not that Collie was afraid of Dominic Maggio, the fat little fuck. Collie towered over the son of a bitch by a good fourteen inches, and he could probably bench-press the bastard one-handed. Still, he'd learned quickly in this business that the less anyone knew about you—or your whereabouts—the better.

"How'd it go?" Maggio said. He was eating something, his voice garbled, and Collie could hear car horns bleating in the background.

"It's done."

"Any difficulties?"

"None."

"And the car?"

"Traded it in outside the county line. Switched the plates."

"Yeah?" Maggio seemed impressed by Collie's ingenuity. "Good deal, man. You need anything else?"

"The money?"

"It's being delivered as we speak," Maggio said. "As promised."

Collie glanced at his wristwatch. It was 4:52 p.m. "I'm gonna call Leo in ten minutes."

Maggio chuckled—a pathetic, wheezing sound that concluded in a series of sputtering coughs. "What's the matter, Collie? You don't trust me no more?"

"That would imply that I've trusted you in the past." His fingers were filthy, black crescents of dirt under each fingernail. "Nothing personal."

Collie hung up. He sat for several moments, drumming his dirty fingers on the tabletop, before picking up the telephone again and dialing zero.

"Front desk." A woman's voice, annoyingly nasal.

"Yeah," Collie said, "this is Room 218. My TV ain't working."

"Is it plugged in, sir?"

From where he sat he could see the plug snaking out from behind the credenza where it fit into the wall socket.

"Of course," he said. "Also, the lights don't work."

"What lights?"

"The room lights."

"All of them?" The woman sounded distant and uninterested.

Collie glanced around. Other than the frosted dome ceiling fixture, he couldn't see any other lights. Not even a lamp on the nightstand beside the bed.

"Yeah," he said. "All of them." He had no interest in dragging this conversation on any longer than it needed to be.

"We'll send someone up in the next ten minutes, sir."

Again, he glanced at his watch. It would give him enough time to grab a shower and clean up, then call Leo to make sure Maggio kept his word about the money.

Hanging up the phone, he scooted the chair away from the table—it banged against the wall at his back—and eased open the bathroom door. Ironically, the bathroom light worked just fine, although the bathroom itself was so egregiously filthy and unattended that he wished it hadn't. The shower head was angry with rust and it looked like someone had recently whipped up a chocolate cake in the toilet. Collie turned on the water, which came chugging through the pipes and resounded in the walls, and let the tub clean itself out before he stripped from his clothes and crawled beneath the lukewarm spray.

While he washed, he thought about the man named Tom Browning, whom he'd murdered no longer than two hours ago. Tom Browning, who'd cried like a baby near the end. The whole drive out beyond the city, bound by ropes in the backseat of the car, the bastard had insisted he knew nothing about Maggio's money. It wasn't until Collie pulled off onto a dirt roadway that cut first through a swath of trees then alongside a field of overgrown bluegrass did Browning start peppering him with questions. Trembling, his voice screechy like a poorly tuned violin, Tom Browning began talking too fast from the backseat—where were they, what was going on, and for the love of God didn't Collie believe him about the money?

"We're getting out," was all Collie had said. He climbed out of the car—one of Maggio's Lincolns—and popped open the rear door. Browning slid out and collapsed onto the ground, his hands and ankles still lashed together.

"Collie—Collie, man—please—*please*—"

"Stop fucking whining, Tom."

When he produced a boning knife from his boot, Tom Browning made a wet, choking sound in the back of his throat. And when Collie bent down toward him, Browning cringed. Collie merely cut away the ropes from Browning's wrists and ankles.

"Up," Collie said, replacing the knife with his Glock, which he directed down at the trembling, blubbering man on the ground.

"Collie, *please*—"

"Get up, Tom. I'm through fucking around."

It wasn't until Collie started walking the man across the field, the gun at his back, did Tom Browning admit he still had Maggio's money. Like Niagara Falls, it poured out of him between sobs and hitching shoulders. And by the time they reached the excavated hole in the ground, Browning was crying freely.

"I'm sorry. I shouldn't have tried to rip him off," Browning managed through his tears. "Tell Maggio, man. Tell him for me. Let him know. Let him know just how—"

Collie shot him in the left thigh. Tom Browning's cries caused a great cloud of birds to burst from a distant tree and take off into the gunmetal sky.

Disgusted, Collie had driven one boot into Browning's haunches. The man crumpled into the hole in the ground with a sickening, hollow thump.

"Collie!"

He tucked the gun back into his waistband and fished a shovel out from under the dense underbrush, where he had hidden it earlier that afternoon, after digging the grave.

While Tom Browning screamed and writhed in the hole, Collie began shoveling dirt onto him.

"Collie, man—please—no! No!"

Soon enough, Tom Browning's screams died off.

Now, beneath the shuddering stream of the shower, Collie rinsed the dirt and grime out of his hair and off his flesh.

Then the lights went out.

Collie froze. Was it the hotel's maintenance guy fooling with the circuitry?

"Hello?" he called. No one answered.

He shut off the water and wrapped a towel around his waist. Back out in the room, Collie expected to find someone in a tool belt fiddling with the electrical outlets, but the room was empty. And dark.

Collie dressed quickly in his clean clothes, pulling his wet hair back and tying it in a ponytail. Then he scooped the TV remote off the table and hammered the power button with his thumb over and over again, to no avail.

Suddenly feeling like an idiot, he realized it could just be the remote. He went to the TV itself and hit the power button. The TV did not turn on. Again, Collie struck the button, more forceful this time.

"What the hell...?"

The plastic panel beneath the screen now held the impression of his thumb. Reaching out, Collie pushed his index finger against the plastic housing of the TV set...and it indented like cheap plastic under the pressure. He tapped the screen to find it made not of a solid glass, vacuum-sealed tube, but of flimsy plastic coated in a sheen of reflective solvent so that it resembled glass.

The fucking thing was *fake*.

Reaching into the credenza, he grabbed the fake TV on either side and yanked it out of the unit. It withdrew without resistance, the plug popping right out of the wall. Practically weightless, Collie flung the hollow plastic box onto the bed. It was no different than the cardboard appliances used as set dressing in department stores.

He couldn't help it. Collie uttered a laugh.

He went to the phone, first to call the front desk and commend them on their little practical joke, then—more importantly—to phone Leo and make sure Maggio delivered the money. But unlike before, this time when he brought the telephone to his ear, he heard no dial tone. Perplexed, Collie jabbed at the cradle but could not locate a dial tone. Chewing at his lower lip, he gradually pushed down against the cradle with more and more force. The thing bent under his finger, creasing. It was made of the same cheap plastic as the phony television set.

But how is that possible? I've already used the phone...

He lifted the phone—it was practically weightless—and turned it upside down to examine the guts.

There *were* no guts.

The telephone was a hollow shell.

Okay, he thought, setting the phone back down. *What is this bullshit going on? Somebody fucking with me?*

This was no longer funny.

He dropped down onto the edge of the bed and climbed into his boots. He'd go back down to the lobby and demand to know just what the hell was going on. If it was some sort of elaborate joke, they'd picked the wrong son of a bitch. And he'd already used the phone, so someone must have crept in here while he was showering to replace it with the fake one...

Collie froze. He felt his bowels clench. For several seconds he couldn't comprehend what he was seeing...or, more specifically, what he was *not* seeing.

The hotel room door was gone.

No, not just removed, pried from the hinges, leaving in its absence a rectangular portal that looked out onto the second-floor hallway. No—the door was *gone*, and there was nothing left behind but an unmarred panel of drywall. As if the doorway had never existed.

Motionless, Collie sat and stared at the wall for what seemed like an eternity. His mind was blank with confusion. Minutes or hours could have passed.

Beginning to sweat, Collie eventually eased up off the bed. The fake TV rolled soundlessly onto the floor. He went to the blank spot on the wall where the doorway had been—where it *should* have been—and stared at it in disbelief. He reached up and touched the wall, feeling for seams that were not there, searching for evidence of trickery in the sheetrock. But nothing...nothing...

Can't be. No way.

He stepped away from the wall, scrutinizing the wainscoting, the trim along the floor. The TV and phone were one thing—items easily manipulated—but the fucking *door...*?

"Hey!" His voice echoed in the small room. "Hey! Hello?" He banged a fist on the wall—the spot where the doorway had been and *should* have been.

Temper rising, he turned away from the wall, running his hands over his hair, trying desperately to shake reality back into place.

Across the room, the bathroom had vanished. He stood facing another plain, blank wall.

No fucking way. I was just in there.

"Okay, okay, okay." He dropped back down on the bed. The springs squealed. "Get a grip, man. Get a hold of yourself."

Panic strummed freely through him now. He kept trying to think of the simplest explanation, the simple little thing he had so obviously overlooked, the thing that would explain away this whole mess. Drugs? Hallucinatory flashbacks? Truth was, he hadn't smoked a joint in over a month, and hadn't done anything harder than pot in seven or eight years.

"Help!" He lashed his foot out and kicked the credenza. "Anyone hear me? Hello? Any—"

He jerked his head to the window. The curtain was drawn but he could still see a glimpse of fading daylight through the purse in the fabric. Launching himself off the bed, he nearly flung himself at the window, swiping away the curtains...only to discover, with unfathomable horror, *that the window was no longer there.* Taped to the wall behind the curtain was a poster of a tropical island beach, crystal clear waters and palm trees bowing across the flaming disc of the sun. *Visit Hawaii,* it said in neon script at the bottom.

"What...the..." The words stuck to the roof of his mouth. He slammed both hands against the poster, hoping without faith that it would tear away and his hands would break through the glass on the other side. But there was nothing but solid wall on the other side of the poster. Frantically, Collie tore down the poster, balling it up in his fists, revealing more and more wall with each strip he tore away, his horror mounting with each exposed section of wall.

Shuddering, he dropped the crumpled bits of poster to the floor. "Think this through, think this through...there's gotta be some...some explanation..."

But what was it?

He took a step backward then, only to trip over the corner of the bed and topple to the floor. Rolling over, he noticed the bed had shifted away from the wall...as if to creep up on him, as if to attack...

But no—not only was that utterly absurd, it wasn't even *true,* because the far side of the bed was still against the wall. Which meant the bed hadn't moved.

Which meant the walls were closing in.

Okay. Stop. Wait. His thoughts coming in Morse code. *Let's not lose it completely. Let's not start thinking the fucking walls are closing in. You've just been stressed lately. That's all this is. Stress. Overworked. What you need is to get a good night's sleep then think about taking a vacation. A cruise, maybe. Ten days in the Caribbean.*

But thinking of the Caribbean made him think of the *Visit Hawaii* poster, which caused fresh panic to rise up in him. He found it suddenly difficult to breathe, the air claustrophobic and unventilated, stagnant—

Ventilation, he thought. *Air vents.*

There was a narrow iron grate in the ceiling. Trembling, Collie fished around in his duffel bag until he located his knife. Then he dragged the desk chair directly beneath the vent, and stood on it. Holding one hand over the grate, he could feel no air—hot nor cold—coming through.

"Hey!" he shouted into it. "Anyone!" His voice was flat, toneless. There was no echo.

No. Please, no…

Hand shaking, it took him several attempts to fumble the screws out of the vent plate with the knife blade. Finally, the iron covering fell away, rebounding off the chair and thumping solidly to the carpet. What he hoped to find, of course, was a darkened, insulated channel of ductwork. But what he found was simply a rectangle recessed about an inch and a half into the ceiling, the inlaid portion painted black.

Defeated, Collie practically melted off the chair. To his increasing horror, he found that the room had become even smaller in the minute or so he'd been up on the chair: the foot of the bed was nearly touching the credenza now, and there was no more room between the wall and the table for Collie to slide the desk chair back from where he got it. Even the ceiling seemed closer to the top of his head, as if it had lowered itself a couple of inches…or perhaps the floor had risen beneath him?

Damn it, if only he had—

He had a gun.

"Shit, yeah," he nearly growled. The hint of a smirk overtook his features. "Fucking *blow* my way out."

Somehow, they'd managed to fuck with him and seal up the door and the window. But the goddamn *hallway* was still there, just on the other side of the wall. Surely—

Not wasting any more time, he pulled the handgun and the magazine from the duffel bag. He slammed the mag into the hilt then chambered a round. Clasping the gun with both hands, he stood directly opposite the spot on the wall where the door had been and leveled the gun.

He fired one hesitant round. In the close quarters, the sound was nearly deafening. Tasting cordite on the roof of his mouth, he squinted at the dime-sized hole in the drywall. A colorless tendril of smoke unfurled from it, wafting toward the ceiling. He'd hoped to see a beam of hallway light pierce through the bullet hole. But that was not the case. Leaning forward, still squinting, Collie could see only darkness. With one finger, he chipped away bits of plaster until a perfect square inch of what was—*impossibly*—a wall of steel revealed itself to him. Embedded in it was the bullet.

A sinking resignation overtook him. Suddenly, the handgun weighed a thousand pounds, drawing Collie's arm down toward the floor.

"Fuck it," he muttered, tossing the gun onto the bed. The bed, of course, was closer to him than before. In fact, the foot of the bed was pressed firmly against the credenza now; Collie would have to crawl over the bed to get to the other side of the room now, if he'd wanted—

However, there no longer appeared to *be* another side of the room: the table and fake telephone no longer existed, the walls flushed up against each side of the bed.

Shaking, bleary-eyed, Collie glanced up. The ceiling had drawn even closer. Haltingly, Collie brought up one hand and, without even having to fully extend his arm, was able to touch the ceiling. As if shocked by electrical current, he recoiled and buried his hand under one sweaty armpit.

A sound erupted from him—a strangled "Uh!"—and his legs suddenly gave out. He collapsed to the floor, the wall shoving against his back and shoulders, the bed encroaching on his knees. He pulled his legs up under him, suddenly able to *feel* the walls creeping closer and closer, closing in on him, suffocating him. He did not have to lean forward much at all to grab hold of the handgun on the bed. With a shaking hand, he brought the gun to his temple and squeezed his eyes shut. Hot tears slid down his cheeks. Eyes closed, he imagined he could actually *hear* the walls closing in—a vague shushing susurration, like sandpaper grazing along a deck railing.

Collie pulled the trigger...and the gun's handle crumpled under the force, another fake plastic prop.

He startled himself by laughing, and chucked the useless gun only a few feet until it struck the far wall and dropped down behind the bed.

None of this is real, none of this is real, none of this is real—

He climbed up onto the bed, having to stoop slightly so that he wouldn't graze his head on the ceiling. He crawled to the center of the bed and, folding his hands atop his chest, blinked the tears from his eyes. The ceiling was a mere two feet from pressing down on his nose. Every corner of the bed was buckling now, the walls drawing in all around it, the bedsprings creaking and groaning and sounding like the inner workings of some giant clock coming undone. Directly above, the ceiling descended in almost imperceptible increments. Then it grew too dark for him to see anything at all.

Collie Burgess began to laugh. He brought his hands up and pressed both palms flat against the ceiling. The wall at the foot of the bed came up to greet the soles of Collie's boots while the bed's headboard put pressure on the crown of his skull. Still laughing uncontrollably, tears spilling hotly down his face, he pounded his fists against the ceiling and kicked his boots against the wall. A second later, he could no longer keep his legs straight...but the ceiling was too low now for him to bend them at the knees. A reverse pushup, the ceiling pressed his elbows down into the mattress, the plaster pressing down against the tip of his nose. The headboard began to splinter...then, distantly, something else cracked.

Collie Burgess screamed into the ceiling, his breath coming right back into his face like exhaust. He felt his knees press firmly into the ceiling, the pressure—the pressure—

Restrained, confined, he suddenly could not move. The sound of his heartbeat suddenly all he could hear, he willed himself to think of wide open spaces—of fields of bluegrass and the unfettered vastness of Caribbean beaches. But in the end, all he could think of were graves.

UNDERNEATH

Many years ago, toiling for some time beneath the weight of creation, a momentary, self-loathing lapse in my own judgment, coupled with the despair of countless failures, caused me to summon him, birth him, afford him a name and a purpose: a Frankenstein pseudonym whose passion and creativity, along with his prolific nature, were frighteningly alien to me, though whose handwriting was more than just a sheer mimicry of my own. Never did I anticipate the final outcome—the resentment laced with irony; the justified sense of personal failure in the wake of unmitigated success; the torment—on the day of his summoning. Throughout the decades and as the success mounted—as the fame rose to proportions dreamt of by starry-eyed young girls in pink gowns and glittered, bejeweled tiaras—we orchestrated a dance, commingling like brothers jumping from book to subsequent book, or like enemies—yes, enemies!—conspiring to work together for the sake and gratification of their individual wants and desires, hopes and dreams, prisoners orchestrating an escape. In the periods between projects, he would vanish, would retreat to the underneath of things—of my life—and float like a shadow through which the motes of ancient dust could pass. And there he would stay until summoned by me, over and over again, to put my words to paper.

Yet now, in my old age, and despite the security of wealth and fashionable circumstance, he visited one last time, and for once without pretense.

Cloaked in the fragrant vapors of nonexistence, he wisped into the room, the worn and cracking soles of his old shoes whispering on the hardwood—a familiar cadence. He was slightly stooped from decades slaving over notebooks and typewriters, his long white fingers fat at the knuckles, aching almost audibly with each creaking flex and bend of their tendons, snapping and popping, settling and unsettling. His face was mine, of course, but it was a withered albino impression of my own darker, healthier features. Had we been twin brothers clambering through childhood, faceless mothers would have whispered about the cruel discretion of God to grant one child with color and life, the other a carbon imprint of his more fortunate sibling. About him wafted the stale scent of sacrifice, of ancient dust and fallen cobwebs gathered like epaulettes on the shoulders of his greatcoat, and that same sacrifice, I could see, echoed in his sad, hurtful eyes.

All these years of believing he'd stolen from me, was it really the other way around?

With a slight agitation of his features, he glanced upward and around, where his name teemed now from the bookshelves, embossed along the brittle spines in gold stamping, testament not just to the depths of his creativity but my own years of success donning his cloak. He executed a flourish with one hand, as if to bring the books to my attention or, perhaps, to address the books themselves. But his eyes turned from them and, on a creaking, pivoting neck, he leveled his gaze back on me. In his pupils burned the accumulation of years of torment, turmoil boiling over like hot pots, a hammer slamming coldly against the dented face of a Chinese gong.

Here I was, a thief facing my accuser...yet the accuser owed me just as much as I owed him, forging between us and through the strands of deceit and tension a sinewy bond, a union of sorts, that resonated simultaneously throughout both our beings like the amplified plucking of a single bass note. So it was inevitable we would jab accusatory fingers at each other, which we did simultaneously, both victims and victimizers alike. Yet the hardship of our lifelong union, to my shock, appeared more profound on him: in his stooped posture and pale, ghost-white face, the sunken, sullen features, that relentless banging behind those steely eyes. How I had laid awake nights, sweating his success, hating his name as it appeared on the title page of every word I had written! A name I had given him! A life I had granted him!

But, oh, what life? To be extracted from a crypt on the occasions my muse was restless, forced—strapped and chained, slave-like—to a worktable, pen in hand, scribbling words upon words upon words at my insistence, at my will? A creature devised from nothingness to vault me to financial success while I stood on his worsening, weakening, bowing shoulders. Suddenly, and for the first time in my life, I saw him from a different angle. How foolish I'd been to be jealous of this man! How ridiculous I'd been to begrudge him his fame! Did we both not cultivate calluses on our index fingers after hours of furious scribbling? Did we both not sigh in mutual relief at the completion of a tale, knowing there was one less story in the world waiting to be told? In short—did it not take both of us to complete each work? We were nothing without each other.

Suddenly, surprising myself, I found I pitied this man standing here before me, dull as bone, futile as a flicker of projected light. After all, he had afforded me wealth beyond my own adolescent expectations, expensive chrome-rimmed automobiles and houses of grotesque elaborateness situated in lavish parts of the world. Likewise, his fame—his name—had seen to it that I'd married not once, not twice, but three times, the totality of them all so beautiful and young, eager women eager to wait on my every desire...while all the while he—this man!—skulked in the darkness of closets, was dispatched to the dampness of basements, stowed away like cargo underneath it all. His foil-stamped name on a lifework of dust-jackets was his only achievement, his only happiness, and I, like the fool, had spent just as long a lifetime resenting the success I'd bestowed upon him! My hands accepting the money and awards, my back accommodating the numerous claps of praise and accolades while I feasted and indulged at dinners and commencements and various other noteworthy engagements in his honor. His name and his fame for my wealth and wellbeing: a tradeoff.

He did not choose this burden; rather, I'd placed it on his shoulders, giving him form lest he disintegrate into particles of dust beneath such weight, giving him hands with which to write alongside my own, and a studious face, black-pitch eyes, cherry-hued pockets filled not with coin—for all his money was mine—but with dust, bone-dust. Ah, that this nonexistent entity could cause me such grief, such anxiety, such contempt throughout my life!

His eyes, as soulless and inanimate as the inks used to line every handwritten page over the years, rolled again in my direction, a feeling of utter despair rising up through me like steam. He motioned me to take position at the writing table, a table we had shared throughout the years, never meeting each other's gaze nor speaking aloud (for speaking aloud was pointless—we lived and thrived in each other's head). I creaked along the floorboards, my old age cold upon me, the taxing, unyielding flex of my prehistoric bones like the corrosion of oxidized copper. He, the man, moved with me in perfect step, our shadows woven into one along the expanse of bookcases along the wall.

Intentions were clearer as he pressed a hand on my frail shoulder and directed me into my chair and, with just two pincer-like fingers, urged a pen in my direction. He, too, sat beside me in his own chair and staring at each other was, for me, like staring into a funhouse mirror. We'd done this for so long, in these very positions, that our chairs would forever retain the twin-hub impressions of our buttocks, the chair-backs contoured to the subtle undulations of our spine.

He slid the notebook before me, motioning for me to open it. So there would be one final story to tell! I gathered up the pen, opened the notebook—he had already picked up his own pen—and we commissioned for one final walk across the mental macadam, opening doors of creation that had been our bread and butter throughout our distinct but inseparable lives, letting the creative sconces burn till the dry-powdered walls caught fire.

We joined in union, as always. None of it was any different than it had ever been, except that our hands moved with equal and deliberate slowness now—we were no longer as young as we'd once been—and our eyes were held, squinting, closer to the handwritten text than we'd ever held them before.

But still—

Sitting at the table, as we had for our entire intertwined careers, we wrote until the life began to slip from my old man bones and my balding, dimpled head thudded soundly, in a final surrender, against the splayed wingspan of the open notebook beneath me. As my pen rolled across the tabletop only to be gobbled up by the fall of space that carried it straight to the floor (where, along the warped and tired floorboards, it continued to roll), he set his own pen down beside the notebook and my dimpled head with his pale and paining fingers. My breath coming in labored wheezes, my eyes were powerless to stare at anything, save for the underside of my eyelids, except the rows and rows and columns and rows of spines proclaiming his name. His name, his name, always and forever his name! By the sheer arrangement of letters that formulated the name I'd given him all those years ago, he was going to live forever, immortalized, while I had become old and withered and plagued with the daily strains of the nearness of death. Edition after edition, supplemented by countless language translations, copyright extensions, nonfictions written about him, using his name, not mine, never mine. On the awards, the countless awards with the engraved plates of brass I'd received over the years, it had always been his name engraved on the plates, always his name on the marquees. And still, given all this, I returned to the endless struggle, the unanswerable question and never-ending debate: who had stolen from whom? Was I the victor because of my wealth or he because of his immortality?

His name, his name, his name!

Here, in this forsaken room surrounded by nothing but his name, I was ravaged not by feral wolves but, quite unceremoniously, dispatched by the fragile hands of time which, in that very moment of my last soured breath and like the sloughing of a second skin, stripped away all I had created.

ALL IS CALM

Following his death, you play Alice and try to push your head through the bathroom mirror. You take off weeks from work, then eventually quit. You sit for a duration under the tortoise-shell reading lamp with a book open on your lap, but do not read. You prepare dinners that will never be eaten. Funny, the way you still set two plates. Funny, all of it. You check your shelves, you check your record albums, you check your clothes. Everything you own is yours now. Everything you own now owns you.

The passage of eons as you stare into the guts of the medicine cabinet.

Ticking clocks.

A showerhead that runs continuous.

You check your pockets. You check the cupboards. You check your books. Funny, how people are so clearly defined by the books they own.

You cannot live here anymore. You are a stranger here. This becomes clear to you. You are not welcome. Nothing is familiar. Everything is familiar. All of it. None of it.

* * *

On a Tuesday, you move into the new apartment. Four Tuesdays later, and it is what it is. Maybe it is the same or maybe it is different. But now you are different. There is an obsession to you now. When you wake up, morning light in your face, morning water in your eyes, you breathe, and it is like the first time.

A new apartment.

A strange apartment chocked with strange smells. A month goes by. Hapless, you wander into the kitchen. You recoil, vampire-like, against the insult of daylight through Venetian blinds. Arranged on the countertops: a display of jars and empty bottles, label-less wines and fruit long soured. Yet it is not the smell of these items that prompts your olfactory retreat; rather, it is your own ruined flesh, ripe with dried and soured perspiration, mucus-heavy, droopy-lidded. You are filthy in your nakedness. So you shower. You shower for a good, long time. You wash the flecks of grit from your eyes and you scrub the scum off your lips. Finished, you towel off while standing in the cramped, foreign bathroom, blurry in the steamed mirror. This is not your apartment. This is not your bathroom. You are scrubbing your crotch now with someone else's bath towel. Nude, you return to the kitchen. The light of day no longer threatens you. You pull back the blinds. Below, in the baking heat of an urban morning, the city is long and rectangular and infused with color, glittering with glass and steel and strung with bands of concrete. Scratching your head, you go to the kitchen to fix some eggs. It occurs to you, while opening the refrigerator door, that you have no idea if there are eggs in this strange apartment or not, but only that you crave them. You search and, behold, there are two left. They are in a small door inside the larger door, sitting patiently side by side, in concave half circles. On the stove, you cook them. You add butter—a lot of butter—and some parsley and some oregano (because there is some in the cabinet next to the parsley). You add pretty much whatever you find. It is suddenly a game: put in as much stuff as you can. You add salt and pepper and, daringly, paprika. Anyway, you think it is paprika, but you're not really sure what paprika is. Then you eat the eggs out on the balcony, looking down on the city. The eggs taste horrible. It is your fault. Too much junk. The game was lost. Or was it won? But the smell out here is not of eggs; it is the diesel exhaust smell of the city. You inhale and think of gas fumes. You go back inside to get dressed and realize you have no idea where your clothes are. Or what your clothes even look like. But you don't panic. There is an obsession to you now, and it is the obsessed part of you that makes things run smoothly. You go to the bedroom closet. There will be clothes here. For certain. You search through the clothes. They are drab and outdated, polyester hostages from some bygone era. Unimpressed, you decide to squeeze into a simple pair of faded chinos and a button-down paisley shirt with a too-big collar. You look like a man and it doesn't flatter your feminine figure, but it's the least offensive ensemble you can put together.

In the foyer, beside the front door, there is a small, circular table with a bowl on it. The table is finely carved and lacquered, intricately detailed with a somewhat oriental design. It looks expensive. Quite the opposite, the bowl atop the table is made of ceramic and, as is observed by the undulations of its contours, not very well made. It has been baked in a kiln and not yet painted. It is the color of bone. You look in the bowl and find a silver button for a sports coat, a keychain bottle opener, two blue rubber bands, and what appears to be a single petrified kernel of corn. It resembles a tooth. There are no car keys, which is what you are looking for. But that's all right. Somewhat amused, you pick up the kernel of corn and examine it with mild interest before dropping it into the breast pocket of your brand new paisley shirt. You feel constipated from the eggs and still a bit groggy, but there is a whole new world waiting for you just out the door. So you leave.

* * *

Before his death, you are watching them dig around for the girl when he comes home.

"Tell me," he says breathlessly, his key still in the door, carrying on his suit the scent of New York City, "tell me, tell me, tell me, tell me you didn't sit here watching T.V. all day."

Because you've started this thing together.

Because you've mutually agreed on a plan, a game plan, and it does not include you watching television until he comes home from work.

That night, in bed, you run your fingers along his chest and he tells you how much of a girl you are sometimes. You tell him about the girl they still have not found and he makes a Jimmy Hoffa joke. You do not find this funny. You tell him you do not find this funny. He kisses the top of your head and says something you cannot fully make out. Sleep is quickly claiming you both.

Because you've started this thing together.

This crazy, crazy life together.

Later, after it is all over, an x-ray and subsequent autopsy would reveal six plastic buttons, a sewing thimble, a pair of gold hoop earrings, ten inches of fishing twine, eleven rubber bands, bits of a colored toothpick, the pull-tab from a can of soda, and seventy-three pennies in his stomach.

* * *

Maggie and Joel convince you to go to counseling. Except it isn't really counseling but a group of people who get together once a week to drink lukewarm coffee, nibble birdlike on cookies, and talk about problems. There are all sorts of problems. You are not comfortable at counseling, but it seems to make Maggie and Joel happy and, anyway, Maggie and Joel were always good to you. They were always good to you both.

Both.

"Both," you say. The word has no meaning. You say it over and over and over again until it is no longer English.

You start reading like it's the end of the world and you need to pass an exam to get into heaven. You find boredom in novels and biographies just remind you of your own personal failures, so you settle on books about strange facts. Because facts seem safe and unchanging.

You learn King Alfonso XIII of Spain was tone deaf, and had in his charge an "Anthem Man" whose duty it was to inform the king when the national anthem was being played so the king would know when to stand.

You learn Grand Central Station accumulates approximately seven pounds of chewed and discarded gum every single day.

For the hell of it, you begin shoplifting. You make off with fistfuls of lipsticks and eyeliner and candy bars until security catches you sniffing around an aisle one afternoon. They do not call the police. Instead, they sit you down in a room behind the walls of the store—a gray, shapeless room, overburdened with video monitors and computers—and the overweight, unhappy-looking security manager begins to ask you questions. You have no qualms about answering his questions. You even inform him that rubber bands last longer when refrigerated, and that if you place a drop of alcohol on a scorpion's back it will go insane and sting itself to death.

"What happened to your face?" the security manager asks after he has been staring for too long. It is a fair question, although one you are rarely asked.

You do not tell him what happened to your face. You do not tell him that, after your husband's death, you played Alice and pushed your face through a bathroom mirror.

Instead, you tell him dolphins sleep with one eye open.

That peanuts are one of the ingredients in dynamite.

"Lady," he says. "Look, lady. Just go home. And don't come back. Ever."

*　*　*

Two months go by and they still have not located the missing girl. You keep forgetting where she is—Alabama? Mississippi? Anyway, it's someplace far from Manhattan, but it could be your next door neighbor, you are so enthralled. Oprah has the girl's parents on one afternoon, and you all but make a party of it. You bake cookies and buy soda and even, toward the end of the hour, fix yourself a cocktail. Police keep searching for a body, says the mother, but we believe she is still alive. The father agrees. So does Oprah. Personally, you doubt the girl is still alive, and wonder what it takes to lie to yourself and make yourself believe that. It must be a parent-child thing, you think. Because when your husband died, you did not lie to yourself. He was right there and there was no denying any of it. You couldn't. Even with Oprah on your side, you couldn't.

He complains of stomach pains a few days before he dies. There is even an appointment with Doctor Mendes on the schedule; you write it on a Post-It note and stick it on the refrigerator. It is the least you can do. He works and you stay home, thinking about being an artist but unable to do it. All you have is shoddy pottery with too many undulations. "Tell me, tell me, tell me, tell me you didn't sit here watching T.V. all day." Of course not—you've made the doctor's appointment and scribbled your own reminder on the Post-It.

In 1906, one of the earliest radio transmissions of actual decipherable sound came in the form of a resonant and eerie solo violin replacing the dash-and-dot theology of Morse code to a group of shipboard radio operators at sea. The tune was recognizable as "Silent Night," and the sound of that lone violin, for only a brief period of history, filled up the entire world.

Because facts are facts.

You cannot sleep without him because he is still here. You feel him in your half-sleep when you roll over. His warmth still spreads across the mattress to your side. Once, you even jar yourself awake when you swear his arm comes across your shoulder and pulls you against him.

Maggie and Joel, the handsome couple, check in on you from time to time. They bring foil-hooded casseroles in hot crockery and practically want to force-feed you. You are too thin, they say. Your eyes are practically sinking back into your head, they say. Almost conspiratorially, Maggie informs you your breasts are shrinking.

But the problem is—

The problem *is*—

* * *

The problem is he never makes it to Doctor Mendes because he is killed in an automobile accident.

* * *

You take part-time work editing a local magazine. You can do it from home, which is nice, and it gives you something to do with your free time. Because all your time is free time and you are beginning to lose yourself. You enjoy working on the magazine and, after a while, even make a suggestion that they should include a segment about strange facts in every issue. That would be something, you say. Because there are so many strange facts. Like sixty percent of all potatoes in the U.S. come from Idaho. Like most hamsters wink instead of blink.

But the problem *is* —

*   *   *

The problem is his car swerves off the road and crashes through the median into oncoming traffic. It is a mess. There is a lot of news coverage. For a while, it overshadows the missing girl in Mississippi. Or Alabama. Or wherever. There is talk that he must have fallen asleep behind the wheel. Some eyewitnesses say the car just slid over all the lanes and crashed through the guardrail. They say he was slumped forward over the steering wheel, although no one is positive he was asleep.

At a bar with Maggie, you tell her how the medical examiner found all that shit inside his stomach, that it was something called pica, where you subconsciously eat indigestible materials. Maggie does not believe you at first because it all sounds so bizarre so you go to the library together and get books. Maggie is shocked. Then she says, "You poor thing," and looks like she wants to hug you but doesn't. As if bad luck is contagious. You tell her he did not fall asleep — that he was bent over the steering wheel because of the severe stomach cramps. You tell her about the appointment you set with Doctor Mendes and how, sometimes, he would have difficulty moving around because the pain was so great.

"It says pica is brought on by great amounts of stress," Maggie says, reading from the book.

You do not want to hear this.

You think, *Tell me, tell me, tell me, tell me,* and do not want to hear this.

* * *

So then a funny thing happens: the distraught mother and father are questioned by the police in the disappearance of their daughter. Maybe other people see this coming, but it takes you by surprise. You keep thinking of the way they held out hope on Oprah, and the way Oprah's hand sat on the mother's knee throughout the interview. If Oprah believes you, does it matter what the police think? They are not charged with anything, the parents—it is simply an interview—but the media throws a parade, and there are awful pictures and headlines in the newspapers the following day.

And still, the girl is missing.

You tell him about the girl they still have not found and he makes a Jimmy Hoffa joke. You do not find this funny. You tell him you do not find this funny. He kisses the top of your head and says something you cannot fully make out. Sleep is quickly claiming you both.

Because you've started this thing together.

This crazy, crazy life together.

The words he says that you cannot make out are suddenly very clear. Because you've been hearing them all along. You've been hearing them for quite some time. *Tell me, tell me, tell me, tell me you didn't sit here watching T.V. all day.*

* * *

At restaurants and shopping malls, alone, you hum "Silent Night." Aloud, you sing the part that goes, "All is calm, all is bright," and are pretty sure those are the words. You also overhear a little girl discussing how Alice slips back and forth through the looking glass to her mother, who listens to the child with passing interest. You smile and order a large iced tea and a salad. At least you are eating again.

* * *

Tell me—
He says, "I'm so worried about us."
You hear him but convince yourself that you do not.

* * *

They find the girl on a Wednesday. Alive. In the basement of a farmhouse in Mississippi or Alabama—one or the other. Two men with grizzled beards and flannel shirts are arrested. Oprah is seen giving a double thumbs-up on her commercials. Police swarm the farmhouse and mill about like one hundred people who've lost a contact lens.

She had been kidnapped and the parents are shown on T.V. clutching each other and clutching their daughter, their faces collapsed into red, sobbing crevices. There is no apology by the news media for their heartless front page renderings and baseless assumptions; it all seems readily and conveniently forgotten in the face of this wonderful news.

* * *

You get a phone call from Doctor Mendes's office wondering why your husband skipped his appointment. You do not tell them about the car accident. Instead, you tell them a pig's orgasm can last for thirty minutes. Then hang up.

* * *

Following his death, you play Alice and try to push your head through the bathroom mirror. They save you by stitching your face up, and although many people stare—and Maggie and Joel shake their heads and look like they want to collapse into tears—it is only the goddamn security manager at some nameless drug store who finally asks about it.

And what do you tell him?

What?

Tell me, tell me, tell me—

Facts. You tell him facts. Because that is all that makes sense. No matter how insane or ridiculous or bizarre, a fact is a fact and it does not change. You find comfort in this.

* * *

Following his death, you play Alice. But they caught you in time and stitched you up.

Next time, they won't be so lucky.

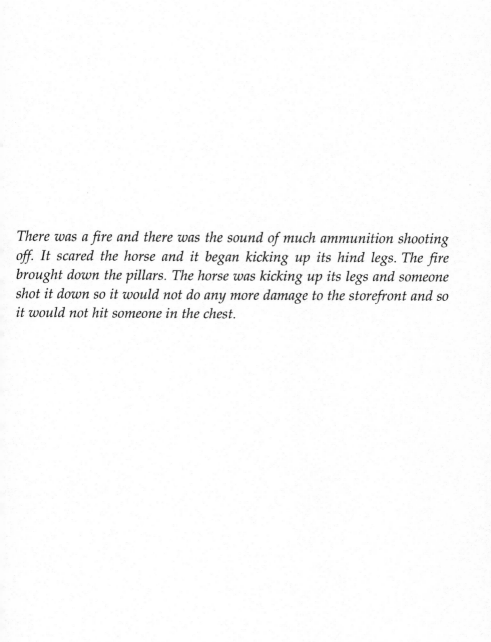

There was a fire and there was the sound of much ammunition shooting off. It scared the horse and it began kicking up its hind legs. The fire brought down the pillars. The horse was kicking up its legs and someone shot it down so it would not do any more damage to the storefront and so it would not hit someone in the chest.

Painstation

There comes a time in every fanatic's life when he or she is confronted—inarguably—with the severity of their own psychoses. It is at that moment a decision is to be made: pursuit or disengagement? It is the mind's way of warning its host that he or she has crossed the threshold of reasonableness and has stepped foot into the muddy trenches of human decline.

Such a realization was made clear to Keanan as he crouched behind the wheel of his Civic in the dark, hidden from streetlights, and watched Casey Madigan disappear into Façade. The notion struck him like a throng—a thousand metal utensils clattering to a cement floor—and he broke out in a sweat. Evenings, he'd stay late at the office because *she* stayed late. Four cubicles down from his, he could adjust his computer monitor at an angle that would reflect her image. She hardly spoke to him. He didn't care. Watching was sufficient.

Keanan cracked the Civic's window. Frigid November air whistled into the car, fragrant with the stink of the East River. Across the street, dull sodium lights flooded the stone front and gold-and-white awning of Façade. He'd never been inside the club, knew nothing about it. Yet, as he watched Casey slip inside the smoked-glass doors, it quickly became a place of severe importance to him. In his mind, he watched the svelte clockwork of her buttocks shift beneath the tight fabric of her skirt; imagined himself running his hands through the breath of her hair; caught glimpses into the pursed openings between the buttons of her blouse, and at the treasures within.

Pushing the car in gear, he spun around the rain-soaked alley and headed back toward his midtown apartment. Once there, he showered, masturbated bitterly, and fell asleep with his pale and knobby legs draped over one side of the bed.

One evening a full week later, as Keanan watched a collection of Mexican janitors with lazy fascination push through the office, Casey strode past his desk. The lilac scent of her perfume coupled with the swoosh of her pantyhose jerked him from his daze, and he watched her walk, stifled by fixation. Sitting up in his chair, he shuffled through the paperwork cluttering his desk until he found the Façade's dining brochure, folded it, and stuffed it into a desk drawer.

He peered around the wall of his cubicle and stared at Casey by the copy machine. His neck felt prickly and his heartbeat was racing. The back of her legs—specifically the creases at the back of her knees—caused him to shudder, and he quickly turned away. In his mind, he embraced her warmth as if she required such affection, needed it from him, and he wondered what her breath would feel like along his neck, what her mouth tasted like. With almost youthful fascination, he contemplated the color, shape, texture of her nipples. He contemplated *everything.*

The swoosh of her stockings was suddenly very close to him. Her head peered around the side of his cubicle.

"Fucking copier is jammed," she said.

He saw her face as something exclusively designed to accommodate his obsession. Eyes, mouth, nose—her perfection was something more than evident. Not for the first time, Keanan wondered how a creature of such exquisite splendor had been created: what sort of god had, in all his malevolence, felt the desire to provoke him with such unattainable magnificence?

He stood, palms sweating against the pleats in his pants. "I'll check it out. Could just be a stuck piece of paper."

When she finally left for the evening, he followed her out into the street. It was cold and the bundle of his coat would hide his face if she happened to look in his direction. She paused amidst a wedge of pedestrians before a crosswalk while waiting for a break in traffic. Vapor wafted from her mouth. Absently, Keanan wondered what it would be like to inhale her exhalations. Would that somehow make her part of him? Almost?

She took a cab to the East Side. Keanan followed at a safe distance in his Civic. With assumed knowledge of her destination, he felt confident keeping a healthy distance behind the cab. Three out of the five nights this week she'd hopped a taxi and disappeared beneath the gold-and-white awning of Façade.

Up ahead, he saw the cab's brake lights flare in the darkness. Tapping his own brakes, he eased the Civic to a halt in the rutted, rain-swept alley. His breath jabbed at the windshield, fogged it up. He saw Casey pay the driver and vanish through the tinted glass doors as the taxi backed up, did a one-point turn, and zipped past Keanan's car. Adjusting his tie, he popped the door and hurried toward the club.

The interior of Façade was poorly lit and only moderately populated for a Friday evening. A pianist at the end of the bar tinkled the high keys. The dull murmur of conversation rose from a sparse arrangement of circular tables to his left. The air, blue and cloudy with cigar smoke, burned his eyes. He pushed alongside the bar to his right, grabbed a handful of cocktail napkins, blotted his eyes. Looking up, he saw Casey pass down a dark, narrow corridor at the back of the club and disappear. To pursue her now, he knew, would be ridiculous. Yet there was something nestled in the creases of his brain, forcing him to continue, to follow her. At that instant, nothing else seemed to matter—his surroundings had suddenly become ineffectual and without consequence.

A clean-shaven bartender in a shirt and tie materialized. "Get you something?"

Keanan shook his head. With the stealth of a drunkard, he wove between a pair of tables and slipped into the darkened corridor. The din of conversation from the bar was immediately blocked out. Sharp, acidic smells filtered into his nose. Two restroom doors stood opposite each other further down the corridor. He paused outside the women's room, absently chewing at his lower lip, a foot tapping on the linoleum. The door was open a crack, the light on. He pushed his head back against the wall and peeked inside.

The restroom was vacant.

Where did she go? he wondered.

Continuing further down the corridor, the echo of his footfalls became more and more prevalent. The stink of acid now burned his eyes. Unable to see properly, he ran one hand along the paneled wall, wincing at the sticky feel of it.

He stopped. There was a closed door at the end of the hallway, a watercolor caricature of a grinning skeleton in a top hat painted on it.

Go home, a voice in his head spoke up. *Go before you embarrass yourself.*

The voice was powerless. His mind—stronger than any voice could hope to be—summoned Casey Madigan in all her angelic grandeur, nude before him like a thousand missed opportunities suddenly united into one perfect instance, one final chance to do what he needed so badly to do.

He pushed against the door and it opened with little protest. Before him, a wooden staircase dipped into blackness. The stink of sulfur now accosted him, potent and unapologetic. Something else, too...

Lilacs, he thought. *Her perfume.*

What was at the bottom of the stairs? There was no light switch—none that he could see, anyway—and there didn't appear to be a railing to hold. Despite this, he felt he could not be swayed; he suddenly needed to see her, at least one last time, before going home. His tenement was getting darker and darker with the passage of each day. How long could he stand there in the dark, listening to the groanings of his neighbors through the walls, while his mind repeated and repeated and repeated and repeated? Eyes closed, he only saw her face. Her image: reflected on the black walls of his cramped bedroom, his cramped mind. Each morning the spray of the shower against his body was her embrace...was individual fingers poking and prodding and caressing. It got to the point where he'd wake up, his face sore and puffy from sobbing in his sleep, curled up in a ball on the bathroom floor. Or in the hall closet. Or on the kitchen counter.

It's been long enough, he thought, feeling as if he were actually talking to her. *I need to take you now. I need another look. Nothing else matters.*

He started down the steps, the planks protesting beneath his feet. The sensation of submergence—of sinking into the earth—grabbed him around the throat and he suddenly found it difficult to breathe. The stairwell emptied into a spacious, cellar-like room with a low ceiling and track lighting. The walls were cinderblock and black with moss. Faintly, he could hear the pump of industrial music vibrating the floor and in his ears. A series of bolted steel doors stood at the far end of the room. A shape shifted in the gloom, its movement giving it away.

"Hello?" Keanan's voice quaked.

The shape stepped into the light. It was a man, constructed primarily of muscle and leather, with a shaved head and deep, insect-like eyes. He acknowledged Keanan without significance, and situated himself on a barstool in front of the row of steel doors.

Keanan approached timidly. Had he been mistaken? Surely Casey had not come down here...

"Brand," the man said.

"Excuse me?"

"No brand?" The man spoke with little inflection. He had a tattoo of a spear etched into the soft well of flesh beneath his left eye. "Two hundred dollars."

"For what?"

The man frowned. "You fuckin' around, buddy?"

Keanan shook his head. "I don't understand."

"Two hundred to get in," said the man, "unless you got a brand. Which you don't, otherwise you'd know what I'm talking about. So—two hundred."

"I...I don't have..." He patted his clothes but knew he had roughly three dollars and seventy-five cents on him. "What is it?"

Irritated, the man adjusted himself on his stool. "Turn and hit it, buddy. It ain't my job to play fifty questions."

"I'm looking for someone." The words were out of his mouth before he knew he'd said them.

"Then it's two hundred."

Is she in there? he wanted to scream. *Is Casey Madigan behind one of those iron doors?*

The pumping music through the walls was making his legs weak. He frowned at the large man and turned, moving back through the darkness. He spent the next hour slinking up and down the destitute streets that ran parallel to the East River, his hands stuffed into his pockets, his mind reeling. He couldn't go home — he knew this, felt it like a premonition. *She* would be there: on every wall, in every closet, crouched in the cover of every shadow. There…but *not* there. Not *real*. Back at home, she was nothing he could touch and taste. Only a figment bent on the destruction of his own sanity. Obsession, he was beginning to understand, was a very angry thing.

Casey Madigan, he thought. *Casey Fucking Madigan.*

In his own unconventional way, he loved her. It wasn't just about attraction or lust. He *loved* her. He could feel her absence now like a fatal wound.

He stopped inside Skiff Laundromat, pumped cash from the ATM machine, and ran back down the length of the alley like a child fleeing a schoolhouse on the first day of summer. His feet splashed through countless puddles; his tie streamed behind him like the tail of a comet. He passed a derelict man with one arm who scowled at him as he ran. As casual as he could be, he moved through the serene atmosphere of Façade and scampered down the darkened corridor like a hound fixed on the scent of a rabbit. As he had done an hour before, he descended the rickety staircase into the underground room. The tattooed hulk was still seated on his stool when he approached the mesh of steel doors.

"Round two," the hulk said.

"I need to see her." As if he owed this behemoth an explanation.

"Two hundred."

Keanan rifled through a handful of greasy bills, produced four fifties, and held them out to the man. Expressionless, the man folded the bills into his leather wristband, stood, and slid aside a steel bolt that ran the length of the two center doors.

"Only rule is to follow the rules," said the man.

"What rules?"

"Pay attention."

With a forceful yank, the behemoth pulled both doors open, filling the outer room with a surge of thick bass and heavy drums. Lights spun and glittered behind the doors. The shapes of people moved in the darkness. A blast of hot air struck Keanan, forcing him to recoil, followed by the stink of alcohol, sweat, and sandalwood.

"Welcome to Painstation," said the hulk, and gave Keanan a forceful shove through the doors.

Blinded by confusion, an army of hands groped for him, held him vehemently. He was toggled and jerked. Something wet was pushed against the top of his left hand while someone yanked his right shirtsleeve above the elbow. Someone shouted, "Bovine!" and he suddenly felt a world of white-hot pain erupt along the flesh of his right arm, screaming down to the tips of his fingers and burning up to his shoulder, where it exploded in a stroke of heat and pain throughout his chest. Like an injured animal, he tossed his head back and howled. He could smell the stink of his own burning flesh.

Someone grabbed a swatch of his hair, yanked his head back until a patch of hair came out. He screamed. Music drummed through his body. Through bleary eyes, he managed to make out a black-hooded figure before him. Something was held up and glistened with iridescent light: a hypodermic needle. Moaning, he tried to struggle free of their grasps, but it was useless. A pair of hands stabilized his head. He felt the needle penetrate the flesh at the base of his neck and draw blood.

Screaming, he brought his arms up to his face, ready to fight the figures off him. But just as quickly as they had appeared, they vanished. Behind him, the steel doors slammed closed. In front of him, the darkness was crisscrossed by intermittent patchworks of light, pulsing to the droning bass-and-drum music. Shapes— human shapes—twisted and writhed in the blackness ahead of him. His heart skipped with each downbeat of the drum. Moving slowly against the wall, he made his way through the rave, his body jolted several times by fleeting shapes in the smoke.

Finally, after what seemed like an eternity, he crossed into a narrow antechamber that amplified his breathing. In pain, he curled against the stone wall and rubbed the scorched flesh of his right arm. It was swollen and tender and hurt like hell.

What the hell is this place?

He found it difficult to summon Casey's face and body in a place such as this. Somehow, even in his mind, her perfection was corrupted by the stone walls and reams of incense smoke. He grappled with the fleeting visage of her face in his head, felt it slipping, slipping, gritted his teeth like an animal. Could he let her slide, let her get away? How could he go home then? How would he breathe?

The passageway emptied into a black, concrete room cramped with velvet sofas and ornately carved statues depicting various sexual acts. The room smelled of lighter fluid. Iron vats hung from chains in the ceiling, draped with burning oil rags. A number of people littered the floors, sofas, and walls, coupling to beat the devil. To his right, a nude couple gyrated against each other like some refined piece of machinery. Further in the room, a shirtless obese man in checkered slacks had his face buried in the crotch of an impish older woman. In a throng of ecstasy, the woman moaned and ground her hips into the fat man's face while twisting the twin bulbs of her nipples between her fingers. A third cluster of people— four or five of them in all, predominantly male—quivered against one another, their bodies accessible and erect, the amalgam of their bodies a mass of floating hands and rigid sex organs.

Head down, Keanan pushed his way through the room to the corridor at the opposite side. A redhead with bad teeth wearing a leather basque nudged past him, leading a naked older man along with a leash attached to his testicles. "Siddy is in for the shit this time," she muttered to no one in particular and grinning ear to ear.

Keanan looked ahead and caught a glimpse of Casey Madigan passing in front of the doorway at the end of the hall. His breath seized. It was like a rush of energy—enough to revivify his mental image of the woman. He'd been wrong—her perfection was still strong here, even among the living refuse. And it was enough to get him moving again.

He hurried to the end of the passageway and found himself in a small, box-shaped room that reeked of urine. A group of naked bodies had gathered in one corner and were administering electric shocks to some woman's genitals. One of her tormentors cracked a whip along the backs of the other tormentors, drawing blood and shrill cries. He turned away in repulsion.

Casey had disappeared behind yet another door.

Is this deliberate avoidance? he thought. And would he ever be able to punish Casey for any intentional mistreatment directed at him? He tried to imagine Casey with metal plugs clipped to her labia while he toggled the switch to send current into her body, to rape her with current, but the notion only caused him to grow weak. He felt his crotch tighten.

Someone bumped his shoulder, hissed at him with porcelain fangs. Shuddering, he pushed forward and slipped through the door Casey had vanished behind.

He stood in a cylindrical hallway with a grated floor and a row of folding chairs against the wall. A number of chairs were occupied, mostly by people who looked very much like—

Like me, he marveled. *They look like me.*

Suits and ties and floral-print dresses. Casey was not here. There was a second door at the other end of the room. Had she gone out the other side? Reeling, he felt like Alice chasing the white rabbit.

The small man in the chair beside him nodded timidly in his direction. "Lights are harsh."

He only stared. "Beg pardon?"

"The lights," the man repeated. He pointed to the bright fixtures just above their heads. "Very harsh. Hurts your eyes, coming in from the dark like that. I know."

"I'm okay."

"Have a seat."

"Did you see a woman just come through here?"

The man rolled his shoulders. "Seen lots of women. What's your name? I'm Craig."

Keanan looked at him. He was a slight, almost comical man, with great knobby temples and huge eyes swimming behind the lenses of his glasses. He wore a tan blazer and a crooked brown necktie, dotted with what appeared to be mustard spots.

"What *is* this place?" Keanan asked. Peering down the row of foldout chairs, he saw their occupants sitting motionless, their eyes focused on the blank tiled wall in front of them. Could they see something he could not?

"Waiting room," said Craig.

"For what?"

"Sim-Sim."

"The fuck is that?"

"Simian Simulation. Have a seat. Wait shouldn't be too long tonight."

A bit cautious, Keanan eased himself into the chair beside Craig. The small man proffered a delicate hand, as if to shake. Keanan didn't take it.

"Craig," the man repeated.

Agitated, he said, "Keanan."

"Craig's not my real name, of course. No one here uses their real name."

"Right," Keanan said.

"Oh." Craig's eyes widened, his thin lips forming a surprised circle. His skin reeked of Skin-E-Dip ointment. "That explains it."

"What does?"

"Your arm," Craig said. "The brand is new. You can tell the way the flesh puckers up like that. See the difference?"

Craig rolled up his right pant leg. He exposed a burn-mark in the shape of a gothic "P." The mark was blue-black and flush like a tattoo. Keanan examined his own mark. It was the same as Craig's, only more vivid. The skin surrounding the brand was red and inflamed, puffed out to nearly the size of a golf-ball.

"I've been coming here for a year now," Craig said. "You're obviously new. That's what I meant."

Keanan peered down the length of the room. Like zombies, the people only stared straight ahead.

"Why the hell do you come here?" he asked.

Craig offered a timorous half-smile. "I'm sorry?"

"This place."

"Painstation," Craig said.

"Painstation," Keanan repeated. In his mind, all he could see was the vague, capering form of the woman he loved—the object of his deepest obsession. In the event of a sudden romance, what would she allow him to do? Would she let him do it all? He'd want to taste, to inhale every inch of her body, every part, and to do so with no reservations. He would love her body in any presentation.

"I come here just for the simulation," Craig said. "I'm not like those others out there. I don't think I could *ever* be that way. But simulation is different. Let's us all be as free as we used to be, as we ever wanted to be." He chuckled nervously. "Almost like a blessing, in this crazy world run by kings and politicians."

The door at the opposite end of the room opened and a beefy-looking figure dressed in a black cloak and hood stepped inside. He tapped the closest two zombies on the shoulder and motioned them to follow him back through the door. They did without a single word.

"Who's that?" Keanan whispered. "Death?"

Craig laughed nervously, twisting his fingers in his lap. Keanan caught the slight bulge of an erection there and quickly looked away in disgust.

"You'll like it," Craig said, his voice cracking. "It's really something else. It's like nothing in the world you've ever seen. Nothing like you've ever been a part of. Ever been skydiving?"

Confused, Keanan shook his head. "You?"

"Gosh, no," said Craig. He ran a nervous tongue along the length of his upper lip and adjusted his eyeglasses. "Don't need to. This is much better."

"Sim-Sim," Keanan mused.

"It's something so special," the strange little man reiterated.

The door opened again and the man in the black cloak stepped into the room. This time, he walked the length of the row of chairs, eyeing those seated before him through the nylon veil of his hood. He paused in front of a plump woman wearing a large gold cross, pointed at her. She stood and moved toward the door, exited the room. The cloaked Goliath continued down the row and stopped between Craig and Keanan. His index finger professed itself, hung in the air like an unfinished thought, then pointed to Craig. Silently, Craig beamed. Goliath's hand rotated and the finger then fell on Keanan. In a twirl of robes, the cloaked hulk turned and advanced toward the door again.

"Come on," Craig said, visibly excited. "It's both of us!"

Keanan stood and followed Craig through the door at the other end of the cylindrical room. Surely Casey must have passed through here. It could be the only explanation as to her disappearance. Yet, unlike the others—and himself—she hadn't taken a seat and waited to be summoned. Perhaps she'd been a member for longer than Craig. Perhaps for years.

This isn't a fucking country club, he thought.

The cloaked stranger stopped Keanan, Craig, and the plump woman outside another set of doors. Behind Keanan, built into the wall, were rows of tiny numbered lockers. With that same pointing finger, the cloaked stranger presented each of them with a number: "Seventeen," to Plump Lady; "twenty-two," to Craig; "six," to Keanan.

With a subtle jerk of his hooded head, the figure nodded in the direction of a copper plaque sealed to the wall beside the set of doors. He paraphrased the words: "Rules. Only one, and with *no exceptions.* This is an authentic simulation of simian life. You must behave in accordance to said environment. That is the only rule. Any violation to this rule, be it deliberate or otherwise, may result in punishment or revoked membership from the establishment."

Revoked membership from the establishment, Keanan thought. *What the fuck is this all about, anyway?*

"Disrobe," said the hooded stranger.

As if reacting to the crack of a starter's pistol, both Craig and the woman began tugging off their clothes. They moved as if in a frenzy, or as if to stay clothed for another second longer would result in their immediate deaths. At one point, Craig glanced in Keanan's direction. A wealth of exhilaration had blossomed across the little man's face. His breath came in quick, excited gasps. Beside Craig, the plump woman had stepped out of her pantsuit. She stood there naked except for her tremendous bra, her ample thighs pitted with dimples, the swell of her belly a network of red stretch marks. Her crotch was a wiry cloud of bristling pubic hair.

"Disrobe," Craig muttered beside Keanan. He was tugging his knobby knees out of his slacks. "Hurry."

Do it, that same prodding voice inside his head said. *Casey Madigan did this very same thing, you know. We're all a part of each other.*

With some reluctance, he began to undress and to place his clothes in Locker 6.

A moment later, the three of them were standing before the cloaked gatekeeper as naked as newborns. From the corner of his eye, Keanan could see the stirrings of an erection between Craig's legs. For some insane reason, it reminded him of childhood fishing trips to Saratoga Lake with his father.

"Twenty minutes," the cloaked figure said. He spun a combination lock on one of the doors. Keanan heard the tumblers slide. The gatekeeper grabbed the steel handle on the door, depressed it, and pushed the door open.

Again—more heat. But filled with moisture. Rainforest. A mist seemed to roll in through the doors. Eager to begin, both the plump woman and Craig hurried through the opening. Keanan tried to follow their example, but moved much slower. When he crossed the threshold, the doors were closed on his back. He heard the lock click.

Before him lay a rainforest wonderland.

For all he knew, he'd just been transported to the Amazon. Immense tropical trees, looming like towers, blotted an artificial sky. Wild ferns grew from the dirt at his feet. Before him, a slight decline in the earth led down to a carpet of lush grass and underbrush which, in turn, gave way to what looked like a mile of dense forestry. With the exception of the wall to his back, he could make out no other visible form of human construction: no walls, no ceiling, no flooring, no vents, no windows. Above him was actual *sky*—or so it appeared. And the light all seemed to be coming from a single simulated sun in the sky, almost as bright and as hot as the real thing. In the distance, he could hear running water and the caws of wild birds.

This is incredible, he thought, standing in awe. *There must be acres of vegetation here. It's Eden.*

Craig and the plump woman were already down the embankment. Like apes, they staggered around incommunicative, dragging themselves through the make-believe forest on all fours. And to Keanan's astonishment, Craig and the woman quickly attacked each other, dropping to the ground. Shrieking like animals, they commenced in rigorous copulation, their bodies thrusting with such audacity that it was almost frightening. Stunned, Keanan only stared.

Movement deeper in the forest caught his eye. Squinting, he could see another couple mating in a succession of quick, reflexive hip-lunges. The woman screamed, threw her head back against a tree. Her partner bent and sank his teeth into the soft flesh just above her collarbone. She cried out in pain, her hands and feet clawing at her assailant, though her face boasted a twisted suggestion of rapture.

He downed the embankment. More couples materialized the closer he got to the body of the forest. He paused once to watch a lone woman crouch, defecate on the ground, then scurry away.

Animals, he thought. *They're acting like animals.*

A man moved past him, sniffing the air, sniffing the ground. For a moment, Keanan watched him with confounded desperation. The man paused directly in front of him, sniffing Keanan's skin.

"Watch it, buddy," he warned the stranger. "The hell is going on here?"

The stranger froze, stared into Keanan's eyes for a moment. There was no intelligence in those eyes, he saw. This freak had left all semblance of humanity out in the waiting room.

The stranger struggled with a frown, then hurried off to some other corner of this make-believe world.

A cold hand gripped his forearm, spun him around. It was another cloaked gatekeeper, though this one was shorter and carried a big wooden stick.

"That's one break," the cloaked figure said. He brought the stick up and thrust it into Keanan's gut. A roiling tumult of pain blossomed in his belly. "The rule is simple, buddy. Don't break it again."

Doubled over in pain, he watched the cloaked figure retreat through teary eyes. Bending down, the cloaked figure opened a hatch in the ground — the *floor* — and descended a stairwell hidden inside it. With nothing more than a bump, the hatch closed behind him.

"Jesus," he breathed quietly. Was that for *talking?* Just for *talking* to someone?

A second hand fell on his back. Tense, he spun around to see the slight, pale form of Craig from the waiting room standing behind him, a meager smile playing over his lips. Craig's small erection jutted from a nest of pubic hair like a baby bird straining for its mother. Disgusted, Keanan turned away.

I got lost somewhere along the way, he told himself. *Somehow, along the way, I lost sight of Casey and wound up here, in this alternate version of reality.*

Casey...

Craig's sweaty hands gripped Keanan's waist and he felt the man's pelvis thrust toward him — felt the biting sting of Craig's cock as it nipped his tender flesh. Appalled, violated, Keanan twisted away from the little man, but Craig's grip was tight. His hips pumped against Keanan's buttocks, his slender prick struggling for access.

"Fuck!" Keanan shouted, stumbled forward, then turned around to face the little rapist. He cocked a fist and drove it into Craig's face. A spout of blood burst from Craig's nose and the little man reeled backward and slammed onto the ground. His eyelids fluttered; his hands came up to his face. His small, red shoulders hitched. His erection quickly receded.

"Rapist fuck," Keanan breathed.

Shaking, on the verge of tears, Craig surprised Keanan by hissing through a mouthful of blood and scampering off into the forest.

This is a nightmare, he thought.

Someone slammed him from behind, knocking him to the ground, a burst of agony rupturing down his spine. Wincing, eyes filling with tears, he craned his neck to see another cloaked figure with a staff standing behind him. The figure introduced the side of Keanan's head to his steel-tipped boot. Keanan felt the world spin and go gray. Faintly, as if from the far end of a corrugated pipe, the cloaked figure warned him about breaking the only rule of Painstation and the Simian Simulation: *do not break character.*

"You're not a man in here," the figure said. "Quit thinking like one."

Keanan remained crouched on the ground until the spirals and stars faded from beneath his eyelids. He brought a hand up to his temple and it came away wet with blood.

This isn't real!

He was suddenly overcome by the urge to prove this to himself—to prove the falsity of this room, for starters. How big could the room actually be? It was all underground, wasn't it? There had to be walls somewhere; he'd just have to run far enough to find them. And how far?

In a frenzy, he darted toward the trees, hurdling over entwined and squirming bodies and brushing past reaching, straining hands. There were walls—had to be—and he would find them and expose this horrendous landscape, this counterfeit world. How could they even keep him locked up in here like this? Anger made him run harder, faster, and it felt good—as if he could do anything he wanted at that moment. Anything at all: rape, kill, bite, fuck, scream...just as long as he did it as an animal, did it without thinking.

There were no walls. The room had to be miles in every direction. Overhead, a flock of large, colorful birds took flight.

Casey Madigan was bent naked over a simulated stream, lapping at the water with her tongue. Seeing this, Keanan froze. A collage of Technicolor images flooded his brain: every make-believe fantasy of this woman now paled to the sight of the real thing. This splendid creature, this rape fantasy. It wasn't just her nakedness that was exposed to him for the first time; it was her *baseness*, the stripped-down, untamed essence of her being in its purest form. There, crouched beside the river like a creature of folklore and myth, her body proffered and rising, sinking, rising, sinking, her aromas filling his nose, his head. He breathed her in and allowed her natural scent to occupy every cell of his body.

Trembling, his mind like a single cable pulsing with current, he advanced toward her, stiffening.

I've seen you like this so many times in my head. So many times, just like this...yet never like this, too. It's this place. We're all different here, aren't we? Here, we can be and do whatever we like until the door opens again and we have to get home. Would you even look at me tomorrow?

He came up from behind, her scent overpowering now, and mounted her. Against him, she shuddered, sighed, rolled her head back. Their eyes met briefly. He pushed into her with a sudden burst of ferocity and she cried out. His body quivered at the sound, the feeling. Her warmth engulfed him. He saw her without opening his eyes: the firm S of her back, the tender flesh of her thighs, the purse of her sex...

She bucked beneath him and a swirl of colors filtered through his mind.

I'm here I'm here I'm here I'm here I'm—

He felt the world pull from his feet, his knees, his spine, and quake through the shaft of his body. A giant network of nerve-endings, his entire physical self convulsed as a tingling wave of excretion erupted inside him. And in the throes of passion, he cried out into the false wilderness.

"I love you!"

Casey stiffened beneath him and wrenched her body from his. Keanan shuddered and nearly lost his balance, slamming against the side of a tree. Before him, Casey clambered away on her hands and knees, her wide eyes glowering at him from over her shoulder. Hot with unrequited passion, he watched her crawl away, needing her now more than ever despite the abrupt conclusion of their act— *his* act.

"Casey..."

Behind him: the sound of creaking hinges. He spun around and saw a number of hidden doors embedded in the trunks of the trees swing open. A regiment of cloaked figures carrying heavy staffs poured out and reached for him, yanked him to unsteady feet.

"No—" he tried to protest.

One of the figures tore his shirtsleeve up the center, scrutinized the letter P seared into his flesh. "Fresh one," the figure said.

A second figure grabbed him by the hair and jerked him backward. "This is three," he barked. "You're revoked."

In a dress of arms, Keanan was dragged toward the open doorway in the body of one of the trees. As if in a dream, he watched Casey Madigan's nude, trembling form slowly grow smaller and smaller. He clenched his hands, made fists, felt the tightening of his muscles beneath the strong grip of hands.

Into the tree. And darkness. The sound of a collection of feet trampling iron steps. Eyes wide, he could see nothing in the darkness. He smelled urine again, and fear. His own.

The beatings lasted for several long minutes. They were administered with the keen practice of seasoned professionals. Several times he thought he would black out but he never did.

I'm here, his mind said, and even the voice in his head faltered.

He was taken to another room. Left on the floor. His own breathing echoed in his ears. He thought of Casey's body shifting and pumping against his own and smiled. He tasted blood. His body was a brilliant tangle of pain.

A door opened and boots clopped toward his face. He was aware of a number of people around him. He thought he heard someone spit on the floor.

"Revoked," someone breathed. "Do you understand, sir? You have violated the only rule of Painstation. You are no longer permitted within these walls."

But what about Casey? he wanted to ask. *Beautiful, beautiful Casey?*

"I love…"

He was grabbed, rolled over onto his back. Hooded silhouettes swam in and out of the light. His vision failed him. Someone grabbed his right arm, squeezed the brand. He groaned. Someone said something else, but he could hardly comprehend words now. He heard the sliding sound of an enormous knife blade…saw it gleam briefly in the sodium lights above…

"Remove the brand," one of the figures said.

Icy pain pierced the flesh of his right arm. It deepened and struck bone. Paused. Broke through. He thought he might scream. But he didn't—*couldn't*. Now, only his mind was capable of operation.

Will Casey Madigan love me with one arm? he wondered.

Discussions Concerning the Ingestion of Living Insects

Mid-October.

Soon-Lee, amongst other things, reflected on flies. Mostly, he considered the way they congregated, purple and black and green, their voices like stinging spikes breaking the air. And he pictured them in a scuttle, like spawning salmon in too-shallow water, rumbling overtop one another like knotted turns in a rope. That was how they were in reality, and how he imagined them in the hours when he closed his eyes. *These things,* he would think, *are most important.* He ate them, ate several of them. He did this only after they became too fat and too lazy to escape him. With one hand, he was usually capable of grasping two or three, sometimes four at a time, and he'd rattle them around and feel them flutter against the flesh of his palm before shaking them into his mouth and biting down. Or swallowing them whole. Sometimes, he liked the way they felt. A living train, receding in lethargic contractions down the back of his throat.

They came in through cracks in the windows—through fissures in the walls and up through crevasses in the floorboards and tiles. Nights, he could hear them coming, working through the foundation of the building like an inevitable doom, building and building only to rupture and expel themselves into the air in a burst of wings and eyes.

And onto him.

And *into* him.

There was no repulsion associated with the acts—neither his nor theirs. It was simply *rotation,* simply *cycle,* the mere spinning of a wheel. And in his mind he could picture that wheel, forever in slow-motion, forty-five revolutions per minute, and he could make out the rutted sound of its churning. It was a grand wheel, aflame with a myriad of colored ribbons and diamond studs. With each turn, a brilliant new light reflected off his mind-face, and he could sense each oncoming color with the same clarity as he'd witnessed the passage of the old ones. All the same, he knew. It was all the same.

When a man dies, he thought, *he leaves several things behind. But what will I leave behind? And will I really, truly even die?*

Often, he laughed. He'd discovered a way outside the wheel, a way to beat the system after all. Eternal life. Immortality. Disenfranchised from the human race. And how many people before him had discovered the same thing? A hundred? A million? None?

Across from his bed and against the far wall hung a calendar. It claimed it was mid-October, but it was well beyond October. Like him, October was long forgotten. A filthy blackness had claimed one corner of the calendar—had withered it and curled it like a burnt leaf. He, too, had been burned...though the details, having grown much too unimportant, were now lost to him. Like many things.

"My name is Soon-Lee." He said this occasionally to remind himself, though he did not know why.

Burned. He remembered something about a fire: the acrid stink of charred wood and a great conflagration...yet nothing was clear. The conflagration, after too much time turning the half-memory over in his head, merely became the wheel itself, spinning colors out of control, powerful and all-knowing the way God is massive and unyielding. And what about God? What about that bullshit? Was there anything to fill that husk?

Soon-Lee laughed. His left eardrum was blown out, and the sound rattled like static in his head.

Between the miserable, segmented hours of his consciousness, Soon-Lee slept. It was a sleep corrupted by violent images and unrelenting waves of nausea. Sometimes, almost blessedly, he would dream of Kilfer and Mines and Tonya—blessed, for these dreams, horrid and painful as they were, represented his last handhold on reality. The specifics of the dreams changed from time to time, but the core always remained the same: they were negotiating a series of narrow, subterranean tunnels beneath the village, walled in on either side, the stink of their sweat in the air. They could hear each other breathing, could hear the fabric of their khakis rubbing against their legs. And the sounds of screaming people, screaming children...

"You hear 'em?" Kilfer breathed. "All of 'em, up ahead somewhere?"

"Children, too," Tonya said.

Kilfer snorted in the darkness. "I don't trust it down here. Let's move topside."

"We're almost to the end," Soon-Lee insisted. "Swab the fucking place."

"Kids," Mines stated to no one in particular, "is just the same." Soon-Lee didn't know what that meant, but continued to listen nonetheless. "Goddamn fountain of youth, little sons-a-bitches. Christ, my head hurts."

Occasionally, the dream segued into the purely bizarre...

"You b'lieve in God, Soon-Lee?" Kilfer said.

"No," he answered, "and God don't believe in me."

"Fuck God," snickered Mines. "What'd God ever do for any of us? Made Tonya here one ugly bastard, that's about it." He laughed. "God can shine my Christing shoes, I'll tell you what."

Kilfer sighed in the darkness. "That's ignorant." He was only a few feet in front of Soon-Lee; Soon-Lee could smell Kilfer's sweat fanning off him in moist waves. "Better yet, what you think about flies, Soon-Lee? You like 'em? They taste good?"

Soon-Lee froze, the hairs on the nape of his neck prickling up. "What you know about flies?"

"I know you been eating them to stay alive. You ever read *Dracula?*"

"I seen the movie once. What's that got to do with me and flies? How'd you know about that?" Even in his dream, he was aware that the flies had not come yet, that Kilfer was talking out of order, that the flies wouldn't become a part of the whole thing until after he was pulled from the tunnels and taken to the hospital, burned and forgotten.

"Don't worry about it, Soon-Lee." It was Tonya, some distance behind him. "He's just bustin' your balls. Forget the flies. We're all gonna die down here anyway."

"Tonya—"

"Shit, buddy, you know that, don't you?"

"What's going on? What are you guys talking about? This ain't how it happened."

And he'd wake up, too exhausted to scream.

Night and day alternated without pause. After many days he lost count and assumed, from the coldness of the walls, that it was sometime in December now. Or maybe even January. Christ, had it been that long? Passing, in the blink of an eye...

He had no feet. The initial explosion had sheared them off at the ankles, the flames working their way up his shins, his thighs. The pain had been exquisite, but he only now remembered this because he remembered *thinking* this, and did not necessarily remember the pain itself. And even the events which led to his arrival at the hospital were fuzzy. Kilfer was there—something about Kilfer, something about Kilfer dying yet saving his life.

Sure, he thought. *Anything you want, buddy. Anything at all.*

"Soon-Lee," he moaned.

Eight of them had gone down into the darkness, yet only four of them had made it to the end. The other men—Soon-Lee couldn't recall their names, though he'd been good friends with all of the Special Operations guys at one time—had split off into separate corridors communicating with equal darkness.

"Up ahead," Tonya repeated. "Trapped themselves down here like rats. And with their children, man. You hear that?" Tonya's face was a roadmap of scars and burned tissue—the only medals he ever received during his tour of the islands. The expression on his face was always one of constant pain, even when he laughed, which was rare.

Soon-Lee shook his head. "How do you know about the flies?"

"Forget it, man," Kilfer said. There was exasperation in his voice. "I didn't say nothin' about no flies anyhow. You're dreaming this, buddy. You got me?"

The screaming of the frightened and trapped grew louder.

Mid-October. Or December or January.

Soon-Lee opened his eyes wide and found himself staring at the calendar on the opposite wall. He wasn't in the tunnels; he was here in the hospital. Alone. And there was no pain. Just immortality and flies. And the cracks in the ceiling. And the graffiti across the walls—CON DIED DEAD and BEG MORT and GOD SPARED ME BLADDER and I WEAR THE ROSE. Words of dead men, all of them. Forgotten, like him. Dead.

Not me, he thought. *Never me.*

"The only way to beat God is to never die," Mines said, creeping along the cinder walls. His booted feet crunched gravel or bone or both. The flame at the tip of his flamethrower passed briefly before his face, bringing his features into stark relief. He looked like a man who'd just been given a glimpse of his greatest achievements, all compiled into one singular, continuous reel. "Other than that, He gets us all in the end."

"All of us," Tonya agreed.

"All of us," chimed Kilfer.

But that wasn't how it went down. There'd been no talk about God, and certainly no discussion concerning the ingestion of insects. In fact, there'd been no talking at all in the tunnels. Was that all really just in his head? Perhaps. But the people and the children and the explosion—those things were real, all right. There was no forgetting them. Not ever.

The only way to beat God is to never die, he heard Mines whisper in his head.

He looked down at his legs now. They were not legs. Two abbreviated stumps—a network of twisted, charred flesh and coagulated blood...of ruined muscle and tissue...a testament to God's cruelty. His skin had gone a pale blue-gray all the way to his upper thighs now, nearing his genitals. They were numb, had no feeling. Looking at them, he felt nothing inside, which would have frightened a more mentally competent human being. Soon-Lee was not that human being; he'd retreated to the darkest recesses of his mind over the dripping passage of days and weeks and months. And was it really months? Could that be?

December? *January?*

His legs couldn't move on their own. It took great effort to shift them, mostly with the muscles of his abdomen and his hands, and while they were being repositioned, they moved like one complete unit, leaving behind red-brown flakes of dried and bloodied skin along the mattress. He could only stare at them for so long until his mind receded again, forcing him to consider the wheel, the spinning cycle of life that he was in the middle of avoiding, that he was nearly mastering. Could he really be that intelligent, that ingenious?

Looking around the room, his eyes fell on scores of empty beds and gurneys. Some were still embossed with the imprint of their occupants, now long since departed. Empty and half-empty IV bags hung from racks or lay discarded on the green tile floor. A bundle of wet laundry lay just outside the doorway out in the hall. The cloying stink of ammonia and perspiration still hung in the air, just as strong as it had been on the day he arrived, screaming and writhing in pain. Even with his wrecked and ruined mind, he was able to remember the room when it had been bustling with people—nurses and doctors and, most of all, the pained and suffering. With surprising clarity, he recalled a young man by the name of Phillips as he was wheeled into the room and established beside Soon-Lee. He was really just a boy—hardly a man, hardly able to fight—and despite the fact that half his left arm had been torn free from the shoulder by a mortar, he remained silent and still, staring wide-eyed and lazy at the ceiling.

Those people in those tunnels, he thought now. *All those children.*

He blacked out for a moment. An image materialized in his subconscious—that of a wild-eyed man dissecting young women and stitching their bodies together to birth some horrific, patchwork monster. This was not a memory; rather, this was part of the insight people are granted into the minds and lives of other people when confronted with the sudden proximity of their own death.

Yet Soon-Lee did not die. Restless, he slept through the night. And was back below the earth inside the tunnels again…

"What do you think they're doing down here?" he asked Kilfer. "All these damn people?"

"Hiding. Some might be locked away, but they're mostly hiding. Some of these villages get a whiff of a Special Ops team on the horizon, they start buryin' their loved ones underground. Whole families."

"Kids," Soon-Lee said.

"That's tragic," Tonya said from somewhere, though he didn't sound too upset.

"Can't trust the kids just like you can't trust their parents," Kilfer continued. "They'll blow up the whole regiment if they could. Pal of mine got killed when one of these island bastards tossed a grenade into his tent while he slept. Whole time he treated this kid nice, didn't do nothin' bad to him, even fed him when he was hungry, you know? Then the kid turns around and pulls a stunt like that. Imagine that, right? Some shit."

"Some shit," Soon-Lee agreed.

"Half of these fuckers still fight like it's the Second World War, diggin' these friggin' trenches in the ground, crawlin' around in 'em like rats. I trust no one."

Up ahead, Soon-Lee noticed small pinpoints of light piercing the darkness. The swell of the people's cries grew. They knew they were trapped and knew they were about to be killed. Soon-Lee felt something banging inside his head. He couldn't wait to get topside, to sit and breathe fresh air and maybe drink some goddamn water.

Tonya noticed the lights, too. "The hell is that?"

"It's them," Kilfer whispered.

The cries grew louder, and soon it became evident that the four of them had arrived at the end of the tunnel, that nothing separated their unit from the rising swell of screaming children other than darkness and a few splintered slats of wood. Soon-Lee squinted, allowing his eyes time to adjust to the new light. He could see them behind the wooden slats, their arms a tangle of bony flesh, filthy and pale. Their cries rose and fell in unison, as if they were all individual parts of one complex beast. Soon-Lee shuddered. What sort of people hide with their children in prisons underground? Didn't they know they wouldn't be safe? Didn't they know they couldn't hide? There was no liberation in war. You had to track and fight, not run and hide. Cowards.

"Shut up, the lot of you!" Tonya barked. His face was alight with passion, hungry for destruction. His eyes were like two celestial bodies, full and glowing. "You filthy little pecks!"

Some of the islanders held torches, which was where the light was coming from. In their close quarters, the flames were either quickly doused or accidentally lit someone up.

Kilfer shook his head. "You see what sort of animals we're dealing with here?"

"Light 'em up," Soon-Lee said, and ignited his own flamethrower. Kilfer and Tonya followed suit. The hot stink of sulfur filled the tunnel, stung Soon-Lee's nose, forced his eyes to tear. The children were screaming louder now, the sound ripping through him like a white-hot charge of electricity. Packed behind the wooden slats like filthy, caged animals, the islanders began to struggle, desperate to break the boards apart and free themselves. There must have been fifty of them trapped in there. A hundred...two hundred...

Mines fired first, igniting the slats and scoring the flailing arms. Once the flames hit, the arms quickly retreated. Or tried to. The screams reached a crescendo, broke into a unified shriek, and then Tonya's flamethrower fanned the entire length of the tunnel. The heat struck Soon-Lee like the collapse of a building. His own flamethrower jammed. He turned it over and pushed the muzzle into Tonya's flame. The flamethrower burst to life and launched a fiery orange stream toward the screaming people trapped behind the burning wooden slats.

Mines was shouting something. Soon-Lee couldn't make it out. Tonya was laughing. Kilfer worked with stern determination, his eyes set, his face expressionless.

And then the explosion hit.

The source was unexplained—perhaps there was a gas pipe down there. Or perhaps it was deliberate, an ambush set by the trapped islanders. Soon-Lee and the rest of the Special Operations unit would never know.

The explosion struck like the fist of God, and for an instant, Soon-Lee saw everything turn white. There was no sound. Then there was too much sound. Something fuzzed and rattled inside Soon-Lee's head, and he felt the hot fluidity of his burst eardrum in his skull. His equilibrium spinning circles, he felt his body lose all touch with reality…and an instant later, he was lifted off his feet and flung into the air. There was no pain. In his mind, he felt the world tilt. It was then that he caught his first site of the spinning wheel, and he acknowledged it with something akin to disinterest, as if he'd seen this wheel a hundred times before, or at least had known of its presence for some time now. It was the wheel that saved his life, for he did not feel the need to sit up immediately after striking the ground, just as the wall of flame shot through the tunnel. Eyes closed, he remained watching the wheel. He was faintly aware of a stinging sensation in his lower extremities. Then, in that second, the pain blossomed—exploded—detonated—erupted—and became something impossibly grandiose, something terrifically heartless and medieval.

And the rest was lost to him: a blur. Except for certain times, staring at the hospital ceiling in the dark, when he remembered that only Kilfer and he had survived, and that it was Kilfer whom had saved his life. Kilfer, dragging his bloodied body through the darkness of the tunnel, whispering to him the entire time just to keep him alive. His words were forgotten, but they were unimportant. It was Kilfer's presence that saved him.

Alive, Soon-Lee thought now. *I am alive. Yet Kilfer is dead.*

He felt a stirring of pain at his waist and knew it was time for more Percocet. He kept the pills on the gurney beside him, and shook two into his hand, downed them. Closing his eyes, he eased his head back down on the pillow. He could feel a million stirrings in his ruined legs. He tried not to think about it.

Keep eating, he thought.

After some time, with the pain numbed to nothingness, he sat up and once again began to feast on the flies. To his delight—and his horror—there were more maggots. As sustenance, they were more fulfilling that the actual adult flies. However, something about their fleshy bodies wriggling within the devastated corruption of his legs disgusted him. He plucked them from his wounds one by one, examined them absently, and swallowed them whole. Process. All one big cycle, part of the same wheel. Turn-turn-turn.

Somehow, Kilfer had managed to drag him topside. There was commotion throughout the village. The explosion had burst through the ground and had set a collection of oil drums ablaze. Several people were killed or wounded. People came and went, rushed by like ghosts in white blurs.

"We done too many things to die right now, buddy," Kilfer whispered near his ear. A team of medics was approaching. "We ain't had enough time to make good of ourselves, if you b'lieve in that sort of thing. You don't b'lieve in God, do you, Soon-Lee?"

But he couldn't answer. He was fading in and out of consciousness, trapped in some cartoon limbo where shapes refused to remain solid and colors bled too bright. His mind replayed the explosion, and several times he began to jerk and spasm, his brain teasing him with replay after replay after replay. What was real? Anything? Anything at all?

"You just hang on," Kilfer said. Then quieter, almost to himself: "Goddamn Mines and Tonya, those poor bastards. Never had a chance to make peace. Not a goddamn chance."

And that was just it. Evil people were afraid to die, afraid of what they had to face. Ideally, given the opportunity, they'd embrace immortality just to stave off the fiery hand of justice in the afterlife.

Poor bastards, Soon-Lee thought now, and almost laughed.

The medics carried him to the hospital. They gave him medication to pull him from his blackout, those little shits, and all it did was make him acutely aware of the pain he was in. Screaming, clawing at their faces, he was carried into the island hospital very near death. Waves of unreality washed over him. Doctors came and went in the frantic tide of emergency, their voices muffled behind masks, their hands cold as ice, their stares as empty and frozen as the tundra. He retreated to peace in his mind, but all he could see was that spinning wheel of light and fire...and he could see that it was beginning to slow, that he was fading and his own time was almost up. *Evil people are afraid to die,* he remembered thinking.

So now—mid-October. Or January. Or maybe time didn't matter; maybe months had ceased to exist. He adjusted himself on his bed, his body bruised and covered in sores, and strained his eyes to see through the darkness. There were a number of windows along the far side of the room, but all the shades had been pulled prior to the hospital's evacuation. Only tiny slivers of moonlight found their way in. A single window above his head, cracked the slightest bit. The air was cold. He was grateful the flies still came. Not really hungry anymore, he forced himself to ingest the flies and their larvae once again, peeling them out of his rotting flesh. It was all part of the cycle, he continued to remind himself, all part of what needed to be done to avoid the destruction of the wheel.

The wheel had to keep spinning.

Thirsty, he managed to ease onto his side and remove the clay ashtray from the windowsill. It was partially filled with stagnant rainwater. He sipped some and saved the rest, uncertain when it would rain again. His throat burned. He began to tremble.

The hospital fell under attack three days after Soon-Lee had arrived. Though he'd been operated on twice and remained stitched and bandaged, the intensity of his pain kept him sedated almost to unconsciousness. When the bombs hit, he was only half awake. The floor emptied out, the nurses and doctors rushing for the exits. Soon-Lee felt the foundation shake. He saw smoke billowing in through some of the windows. How badly were they hit? Would troops move in? What had happened to the defense, the fucking barracks?

Most of the patients were able to leave on their own. Others tried and were trampled and crushed in the hallways and stairwells. A few compassionate nurses managed to gather the remaining few. Except for him. They'd left him. And perhaps it was only his imagination, but he was fairly certain that a young female nurse had paused at the foot of his own bed, had locked eyes with him, debating whether she could carry him or not...and then fled.

The entire floor was empty in a matter of seconds; the entire hospital in a matter of minutes. And then the gunfire started outside. He could hear it through the walls, the cracked windows. Had they all been killed? Kilfer? Yes—he knew Kilfer was dead. He could feel it. And yet Kilfer returned to him several nights later.

He appeared as a shadow in a darkened corner of the room.

"Step out," Soon-Lee insisted.

"No."

"I want to see you."

"I won't."

"Damn you, Kilfer." He bit his lower lip, drew blood. "What's the matter with you? They killed you out there, didn't they? They shot you."

"Yes."

"What is it? What do you want?"

Kilfer's voice sounded very far away. "It's bad where I am, buddy. Just like I said. I know you don't b'lieve, but it's bad. *Real* bad."

Soon-Lee started to shake. "The hell you talkin' about? You tryin' to drive me nuts?"

"I'm telling you."

"Fuck off."

"Fight it, buddy. Stay alive. Don't die. Don't ever die. It's bad for guys like you and me. Very, very bad."

Soon-Lee's mouth was dry. "The wheel..."

"Keep it spinning."

"Cycle."

"Yes. Keep it spinning. Recycle the whole damned thing. You understand, buddy? You get me?"

He nodded. He was sweating and had a fever. "I do." He looked at his legs, disfigured and mummified within a roll of gauze bandages. A few bloodstains had surfaced on the gauze over the past few days and Soon-Lee had immediately noticed how quickly the flies in the room lit on him, sucked at the bloodied bandages. Frantically, he had swatted them away...but all the while, he'd been thinking in the back of his mind.

"Yes," Kilfer told him. "You know it."

So he unraveled the bandages and stared at his scarred, stitched-up legs. Gritting his teeth, he systematically popped the stitches and broke open the skin to become his own bait. He cried out countless times. And the flies came. For days...and weeks...and months. The more that came, the more he caught and ate...only to have more come again. They seemed to be the product of an infinite well, coming and coming and coming and never running dry. And the cycle was simple. *They eat me,* he thought, *and then I eat them. This way, I never die. I remain.*

I remain.

Mid-January, closer to February. He understood Kilfer's apparition to be just that—a figment of his own imagination. However, Kilfer's image did provide him with useful advice. Was it possible to beat the system, to beat God?

"My name is..." He paused. Considered. Looking down, he saw that the skin around his genitals had turned black and hard, and he could no longer feel his thighs. His abdomen was bloated and pasty. He could tell his body was wracked with fever.

"Kilfer!"

But Kilfer had ceased appearing to him months ago.

What happens when the flies stop coming? said a voice in his head—a voice very much like his own. *What will keep the wheel spinning when the flies stop coming?*

"They'll always come." His voice shook, trembled. "They'll always be here."

Night and day continued to alternate.

I must have been here five months by now, he thought. *Five months. Damn it all, that calendar is wrong!*

He could hear screams echoing down the hospital corridor— the screams of the burned and dead islanders from the tunnels beneath the village. Did they know he was here? Were they coming for him?

"My name..."

He shuddered. His entire body had gone cold. There was no feeling in his fingers, in his face. He tried moving his tongue around his mouth and found that he couldn't.

Six...seven months, easy...

He knew he had to keep eating. Even in the darkness he could see that there were plenty of flies on his legs, that there were plenty of wriggling grubs burrowing in his flesh, yet he could not bring himself to consider eating them. He couldn't even move his hands to properly operate his fingers even if he'd wanted to do so. His body was slowly seizing up on him. The wheel, he knew, was beginning to slow.

"Uh…"

Evil people, he reminded himself, *are afraid to die.*

He managed to maneuver his hands in the bloody pulp of his legs, to fish out the maggots…but there were only a few. He'd been wrong—there were hardly any at all. And even the fattest, slowest flies were faster than him.

Panicked, he looked around. Beside him, resting on the gurney with the Percocet, lay a number of hospital tools. Among them was a scalpel. Its blade glinted moonlight.

He didn't need the flies. They were an inconvenient cog, the middle-man that needed to be cut. This was nothing he couldn't continue on his own. Ingestion equaled digestion equaled regeneration. It made sense. He didn't need the flies. He'd *never* needed the flies.

It took him several tries to finally grasp the scalpel. With much difficulty, he managed to bring the blade down into the soft, scored flesh of his ruined left knee. He cut a piece of himself—a piece big enough to require chewing—with effort, and it took several drawn-out moments for him to finally get the piece into his mouth.

It was October twenty-seven.

Years after the war, a few of the old boys got together at the local lodge in the city. It was a quiet and modest event and none of the wives were in attendance. Jonesy was there and he plucked his harmonica from his chambray work shirt and started to blow and it was just like being in Europe all over again. In fact, it was so real that the lodge grew quiet and somber and many of the men did not speak much about the war for the rest of the evening. For a long while, Jonesy looked at his harmonica and turned it over in his big hands and looked as though he did not know what it was. After ten o'clock, when most everyone had left, I looked over and saw Jonesy's seat empty and his coat missing from the coat rack. He'd left his harmonica on the table.

Then There is Boston

For Deb, 2004

Then there is Boston, and the storm comes in and makes everything white. Snow covers the city. We stay for days by the hotel fireplace, drinking pinot grigio and eating too-hot clam chowder, our bodies together and shrouded in a knitted Indian afghan. We spend early mornings in the cafés and bistros and walking the Quincy cobblestones, she beautiful in a brown jacquard cap, I beautiful because of her. The sky misted with cold, the cityscape a frozen horizon of neutral pastels in the predawn moments before sunrise, we crest Broad Street in time to see the sun break behind the buildings. She sighs and says it is something beautiful and I say yes, it is always something beautiful, and there is nothing between us and we are all open and new. I tell her I have never felt so new and she knows this and feels this, too, and holds me in that way that makes me think she will never dare let go.

Nights and we are assembled poetry, a haiku of intermingled arms and legs, sambaed as if in dance, rhyming in all our passion. There is no greater togetherness. I am overcome by moments, some moments, and try to communicate to her the effortlessness through which I have been conquered—through which she has conquered me—yet I am powerless to get her to understand through words. I tell her this, and tell her that words are all I know, that words are how I am powerful and are what I command, so how can I not tell her what is inside? How can I bring the inside out to her? "But I know your words," she whispers, and pulls me close. And she does. And she does. And there is the warm fall of her breath across the summit of my shoulder, and there is the ghostly tickle of her curled hair against the side of my white face, and there is the physical silhouette of her against me, the cascade of skin, and I can think of no words and I am rendered defenseless and cannot wander.

I write in the lobby while she sleeps. I do this for us, and to keep these things down, all these things, so they will always be there to look back upon. My words come and they are free and uninhibited, but they are not perfect, and I cannot uncover, with any ounce of sincerity or personal gratification, the truest trueness behind what it is I am experiencing and in the telling of such experiences. I cannot tell it. It is there and all around me and I have slowly become infused with it, with all of it, but I cannot tell it. And I am taunted by the not telling.

"Your wife," says the older woman who refills the brochures at the front desk of the hotel lobby, "she is very pretty."

"Thank you, but she is not my wife," I say.

"She is still very pretty."

"She is," I say.

"She is asleep?"

"Yes. We were up very late."

"She is a very beautiful young lady."

"Thank you."

"You are here to work?"

"No. We are vacationing," I tell the woman. "We are from Maryland."

"This is some storm," says the woman. "You came just in time for some storm, the two of you."

"I suppose."

"You are in love, and very deeply. I can see it in the way you write."

"Can you?" I say.

"You are pushed very far over your writing and you are hungry to get the words out, all the right words, but you do not write so fast while pushed very far over. You sit and you think, but you are still so very hungry for the words to come, and so you wait." She says, "There is an innocent and beautiful frustration to you."

"I don't know how to say it," I confess.

"You don't need to say it. Write it simply and honestly and how it is. There is no need for splendor. This is not poetry; this is life. And," she goes on, "it is good to be so young and twenty-something and in love."

"It is very good," I admit, smiling.

"You should enjoy it."

"I enjoy all of it," I say. "Every second."

"You are a fool, then," says the woman.

"A fool?" I say. "For what reason?"

"For her not being your wife," says the woman.

I write until I cannot write any longer. I purchase a bottle of Cavit champagne and some freshly baked sesame bagels and carry everything back up to the room. When I get there, she is coming from the shower, and there is a twist of towel about her head, and nothing else. I set my writing tablet, the champagne, and the plate of bagels on a table and watch her move across the floor and to the bed. She is smiling and whispering to me, prettily and easily very womanly, and I am suddenly and once again overcome by my love for her. She pauses in her stance, all too briefly, and remains as a dark figure suspended before the bright rectangle of window at her back. I know every part of her, and I know it from watching and holding.

"What are you doing down there, baby?" she says, and lets herself fall back onto the bed.

"I am writing," I say. "I am writing all of this down. I want us to have it all."

"We already have it all," she says.

"I want you to have more."

"What more is there?" she says. "There is no more. I would be terrified, baby, to learn that there is more."

"Are you happy?"

"Always."

"Then I am happy, too."

"Then it is very simple," she tells me, "for us to make each other happy."

I agree that yes, it is.

Some indoor markets are not bothered by the snow, and so we visit and we buy boiled peanuts and eat them out of wax paper pouches. Faneuil Hall is not very busy as it is not the season for business. We watch a puppeteer perform with marionettes from one cart, and he works both puppets on his own and without assistance, and it is funny because one of the puppets—the not-so-smart one—is named after me. We laugh and it is all very funny. When the performance is over, the puppeteer tries to persuade me into buying one of his puppets. I do not buy any puppets but we give him a dollar, which I stuff into a slit in the lid of an old can of Maxwell House coffee.

"I would like to maybe see Fenway Park," she says, "and maybe the Boston Public Garden." She is reading a pamphlet.

"I don't think the Garden would be much to see in all this snow."

We stay in the hotel that night, and carry all the bedclothes and pillows to the window parapet. We curl like cats in the bedclothes on the parapet and look out on a snowy Downtown Boston. She kisses me and I smile and turn and fog the windowpane with my breath. With her index finger, she draws a heart in the blossom of fog.

"Tell me a story," she says.

"I don't know any stories."

"You always say that."

"It's always true."

"It's not," she insists. "You write all the time. You stay up late writing in the lobby after I'm asleep. Can't you tell me a story?"

So I tell her a parody of the way we met, and I make it humorous but sweet and very gentle, but also somewhat rough and overdone in the parts I feel require to be somewhat rough and overdone. She laughs at some parts and frowns playfully at others but, mostly, she just listens and puts her head against my chest and, just as I finish the story, she tells me how loud my heart sounds in her ears.

Much later, and I am writing again in the lobby, and the words are still finding it difficult to be born. I write and then read what I've written and I find that I have not captured any of it, not any of it at all, and I do not know what to do about it. I can only tell what happens and try and tell how it makes me feel, but there are no words strong enough, and I am incapable of uncovering and divulging the magic and mystery of the beauty.

"It comes better for you tonight?" asks the woman as she refills the brochures.

"It is difficult to find the right words," I say.

"Maybe you try too hard."

"I want to write it as it is, so we will be able to look back on what is written and remember what it was like to have lived it."

"Because," the woman adds, "these are fantastic and wonderful times, correct?"

"Yes," I say, "fantastic and wonderful. Two adjectives."

"She is asleep now, your pretty young lady?"

"Yes."

"What do you suppose she dreams of?"

"All of this," I say. "At least, I hope she does."

"It is good," says the woman, "to live it in the day and dream of it in the night."

"I can't find the words," I say.

"Maybe," says the woman, "you are just trying too hard."

I finish and sneak up to our room and creep into our big bed. She moves and shifts and says something that I think is sleep-talk until she speaks again.

"We won't let little things ruin us, will we, baby?" she says.

"No, sweet."

"We will try very hard, won't we?"

"Yes," I say, "but it won't be very hard at all. Not really. Not for us."

"I don't want it to be hard."

"Nothing will be hard," I say.

"Do you promise?"

"I promise."

"Did you do much writing tonight?"

"A little."

"Can I read any of it?"

"Not just yet."

"How come?"

"Because," I explain, "it is for later."

"When?"

"Much later."

"How much is much?"

"Later," I say, "like when we're different people and we may want—or may need—to look back on things like Boston."

"That is very pretty, to think something like that, but it is also very sad."

"There's nothing sad about any of it," I say.

"Well," she says, "it doesn't matter because I like how you think, and I like how you take care of us that way."

"It's all I can think," I say, "and it's all I know how to do."

Come morning, the snow has started to melt. We take pictures standing beside the enormous stone columns of Quincy Market. We drive and lunch at a small riverside café, where we drink mimosas and share a large bowl of cream of crab soup. By late afternoon, the streets are clear enough for horse carriages to appear, and we watch the carriages campaign up the steep incline of road along the river while the day warms up around us. Later in the evening, we go to a small restaurant for dinner, and there is a band and we dance primarily to the slower songs. I am a poor dancer and I slip my fingers into the belt-loops of her slacks in an effort to keep rhythm. She laughs and she has been drinking too much wine and she dives in and pecks at my cheek whenever she finds our positioning favorable enough to execute such a maneuver. It reminds me of us from so long ago. I think it but do not bother saying it because I can tell she is already thinking it, and that she already knows I am thinking it, too. We are good that way. So we dance and she pecks and, just once, I stop her from dancing and just press her hard up against me and hold her that way, unrelenting, and her face is suddenly very close to mine and very open to mine, and there is nothing else in the world that I can see.

"Say something," she tells me from nowhere, and she says it very quickly and breathlessly.

"You make me want to stay like this and not move," I tell her. "Ever."

She smiles, and it is in that way that makes me aware that I have touched something important and vulnerable and secret deep inside her, and that makes me feel good, and it is always good to know that her vulnerabilities are always right there for me to touch and that she so truly trusts me to touch them and never, ever hurt them.

"You say the right things," she says, still smiling.

"Rhubarb," I say, also smiling.

And when it grows too late we are back in the hotel room, and she is coaxing a small fire from the hearth near the foot of the bed.

"This is my favorite trip," she tells me.

"Mine, too," I say. "But I don't go on many trips."

"You always have to ruin it."

"I'm joking. No," I say, "this is as good as it gets."

She says, "It's as good as anyone is allowed to have without it being criminal."

"I think sometimes it's criminal."

"Is it?"

"Just sometimes," I say.

"And why is that?"

"Because you can be very, very dirty."

"Shhh," she says. "Don't tell."

So then we are very, very dirty together and, afterwards, I am back down at a table in the lobby with my writing tablet open before me. The lobby is very quiet and it is late and there, too, is a fire in the large fireplace across the lobby floor.

"This writing is like insomnia," says the woman refilling the brochures. "It is like the midnight disease."

"I feel very anxious to get it all down."

"Why?"

"Because it's important. It's important and I would never want to lose any of it."

"Why would you lose it?"

"I just want to have it down," I say. "It would be something good to have."

"Perhaps," says the woman. "But," she goes on, "there are more important things, I would think."

"Like what?"

She does not leave the counter, and says, "What are you writing?"

I look down and then look up and then look down again. "I am writing about today and about tonight. I am writing all the things we have done and how it all makes me feel."

"It is difficult?"

"Of course. I am trying to make it as beautiful on paper as it is in reality."

"Because," the woman says, "it is so much more beautiful in reality."

I say, "Yes."

The woman says, "Then why are you sitting here now?"

I look at the woman for a very long time.

Finally, she says, "I think maybe you are trying too hard."

Back upstairs, I am quiet upon entering the room. The fire is dead and the room is cold. I can see a slight, curled shape in the bed beneath the tumble of blankets.

"Hello, sweet," I say, climbing beside her and moving up and over and against her.

"It's you," she says.

"Who else would it be?"

"I missed you."

"I am back."

"Did you get good writing done?"

"Yes," I say, "I did."

"Have you finished?"

"Yes."

"And I have to wait until forever before I can read any of it, right?"

"No," I say, and hand over my writing tablet. "It is for you and it is for us. You can do whatever you like."

"Seriously?"

"Yes."

"I want to read it all," she says, leaning over and switching on the tiny lamp on the nightstand. The room falls to a pale yellow. "But first I want to read the thing from a long time ago. Remember? It is the thing you said I could read sometime later. I want to read it first."

"It's there," I say. "It's right in there. You can read it all. But," I say, "I do not know if any of it is any good. I tried very hard to make it good," I say, "but I do not know if any of it turned out that way."

"You try too hard," she says, opening the writing tablet.

"It just may not be very good," I continue to warn her. "I have not captured everything perfect, as I'd wanted to."

"Let me read," she says.

I say, "It is not perfect."

"Let me read."

I say, "It is not as beautiful as I'd wanted."

"Let me read."

I say, "It is not poetry."

And she looks at me, almost injured, and says, "But it is to me."

Ronald Malfi is the award-winning author of several horror novels, mysteries, and thrillers. He is the recipient of two Independent Publisher Book Awards, the Beverly Hills Book Award, the Vincent Preis Horror Award, the Benjamin Franklin Award for Popular Fiction, and he is a Bram Stoker Award nominee. He lives with his wife and two daughters along the Chesapeake Bay, where he is currently at work on his next book.

CPSIA information can be obtained
at www.ICGtesting.com
Printed in the USA
LVOW03s0848031017
550957LV00001B/1/P